blue
rider
press

A Guide for Murdered Children

A Guide

for

Murdered Children

⊸⊸⊸⊸⊸⊸

Sarah Sparrow

BLUE RIDER PRESS

NEW YORK

blue
rider
press

An imprint of Penguin Random House LLC
375 Hudson Street
New York, New York 10014

Library of Congress Cataloging-in-Publication Data

Names: Sparrow, Sarah, author.
Title: A guide for murdered children : a novel / Sarah Sparrow.
Description: New York : Blue Rider Press, 2018.
Identifiers: LCCN 2017022133 (print) | LCCN 2017031872 (ebook) |
ISBN 9780399574542 (eBook) | ISBN 9780399574528 (hardcover) |
ISBN 9781524743833 (international edition)
Classification: LCC PS3619.P3723 (ebook) | LCC PS3619.P3723 G85 2018 (print) |
DDC 813/.6—dc23
LC record available at https://lccn.loc.gov/2017022133
p.   cm.

Printed in the United States of America
1   3   5   7   9   10   8   6   4   2

BOOK DESIGN BY AMANDA DEWEY

For the children

——A simple Child,
That lightly draws its breath,
And feels its life in every limb,
What should it know of death?

—William Wordsworth

book one

Closely Watched Trains

―⏤⏦⏤―

I know it's all a bit overwhelming (to put it
mildly!) but in time you will understand your
purpose here. So WELCOME HOME, everyone,
and GOD BLESS every one of you!

—from "Hello and Welcome!"
(the Guidebook)

WICKENBURG, ARIZONA

Present Day

WATCHING THE DETECTIVE

In rehab now—
    —again.

Detective Willow Millard Wylde.

Fifty-seven years old: shitty health and shaky spirits.

Kind of a fattie . . .

Which is usually what happens to him at the end of a run.

He was drinking around the clock. Burning his fingers, his mattress, his couch, and his car seat with those bullshit alkie Marlboro Blacks. Burning down his anxieties and dreams. Chugalugging pain pills with Diet Dr Pepper from the moment he awakened to the moment he passed out—and even in the middle of the night, after being startled to wakefulness by his own stertorous snores and otherworldly screams.

No diabetes—yet.

No prostate cancer—yet. (Though tests showed peskily chronic microscopic amounts of blood in the urine, etiology unknown.)

Just some scabby, top of the head, sun-induced cancer, but no melanoma. Yet.

Still no tangible signs of early-onset dementia . . .

Cialis seemed to work most of the time for those few and far-between afternoon delights. Sometimes he had little romantic dates with himself when chemical enhancement wasn't required and performance wasn't the issue. But generally he's lost the urge.

Generally lost all urge.

Willow—that haunted half-oddity of an eccentric name that his grand-mother bestowed on him, a name he love-hated, a name he'd always been forced to explain (women were enthralled, men were suspect)—Willow Wy-lde, that complicated, beautiful, ruined American mythic thing: Washed-Up Cop. That luminous travesty of premium cable, movies and fiction, high and low: retired alcoholic homicide cop (one of his exes called him a "functional assaholic"), bruised and battered three-years-into-forced-retirement cop, un-lucky in love, depressed, once flamboyant, once heroic cop, decorated then dirty then borderline absolved, now demolished, a revolving door AA mem-ber too played out to be a suicide threat. Friends used to arrive en masse to take his weapon away but after the first few interventions bailed in the ensu-ing months then years of relapses. In time, "Dubya"—he had the nickname long before George Walker Bush but didn't mind sharing it (sometimes he just wasn't in the mood to be Willow)—alienated even his die-hard boosters. Their patience and goodwill expired, and they were dispatched or dispatched themselves from his life one by one.

On *this* day, late June, in the Year of Our Damaged, Dysfunctional Lord:

He walks from building to building in the absurd, nearly intolerable blast furnace of Sonoran Desert heat. It gives him solace to singsong-whisper under his breath the mantra, "I'm broken. Broken. Broken . . ." The tidy personal prayer seemed to go well with the rehab's favorite motto, "Hurt people hurt people."

Oh, true dat.

His daughter Pace went online and found a place called the Meadows. She read that famous people went there. Well maybe they did but all Dubya knows of *famous* are a European automobile heir who looked like a comic book prince and a jovial, forgotten, once sitcom actor who resembled a spooked and bloated farm animal—mixed in with the usual head cases, drunks, dope fiends and sex addicts.

Willow's wrist is in a cast, the bones having been broken in the collision with a barroom wall. A long pin crucifies the hand to secure the fracture. A tiny red button caps the pin and sits below the pinkie like a ladybug.

Still limps from an old gunshot wound to the leg, when he worked narcotics in Manhattan . . .

It's 118 degrees—he can't figure out if that's in the sun or the shade, as
if it the fuck matters! The only place hotter in the world is Death Valley.
Once a week, the two shit kilns have an apocalyptic do-si-do, competing for
Hell's honors. He could never wrap his head around the fact that the hottest
place on Earth was in the U.S. of A., not the Sahara or Bum Crack, Syria,
and now, courtesy of his beloved codependent daughter, he's in rehab in
literally the hottest place on Earth—more or less—and shakes his head, muttering, "Broken! Broken! Broken!"

His only real family is the rehab tribe: counselors, doctors, RNs, kitchen
workers, fellow inmate-travelers. They detoxed him for a week in a room
next to the nursing station. Rx: Seroquel for sleep and anxiety, trazodone
for sleep and anxiety, donuts and Hershey bars and four packets of sugar/
four of stevia in black coffee for sleep and anxiety. Jacking off in bed and
cigarettes 'round the smoke pit for sleep and anxiety . . . His besties are
a Rimbaud dead ringer—a crazy-handsome seventeen-year-old poet whose
arm is also in a sling, due to deep tendon wounds from a suicide attempt that
put him in Bellevue for three weeks, and a black fire chief from Fort Worth
who peaked at sixty Percocet a day. (Willow marveled at that. The most he
could ever manage was ten.) And a wry gal, a gay Buddhist from Fort Lauderdale who refuses to call him Dubya ("Willow is such a beautiful name.
And Willow Wylde is wildly beautiful"). She's droll and way broken too
and he feels better when Renata's around. She used to be pretty—everyone
used to, even ol' Dub. He tries feeling sexy about himself and people in
general (hey, anything to pass the time), but sexiness corroded a long while
back, along with everything else.

It's tough to feel sexy when you're wheezing, broiling and broken, sharing a room with three men, two of whom have sleep apnea and use angry-
sounding, portable CPAPs at night. It's tough with a long ladybug pin stuck
impaling your walloped writing hand . . .

Yet still somehow he possesses that irrational, mandatory—yes, *sexy*—
certainty that somehow all will be solved, all will be made right . . .

tomorrow! That knowledge, a reflexive fallback, that a victim's family will be assuaged and justice will be served. Justice! Because contrary to popular opinion, there *was* such a thing as closure and screw anyone who said otherwise. Hell, he lived for closure. As a homicide detective, he'd always had a different interpretation of the word. Trouble was, people had the idea that closure was about feeling good—feeling good was the bottom line, the secret of life, everyone always just wanted to *feel good*, but nothing ever felt good about murder and its aftermath. No: closure wasn't relief or release, it was a balancing of scales, that's all. When the scales were balanced, order and some kind of serenity returned to the world, in spite of oneself. A detective's job was to restore balance. That's why he became a Cold Case guy, even though he fucked that up like everything else. The natural order of the universe was balance and symmetry, not justice, but balance *was* justice; give him a ninth-century mummy with a dagger in its chest and Willow Wylde would get his ordered, just results. It was nothing but a crossword puzzle designed by the Creator and he was good at what he did because he saw that, knew that and was never blinded by the personal.

Now, though, the imbalance was . . . himself.

He was his own cold case and didn't have clue one. He wondered if the solution to the crime of Mr. Wylde lay in the idea that hope itself hadn't died—yet—and laughed at the brilliant idiocy of that new notion. True dat: it was a glorious mystery that he still awakened with the buoyancy of Hope. It gave him a spring in his step as he strolled from building to building in the infernal square dance of punishing heat. He wasn't even sure what Hope meant anymore, just another bogus word but there it was, his lifelong companion, a big friendly dog, a shaggy dog story that he recognized for better or for worse as his soul mate. When the dog died, where and who would the bereft Willow be?

He strung together the grimy beads of all those tropes—Order! Balance! Justice! Closure! Hope!—like a necklace of cheap pearls. They still made him feel pretty.

Such is the travesty of the broken cop—

As he soaked in the tub of his dorm room, sobbing, his good hand instinctively washing the wounded one as if neither belonged to him (a van drove him to the Mayo Clinic in Scottsdale yesterday to finally have the pin and cast removed), an idea haunted him: that one morning he'd awaken to find the big dog dead in a field, the soul mate gone maggoty and swollen to near bursting in the heat. *Hope abandoned*—He'd seen the blessed illusion of Order and Balance disappear in those in whom they burned brightest. He saw what happened when the landlord Hope departed—

—its tenants became ghosts.

Another thing should have haunted him but didn't. Instead, it capti-vated and puzzled, holding him an intrigued, almost genteel hostage. It wasn't yet fully formed yet rather was a mirage of what was soon to come.

A persistent vision.

The vision started on the plane, on his way to the Meadows. He was crammed into coach, still drinking but no longer able to get drunk. Like him, the vision too was a complicated, ruined thing, though not of this world. It was a thing that was coming, a thing that lately had begun to intrude on waking life—like it did the other day when he passed the "talking pipe" to his neighbor at the big Saturday men's stag share—a hallucination he'd re-frained from sharing with the Meadows' counselors. Though he did men-tion it to Renata, who was gracious enough to call it "weird and sort of gorgeous" (*gorgeous* being her favorite word).

The vision, more a visitation, of a train whose stained-blue passengers were phantoms.

Not of those he once knew, nor those that Hope had abandoned, but a vision of another world. What world? The bluish *whoosh* of cabin cars came like a comfort—Willow felt the wind as they roared past—a horror yet a new kind of hope.

Somewhere in him, he knew it was the last hope.

SAGGERTY FALLS, MICHIGAN

July 4, 2000

TROY AND MAYA

Cul-de-sac bustle.

Independence Day festivities, chez Rummer: Elaine, Ronnie and the kids.

Exurbia unbound.

The mise-en-scène unfolds about thirty miles north-northeast of Detroit, in the leafy, semirural village of Saggerty Falls, a 2.5-square-mile community in Lenox Township, Macomb County, in the "lower thumb" of Michigan.

They used to make engine blocks there but the foundry's defunct . . .

Pop: 3,073.

Number of families: 783.

Median family income: $45,489.

The Salt River runs through it . . .

A Fourth of July afternoon—

—and the little ones run amok on sugar highs, starbursts of growing bones and neurons. Elaine and her galfriend Penny are baking cookies in the kitchen. Elaine uses that word, *galfriend*, having inherited it from her mother, who'd say about a movie or whatnot, "Why don't you take a galfriend?"

"I want to fix you up with someone," says the lady of the house. (Her mother used to say that too: *fix you up.*)

"Not interested, unless it's Richard Gere."

Penny the newbie divorcée moves on to spinning salad, the foundation of her new aerobics empire. She wryly says, *My salad-spinning workout video's gonna make me shit-rich.*

"Well, he ain't Richard Gere but he's *close*," says Elaine, nodding toward the window overlooking the backyard, where the men hover by the barbecue.

Penny takes a gander and says, "Your husband?" Galfriend Elaine guffaws. "You know," says Penny, contemplative, "I might not be comfortable with that—I'm not saying I couldn't *get* comfortable. Don't think I haven't had my fantasies . . ."

"I'll bet you have, Miss Horndog. Miss Horndog Divorcée." Elaine gets more specific and points Roy out. "*That's* your man."

"Roy Eakins?" says Penny, in that sly way of hers that makes you wonder whether she's completely repulsed or thinks the idea may be worthy of her consideration. "I don't *think* so. Though I *might* be interested if he looked a little more like Demi Moore."

"The hair's close," says Elaine lightheartedly. "Oh come on, Penny. He's *smart*. And *funny*, in that off-way you like."

"Not my type," she says, returning to her spinning.

"He teaches *history*."

"Teaches history? Like, that's all you got? *Teaches history?*"

"History teachers are supposed to be seriously well-endowed," says Elaine, in licentious good cheer.

"Oh right, that's totally their rap." She squints her eyes at the man, saying, "Kind of an odd duck, no? With that super-weird kid?"

"Grundy? He's sweet."

"As in retarded, potentially violent sweet?"

"You are so mean!"

"He *isn't* sweet, Ellie, he's like friggin' Lennie from *Of Mice and Men*." The girls howl at that; they've been drinking and are feeling no pain. "How *old* is that kid, anyway?"

"Thirteen?"

"Are you serious? He looks like he's in his—forties!"

Again they howl. Funniest thing ever.

"Grundy's 'special needs,' " said Elaine. "And so?"

"Look who's being politically correct."

"He's probably some kind of genius. He's on the spectrum."

"Just like me, milady."

"Exactly. That's why I think y'all'd be perfect together. Though you're actually more on the spectrum . . . of growing cobwebs on your vagina."

They lose control again and take the opportunity to finish what's left in their wineglasses.

"Look, history nerds and their mutant offspring aren't really my thing," says Penny. "I like the tall, dark, childless type."

"Oh come on, honey, Roy Eakins is a friggin' action hero. He's a great dad and that says a lot. He's single and quirky and brilliant—which means your *kids* would be single and quirky and brilliant."

"Ha!"

"Plus he's friggin' *funny.* He's very dry."

"Just like my pussy."

"We can remedy that!"

"We'd make pretty spectrum babies. You know, all scary and autistic."

"You'd be cute together. And whatever—you could do it *one time*, to break the ice. You know, that's formed between your legs."

"Can you leave my pussy alone, please?"

"I'll join the club! Know what I heard Roy say? 'History doesn't repeat itself but it sure does rhyme.' Don't you love that?"

"That's Mark Twain, brainiac. Now Twain, I'd fuck."

"I'm serious, Pen, we have got to hook you up. With *someone*."

"The ink on the divorce papers isn't dry, Ellie."

"Oh, bullshit. Use it or lose it, girl. How long has it been?"

"Since—?"

"*You* know."

"By my own hand? A few hours ago."

"You are such a slut."

"Actually, I meant a few minutes ago. In the guest bathroom."

In paroxysms again.

. . .

A t this same moment, Ronnie Rummer stands by the grill in a spat-tered GOTTA PROBLEM WITH THIS? cook's apron, tiny American flags tucked over both ears. Next to him is the action-figure history teacher Roy Eakins, oblivious to the tipsy, prying eyes apprising him from the kitchen window. Ronnie goads the meat until it sizzles, then gyrates triumphantly, embarrassing his son, Troy, but delighting daughter Maya, provoking her to buffoon-salacious imitation. The nine-year-old is a freckle-faced Alfred E. Neuman doppelgänger; his younger sister's hair a fiery red torch, a geyser, a local attraction that Elaine maintains with religious devotion.

Through it all, Roy's son stands apart, examining his own man-sized hands—deep in the solving of their mysteries.

As if called by a sovereign voice, Troy rushes off and Maya follows like one attached by rope. Grundy looks up and moves toward them before Roy commands, "*Stay.* You stay with us."

Penny and Elaine exit the house bearing full glasses of wine. Enter De-tective Willow Wylde, in from New York to surprise his daughter with a puppy on her Sweet Sixteenth. (Word is, she knows he's at the barbecue and is dodging him. She's been dodging the world for a few years.) Willow has a rep as a rake and a bad boy and likes that the girls have had a little too much. He's already been working Penny, who he always thought had a thing for him back in the day when he was a policeman in the Falls; his upgrade to the Manhattan big leagues can only have helped his case. Willow's research in the field had proven that certain women, particularly divorcées, couldn't resist the glamour of a big-city cop, particularly the glamour of a New York City narcotics cop. He and his NYPD drinking buddies liked to call it the job description that launched a thousand blow jobs. When they said their prayers, they thanked the TV procedurals for that.

The Rummers had invited Owen Caplan, but he politely declined to at-tend. Willow and Owen once were patrol-car partners, the local Starsky and Hutch, before the shit blew up between them in so many ways, and in the years since he'd left for the Big Apple, Owen had been appointed by the city to be chief of the five-man Andy of Mayberry department. (He'd always been ambitious, and Willow thought, *Good on the little fella.*) Adelaide, Willow's ex, had also been invited but politely declined. *Hmmmm.* Pace, Willow's child with Adelaide, was invited too, but MIA—to be fair, his daughter hadn't actually RSVP'd (not being a student of Emily Post) and Willow still hoped she'd turn up. If Pace didn't care to see him (it seemed like half the world didn't care to see him), she might just give a shit about seeing the $650 puppy he brought. If Dad had been unreliable in everything else, he'd at least been consistent with guilt-induced, over-expensive birthday presents.

Like most of the neighborhood men, Ronnie Rummer had done a lot of thinking about Penny and what it'd be like to have her. She had a wild streak that she didn't try too hard to conceal, and they'd always had one of those easy, flirty things going on, or at least he thought they did. He'd have to watch himself a little because the low stone fence of Penny's marriage was now gone. His own fence was tall and strong, but like any suburban Superman he could see himself leaping over it in a single bound.

The fire in the grill goes out.

Ronnie squirts the can—no lighter fluid.

He turns his burger-flipping chores over to Dubya and goes to find the kids.

Troy's in the meadow behind the house with a sparkler. On the front of his T-shirt it says BE EXCELLENT TO EACH OTHER. On the back, AND PARTY ON, DUDES.

"Hey! What'd I *tell* you about sparklers, Troy? You wait until *tonight.*" Troy casts his eyes to the ground while his little sister cavorts to unheard songs. "I need you to go to Ebenezer's for lighter fluid."

"Can I take Maya?"

"Okay. Ride on over but don't be long."

The smile returns to his son's face. Reinvigorated by a mature, useful task, he looks at the sparkler and then looks at his dad—what to do? "Put it in the ground," says Ronnie. He buries it and, with that task done, is ignited anew. (Nine-year-old boys are all about ignition.)

The siblings run off, the invisible rope between them taut.

. . .

Wmant grill? No—more than that, more a sickening familiar vortex
than a shiver—a fluish, dizzying, feverish gust that raced his pulse and seemed
to make gooseflesh of his very soul, nearly knocking him off his feet.

Standing at the barbecue, a sense-memory déjà vu turned his stomach . . .
and with it came that blueness again, age-old, without origin, without earth-
liness. (In his mind, he always called it the Blue Death.) Nana used to
nurse him through what she called "the fits," but Willow's mother didn't
like the term, hated it, countering that it was merely "the ague"—that odd,
antiquated word—no, Mom didn't like the spooky way Nana fussed over
her boy's ague at all. His grandmother would then submit to her daughter
before faking her out in order to comfort him, sneaking into his room and
whispering in his hot pink ear through the blue delirium. He never understood or recalled what she was saying, so dreamlike, yet still it soothed, but
the nature of the elixir remained forever tongue-tied and unknown. Nana—
how he loved his Nana!—was for sure some kind of Old World witch. One
time when "the fits" happened, Willow heard barking in his head; Palomar,
their runaway German shepherd, was in the midst of dying crosstown, im-
paled on a fence by three neighborhood sado-punks. *The Blue Death* . . . The
Wyldes hadn't even known the dog had escaped the house.

Guests begin arriving with Tupperwares of egg salad and coleslaw, med-
leys of macaroni and fruit salad, potpourris of this and that from family reci-
pes. And desserts: brownies and apple pie, peach cobbler and s'mores, banana
pudding and Oreo creations, the whole Great American Sugar Songbook.

Maya pedals furiously, that rope between she and her brother too tight
then too loose, the wild garden of hair on her head burnt-orange in the midday sun. Troy exults in his superior strength and locomotion, leaving her in
the dust. (Nine-year-old boys are all about lording it over little sisters.) Her
unicorn is in the flowery bicycle basket—she made a daybed for it with a
silk pillow Mom had given her. When she isn't looking toward Troy, she
glances at the sleeping creature with the devotion of a rehearsing mother.

Troy races to Ebenezer's amid the distant ambient sounds, some near but mostly far away, of Roman candles and firework rat-a-tats. Apparently not everyone got Dad's memo to wait until dark. The pulse of his heart accelerates at the hijinks of the taboo breakers but he isn't envious, only becoming more excited about tonight's celebrations.

A block from Ebenezer's, he turns to look back—sister gone.

She isn't dead, not yet, but will never speak again or have recordable conscious thought. Maya's body has a week left of breathing and making all manner of unrecognizable sounds, an animal's involuntary reaction to the work being done. Troy will soon be in water, reunited (in a sense) with his sister-princess, looking on with supportive, sightless eyes like a figurine propped on the balcony of a decayed castle in a forgotten aquarium.

THE MACOMB ORCHARD TRAIL

Present Day

BEFORE THE DEATH OF LYDIA

The body lay in a gulch, about a hundred yards off the hiking trail.
   Is it naked?

No—this isn't a homicide, so why should it be?

What is it wearing, then?

All those things that say *runner/hiker*.

Sex?

Female.

No mystery here.

This is no crime scene . . .

The "Orchard," northwest of Saggerty Falls, runs alongside the abandoned Michigan Air-Line Railway, stretching from Richmond to Dequindre Road, where it connects to the Clinton River Trail. The path the woman traversed was in an area unfrequented by trailbirds, but Lydia Molloy is—*was*—a solitary hiker by nature. Her last repose is an almost miraculously hidden spot that cannot be seen from the air, should there have been a rescue effort. There will be no cause for that, at least not for some months.

Still, there is no mystery.

We know her name and occupation.

We know how she died, and it wasn't on duty . . .

She was—is—a Macomb County Sheriff's deputy, age thirty. If the body had been collected, toxicology would reveal low levels of oxycodone. She injured a rotator cuff while wrestling with a suspect a few years back, and the two pills a day that she took to deal with the pain had become a mostly man-ageable habit.

She was listening to her Spotify playlist. Inexplicably, she preferred classical music while hike-running but only played "my ladies" when at home—Sia, Gaga, Rihanna.

At the time of death, the particular track she was absorbed in, Mahler's *Kindertotenlieder*, is notable, but for reasons to be later revealed.

How is it, then, that there is no mystery?

What happened?

She saw something off-trail, glinting in the sun—

It was that sort of thing one hears about all one's life, the bad-luck fall that cracks the neck or bleeds the brain. The friend of a friend falls from their bike and their head hits the curb or trivially stumbles and destiny con-spires to end everything—memory, desire, breath, life—in an instant. Usu-ally, it's bodysurfers into sandbars and divers into shallow pools that one reads about. In the deputy's case, she tumbled down the maw of the gulch before coming to an abrupt, hidden rest. In the moments that Lydia was falling, what was she thinking? She wouldn't have had time to voice—or think—more than *Shit!* though *not surviving* couldn't have been in her mind-set, not remotely. A gross and damnable inconvenience, yes, but never the end of all things.

If there was a witness, what would they have seen?

Woman on trail, walking with resolution. Something ten yards ahead gets her attention. Casually curious, she leans to investigate and then trips and tumbles. A nasty fall but the grassy, sloping terrain is such that a sense of fatality isn't in the air. The spectator draws closer, their drone's-eye view hovering over where the hiker has come to rest. The witness zooms in on the rock—the rock of destiny, ending memory and desire—and thinks, *What terrible luck*. The witness stays a few frantic minutes, uncertain if the hiker is dead (we know otherwise), and is about to go for help when something remarkable happens. The lifeless body has a great seizure, a moment of elec-trified cosmic astonishment to flesh and bones. It stands, haloed in blue. (What *is* that otherworldly blue?) The hiker's anguished and astonished face, like that of a child roused from deep sleep, contorts in tears, the mouth letting out a great yawp—more like the scream of a little girl who lost her parents in a department store of the dead. The witness is transfixed, more by the eerie phenomenon of what they see than by the hard fact of the woman's sudden reanimation.

The face becomes a mask of serenity, regal, timeless. The body remains in place, stock-still. Rigid, though not in the sense of rigor mortis.

A monument now.

A sphinx.

And the gulch—the entire valley—is bathed in the *parfum* of blue mist, sprayed from a nebulizer of the Unknown.

The body that was Deputy Lydia Molloy and will improbably remain Deputy Lydia Molloy a few months longer begins its slow, labored, somehow elegant ascent from the ravine.

It stops short of the trail and sees something glinting. Not the glint of the original thing that stirred her curiosity—an inexplicably discarded silver belt buckle, of all things—but rather the iPod that flew from Lydia's grasp at the beginning of the fall. (Though the earbuds remained attached to the body throughout the fall.) The arm of the body reaches out to retrieve it. The hands of the body plug in the earbuds and she resumes listening to the music.

Kindertotenlieder . . .

As Lydia makes her way back to her car, wobbly as a foal yet growing stronger and more resolute with each step, she hews close to the tracks, stepping over a rusted rail, making a game of walking over the buried, blown-out ties just as a child might, arms outstretched as if balancing on a tightrope.

A small smile comes to her lips as she imagines a lumbering, clacking train springing up around her—

At last, she knows she is home again.

AFTER THE DEATH OF LYDIA

I.

We've grown accustomed to these, sometimes preceded by a *WARN-ING: What You Are About to See Will Be Disturbing to Most Viewers.* The call of the global village's electronic tom-toms . . .

Bodycam tapes, not of the controversial racial genre, but those outlandish in their wholly unexpected outcome: like the Seattle slacker who was asked to show his ID by a cop on beat patrol. The kid is quiet and cooperative, charming even, diffident and polite—looks like, who's the actor, Jesse Eisenberg?—the tousle-haired, archetypal, benignly twisted boy next door, such undeniable sweetness there, possessed of gentle smarts and nerdy passivity. The cop lowers his guard, because who wouldn't? There is zero threat. The officer's even enjoying their friendly exchange and is moving things along into a cozy wrap-up of conversational banter when the millennial pulls a gun from his backpack and shoots him.

Kills!

Scroll down for video, scroll down for frisson of shock and horror. Scroll down for madness and perversion, scroll down, scroll down—

Here's this one:

A 911 call at 9:03, dispatched to the Saggerty Falls Sheriff's Substation.

What's the problem? (Is there really one?) The manager of Tim Hortons seemed to think so. A gentleman in his forties, wearing a natty suit but no shirt or shoes. That in itself is no particular cause for alarm. He's been there since they opened at 5:30 and now it's 9:00 A.M. and he's been singing for half an hour. The manager told him to please stop but he won't. It started with Ed Sheeran, soft and on-key enough to be mildly confounding yet amusing to customers before seguing into an aggressive version of Panic! at the Disco's "Death of a Bachelor." Now he's doing that song from *Suicide Squad* with "please don't make any sudden moves" and it's riding on the collective nerve.

You're lovin' on the psychopath sitting next to you
You're lovin' on the murderer sitting next to you
You'll think, how'd I get here, sitting next to you?

The cruiser with Deputies Lydia Molloy and Daniel Doheny is the first to arrive. They wear shoulder-mounted cameras—mandatory in Brave New Video World, even in a small village like Saggerty Falls. A patron or two has already posted cell phone mini-movies of the idiosyncratic soap opera on Twitter. "The whole world is watching" mantra is obsolete; now the whole world is watching itself watch . . .

Lydia hangs back while Daniel approaches, interrupting the song. The gentleman's muscular chest is bronzed and shaved, like some *GQ* model. *GQ* smiles a wry "my bad" smile at the deputy. Daniel's cool—he's always cool, and attuned to the quirkiness of whatever encounter, which is after all what makes work interesting. There's a brief, unhassly exchange before he motions the gentleman to step outside. He complies. Lydia waits on the sidewalk for them to emerge, hand on gun. When the gentleman hits the street, he stretches out his arms like a sun worshipper and yawns dramatically before letting go an animal bellow of Dionysian bliss. Daniel doesn't have a particular vibe (other than the oddness of it), but the detainee is built enough to warrant caution. Plus, experience has shown that when he *doesn't* have a vibe, well, that's usually not a good thing. Meth and/or mental illness can mask as anomalous eccentricity.

The gent refocuses and folksily says, "It's that bad, huh?"—Daniel knows that he's referring to his singing voice.

"I've heard worse," says Deputy Doheny, to defuse.

"Guess I should cancel my audition for *The Voice*—"

With that, he shoves the deputy into the plate glass with enough force that it thunders and cracks. Then wheels around to Lydia, smiling calmly as she draws her gun. Inside the establishment, gasps and herd-scatter, but no one emerges—they rush toward the front counter instead to take cover. On-lookers make movies from across the street and from office windows.

Deputy Lydia Molloy points her gun.

"Get on the ground! Now!"

Her partner is already on his feet and tases the assailant, who plunges a Buck Knife into his chest. GQ reels, pulling the dart from his hairless sculpted torso, and turns back to Lydia. He cranes his neck to the sky and gives the dark Gods an offering of a piercing banshee cry. He charges her and Deputy Molloy shoots, three times. Squat-frozen in combat stance, she holds her aim and, when it's unquestionable that GQ is dead, rushes to Daniel as he struggles to yank out the knife.

Three squad cars arrive.

Everything's happened in under thirty seconds.

Lydia was directly behind GQ, which was why Daniel had tased and not shot, fearing she'd be struck if he missed. Daniel is bruised and minorly punctured, his vest and ego taking the brunt of the blow.

2.

They lay together that night at Lydia's place in Richmond, half in shock, half exultant. (One of the quirky things they discovered about each other since beginning their "sleepovers" was that recently—independently—both had developed a thing for wearing kids' pajamas.) "I don't think you under-stand," said Lydia. "If something happened to you, I know I would die." Her words surprised them and moved her to tears. He put an arm around her, wincing from the knife wound. (Some stitches there.) "Don't worry. I'll always protect you. As long as you're there to protect *me* . . . after I fail to protect you." They laughed at the sardonic remark.

She didn't know why her feelings toward Daniel were so strong. *Am I in love with him?* They'd been working together a few months and she'd never felt any sort of attraction. But something changed after she fell on the Orchard Trail—she'd become almost obsessed. Then one day, not long before the shootout at Tim Hortons, he confessed that something had changed in him too. Gossip among the deputies had it that they'd "hooked up," though they hadn't, not really, but their denials only made things worse. They *tried* being with each other in that way. They fucked a few times but neither one seemed to be all that interested. Eventually the love-making became rote, an awkward going through the motions before it actually became embarrassing. At first, each was hurt. *Am I not sexy to him/her? Does he/she just want to be friends?* They finally had a talk about it. "What's the matter with us!" they said, laughing. It was nice that it never got heavy. They decided that whatever they shared was pure and special, lovely and different, something they'd never experienced with anyone else before. A special bond that didn't require explaining and just "was."

The GQ killing was big news. Even Detective Willow Wylde (ret.) read the Internet item aloud during Sunday-morning roundup in his duties that week as elected "mayor" and all-around director of entertainment of the Meadows. Nothing like a singing, Tom Ford lookalike psycho to capture the cynical hearts and minds of rehabbers. The Macomb deputies vivisected the publicly released bodycam footage, celebrating Lydia and razzing Daniel for trying to tase a male model but getting stabbed instead. A lot of emasculating jokes when the two of them were present, like asking Lydia about Daniel, "How's the missus?" Sheriff Owen Caplan was so pleased that he threw a press conference from his administrative office in Mount Clemens, the county seat, with Deputies Molloy and Doheny front and center. It was the sort of feel-good justifiable homicide that did wonders for the department's public image and morale.

Daniel left the bedroom to take a call. Lydia knew it was Rachelle, his wife, from whom he was separated. She heard him talk in low tones from the living room, assuring his ex that he was all right, the knife had barely penetrated the skin. She went to the door and listened to him lie to Rachelle that he was back at home, in the little place he'd moved to in Smiths Creek after their marriage fell apart. Lydia didn't intrude on that space because she loved him, she wasn't *in* love (am I?), but rather it was his very special friendship she didn't want to lose. If that were to happen, if she nosily fudged boundaries and lost him because of that, she knew that what she said earlier would come true—it'd be the death of her. Each day they grew closer and neither could explain the reason or depths of that.

It was like a union of blood.

During his private conversation, the vision came to Lydia again. The first time it showed itself was when she rose from the gully grave and walk-straddled the tracks of the Orchard Trail. But it wasn't vivid then, not yet, it wasn't otherworldly and panoramic until that night at home after the fall when she sank into bottomless sleep. Now she was starting to have it again, to *feel* it, symphonically, everywhere, in waking hours—with the smallest effort, she could summon it. A profound warmth accompanied the vision; the only way she could describe it was that it felt like family.

She wondered if it might be religious in nature. As a girl, she prayed to God to make her a saint.

The imagery was of a train filled with people, but the features of their faces were blurry and impossible to discern. The first time the locomotive roared past—a silent roar—it moved too fast for her to see the figures behind the windows. It blew by like an express, as if belonging to someone else's sleep, someone else's dream. Then it slowed down, the way trains do when entering cities. Tonight, lightly focused on Daniel talking in the other room, Lydia imagined, *felt* it slowing to a stop, as one notices a moth alighting on a book.

Daniel wrapped up the call. It was semi-awkward and besides, he wanted to get back to Lydia. His wife asked if he was sure he didn't want to stay in St. Clair tonight, at the house they used to share, "in case you need company. I'm worried about you." The offer was more about sweetness than it was a come-on, but Daniel said, *No, I think I kind of need to be alone.* Rachelle acted like she wasn't hurt—she wasn't, really, because by now both had a lot of experience pretending not to be hurt, enough so that they weren't sure if the hurting was even possible anymore. One thing would injure her, though: if she knew the emotional gravitas of his involvement with Deputy Lydia Jane Molloy.

He was glad to be off the phone. On his way back to the bedroom, he passed two big shopping bags Lydia had picked up from the Dollar Store, filled with tiny unicorns.

There must have been thirty of them.

AFTER THE DEATH OF DANIEL

Deputy Daniel Doheny wondered why he hadn't spoken to his partner about it. He felt as close to Lydia as she did to him, yet it was a barrier he couldn't seem to cross.

He and Rachelle had been through hell. In Afghanistan, he killed three men and a child, a little boy, and nothing—certainly not the circumstances, which cleared him of wrongdoing—could exculpate him. After coming home, he had violent night terrors, occasionally injuring himself when his demons launched him from bed during sleep. He stopped sharing a bed with his wife, fearing he would hurt her. He bought pot and pills off the street, Xanax mostly, never seeking professional help because he still had the dream of becoming a cop. Severe PTSD would have been too much of a strike against him. When they lost their baby boy to crib death, Daniel was convinced it was the result of paying off the karmic debt incurred by the Afghan boy. They tried again to get pregnant but it didn't happen. When he learned that Rachelle was having an affair with the fertility specialist, he walked. She got depressed and agoraphobic and wouldn't leave the house for a year. Daniel didn't go through with the divorce because he thought that without the anchor of marriage, flimsy as it was, she would kill herself. He went to work as a corrections officer, one of 250 at the Macomb County Jail.

He wanted to be a cop, *needed* to be; it became his only salvation. He would do his time at the Macomb County Jail and become a street deputy, then maybe a sergeant or lieutenant or even captain. Who knew? A year into the job, just before he was scheduled to take his Academy physical, he got into a scuffle with a tattoo-faced convict who "gassed" him with feces. That night he had shooting pains in his arm that continued into the week-end, unrelieved by heroic amounts of Aleve, Xanax and some cortisone of Rachelle's that was way past its expiration date. He thought that he'd hurt himself in the fight and ignored it. When he finally went to the ER—something told him to drive the ninety miles to Lansing, "incognito," to es-cape the prying eyes of someone in health care who might have dealings with the jail—they said it was a serious heart attack and he couldn't believe it.

His cop career was over.

The trite fantasies about going on a suicidal killing rampage embarrassed him. When he found out that the man doing cadet physicals was none other than Dr. Orvill Wirtz, he couldn't believe his luck. Wirtz was the specialist whom Rachelle had sowed her mild oats with. The doc was married and had a lot to lose, including his license. He was weak, and disgusted Daniel; he couldn't even believe the asshole had a half a dick to fuck his wife with. He'd been cuckolded by a milquetoast. He blackmailed him into supplying a healthy EKG and voilà, it was official: Daniel now had the heart of a teen-ager. A few months later, he mustered out of the jail in Mount Clemens and joined the day shift at the substation in Saggerty Falls. (Sheriff Caplan per-sonally approved the application; he had a soft spot for vets.) That was where he met Deputy Lydia Molloy. Like him, she began her career as a corrections deputy but had left six months before he started work at the prison.

The last time he slept with his ex was about a month ago, before he and Lydia began "seeing" each other. He'd had one of his recurring nightmares and out of desperation called Rachelle from his bachelor pad in Smiths Creek. In the dream, they were at Macy's shopping for baby things. There was gunfire in the streets and parts of the store were demolished, like some cav-ernous World War II cathedral. The dapper salesman—he looked a little like the wacko GQ model from Tim Hortons—showed them cribs while politely speaking through a gurgling hole in his throat. When Daniel awakened, he picked up the phone but could barely talk. Rachelle said to come right over.

That was the night Daniel died, two hours and twenty minutes after they made love. He clasped his chest and fell off the bed to the floor, but Rachelle, out cold from the tranquilizers and the wine, was snoring and oblivious. Approximately a minute before brain and heart would die, a kind of gale blew through his body and as consciousness returned he found himself dreaming not of Macy's but of the Afghan village that unraveled him. He was shooting and shooting, yet this time his pursuers wouldn't lie down. The villagers of the damned stood staring and impervious, without fear. Then came a screech of metal—nothing like incoming artillery or any-thing he'd ever heard in combat—growing louder until it was deafening. When he stepped outside, the blown-out landscape crowded with bodies that kept staring yet would not fall, there it was:

A train, like a giant version of the Lionel set he loved so much as a boy. It waited for him and he boarded.

In the morning, he was confused. He realized he had wet the bed. He could have turned the soaked mattress over while Rachelle was in the bath-room but flipped it around instead so that the urine was on her side. When she groggily came back he touched the sheet and said, "Hey, babe, I think you might have made a little water here." She inspected and couldn't believe it, blaming it on the Ambien. "Oh my God," she said. "That hasn't hap-pened since I was in college."

When he left, Daniel was unsteady on his feet though weirdly invigo-rated. The world looked strange and new. His left arm and chest ached, as if badly bruised. That day in the locker room of the substation, he did a hun-dred push-ups.

A month had passed and he wondered why he hadn't told Lydia about the train. It was with him now and seemed always to have been. In the week since he had "boarded" he noticed that his night terrors ceased. He stopped taking pills and smoking weed because the train calmed him, like a form of mindful meditation. *Meditation in blue*, he called it. Often, he re-treated to one of the luxuriously wood-paneled cabins and sat waiting. (For what, he wasn't sure.) A porter eventually appeared, an elegant woman in her sixties who brought milk and freshly baked chocolate cookies that tasted like the ones his mother used to make. That went on for a week or so—a week of lucid dreaming and cookies—then one morning the porter brought a little girl into the cabin. She sat beside him and smiled at his milk mustache. He smiled back. Night after night he waited expectantly for the porter to usher her in and when she appeared, the girl sat and smiled before gazing with a kind of contented promise at the dark, rushing void outside the cold window. He stole glances. She was so familiar to him. He knew he loved her and that he would until the end of time. Her hair was fiery red and always there was a vaporous halo of blue. She wore her blueness so lightly, so elegantly—sometimes like a shawl, sometimes a chiffon collar, sometimes a dancing rosary of periwinkles.

He caught his own reflection in the window but did not see himself. He saw not an adult but a child, a boy of nearly ten years old, but he didn't have the features of the boy that Daniel remembered he once was.

It wasn't him . . .

The girl put her hand on his. Daniel's revived heart soared and ached and broke and it wasn't until the night the train arrived at the station that he knew it was Lydia.

THE PORTER

Annie had the same ritual before every Meeting.

She organized the *Guides* by first names. She wrote the names on the covers in cursive and sorted them into neat stacks before putting them in the old leather satchel that once belonged to her mentor. The *Guides* were like living, sacred things. She thought of them as her babies. If there was a birthday that night—there were usually one or two a week—she put candles and a disposable lighter that she bought at 7-Eleven in the satchel as well. Then she lit a stick of Om Nagchampa incense, also from 7-Eleven (the franchise was owned by an Indian family), and sat cross-legged, breathing deeply. She'd done this for sixteen years.

She lived in an SRO on Detroit's Skid Row, beloved and protected by its denizens, many of whom called her Mother. She dispensed money when she could, bandaged and cleaned wounds after brawls and drunken falls, assuaged the despair of what had been irretrievably lost. They brought Annie small, heartfelt gifts and wrote poems to her singing her praises. She shaved her head like a monk; two decades ago, the hair had vanished during chemo but she stayed with the look. The cancer hadn't recurred but she knew it would one day.

She knew things.

Sixteen years ago, when she presided over her first Meeting, there was only one group a week. The *Guide* wasn't even printed—it was passed down by oral tradition. Back then, rules and regulations were spoken out loud to guests, who were asked to memorize what they heard. It was done that way because Annie's mentor and supervisors were concerned there might be "problems" should the *Guides* accidentally fall into the hands of those not meant to see them. But she cleverly found a way around that because she thought it was important that her guests had something on paper to refer to, a resource they could turn to in moments of anxiety. She told her mentor that to outside eyes, the *Guides'* cryptic content could easily be explained as "jottings" or samples of creative writing. Works-in-progress. Snippets of speculative fiction.

But now she had no overseers, no mentor or supervisors. They'd all vanished as subtly as they had long ago appeared.

She always *felt* when new children were coming. The sound of the train would grow louder but less *whoosh-y*. And then it just happened: she found herself on board, walking down long, dark corridors carrying trays of hot tea (the very same flavor she brewed in her tiny rented room) or lemonade, milk and cookies and brownies, all sorts of sugary whatnots. That was how Annie greeted each new arrival, and the ritual always touched her heart. Their blueness appeared to her in the form of jewelry: necklaces, earrings and rings, sometimes tiaras and crowns of cerulean. She never wanted to know what had happened to them—the specific horrors that brought them to this long ride through nothingness—no, that was anathema. Such information wasn't hers to possess. She was merely happy to serve drinks and cookies and solace, and direct them where to go after the train pulled into the station.

She used to be a schoolteacher, but that was so many years ago. They fired her when she began hearing voices. She wound up in Ann Arbor at a psychiatric hospital called Swarthmore. She had already twice tried to kill herself when a scholarly-looking fellow began to visit. He told the authorities that he ran a halfway house for schizophrenic women in Detroit. His name was Jasper. He was a presentable, reputable man with a nattily manicured white goatee. Over the months, making the forty-five-minute drive from Detroit three times a week, he won Annie's trust. He went to court and eventually secured her release to his care. He drew her back to *this* world by tenderly and methodically telling her about the *other*, the one the trains came from. He told Annie that she was a lot like him, they shared much in common—and that people like them were rare and highly sought after in his line of work. She asked, "What line of work is that?" He said that he was a "Porter" (when he wrote the word, it was always capitalized), and in time she came to know what he meant.

He taught her everything. She loved him like a father. Not long after she joined him, Jasper got sick and she cared for him until he passed. When he died he had no possessions, excepting his leather satchel and a beautiful an-tique cabinet of dark wood that was filigreed in mother-of-pearl, a parting gift from the Porter—a woman—who had mentored him.

He gave both to Annie and it felt like he had given her his heart.

She usually took the bus a good two hours before the Meeting, to be safe. Jasper taught her that being late was a sin. Besides, she needed to pick up Bumble. He didn't have a driver's license and liked to ride with her.

She wasn't training him to be a Porter because that just wasn't how it went. Being a Porter was a matter of destiny, not schooling. Yet all Porters needed what Jasper called "sentries," to assist during Meetings. He taught her that the best sentries were the "backward" ones, those who were blunted or socially inept, and indeed, Bumble was a brilliant young man afflicted with Asperger's. Though Jasper *did* become Annie's helper for a time when he got too sick to be a Porter. She suspected he had an ulterior motive, wish-ing to lend his support through that first critical month when she essentially ran the Meeting by herself. He also told Annie that sometimes sentries were Porters who'd gone mad, having crumbled under the pressure of their duties, but that was a rarity.

The sentries stood at the door to make sure only invited guests attended. Because the Meetings took place in a church—the churches were under the belief they were being rented out for 12-Step meetings—outsiders occasion-ally wandered in, thinking it was AA or Al-Anon. But once all of the chil-dren from the train arrived, Bumble locked the doors. The Meetings lasted ninety minutes. At each, there were usually five or six "landlords," Annie's word for the ones whose moribund bodies housed the children who had returned. (The Porter encouraged them to think of the childtenants as "roommates.") It took a moment for the landlords to even find their way to the Meeting, because the absorption of the train kids was disruptive, to say the least—as if being resurrected from the dead hadn't been disruptive enough. For a week or so, both children and hosts were severely disoriented and depressed, not only clobbered by the bizarreness of whatever it was that had happened to them but also struggling to adapt to having two sets of memories; they'd become little ones and grownups all at once. Ultimately, it was the child who would dominate, while drawing on the energy, intellect and experience of the landlord in whom they resided.

Annie could *feel* that she wasn't long for this world and knew as well she would not be traveling to the other. To journey at life's end to the place the trains came from was a privilege afforded only to the most powerful of Porters, and while she'd done well in her vocation, Annie never believed she was that special. No, she would die here, in *this* world, like her mentor. She had been a Porter far longer than any she'd heard of, longer than was meant to be. She had such knowledge from whispers overheard in the long, dark corridors of the Pullman cars while she carried trays to the cabins of her guests. She eavesdropped on other Porters, old and new, as they congregated in the locomotive's nooks and niches, discussing her longevity in a respectful hush. They stepped back in obeisance, even awe, as she swept by with her tray of treats on the way to greet a new child . . . and she *was* an anomaly. Porter work wasn't amenable to a long life; it took too much. Yet somehow, by fate or physical constitution, she had persevered.

There was much she would never know. How many Meetings were taking place throughout the city, the country, the world? How did it all begin? And what did any of it mean? (The impossible question of impossible questions.) Not since she was a young girl who awakened one morning with a shock of apprehension that *everything* was a dream had Annie doubted that life (and death) could hold such mysteries. Still another unanswerable question haunted and persisted: Why would Mystery be used to such vengeful ends? Yet through the years, Annie's curiosities had ended, the leavetaking perhaps another mystery in itself. All she was certain of, all she had, was Love. She'd even begun to love the murderers—hadn't they brought her all the beautiful children? But she suppressed the heretical feeling whenever it arose, suspecting it might cause harm to her innocent wards.

Now the old, haunting curiosities had come back, and she wondered what that meant . . .

Tonight, new arrivals were due. As always, Annie wasn't sure they'd make it. Everyone of course had the address she handed them on the train, but it usually took a week or so for them to appear as landlords at the church. It was inevitable that they would; it simply had never happened that a child from the train hadn't. And when they did, all would be well.

She wrote the boy's name, Troy, on a *Guide*, in Roman-looking letters— very masculine but still fun. On another she wrote the girl's, Maya, in gold. Then she drew a little unicorn head without knowing why, dusting glitter over the sprig of Elmer's glue that made its horn.

WILLOW UNBOUND

I.

The Meadows staff strongly suggested that he transition to a halfway house. (In the final days of rehab, they always pushed hard for a "plan.") The flowcharts demonstrated that your best shot was to move into a sober living situation. *If you run straight home and stop going to meetings,* warned a counselor, *relapse is one hundred percent.*

The Big Book said "half measures availed us nothing," but Willow compromised and decided to stay with his kid. He'd only visited the house in Marlette twice—once for the birth of his grandson and another for the burial of Pace's dog, the same guilt-puppy he'd flown in from New York to give to his daughter on her sixteenth birthday. It died last year on her thirty-first.

Geoff, Pace's husband, grew up in Marlette, a city in Sanilac County that was even smaller than Saggerty Falls. He tended bar and was an all-around decent fellow who actually looked up to Willow—a lucky turn, because he'd never have agreed to the layover if Geoff was an asshole. The cottage was lovely and well kept, and it was wonderful to see Larkin. He noticed the toddler was walking a little funny. Pace said the pediatrician told her it was a muscle thing that he'd grow out of. "He said it's really common." Really? *Right,* Willow wanted to say. *He's just like the millions of*

other kids out there hopping around like fucking wounded kangaroos. He pictured Geoff breaking the boy's leg in a fit of anger but dismissed the brain
video as a dark, reflexive cop fantasy because it didn't remotely fit the picture. Larkin was happy as a clam and clearly loved his daddy.

So there he was in Marlette, "the heart of the thumb," an hour due
south from the unmanicured tip of the nail, Port Hope, where the detective
resided—and an hour north of the old Saggerty Falls stomping grounds.
There he was, in yet another borrowed room. This one happened to be in an
attic. He'd become a squatter in other people's lives, a grizzled rehab gypsy,
a stranger in other people's narratives, not to mention his own. At least he
didn't have to share *this* room with drug addicts, drunks and sundry other
dueling disorderheads, a detail that for the moment offset the unmentionable
negatives—that he had $17,346 to his name and an iffy pension; that he was
lost, adrift, aged out, invisible to the unfairer sex; that his future looked the
same as his bleak, checkered past. Was there even the old standby left called
Hope? Dubya still named it that but the edifice was in the midst of collapsing into itself, like a slow-motion film of a demolished building.

The meeting at First United Methodist, five miles from his daughter's
home, was decent enough. There were some attractive ladies—garden-
variety 12-Step newcomers with the world's shortest dresses and shittiest
tattoos—but try as he may, he couldn't even make eye contact, let alone get
any action. He'd lost the thread of what was "attractive," anyway. Attractive in rehab and Alcoholics Anonymous was different from attractive in
the world. One thing he *did* know: he wasn't sexy anymore. He wanted to
get the fuck out of there. He was tempted to stay till the end so he could at
least hold one of the hotties' hands during the Lord's Prayer, but the goal
was just too pathetic.

He got up during a share, poured himself a cup of coffee and walked
right out the door.

As he left the church parking lot, he thought it might be time to refill his Cialis prescription. Trouble was, it was so damn expensive. Everyone bitched and moaned about the high cost of EpiPens and cancer pills but no one said boo about the usurious cost of dick stiffeners. Where was the outrage? Maybe he'd talk to his son-in-law about getting some over the Internet. Maybe Geoff had his own secret stash. But why even bother, when he was nonexistent to women? At least he was out of rehab and half-way home.

He'd been on the fence but Pace insisted he come. "I want to cushion your reentry, Dub-Daddy," she said. What shocked Willow was that he'd acquiesced. *Must be gettin' soft.*

They sat at the dinner table while Larkin watched TV nonsense from a beanbag chair.

The fried chicken was very, very good.

It was more than very good, considering what he'd been eating at the Meadows. Which hadn't been all that bad, but there's just something about the taste of food when it's been cooked for three versus a hundred. He and Geoff shot the shit about this and that. His daughter didn't say a word. She was biding her time. Finally, she said, "So how was it?"

—the dumb, elephant-in-the-room question that had been on respectful moratorium, waiting to be voiced.

"Well," said Willow. "It was weird and it was beautiful."

Pace smiled wryly. She loved her dad's way. "Any celebs?"

"Not really. Maybe a pop singer or two."

"Oh my God, *who?*"

"Didn't catch their names."

He was fucking with her just a little.

"Are you serious?" she said, outraged.

"Didn't see the superstars all that much. They were in a different group—with the sex addicts. There was *one* . . . a dark-haired gal."

Pace didn't know if he was kidding. "Selena Gomez?"

"That doesn't ring a bell."

"Daddy, if you don't remember her name, I am going to *kill* you."

"Hell, he couldn't tell you her name even if he knew it," said Geoff. "It's an *anonymous* program." He winked at his father-in-law. "Right, Dubya?"

"The man is absolutely correct," said Willow. "Anonymity is the spiritual foundation of all our traditions, ever reminding us to place principles before celebrities."

"Don't give me that bullshit! *Nothing's* anonymous anymore. You better call some of your friends who were there and *ask* them."

"Listen to your husband. I could never rat out my trudging buddies, Baby Girl."

"Oh right," she scoffed. They were all enjoying their fun.

"And it *especially* applies to me," he said. "I mean, as a retired law enforcement officer."

"I'll get it out of you yet."

"If you need some cash," said Geoff to Willow, "you could always sell that shit to DMZ on the down-low."

"It's *TMZ*, dipshit," laughed Pace.

"That time may already be approaching," said Willow.

Pace let it go and said, sincerely, "You look great, Dad."

"She's right," said Geoff. "You look rested. Healthy."

"Well, thank you. I feel pretty good." What else could he say? He added his signature sign-off: "Onward."

2.

A few hours after dinner, there was a gentle rap on the door of his room in the attic. He was feeling like Anne Frank up there.

Pace had a plate of cookies and a thermos of ice with Diet Dr Pepper, just how he liked it. She sat cross-legged on the floor.

"I'm so, so proud of you, Dub-Daddy."

"All right," he said modestly. "Come on, now."

"I'm serious."

"Don't blow too much smoke at me, it's bad for my recovery."

"It's such a big thing that you did. And I know how hard it is. How hard it's been."

Her words made him feel good—*right-sized* was the term they used in the Program.

"Thank you, darlin'. It was pretty harsh there for a while. I spent two weeks plotting my escape."

"I'll bet you did," she laughed.

"Then something kind of happens and you start to ease into it. You stop fighting. And you look around and see a whole bunch of other people who blew up their lives and it's comforting somehow. I guess they call that sur-render." He smiled at his beloved. "And hey, I should be thanking *you*. For finding a place for your crazy old man to dry out."

Pace touched his hand before worry clouded her face. "Are there AA meetings in Port Hope? Or anywhere close to where you live?"

"Oh, sure. AA's everywhere."

"Okay," she said, tentatively. He knew where her head was going. "Have you thought about going back to work?"

"Not really," sighed Willow. "Not yet."

"Well, give yourself a moment," she said, with can-do resoluteness. Then she wavered. "But don't you think maybe it'd be a good thing? To go back to work?"

"Market's tough out there for an ex-cop. An *old* ex-cop. They're giving all the high-paying jobs to wounded vets—you know, graveyard security at tow yards, that sort of thing. Most of the really prestigious jobs are taken. Like guard positions in parking lots at Walmart."

"Very funny. Don't be so cynical. Why don't you raise the bar? You could open up a private-detective agency."

"Maybe I could," he said. "Hire myself to find myself."

He was trying to keep it light.

"I think part of the problem," said Pace, "might be that you're not—you need to keep your mind active."

"It sure was active at the Meadows. They saw to that. There was the journaling class, painting therapy, movie night . . ."

"You know what I mean, Daddy. Now that you're out, it's important to use that head of yours. Because you're brilliant. Have you called any of your old contacts in New York?"

He shook his head. "The only so-called contacts I didn't burn are the bartenders, and I burned quite a few of those." Pace's face darkened as she stared at the floor. "Hey now, it's all gonna be okay, Baby Girl. I'll find something, don't you worry. Okay?"

"I do worry. I worry about you."

"Well, I'm fine and I'm going to *be* fine." He waited for her to eke out a smile. "Talked to your mother?"

She knew what he meant. "I don't tell her stuff about you, Dad."

"I didn't mean that—though maybe I did. I guess I was a little curious about how much she knew."

"Nothing from *me*. Not that she wouldn't be happy to hear you're sober. She'd be thrilled."

"Whatever. I just want to be the one to tell her."

"And why would you do *that*? It's not like you give her regular updates. When's the last time the two of you even spoke?"

"I guess it's been awhile. She doing okay?"

"She's good—they're good. They just moved."

"Oh boy. Adelaide *hates* to move."

"I know, but they got a bigger house so I think she's okay with it."

"A bigger mousetrap," he said cryptically.

Father and daughter grew quiet. Pace's brow furrowed and Willow thought she was going to yap again about worrying over him. Then he realized her thoughts were elsewhere. "What's going on?"

"I wanted to tell you . . . about Larkin's leg."

Willow stiffened. "Did Geoff do something to him, Pace?"

"Are you serious? *Fuck* no." She shook her head in chagrin at Dark Cop, Dark Dad. "Larkin has a little problem with his hip, that's all."

"What kind of a problem?"

"Apparently, he's had it from birth. They didn't think it was serious."

"Why didn't you tell me?"

"I don't know. You've kind of had a lot going on. If you haven't noticed. I didn't want you to freak out but Geoff told me you wouldn't and that I was being dumb."

"Is it serious?"

"Not *serious*-serious. Kind of, I guess. They say if he doesn't have surgery, he might have trouble walking."

"He already has fucking trouble walking!"

"Don't yell at me!"

"I'm sorry," he said contritely.

"I mean as he grows, it's going to get worse. They said it's probably best not to wait."

"It's not a cancer or anything?"

"No!"

"Okay," he nodded. "So we're talking when. For the surgery."

"Soon. Sometime soon, I guess. They say it's not that big a deal. I mean the actual operation—that it's kind of basic. The doctor says he does them all the time. I mean, if it needs to wait, they said that's okay too. But the sooner the better."

"How much do you need, Pace?"

"I don't know," she shrugged. It embarrassed her to talk about money with her father. "Geoff's group plan is supposedly going to cover some of it—why does anyone even have insurance if it always only covers *some* of something, and, like, the smallest part?" She scowled in exasperation. "But it's going to be okay. I'm in the middle of hassling with them." She sighed. "The doctor needs fifteen thousand off the top. I'm pretty sure we'll get most of that back. But I don't trust the insurance companies for shit."

"I'll give you ten tomorrow."

"Dad, you don't have that kind of money."

"You don't know what I have."

"I didn't go to Mom yet because—she gets so flipped."

"You don't need to. You let me handle it."

She came and sat next to him on the bed and Willow held her like he used to when she was small, when she got a booboo or had a bad dream and cried in his arms, before the divorce, before he moved away.

Years later, when Pace visited him in New York, he tried holding her but she'd squirm away. She never forgave him for leaving her and Adelaide, never knew or understood the reasons why. She could never understand— how could she?—and he resented her for that until he came to know that wanting a child to understand was the most selfish and grievous of sins.

MINIATURE DREADS

Port Hope—could the name of where he lived (he thought to himself) be any more magnificent, more ironic, more absurd? Detective Willow Millard Wylde—tired, retired, refried and broken—was actually living, in what felt like the end of days, end of *his* days, in Port Hope! He'd been there since his forced retreat from the NYPD and the world . . . On arrival home from his sojourn to his daughter's, Dubya had his ashes hauled—what could have been more hopeful? Miranda, an overweight "bodyworker" who worked at Menard's Home Improvement, made nighttime house calls until she built "a full-time massage therapy practice." She gave a pretty good half-hour rub before improving his home by jerking him off sans oil. Miss Miranda had beaucoup cleavage and let him touch her fat thighs, which the recovering cop kneaded with the rough fingers of his still-healing hand—way better than doing those P.T. exercises with Silly Putty the doctor at the Mayo suggested. (No amount of Miranda or putty would make his bullet-shattered leg right again.)

After the transaction, she used a warm washrag to clean him up, like the gals in places he used to frequent as a Cold Case cop in the Big Apple. He wondered where she learned the technique. Maybe it was just a universal hospitality thing, like stewardesses handing you the hot towel.

How strange was the world of bodies! That a lonely, mountainous, thrown-away gal could make him feel better with her cut-rate fumblings, could *heal* him, albeit temporarily—how amazing that a crude, perfunctory act resulting in 5ccs of seminal expectoration could allow him instant access to his old friend Hope! How strange and comical, how sweet and grotesquely sad . . . but in the end, it was just life, or signs of. And where there was life, there was Hope. (Not necessarily Port Hope.) Even though Willow knew that wasn't necessarily true—*Where there are signs of life, there are signs of death*, intoned Dark Cop—it *seemed* to be true. Like the proverbial glass, a person could look at a body and see it as half-alive or half-dead. He preferred to see himself as the former.

Thirty dollars to be healed. Thirty dollars to feel connected to something larger than himself. For bookkeeping purposes, he put the Miranda invoice in the "necessities" file, like water, electricity and tithing.

After the check he wrote to Pace, his account was left with about seven large. The 10K for Larkin's surgery was in the necessities file too; Willow hadn't helped the girl in her suicidal teens and he'd be damned if he didn't help her now. But she needed more than that kind of help, she needed a father's unconditional love, support, protection. A Band-Aid wouldn't do—reparations and future deposits were in order. By the time he left the planet, he needed to leave behind a trust fund for his grandson, say, two hundred grand for his education, and something for Pace as well. He'd flushed his earnings as a detective, eating his way through whores and fancy restaurants, losing at horse tracks and gaming clubs. For a few years he went on a Rolex binge, trading up and up and up, and the thought of it turned his stomach. He must have stolen a quarter million from drug dealers but had nothing to show for it.

Asshole.

He put on his faves, Rachmaninoff and Mahler—CDs, because he still hadn't gotten the Bluetooth/iTunes thing down—and stared into the mirror at his sad sack self. He wore the gift Pace ordered off the Internet, a nightshirt emblazoned with HERD PEOPLE HERD PEOPLE with a cartoony shepherd and flock of sheep bunched below the letters. (He had told her the "Hurt people hurt people" mantra on a phone call from rehab, and this was her retort.) The shirt was in a crazy XXXXL that came down to mid-shin. Willow moved closer to the mirror, peered into his eyes and saw the shadow of death already upon him. He thought of the line he'd read in a Graham Greene novel that he borrowed from Renata at the Meadows—"the anxieties which are beyond the reach of a tranquilizer"—and knew he was beyond tranquilizers, beyond alcohol now.

He hoped he wasn't beyond solace, and a measure of peace.

L ast Sunday, before returning home, he took his grandson to Marlette Park.

Now that he was privy to the backstory, Larkin's waddle seemed more pronounced and Willow treated him with an excess of devotion and tenderness. No reason to be maudlin about it—just a musculoskeletal problem that a surgeon can fix—but he couldn't help getting mushy. His defenses had crumbled since he got sober. The world was, after all, a poignantly lacerating, sentimental place. It always had been. Booze just softened the edges, making the epic heartbreak of being human manageable. He wept throughout the day, never knowing what might set him off. He covered a post-orgasmic crying jag with a long, stagey cough while Miranda dutifully fetched the après-sex washrag.

At the park, watching Larkin play, he thought of Pace and the adolescent hell she'd gone through, the hell he'd been absent for. He thought of her mother, Adelaide, and how he once loved her—loved her still. Watching his feisty grandson's clumsy, twisted, joyful movements, he came to think of other small bodies long gone: Troy and Maya, whom Pace once babysat. Their disappearance really did a number on her. Him too. Because all his life, he'd perversely considered such an event befalling his own, not just Dark Cop's fantasy but every parent's. When that terrible day finally came—for the Rummers—the hard-core possibility of such a loss entered his body like a slow-growing, inoperable cancer.

Pace had just turned sixteen when it happened. Willow was in his early forties, on a surprise visit to the Falls from New York, with a birthday puppy in tow. He had moved to Manhattan at thirty-seven, in flight from Adelaide, the woman he loved—the cheater who mauled his heart. (Of course he ignored the truth, for a while anyway: she'd never strayed until there was nothing left of the marriage, never strayed during his dalliances with wait-resses, strippers and whores.) Willow hardened and polished the hurt and humiliation until he hyper-shined as a rookie in the NYPD. Pace came to stay at his place in Midtown whenever his impossible schedule allowed—which it never really did. He invited her twice a year, often canceling at the last minute. As her father's fuck-yous became predictable, her heartbreak matured into rage, her rage into dangerous act-outs of rebellion. Adelaide blamed him for their daughter's dance with death—and who was he to say she was wrong?

When Addie got too crazy and begged him to intervene, he would fly back to Saggerty Falls for long, stressed-out weekends, the travesty of a heli-copter parent—a tourniquet parent, crashing with friends and doing triage on his baby girl, if and when he could find her. At the end of his marriage, he fled the Falls to save himself, taking die-hard heed of his therapist's en-abling counsel. "How can you show up for your daughter until you show up for yourself?" During his oh-so-courageous reinvention and self-renewal, abandoned by her warrior-protector, Pace got badly burned in the not-so-friendly fire.

Hurt people hurt people.

The damage done was the great, consuming shame of his demolished life. When the Rummer kids vanished, it seemed to Willow they'd been sacrificed for his eyes only, a primordial, custom-made metaphor of the con-sequences of abandonment that caused him to lose his daughter. The detec-tive was forever changed. Brother and sister became twins in a derogatory constellation of transposed grief, a frozen cell slice of his own tragic DNA—Pace became Maya, and Willow became Troy, the older one who had fatally failed to protect.

Watching Larkin and another boy on the slide at the park, Willow won-dered what his grandson would become. Genes often skipped genera-tions, which meant the boy just might be heading for rehab and general despondency . . . "We're saving a seat for him" was how folks put it in AA.

He remembered the haunting desperation in Adelaide's voice when she called him in New York at 3:00 A.M. to say she couldn't do it anymore. They needed to hospitalize Pace, commit her, restrain her, do *something* or their daughter would surely die. She'd just had Abortion No. 3, overdosing in a seedy motel in its wake, and Adelaide told him that Pace was turning tricks with men she met online. She was no longer living up to the family name, as Grandma Wylde used to say about family members' misadventures, but dying up to it.

Yet she turned out okay. How did *that* happen? Dark Cop knew it was just a numbers game. If they made it through their teens without getting hit by a drunk or coming down with a TV-movie disease or getting taken out by bad H—*or being shot at school or getting abducted, raped and murdered*—actually, they had a pretty decent chance of hanging around awhile.

Willow went over and pushed his grandson in the swing. He drifted back to his own boyhood, remembering the mothball smells and dark wood of his grandparents' home. He pictured the faded red metal canopy of the deck overlooking the leafy backyard and recalled the visions he'd had as a child. Once, he had a nightmare that Nana had died. He saw her standing at the foot of his bed in a luminous blue wedding gown; when his mother rushed in to comfort him and Willow told her what he'd dreamed, she immediately picked up the phone to call his grandfather. The old man was startled and told her the ambulance had just arrived. Nana was dead in a few hours. After that, Willow stopped sharing his dreams and visions. He didn't want to cause his mother, or anyone, pain like that again. But he loved Mom for taking his vision seriously, for honoring his gift and giving him that kind of respect. Willow wondered if she'd always known that something was wondrous and peculiar about him from an early age and if such knowledge forced her to listen. To make that midnight call to her father.

When he got older, the dreams and visions stopped. They didn't go away, not exactly, but he stifled them, believing them to be useless and borderline destructive. In his late forties, around the time Willow left homicide and began working Cold Case in New York, the visions returned. He stuffed them again. He grew tortured, wondering if their suppression was an act of selfishness and cowardice, of weakness. In the middle of these

musings, a chill came over him. The chill was accompanied by a dreamlike
whoosh, now familiar—

—with a shock, Willow realized he'd been standing there lost in thought
and that Larkin was gone from his swing. When his panicked eyes found
the boy, he ran over to him dramatically enough that it seized the attention
of the other parents and guardians. Sitting in the red caboose of the kiddie train, startled by his grandfather's near-violent, beneath-the-armpit ex-
traction from the car, Larkin burst into tears. Willow carried him to a park
bench and sat the toddler on his lap as he tried to soothe. The boy's tears
and squirmings were quickly blotted out by the sight of the small train,
soldered to its decorative track for safety. Willow stared at it, shivering with
recognition—but recognition of what? Where had he seen it? He remembered now, though the *feeling* was in fragments. Still, he wasn't certain if it
was a throwback to one of his old-time visions, or something new.

He was suddenly possessed by the irrational thought that *no* child deserves to be on a train, any train! But he couldn't explain his sensations; nor
could he trace the feelings behind why a little boy's benign and playful
presence in a miniature locomotive was a mournful and disastrous thing.

LYDIA TAKES A MEETING

I.

When a cop killed someone—a fairly unusual occurrence here—department policy mandated a visit to the shrink. If a deputy was shot, he had to do therapy too. (America's newest religion was the cult of Trauma.) Daniel Doheny already had his session.

Lydia hadn't given a second thought to the "death of the bachelor" (for a few weeks, whenever her substation colleagues saw her they broke into the Panic! at the Disco song the madman was crooning at Tim Hortons), at least not in the conventional sense. If anything, the incident stirred up questions she would never have brought up with the police shrink. No, they were issues more along the line of things she'd talk over with Annie, the woman who led the Meeting and called herself "the Porter."

Lydia wrote them down on a pad so she wouldn't forget.

Questions! There were so many that even the idea of them was absurd. She was definitely still Lydia—but how much of Lydia? And just how long would the "landlord" Lydia dominate, in brain and in body? She certainly *felt* like Deputy Molloy; all of those woman's memories were intact and accountable. She even remembered that ill-fated hike . . . drifting in recollection, she knew she was wholly Lydia, more or less, in the moment. She liked the food and clothes and smells that Lydia liked, and the music too—classical (Copland and *Kindertotenlieder*), hip-hop (Nicki and Kanye and Big Sean) and Top 20 (Adele and Rihanna). Plus, there were certain men and women whom she worked with (except for Daniel) or passed along the street who made her feel what she called *sexybody*. But what of the other memories and feelings, those of her tenant-"roommate"? What about being able to recall a set of parents different from her own? What about holding the stuffed unicorn close to her so she could sleep? (Lydia had *never* been a fan of stuffed animals.) What about her craving for cotton candy—she was a vegan who was nearly phobic about sugar—or when she made plans to buy turtles and goldfishes. What about when she zoned out in front of the TV in front of *Rugrats* and *Dora the Explorer*?

Lydia favored shows like *Dr. Who* and *Black Mirror* . . .

Friends still called her cell and she had no trouble talking to them, no trouble at all—a bunch whom she hadn't heard from came out of the wood-work right after the shooting—but once Lydia hung up she drifted again, feeling ten thousand miles away. Her mom and dad, proud and worried about the whole Tim Hortons thing, came in from Minnesota to stay with her and she was fine with them too; she loved them in the same way she loved the other parents, Maya's parents, though Maya's were so pale, so hard to summon. Lydia was aware that she seemed "different," especially to her folks; she would have had to because she wasn't their Lydia anymore, not completely. They never made any remarks about it (though sometimes seemed on the verge), but she also knew that whatever part of her that ap-peared anomalous or strangely new—being spacey or whatever—would be written off by them to the post-traumatic stress of the Tom Ford lookalike kill. After a Meeting, Annie told Lydia that she was actually fortunate to have had that incident because it was a good "cover" for odd and unfamiliar behaviors.

At the time of her death, Lydia had two half-casual lovers, a man and a woman, sweet *sexybody* buddies from different counties, neither of whom knew about each other. But she ended all that because, well, Maya wasn't exactly thrilled. (One of them even showed up when Daniel was there. *Awkward.*) They managed their hurt feelings by attributing Lydia's cooling passions to her shooting that crazy man; the Porter had absolutely predicted how they'd rationalize her pulling away. Out of weakness, she let the man play with her body for a few weeks and it *did* feel good, but Maya was weirded out so Lydia chose to stop—she was overruled. That's why it felt so nice to be with Daniel, because he understood. They started talking about secret things, not in detail but enough for Lydia to know that he felt the same way she did. He never talked about *his* lovers and she wondered if he was in the closet. Not that it would have mattered. She just felt lucky to have found him. It was like a miracle.

There were so many things to ask Annie, though most of her questions and concerns would soon fall away, the way they always did in a landlord's journey. They would migrate and become the concerns of another, someone already on their way to the station to greet the train.

2.

The first time Lydia went to the Meeting, she was almost late.

How had she even gotten there?

She dreamed she was back on the train. The Porter came to her cabin with the usual tray of cookies and lemonade and everything was so clear, unlike the fuzziness she was accustomed to when trying to conjure the same tableau during waking hours. There was a little boy there too but he was fuzzy, even in the dream. The Porter—Annie—told her they would be arriving soon and it was of great importance that she come to see her. She wrote the address down on the back of the coaster the lemonade was on and told the little girl she should commit it to memory. Maya said that she was terrible at remembering things, but Annie assured her that she wouldn't forget.

"When should I come?" asked Maya.

"You'll know," said Annie, then smiled and left.

Maya turned over the coaster.

The Divine Child Parish
276 Lafayette Circle, Detroit, MI 48206
Be there or be square!

She was supposed to have pizza with Daniel that night but told him she had to meet a friend. He raised an eyebrow, implying she was having a rendezvous with one of her old *sexybodies*, but was funny and permissive about it. At the last moment, Lydia said, "You didn't have the dream?"

"What dream?" he answered, and she felt foolish.

She said she'd be back at ten.

Detroit was an hour south of Richmond, where she lived (sharing her home more or less with Daniel now), and she *did* have trouble with the address Annie gave her—Lydia wasn't so wonderful with directions, even with GPS. When she arrived at the church, she couldn't for the life of her make sense of where she was supposed to go. She'd forgotten that just before leaving her cabin, Annie added that the room she'd be looking for was in the basement. The block was so dark and there were tall, tall trees, what looked like a forestful. She was in tears and about to leave when a funny-looking man with a twitch came out, looked around and waved her over; she got the feeling he'd been sent after her. He introduced himself as Bumble and said he was "the sentry—I help Annie." He was very odd, to say the least, but his smile disarmed her. Bumble beckoned her to follow and they took the stairway down. At the bottom, he pointed to a half-open door. She smiled at him nervously and he politely but firmly encouraged her to go in. When she gently pushed through, she saw that the Meeting was already in progress.

Five people sat in chairs that formed a circle in the center of the smallish room. Annie presided, looking more beautiful to Maya than she did on the train. She wore turquoise jewelry, a silver pin in her collar and a long black dress like the ones Spanish royalty wore in the paintings Lydia saw when she visited the Museo Nacional del Prado during gap year. Annie stood and went to the door to hug her. Then she turned to the group and said, "Everyone—this is Maya." They smiled and shouted, "Welcome!" Annie pointed to one of two vacant chairs and the newcomer went to sit. But before she did, she picked up a pamphlet resting there—*Maya* was written on it above a glittery unicorn that warmed her heart. Then she glanced at the empty seat beside her; the pamphlet on it was addressed to *Troy*.

It was hard for her to focus during the Meeting. When she looked around, it seemed a lot of the others—so-called landlords and their invisible child-tenants—were similarly bewildered. One of them, called Dabba Doo, looked to be somewhere in his sixties. He had a quirky sense of humor and wore a tweed suit without shoes. Another was a blond girl named Violet, an absolute stunner. Most were well-dressed, except for a wiry black fellow in sweatpants; apparently, he was a yoga teacher. During the Meeting, some of the guests burst into tears without provocation, while others simply doodled on their *Guides*. Violet and the yogi peppered the Porter with questions that seemed either to make great sense or no sense at all. Annie was patient and motherly, occasionally dispensing hugs and Kleenex to the frustrated and distraught.

At Meeting's end, everyone stood and held hands for the Serenity Prayer:

> *God, grant me the serenity to accept the things I cannot change, the courage to change the things I can, and the wisdom to know the difference.*

Lydia had been to a few AA meetings with alcoholic friends, but that was years ago. She wondered how she could have known the prayer so well. It was an easy one, but easy to stumble over too—maybe it was the effect of saying it en masse. Before Annie walked Lydia to her car, they said their goodbyes to Bumble as he restored order to the room.

Once outside, the Porter said, "I didn't expect you so soon."

Lydia forgot about the list of questions she'd prepared; suddenly, all of them seemed to evaporate.

"I'm not the best artist but I hope you liked the unicorn," said Annie.

"Oh my God, I *loved* it!" she exclaimed.

"Things will become clearer—you'll be surprised how quickly that will happen. But at first, it's a bit of a struggle. Just try not to think that much. *Trust*—that everything is as it should be. Turn your head off! Do you think you can do that, Maya?" She really didn't know what Annie meant but said yes. "And I know it's confusing but I like to call the children by their birth names, not the names of their landlords. It seems to help with the . . . well, it just seems to help." Annie saw that along with Maya's *Guide*, she was clutching the one with Troy's name; Lydia couldn't remember having picked it up. Annie took it from her hand and said, "He'll be at the next one—the boys are always a little bit slower to get here than the girls. It's best he take it from the chair himself, when he comes."

Lydia didn't know what she meant. She didn't know what any of it meant but right then tried to turn off her head, as the Porter had advised.

"Do you know who he is yet?" asked Annie, with that lovely smile. "Do you know who Daniel is?"

"I don't even know who *I* am!" she answered, bursting into hysterical giggles.

Annie delighted in that and giggled along. "Good Lord. That is the truest and most charming thing!"

"Am I Maya or Lydia?" she asked, solemnly.

"A little of both," said Annie. She hugged her close. "Don't worry—I'm afraid I don't know who I am either! But I've turned my head off so long, I don't need to know. Not anymore. I'm just . . . grateful. And you will be too. Be patient."

Lydia got in her car and rolled down the window.

Annie leaned down and kissed her cheek. "I love you," she said. "I really do, you know."

"I love you too," said Lydia—the first thing all night she was certain of.

3.

Daniel was in his PJs, fast asleep on the couch, when she got home.

The TV was on mute. He'd been watching an old episode of *The Rifleman*. Lydia sat down next to him, overwhelmed with the night's experience, overwhelmed by love. She closed her eyes and fell right to sleep. It was the first time since she had died that her sleep was dreamless.

No anguish, no *whoosh*—no train.

When Daniel awakened, he was happy to see her beside him. His heart leapt within as he kissed the crown of her head. The mouth of her purse gaped open and he plucked out the *Guide*. He saw *Maya* written on its cover and was puzzled.

He opened it to the first page:

Rule Number One: Be GOOD to your NEW BODY!!! Treat it with RESPECT and it will RETURN the favor!!!

He wasn't all that interested; he was nearly as tired as she.

He stuffed it back in her purse.

Lydia let him sleepwalk her to the bedroom, where he changed her into pajamas that were dotted with little lambs. He tucked them both in; with eyes still closed, she whimpered. He knew what she wanted. He got out of bed to retrieve the stuffed animal that had fallen to the floor. He put it in her arms and she held it to her body, smiling in her sleep.

He held her as tightly as she did the unicorn.

"Sister," said Daniel beneath his breath, though their relationship's provenance had yet to surface in his consciousness. He joined her in sleep and was soon in his compartment on the train. A woman came with a tray of toy soldiers, French fries and a milkshake. She said they'd almost arrived at the station and told him to remember an address.

Boys were better at memorizing things.

HONEYCHILE

1.

That Saturday, while others his age were goofing or loitering, one boy knew exactly what he was up to. He was biking to meet a friend at the Cherry Street Mall in Mount Clemens to look at new video games—his real plan being to sneak a peek in the department store window at new fashions for ladies. That's what he wanted to be: a designer of beautiful clothes for women. A few Christmases ago, his mother got him a subscription to W, and he had stacks of them at home.

Winston Collins was eleven years old.

He wore gel in a shock of green hair (did the dye job himself) and prescription sunglasses with crazy lime frames, a birthday gift from Mom.

Favorite show: *Project Runway*. On the walls of his room were pages clipped from magazines featuring his Dream Team: Kendall Jenner, Cara Delevingne, Kaia Gerber. Winston was old-school. Karl Lagerfeld was his icon and the boy-ingenue obsessed about meeting him one day, was *certain* that he would.

Wrong about that.

Two thousand children go missing each day. The number abducted by strangers is more than a hundred a year.

Most, like Winston, are killed within twenty-four hours.

The thirty-seven-year-old woman sported glasses that, unlike her victim, lent a serious big-box shopper look. She was pregnant, so it was easy to lure him to the minivan—she asked for help with a package, just like Buffalo Bill did with the senator's daughter in her husband's favorite movie, *The Silence of the Lambs*. Laverne was in charge of the binding and gagging (not her forte, which she'd proven time and again), but hers was not to reason why; she did what her man ordered or suffered the consequences.

From Mount Clemens it was twenty-five minutes plumb north to the three-acre home in Wolcott Mills (bought four years ago at auction with a loan from her father-in-law). She enjoyed living in the unincorporated village, with its thickets of elms and tulip trees that called back her childhood. She was house-proud; it was the first place anyone in her family had ever owned.

Her husband carried him down to the rumpus room. (He was wrapped in a carpet by then.) After the Mister left, Laverne looked in on the panicked, wriggling body while she vacuumed, a little ritual that calmed her nerves. When Winston surfaced from the chloroform haze, he choked on the gag and immediately had the urge to vomit; for that very reason, she had been schooled to closely supervise their guests, because he didn't want anyone aspirating and dying before their time. The young fashion maven's ears were stopped with hot wax, another predilection of her husband's that she never "got." The pain was grotesque and strange—parts of his body had been burned—and a regressive voice inside said, *Mama I skairt to be kilt.* Yet somehow he still conjured the strains of "Rise." Winston taught the song to his mom and they made a lip-synch duet for YouTube that he thought was as good as anything Emma Stone did on Jimmy Fallon. Well, almost.

There it was: Katy Perry's pellucid voice ringing *You're out of time, but still I rise* throughout the room and the world itself, belting it out like a private concert for him alone.

When her man finally came home there was a bit of disruption—Laverne had already removed the gag because the boy "wasn't breathing right," which pissed him off. He smacked her to the ground, bloodying her nose. She couldn't understand why, because she was only doing what he had told her to under those particular circumstances. But he didn't hit her as hard as he used to, back in the time before she was in the family way.

He turned his attention to Winston. To have a prepackaged quarry "dressed" and waiting for him was the most exciting thing, like a feast after the hunt. He usually left them in his wife's care while he made a trip to the Laundromat (he had his rituals too), to mentally prepare. The anticipation gave him butterflies that soon became hawks, the skies of his head darkening with them, and when he was ready to feed he made Laverne turn her body to the wall like the kids in his other favorite movie, *The Blair Witch Project*, while he attended to the visitor, impaling him the same way he did his wife, on this occasion timing his release to Winston's final breaths. He liked keeping them alive for a week or so but sometimes it didn't work out that way, so he kept them dead.

The last thing Winston saw was the bad man's T-shirt with the naked woman and huge angel wings.

He thought of Katy, whose voice he heard till the end.

That night he took Laverne to the Sirloin House, close to where his father lived (though he never invited the old man along), a postmortem celebration that she always looked forward to. For a few hours anyway, she relished the loosening of her master's reins. *This is the real him,* she told herself. *Funny, sweet, romantic.* It was a perfect moment for Laverne to begin another ritual: erasing from memory the details of what she—they—had done. Still, she wouldn't have had it any other way, because how dull would her life be without the spice of her man's darkness? He was the only one who ever knew about *her* dark places, without her having to say a word, and she cherished him for that. On those victorious nights, dining out like a normal couple, there was even laughter, which almost never occurred in the house. (She didn't get around much anymore.) She especially looked forward to steak and ice cream because at home, her diet was strictly regulated. He always left the server a big tip. This time the waitress shook both their hands and nearly wept for the random acts of kindness in the world. Laverne glowed with pride.

She wasn't wild about the long, hot shower he always made her take before such dinners. It scalded. He stood by the open glass door, keeping a close eye. He wanted to make sure that she didn't adjust the temperature. She thought it was silly, standing there like that, because why would she ever go against him? She had a mischievous streak and, when he wasn't looking, angled her body so less of the hot water fell on her—Laverne's way of getting one over on her man. But she liked that he stood there, she really did. There was something protective about it. She felt extra-special, extra-loved. She was his wife and his woman.

He never showered after his business was done. Sometimes he didn't wash for a whole week, which she wasn't wild about either. There were so many smells on him. But that was his way. And he never laundered his "executioner" shirts: Mötley Crüe, Black Sabbath, Metallica. There were five of them that he kept in a secret drawer.

Now there were six.

2.

Suppertime.

A half hour's bike ride away from the Cherry Street Mall, Honeychile—aka Renée "Honeychile" Devonshire, née Matlock—had been partying with friends from Mount Clemens High ("Home of the Battling Bathers") on her Not So Sweet Fourteenth. That's what she called it on her Evites.

The Devonshires, Harold and Rayanne, adopted her at ten years old, and she was their full-on miracle girl. How was it that no one had wanted her until they swooped in? That's what Rayanne asked herself all through the eighteen months before she was legally theirs. *Our child.* It was fate that we got her, said levelheaded Harold. *How could no one have seen the beauti-*

ful soul behind the health issues? Each day, Rayanne's heart gurgled like a summer fountain over the eccentric, willowy child with the cartoon body and sweet, funny mouth, the infectious laugh and piercing green eyes. Harold and Rayanne spent ten years trying to have a kid—ten years!—and at forty-six, she decided: enough. She was fifty now and realized that Honeychile had saved her, in more ways than she could ever have imagined. The pride and joy, as they used to say, of Rayanne's life.

Honeychile had cleidocranial dysplasia, the same thing as the boy on their daughter's favorite show, *Stranger Things*. She was five feet tall, with shoulders that were almost nonexistent. The Devonshires had her extra teeth pulled so the adult ones could arrive without being mobbed. Rayanne told her husband that she looked just like the young Christina Ricci, but Harold insisted her birth mother had to have been Amy Sedaris. (Harold was wry and bookish and loved all the Sedarises.) She had asthma, which the doctors said was also genetic, but Rayanne blamed her other troubles— quote-unquote behavioral stuff—on the biological mom, "that horrible Matlock woman," a bona fide crackhead, reprobate and God knew what else. Honeychile could get beyond moody and one time physically lashed out; when Harold sternly told her that would *not* be tolerated, she was genuinely remorseful and never did it again. Rayanne loved that about their daughter; that she could listen and learn. Still, they hoped she wouldn't get too crazy when her period started. Rayanne didn't think it was funny when Harold quipped, "Hope not. You remember that movie *Carrie*, don't you?"

But oh, *this* one! exulted Rayanne. She was an armful but was worth it. And holy shit is she ever funny and smart, and all heart too. One of those "unforgettable characters" that you're blessed to meet in this life.

"Ma-ma? Pa-pa?" she said, in her best-worst posh British accent. All her girlfriends had left except for her BFF, Zelda, who was lounging upstairs. They were having a sleepover. Honeychile ceremonially gathered her parents in the den, her favorite place, where she liked to read thriller-mysteries like *The Light Between Oceans*. "I have something for you," she said. She brought out a box that was as beautifully wrapped as one of her birthday gifts.

"Sugar, you can't be giving *us* a present," said Rayanne. "It's your birthday!"

Honeychile protested with a crazy-funny version of "It's My Party and I'll Cry If I Want To"—oh, this girl, this girl! Rayanne (because she was Rayanne) was already shedding a tear, which was Harold's cue to step in. As he grabbed the gift, the birthday girl took the opportunity to admonish. "First Rule of *Fight Club* when given a present? You do not say no to the present! Second Rule of *Fight Club* when given a present? You do not say no to the present!"

He tore off the paper, revealing a snow globe. On closer inspection, they saw what she'd done. The small figure of a girl was being sandwich-hugged by the artful representations of Harold and Rayanne. They held it to the light and stared in wonder—the sculptures had their exact faces. "I worked on it after school for, like, a *month*. Do you think they look like us?"

"Yes," said Harold. "It's amazing."

Rayanne couldn't even speak.

Honeychile was pleased. "I just wanted to give you something special because of everything you've given *me*." Her mom was crying but the tears came out in a weird, gloopy string of giggles that made everyone laugh. "I was going to tell you that I actually found my birth parents and was leaving *tonight*—but that would have been too mean!"

"Well, I'm glad a cooler head prevailed," said Harold.

Honeychile's humor could have a dark streak. Rayanne smiled and let it slide, focusing on the globe. "It's the most beautiful thing I've ever seen," she said. "Thank you, dearest, dearest daughter."

"Time for snow globe reenactment!" said Honeychile.

She took the gift, dramatically planted herself in the middle of the den and waited for them to join her. Then she held the globe aloft in her hand, its snowflakes flurrying over the tiny figures within, as the three of them imitated the group hug.

"See?" she said. "Are we not the adoption poster family of all time?"

3.

The walls were covered with photomontages of Honeychile's favorites: Bowie, Pink, Nick Cave.

Zelda was poring over Instagram.

"Oh my God," she said. "Roxanne took, like, *ten thousand pictures* of your party."

"Did you see what she was wearing?" said Honeychile.

"She was totally dressed like a slut!"

"I *know.* I don't think she left her *house* like that—she probably changed in the bushes. Even my dad said something."

"Oh my God, I heard him! He told her to put on her sweater."

"There weren't even any *boys.*"

"*Roxanne* didn't mind. I think she's totally found her Inner Dyke."

"Really?" said Honeychile.

Zelda lowered her voice to a conspiratorial whisper. "Jasmine told me something but you *cannot tell anyone.*"

"What!"

"You have to *promise.*"

"I promise, I promise—"

"Jasmine said that Roxanne told her that she *masturbates* to Kristen Stewart."

"*No . . .*"

"I think when Kristen started having hundreds of *girlfriends*, it like gave her *permission.* I mean she was *always* attracted to Kristen. She used to lay in bed and watch *Twilight* in *slow motion*—now we know what she was doing!"

"Who *isn't* attracted to Kristen Stewart?" said Honeychile, wryly.

"Oh my God, *I'm* not. Not in *that* way."

"Speak for yourself," she said roguishly.

"Honeychile!—"

"Oh come on, Zell. She's *hot.*"

"She *totally* is but so is *Selena* and *Hailee* and *Kendall* and *whoever.* But it's like a whole other level to think of them while you're like *pleasuring* yourself with a vibrator."

"Is that how she does it? With a vibrator?"

"That's what Jasmine said."

"Maybe she and Jasmine . . ."

"I don't think so. Jasmine is totally penis-obsessed!"

"When do you think you'll do it?" said Honeychile.

"Masturbate—?"

"When do you think you'll *fuck*."

"—because if you meant masturbate, I'm already pretty much a professional."

"You are not."

"I so *am*. And you better *start*, Honeychile. You need to be *prepared*. You have to have been doing it awhile before a guy puts his dick in you."

"You are so repulsive!" said Honeychile. They laughed and swatted each other. "I guess you should have gotten me a vibrator for my birthday! Because it's actually kind of hard to masturbate with a Walmart gift card."

"You can *try*," said Zelda.

They were laughing so hard that Rayanne came to the bedroom door.

"Girls? I hope this isn't going to go on all night."

"It won't, Mrs. Devonshire," said Zelda obediently.

"Mom," said Honeychile. "Can you just chill?"

She started belting "It's My Party" again but Zelda was too shy to join in.

Rayanne shook her head, smiled and went to bed.

I n the middle of the night, Honeychile had the worst asthma attack of her young life.

The scary episodes had happened twice since she'd been with the Devonshires. She would turn completely blue and then be revived by a shot of adrenaline that Rayanne kept on hand. This time, a minute before, Zelda awakened from a nightmare and crawled from her sleeping bag to rummage in the fridge. She made a bowl of Cheerios with soy milk that she heated in a saucepan, thinking it would calm her nerves, then sat at the table to read a story about Dakota Johnson and Zayn Malik in a magazine that she brought from home. When she got back to the room, Honeychile was on the floor gasping. She switched on the light: her skin was a shocking, diaphanous white, made more horrifying by the bottomless wishing wells of half-open eyes when her BFF tried to rouse her.

She bolted from the room screaming.

In the brief moment when Zelda ran down the hall to pound on their door—Harold leapt from bed and ran to his daughter while Rayanne retrieved the EpiPen from their bathroom—a paroxysmal shiver flooded the cold, dead body, bestirring it to life. Of course, the injection was of no use, but everyone was convinced it had saved her. Her lids fluttered. Honeychile looked at them in shock and awe, saying, "Oh," then "Wow." Her mother held her in her arms while the revived girl began telling everyone she was sorry. Rayanne told her not to be silly, to just lie quietly, that she was going to be all right now. They lifted her from the floor and put her in bed. Harold asked his wife if they should take her to the ER and Rayanne said, "We'll see. Let's see. Her color's coming back. I'll sit with her." (Rayanne was actually cooler than Harold in such crises.) Honeychile said she was thirsty and Zelda brought her a glass of water.

After a while, she recovered enough to say that she wanted to go to her sanctuary. Rayanne said she didn't think that was a good idea—the den was all the way downstairs, too far from their bedroom—but the girls wound up camping there, with quilts that Mom provided. Rayanne slept alongside them, or tried to for an hour or so before Honeychile kicked her out.

Unchaperoned, the girls proceeded to eat about a gallon of rocky road. On their third trip to the kitchen, this time to make popcorn in the microwave, they were overtaken by a mood of giddiness and abandon.

"Oh my God, Honeychile, I wish I had taken a picture of you on the floor!" said Zelda. "You *totally* looked totally dead."

THE SLEEPLESS PORTER

S omething was wrong.

    Something had felt wrong for weeks now and it wasn't just her interrupted sleep (which hadn't really occurred since chemo) that was the culprit. Rather, Annie felt the source of her discomfort lay in the nature of the anomalies she had begun to encounter during her rounds on the night train.

Last night, for example.

A rowdy girl appeared in one of the cabins, causing havoc. She was almost completely out of control. Occasionally, such a thing happened with new arrivals—Jasper, her mentor, called it "transition anxiety"—though in most cases, fright quickly dissipated into agitated calm. This one was different; it was as if she didn't belong there, and knew it. When the girl fled from the dark-paneled cabin, Annie was forced to summon help. Thankfully, the ancient, shadowy beings called Subalterns—the train's rarefied equivalent of sentries—were always close at hand. After she was forcibly led back to her room, Annie brought a tray of lemonade and cookies that she naively thought would soothe, but the hellion sent it flying.

There was something else that caught the Porter's attention. Most of Annie's wards on the train were between the ages of five and eleven—sometimes a twelve-year-old would find their way—but *this* one was a full-blown adolescent. Short and odd-looking, the fearsome interloper was physically deformed as well, though there'd been precedents for that. Annie remembered a boy a few years ago who appeared in his cabin in a wheelchair. (He had a taste for pizza with chocolate sprinkles.) There was no rule that said so, but able-bodied children had been the norm.

What did it mean? That she'd soon be hosting murdered teens and young adults? The middle-aged? And if that were true, what difference would it make? As if she had a say! Had she become complacent and arrogant in the mysteries of her custodianship? Did she dare to believe that the incomprehensible could ever become familiar? She was there for one thing only: to serve. Nothing that went on was up to her, nor ever had been. It'd been a long while since Annie felt the astonished apprehension of her vocation, and now she scrambled to reclaim that sacred feeling because she knew it was essential. One must stay humble or go mad.

She lit incense and knelt before her mentor's cabinet, bracing herself with a prayer of humility.

Yet still . . .

She felt aged out and in over her head.

S he was contemplating the freakish new normal when the physician came to the examination room and invited Annie to his office. That was where he told her the cancer had returned.

He was startled yet relieved when a smile came to her face. It was always better when the patient, by denial or disposition, didn't break down in front of him. He had walked this woman through her illness for twenty years and gotten to know her as best as anyone could. He'd never met anyone like her. She was an open book and a riddle all at once. He didn't know what she did for money—knew nothing, really, about her life. What she *had* told him was contradictory. She once mentioned an inheritance but the doctor knew that she lived in a building on Skid Row. She said she was a volunteer in the pediatric wing of Macomb General. He had a friend on staff there who confirmed Annie was a "legend," beloved by all, though apparently she had resisted the hospital's overtures to put her on salary.

Her type of cancer was of the unlucky variety that can never be declared cured. When he showed her the CT scan of inoperable tumors, her reaction was the same as in the past, when he would tell her, "Annie, you're good as gold. See you same time next year."

She cried on the bus ride home, not with self-pity, but from gratitude. Jasper had told her this day would come and now it was here. He also said that when her time as Porter was nearing a close, she would begin to experience "turbulence," but she never pressed him about what that meant. Now the anxiety of the last few weeks made perfect sense and filled her with a measure of relief. Looking out the window on the familiar, rain-slicked streets that grew more derelict as she got closer to home, Annie understood. She took solace in a sudden, secret knowledge, no longer hidden, that help was on the way. Someone was heading to the station—her replacement. She could *feel* it. She would do for them as her mentor had done for her . . .

How honored she was.

Walking from the bus stop to her apartment, she was greeted by shouts and tender whispers of "Mother" by the scavengers and outcasts. Each asked if there was anything she needed, eager to provide a service, any service—the service of Love. The whole wide world was filled with mothers and fathers and it made her heart thrum. The children of the train were mothers and fathers as well, and teachers too, long after their lives had abruptly ended. Love was deathless. The fruitless children of the train had parented her.

She showered in the hallway's communal bath. When she returned to her room, Annie took special care in front of the mirror as she prepared for sleep. She put on the dress she was wearing when she and Jasper first met (Annie hadn't worn it since), then riffled through drawers to find the necklace he gave her on the day that he died. With loving thoughts of the one who had rescued her from obscurity and madness, the Porter lay atop the bedcovers. She smiled to herself, thinking she must look like a corpse at a wake.

That night, when she boarded the train in full dress, the Subalterns emerged from the shadows, as if in respectful salute. They knew. It sent shivers down her spine.

It was the one time—and the last—they would dare to show her their faceless faces.

WILLOW IN NEW YORK

I.

It was a long while since he'd been back—and the feeling wasn't good.

If Rafael had been a tad more enthusiastic about seeing him, Willow might have been in less of a funk. But what did he expect? He'd left Cold Case under shitty terms and the terms were shitty still. It was likely Rafael knew why he was coming to see him, but at least he had the decency not to get into any of it over the phone. Or maybe it was *indecency*, because if not being rehired was a done deal, the pilgrimage to the city would be a humongous jack-off. Groveling was humiliating enough, made worse by a monster toothache. He'd been popping four Advil every two hours since he left home, to no effect. If his kidneys shut down, so be it.

Abandon Port Hope, all ye who enter here!

My life is fucking absurd.

The appointment at the precinct was a few hours away and his best idea was to find an AA meeting. It made no sense but Willow suddenly got paranoid about running into anyone he knew; say, a cop in recovery. His life being the absurd one it was, of course he ran into a familiar face: a confidential informant straight out of the Way Back Machine. They nodded to each other, and throughout the hour their eyes furtively met. As was his habit, Willow bolted to the street right after the Lord's Prayer, but the CI caught up.

"Dub!"

"Hey, Marlon."

"Buddy, how ya doin'?"

Willow kept walking. "Good! I'm well."

"Man, I haven't seen you in what, three years?"

"'Bout that."

"I thought you overdosed!"

"Fuck you."

"Just teasin', man. How's the leg?"

"I'm still using it."

"Dude, how long you been sober?"

"Three years."

Marlon knew it was a lie. He could sniff sobriety dates like dogs that sniff cancer. The lowlife knew everything; that's why he'd been an invaluable informant. He wasn't like other snitches Dubya had enlisted through the years—the man had a kind of morality code, which turned out to be a lucky thing for Willow. (A very lucky thing.)

"That's awesome, Dubya. I'm here on a fucking court card, can you believe it?"

"Outrageous," said Willow, deadpan.

"You still funny!" said Marlon, his face cracking open in a smile. "So—you a detective again?"

"I'm retired."

Willow hadn't stopped moving, hoping to shake him.

"Good on ya! I figured that, 'cause otherwise I'ma hear from you. Your shit went *dead*. Where you staying?"

"Staying?"

Marlon wide-grinned at his old employer's superior, game-playing bullshit. "Downtown?"

"I'm *staying* in Maui."

"Maui? No shit. Isn't that where Woody Harrelson and all those rich, dope-smoking *celebrities* live? You hangin' with Woody?"

"You ask a lot of questions. You should work for the TSA."

"The TSA don't ask *shit*. Hey, lemme give you my digits."

"That's okay, Marlon," he said, wincing at the asininity of that word.

"Come on, man—we'll cut up old times."

Willow winced again as the CI pressed a slip of paper into his hand. He must have written his number down during the meeting.

"I'm into some shit that's a little bit . . . *inneresting*." Which was code for money. "When you burn out on all that smokin' and surfin' you're doing with Woody, you should hit me up."

Marlon was fishing. Willow could read the damning *once dirty, always dirty* in the snitch's conspiratorial eyes.

"Later," said Willow, power-walking away.

"Don't lose that number! And say hi to Mr. Harrelson!" Then, after Willow was a hundred yards gone: "We owe each other! Forever!"

2.

"I'm sober, Rafael."

"Good for you," he said, genuinely glad. "For how long?"

"Three years—from about the time I left the department."

May as well feed the lie. Besides, if they made him pee in a cup, he'd ace it. Willow had been clean a few months now and they hadn't yet invented the test that measures for how long. Though they might be able to detect marijuana in the hair follicles, because THC hung around in the system.

"How's Pace?"

"She's good—she's great. Perfect. Gave me a grandson."

"Isn't that wonderful?"

"Yes it is," said Willow. "He's really somethin'."

"I've got a few of those myself now. Though 'Grandpa' on the CV can be a bit of a cock-block. I tend not to mention it to my Tinder hookups."

"You're on Tinder?"

"Can't imagine life before it. 'Love Me Tinder'—Elvis said it first." Rafael took a harder glance at his old colleague. "What's going on with your jaw there?" It had swelled like a tiny cantaloupe.

"Toothache. Haven't had one since college."

"Could be an abscess. They're a bitch."

Willow knew it was time.

"Rafael—I appreciate you seeing me. I really do. And I know you didn't have to, so I thank you for that. Being sober awhile, I've had a lot of time to think. About my mistakes. And all my . . . horseshit." Rafael cracked a smile and that was a good thing. "And a big part of why I'm here is to make amends to you—to the whole unit, really—but that's not the only reason. Which you probably already know." He took a long, reflective pause, footnoted by contrition, humility and steely resolve. "What I'm saying, Rafael, is I'd like to come back. It's different for me now and I think I could be an asset. I know I could. I've done a helluva lot of growing up."

Rafael nodded, hands clasped together, avoiding his eyes. In that moment, Willow still thought it could go either way. His old boss stared down at the desk, making minuscule adjustments to a letter opener and scorpion paperweight.

"I know that," he finally said. "And I'd love to have you. Problem Number One is that we just don't have any room. Not in Cold Case, anyway. We have a pretty tight group of folks right now, Willow, and you know how tough that is to achieve."

"I do. I do. That's fair."

"Takes awhile to get the chemistry right."

"And Problem Number Two?" asked Willow, trying to be wry and lighthearted about the whole fiasco. "Or would that be Problems Two through Ten?"

"Dubya . . . you were a *terrible* Cold Case guy." Willow cringed at his candor. "Some folks just don't have the aptitude." The qualifier stung him more than the opening salvo. "Which I have to say was a surprise. What we do in that unit is kind of a black art. My gut told me you'd take to it more than you did. So that's on me."

As he sat there and faced the music like a hapless adult-child, he experienced an unexpected sense of liberty. He'd made his little play and got checkmated. A consistent theme in his life was that whenever a door closed—and they always did—he sighed with relief. Rafael, who was actually fond of him, took pity, offering the consolation prize of a promise to have a word with his cronies (all of them men with whom the remorseful detective once worked) about upcoming vacancies in the homicide division. Willow demurred, using the excuse of not being "street-legal" due to his leg injury, which he said had been acting up and might need a surgery (another lie)—*leg injury* being an unfortunate callback for the putative source of his addictions and the three rehab stints the union wound up paying for. Rafael, himself relieved, didn't pursue. What they both "understood" was that homicide would never take him back. Toward the end of his eleven-year tenure in narcotics, Willow got ambushed by some dealers he'd busted. He killed two and was shot in the process, becoming some kind of hero—which was how he finagled his way into homicide, his dream gig. But life in that ecosystem quickly became insupportable. In-house suspicions that he'd ripped off said dead drug dealers (and had been doing that for years) began chasing him around like a cartoon storm cloud. Nothing was ever proven, but the "cronies" were glad when he finally asked for a transfer to Cold Case. He owed Rafael for making that possible; the man never believed the scuttlebutt.

Maybe everyone would have been better off if he had . . .

The mentor stood, reaching out his hand. Willow shook it and thanked him again.

"I'm going to give you a number to call," said Rafael, scribbling something down. When he handed it to him, it made him think of Marlon, his old CI, doing the same. Willow's head scrambled—it seemed a bizarre notion, but maybe Rafael wanted him to contact one of the influential investigators directly and begin a grovel-fest that might topple the dominoes of inter-departmental opinion that was set against him.

"What is it?"

"My dentist," said Rafael. "She's awesome. You oughta get that taken care of before you get an infection in your brain."

3.

He came to New York on a Hail Mary pass but the Gods had other plans, decreeing him worthy of a root canal he couldn't afford. Just another watery notch in the belt of shit around Willow Millard Wylde's pasty, post-rehab paunch . . .

He put it on the unused emergency Visa with the $6,500 limit.

Willow seethed with anger while the doctor yanked and suctioned. *You were a terrible Cold Case guy* rang in his head like the voice-over flashback of an old B movie—a fair description of what his life had become, or maybe always was. *Some folks just don't have the aptitude!* Which royally pissed him off because in his mind he knew he was the "black art" prince; hell, he was a fucking Marvel superhero. But looking back on his time in the Cold Case unit, he was ashamed. He winced as he saw himself futzing around the Spirit Room like some Barney Fife. He would never be able to share with Rafael—or anyone—how he made himself that way by suppressing his natural gifts.

The Spirit Room . . . where DNA, rape kits, and cartons of flatlined cases were stored. When he first took the tour (a month before crossing over from homicide), the voices overwhelmed. It'd been so long since Willow had heard voices like that—the symphonic choir of the departed—and this time he *felt* them. When he finally joined Cold Case, they grew quieter over the months, a muffling result of the mixture of self-will and opiates. It made him physically sick to hear them. Still, he was drawn to the Spirit Room, where he torturously loitered, wandered and even sometimes napped. How had he been so arrogant to believe he could acclimate himself to the radioactive field of the forgotten, unburied dead? He could dial down the voices (a skill he'd honed since boyhood, after the death of his Nana), though in so doing Willow suffered the consequences. The expenditure of energy required for their suppression had the effect of turning him into a caricature of incompetence bordering on the cretinous. (Enter Barney Fife.) For the first time in his profession, he felt like a fool. His cohorts nicknamed him Special Needs and he laughed it off but it hurt. Whenever Rafael was on the brink of firing him, Willow allowed himself to briefly tap into his verboten gifts; the voices led to small and occasionally larger triumphs. But most of the time he came off like an ass, a dunderhead, a misfire.

Like some kind of mutant mistake—

With his Visa drained and a face numbed by Novocaine, Willow walked to Duane Reade to get the Vicodin script filled. He bought a can of Diet Dr Pepper and a box of straws. Stepping outside, he stood on the sidewalk sipping his soda and peering into space, captive to the black void of his mood. When he came to, he was staring at the bar across the street. Like a man under hypnosis, he walked toward it in a straight line through traffic.

The darkness and quiet pleased him more than it seemed possible. The bartender was unfazed when he pulled a straw from the box to suck up his Tom Collins. The first taste was so good that he wouldn't have cared if it were his last. The second was even better because he used it to wash down three Vikes.

What now?

His thoughts turned to confidential informants . . .

Willow wondered just how "inneresting" Marlon's shit might be. He fantasy-calculated the size of a score that would make his life, at least temporarily, copacetic—25K? Thirty? What would make it more than copacetic too . . . a hundred large? Hell yeah. If whatever Marlon was promoting was in the neighborhood of ten grand—or five—or three—would it even be worth the risk? Possibly. Hadn't he already risked everything (or what was left of it) with the relapse? Hey, 2K and change would at least pay for the root canal . . . What he really needed was a lotto-size win, something over a mill. Five mill had a nice ring to it. He'd buy Pace a house on a few acres and give her a mill for herself. Maybe buy Geoff a Harley, just to be sportsmanlike, and put two million in trust for Larkin. Then maybe he *would* move to Maui. Smoke ganja and star in Harrelson home movies for the rest of his days.

He felt a warm buzz from the booze, though it'd be another twenty minutes or so before he came on to the pills. Liquor would potentiate their effect and he was looking forward to that—*old times*, he thought, before amending it to *not so old times*. As he waited, Willow reminisced about his legendary caper from yesteryear. When he first joined the NYPD, he worked narcotics and within a few years had a sweetheart deal with Marlon, his CI—Willow robbed dope houses Marlon tipped him to. His method was to smash in, cuff the dealers and then take the money while calling in the bust. They never got too greedy because the whole enterprise was risky, to say the least. There were a lot of moving parts. And they couldn't do a "lick" too often because Willow always needed a plausible reason why he'd gone in without backup.

So Marlon told him about a trap house that always had at least $25,000 on hand, guaranteed. The plan was for Willow to pocket fifteen and give his CI five (leaving five for show), which he did. But the stash was closer to 200K and Willow took 125. When the dealers made bail, they somehow found out about Marlon and tried to assassinate him. Unfortunately, the attempt occurred at the very moment the dirty detective was giving his partner his cut outside Katz's Deli on East Houston. Willow saved the CI's life by blowing two of the felons away but was shot in the leg in the process. The tabloids made him a hero, which made it easier for him to transfer to homicide a few months after leaving the hospital. Getting shot was the best thing that could have happened, because his hero status had the effect of tamping down, temporarily anyway, the rumors of illicit gain that had been spreading in the department to explain the source of income behind Detective Wylde's whoring, gambling and Rolex sprees—

—Oh. Oh . . .

Now he was stoned and fuck if it didn't feel good. Nirvana time. And with that sumptuous, familiar feeling, his plan of action became clear. As Willow worked himself up to making the call to Marlon, he killed time by reflecting on the Meadows. He wondered where Renata and the black fire-man and the Rimbaud boy were—wondered if they were sitting somewhere loaded, like him. In the same way he had sleepwalked to the bar, he slid off his stool and strolled to the pay phone outside the restroom.

He put his hand in his pocket, feeling the paper with the CI's "digits." Then his copness kicked in. He went back to his perch, laid down a twenty and told the barkeep, "I shall return."

He sun-blink sauntered to Duane Reade and bought a disposable phone—a burner that couldn't be traced. Returning to the sepulchral quiet of the bar, he stood at the pay phone and dialed. A voice answered:

"This is Detective O'Connor, who's calling?"

Startled, Willow hung there a beat before frantically searching for what-ever button would end the call.

What the fuck?

Had he been set up?

No way—no way would Marlon would pull a stunt like that . . . and for what reason?

The phone had been answered with that flat, clue-seeking aggressive-ness of a cop at a crime scene.

He left the bar in a panic-sweat and stomped the burner into pieces. Threw them in multiple trash bins, just like the asshole perps in his favorite cable shows. A battered Lincoln Town Car pulled up. The gypsy driver asked where he was going.

"Penn Station," said Willow, his heart nearly hammering him into a blackout as he settled into the backseat.

4.

He had come by train and was glad to be leaving that way. Airplanes and airports made him nervous. Trains brought out the Dr. Richard Kimble. They were romantic and catered to his fugitive sensibilities. He swallowed five more painkillers at Tracks, the bar in the station.

It was time to put a smiley face on the wreckage. He had a few hours before embarking and was way, way high. He had a brainstorm and vacated his stool; there was a place he urgently needed to visit. He approached an Amtrak employee—in retrospect, the man looked closer to some kind of scruffy, patchwork character in a dream—to ask directions.

Willow threaded his way through a hundred travelers, then descended...

As he traversed the gently sloping ramps and jittery-solid iron staircases, it grew cooler and less populated. He made peace with the thought of never again surfacing to see the light. He decided that it would please him immensely to become a Phantom of the Underground. He thought of a documentary he once saw about the "mole people" who lived in forgotten tunnels that stretched from Penn Station to Harlem. In his stonedness, Willow knew that entering *that* dream would be infinitely preferable to the nightmare he was living.

He couldn't determine how many levels down he'd gone. He mused about throwing himself in front of a train. At the Meadows, he became friends with a Londoner who did just that—a posh, witty man whose injuries forced him to scuttle through the rehab halls like a drunken insect. The fellow's brain was damaged as well but his droll, mordant humor was thoroughly intact. *I'd never be that lucky*, thought Willow. *I'd never live—but if I did, it would be in a hell of physical pain and permanent confusion.*

He was about to plunk himself down on the cold concrete floor and wait for the mole people to claim him when he saw the signage:

AMTRAK EMPLOYMENT OFFICE

He roused himself and stumbled toward his destination, feeling nearly whimsical. It was astonishing how quickly one's mood could change—was *nothing* real? The reedy, serious-looking Ethiopian with high-boned, acne-scarred cheeks skeptically took him in.

Willow pulled himself together and said, "I'm interested in working on the train."

"I'll give you a form to fill out."

"Is there a union?"

"Yeah, there's a union."

"I want to be a porter."

"We don't call them that."

"What are they now, concierges?'"

"Service attendants."

"How long is the training?"

The man half-smiled, half-scowled. "I don't have time for this shit."

"Say what?" said Willow.

"Tell you what. If you want to take a urine test—and that test declares you are drug and alcohol free—I'll get you a uniform and you can start right motherfucking *now*."

"Done!" said Willow, triumphantly.

The smile-scowl instantly became a mask of brusque indifference. "Listen, mister, sober up and come back Monday when the lady in charge is here. 'Cause I cain't do shit for you."

Willow saluted him. "Thank you, broheem."

He had no memory of how he found his way back to Tracks; it was as if he'd simply materialized there (same stool as before). With some curiosity, Willow noticed he was watching NY1 on the bar's big-screen. Like a person regaining consciousness, the images slowly coalesced. A street reporter was talking gibberish until the words started making sense . . .

A shooting in Chelsea—drug deal gone wrong.

Then, an old mug shot of the dead man filled the screen:

It was—

Marlon?

Holy Jesus, thank God for the burner!

The death of the CI was an omen of unimaginable proportions. His trip to New York had been nothing less than a snapshot of the disasters that awaited . . . even the root canal loomed large. Again, the detective thought about jumping in front of a train—maybe, like his British friend, he'd survive, returning to scuttle among the tunnels as the Mayor of the mole people.

He staggered aboard.

He didn't even bother telling himself the Big Lie, the Relapser's Affirmation that falling off the wagon was an essential part of any drunk's sobriety story . . . what didn't kill you made you stronger . . . all is God's will. The lie that when he got home, he would surrender anew to powerlessness, one day at a time.

He did think about telling Renata he'd picked up again. Though maybe he'd tough it out, keep his own counsel. More will be revealed . . .

Run silent, run deep—

If he *did* throw himself under the train, Pace would get a check for $250,000—he took out a policy in his late forties, when he became certain his hijinks would get him killed. Bullet to the leg notwithstanding, the odds of being killed on the job weren't great; suicide was by far the biggest cop casualty. Self-removal nullified the contract only in the first few years, so he was good to go.

He was golden . . .

The train rumbled, pneumatically hissed and squeak-squealed. He fell into a deep, sweaty sleep, dreaming that he was on the train—not in the passenger car where he was now but a plush private cabin. A handsome, stately older woman came in to see him, carrying a tray with refreshments and a linen napkin. She whispered in his ear but he couldn't understand what she was saying. At least she'd been kind enough to bring him a drink.

When he awakened, they were arriving in Pittsburgh. He frantically felt in his pocket for the piece of paper with Marlon's cell phone number before remembering that he'd torn it up and thrown it away in the street after dismantling the burner. That was when Willow realized it was a different slip of paper he was searching for—the one with the address the woman on the train had given him. But there was no paper. Fragments of her whispers came back to him now.

She told him to memorize it.

And indeed an address stuck in his head, as if illuminated.

MAYA AND TROY

I.

It was notable that while Lydia intuited that the empty chair beside her was being saved for Daniel (the name "Troy" on the *Guide*'s cover still seemed to carry no particular weight), she hadn't given a single thought to his imminent arrival, not even by her third Meeting. Her indifference had more to do with the fact that everything was still so amorphous—that Lydia's waking moments lived outside a kind of parentheses provided by the blurry, *whoosh*ing train that had brought her tenant, Maya, back to the world, *this* world, the earthly world of that little girl's long-ago home. Lydia's daily life, her practical, deputy life, seemed to be going just fine. Not too many glitches other than a general spaciness that friends and colleagues wrote off to the effects of PTSD related to the Tim Hortons shooting.

She looked forward to Annie's church basement gatherings and even began to consider her fellow participants as friends. Not in the sense of grabbing a coffee and learning more about their lives—which the Porter actually discouraged, cautioning that it "pulled focus"—but thinking of them as she would family members. Conversation among the group before Meetings was typically confined to where they grew up and where they went to school. (Some bashfully said, "I stopped halfway through second grade," meaning that was when their lives had ended.) Everyone seemed to know they were here for a single purpose, even if their shared goals were in various stages of fogginess or razor-clarity.

The common denominator, the heart glue holding the room together, was Annie. She gave out hugs when they came in and all lined up for hugs at Meeting's end.

The ninety-minute Meetings were divided in two. In the first half, the shares tended toward a discharge of frustrations, worries and general fear, a "clearing of the table," as Annie put it, in metaphorical preparation for the meal about to be served. Landlords and child-tenants both experienced "transition anxiety" (Annie's phrase, again), rooted in the confusion of the old and new lives that were suddenly conjoined within. Considering the cir- cumstances, it was amazing they hadn't gone stark raving mad. But the Porter said such a thing never happened, "even if you *do* sometimes feel like you're losing your marbles." Everyone tittered at that old-timey phrase. She assured them that the longer they were here and the closer they came to fulfilling their purpose—what she called the *moment of balance*—the more focused they'd become, the more grounded, integrated and less afraid. Some, of course, were more integrated than others because they had been here longer. Like Dabba Doo, an older, bookish man who favored three-piece tweed ensembles but eschewed shoes and socks. He'd been coming to Meet- ings for seven months now, though at some point Lydia remembered Annie saying that six months was the "term limit."

The second half was a Q&A devoted to "practical living." There were a lot of awkward shares around the barfy issue of what Annie called "romantic stuff," such as the sexual attention of current boyfriends, girlfriends and spouses. When the children of the train first arrived and became tenants, there was a requisite doldrum period of dormancy and indifference. "Land- lord sex" confused them, but was no big deal; they were on autopilot, along for the ride. But as their time in the world grew more limited and they moved closer to the *moment of balance*, the children became dominant. Not only did their landlords lose interest in the sexual act but they found it phys- ically repugnant. When partners and lovers were rebuffed, those individuals grew insecure and tended to become more vocal about their needs. Annie walked the group through various defensive strategies. "Depression and moodiness, backed up by visits to a shrink" was always a good tactic, she said. A protracted, nonspecific illness like mono or Lyme disease was another—anything that provided a plausible excuse for disengagement and overall lack of drive. "Be gentle. If you're gentle about it and tell them to be patient with you, they usually understand. It will buy you time. Some will get the message, some won't. Most *will*. Anyway, by the time you're focused on your mission, none of that will matter." In some cases, she advised a breakup as the only solution. "You'll know what to do, in time," she said, with that Mona Lisa smile. For thornier issues, she made herself available after Meetings for one-on-ones.

"Mission"? What *was* their mission, what *was* their purpose? She called it the *moment of balance*, but what was that? It was the elephant in the room that was rarely discussed, because Annie said it needn't be—*more shall be revealed*. The only thing that was required to know, she said, was that they all had one, a mission and a purpose, and it was "very, very special." And as long as Annie was calm and confident, well, they were too. She made each of them feel like teacher's pets.

At the end of the Meeting, they stood in a circle and held hands for the Lord's Prayer. After *Amen*, the group shouted, "More shall be revealed!"— their favorite part. To top things off, the Meeting's goofiest, most senior citizen (Maya's favorite) would exultantly crow "Yabba Dabba Doo!," sending the room into paroxysms of laughter that Annie seemed to delight in as well.

One night Daniel finally came.

He was late, just as Lydia had been her first time. He smiled at her and went straight to his chair. Annie paused and introduced him to the others, addressing him by the name she'd written on his *Guide*.

Ten minutes before the Meeting ended, Maya felt Troy's hand touch hers. At the moment of contact, they briefly glanced at each other, then kept watery eyes on the Porter while struggling to retain composure; intellectually, it was all still a puzzle to them. Annie was in the middle of responding to a guest when she glanced over—nothing escaped her—and her voice broke with emotion. She quickly looked away.

The presence of siblings in a Meeting was another anomaly, another omen, because such a thing had never happened, at least not on Annie's watch. (And *why* hadn't it? It wasn't as if a brother and sister had never been murdered before.) The Porter had the feeling they'd been killed by the same person and at the same time; that they'd died together was almost too much for Annie to bear, and the emotions that washed over her were new as well. How was it possible she was feeling such anguish, such despair? That puzzled her because she would never have survived the last sixteen years if she had felt the way she did now.

She took it as another sign that her sacred hours with the basement children were coming to a close.

2.

It was a strange time—a strange time within manifest strangeness.

Daniel had moved into Lydia's home because neither one of them wanted to be alone. But now, something much more than human need drove them. More had been revealed . . .

Brother and sister were unembarrassed by the initial sex play that occurred between them when they first inhabited their landlords. It seemed "natural" enough. But as they grew into who they were, or once were—sibling children—they stopped all that without too much fuss. Meanwhile, they employed Annie's stratagem of keeping the wolves at bay by no longer bothering to quash innuendo or refute their "relationship" among coworkers and peers. They cagily didn't flaunt it either, their coyness sealing the deal for those who were still unconvinced that they were lovers. Touching hands at the Meeting, they received spontaneous transmission of who and what they were—Maya and Troy—and if they knew nothing else, the secret knowledge was more than enough for now. They came to perceive the design of their return as being "perfect," even though the concept and meaning of that return still drew a blank. The maturity and animal strength of Lydia and Daniel (Troy and Maya called the landlords their "sleepover friends") protected them like a nautilus shell or even a parent. There seemed to be just enough of the right ingredients that the recipe appeared to be flawless. But the nature of the meal—its mission and purpose—was unknown and still marinating.

Where did that leave them?

In other words, what had happened? What were they doing here? What were they doing *anywhere*? Annie cautioned that such questions were too large, and irrelevant to the moment. But smaller ones abounded, presenting themselves as swatches of entangled memory. All those unicorns! They made sense to Daniel now—just as the taste he'd developed for mixing black licorice and popcorn made sense to Lydia.

It was early enough in Maya and Troy's arrival that the minds of their landlords still dominated, struggling to make sense of their fractured beings. Lydia and Daniel chased down surreal theories, informed by pop culture, film and television (though *surreal* came up short in describing the impossibly outlandish circumstances), like having been in an accident together as kids and emerging from double comas years later to find themselves partnered as cops. Which really did sound like some god-awful show from the eighties that never made it past the pilot episode. Like cosplay fans at a convention, they obsessed over Annie and everyone else at the Meeting, especially the scholarly, barefooted Dabba Doo. Daniel, being the resident sci-fi nerd, blurted out, "What if we're just characters in a new Netflix series?" Lydia laughed so hard she almost peed. They knew that the ingredients of the perfect recipe were there (trusting Chef Annie unconditionally) but at this stage, while they could smell the aroma of what was being cooked, they were clueless to the whereabouts of the kitchen.

They still called each other Daniel and Lydia, unwilling or unready to take that next step of spooky ratification. So much *hadn't* been revealed—they knew they couldn't see the forest for the trees—but the little spiders spun their little theories, usually while lying next to each other in their PJs at bedtime. Sometimes they used a flashlight to read the *Guide* together before sleep, covering themselves with a blanket.

Welcome to orientation! You are not expected to know anything— this is not a test or an exam, so you can relax. (Easier said than done!) It is not an audition either—if you're here, you've already won the part! So take a deep breath and know—TRUST!—that more shall be revealed. I know it's all a bit overwhelming (to put it mildly!) but in time you will understand your purpose here. So WELCOME HOME, everyone, and GOD BLESS every one of you!

If they weren't too drowsy, Daniel kept reading aloud until Lydia drifted away . . .

Rule Number One: Be GOOD to your NEW BODY!!! Treat it with RESPECT and it will RETURN the favor!!!

Rule Number Two: It is perfectly normal for the "old" you to occa-sionally feel sadness. These feelings WILL diminish as you get closer to your *Moment of Balance*. But if you DO feel sad (you sometimes will) it is TO BE EXPECTED. Remember: take a deep breath and TRUST!!!

Rule Number Three: As time goes by, you will find that you are becoming more "yourself." But *remember*—while ADULTS are PLAYFUL, and CHILDLIKE qualities are usually tolerated and en-joyed, do NOT call ATTENTION to yourself with too much CRAZY HORSEPLAY! Listen to your Landlord!!!!

The *Guide* would fall from his hands as he tumbled into his sister's dream. It was always the same. They dreamed that their *moment of balance* had been achieved and their work here was done. Lost in a city, they asked random strangers for directions back to the train station. The people they approached didn't have faces, but that didn't frighten them. Each time Troy and Maya moved on to the next bystander, the one before suddenly grew eyes and ears and a mouth and a nose, like a flower blooming in time-lapse. In the dream, they stopped worrying where the station was, because they knew they would find it again when they had to.

But that time was not now.

3.

Owen Caplan has been a career cop since the mid-eighties. His education began modestly, at community college, and he was a decorated vet in the Marine Corps. A lifetime resident of Macomb County, he lives ten miles northwest of Saggerty Falls, in Armada. He's an active weekend hiker on the Orchard Trail.

Originally a station on the GT Railroad, the Falls was incorporated as a village in 1869. It never grew large enough to become a township. In 1991, its sleepy police department boasted four full-time officers, one of whom— the childless bachelor Owen—was the "designated detective" because he had a B.S. in criminal justice from Wayne State University. (Willow Wylde became his partner in '93 and then moved to Manhattan to work narcotics five years later.) In 1999, eighteen months before the disappearance of Troy and Maya, Owen was upgraded by the local governing body and made chief. It was an ill-fated incumbency; the Rummer case effectively broke the back of the Saggerty Falls PD.

The abductions received so much press and political attention that the village was forced to dismantle its overwhelmed, undertrained police department and contract out to the Macomb County Sheriff's Office. With its eighteen jurisdictions and multiple municipalities, Owen couldn't argue against the Sheriff's superior manpower, resources and skill sets. "Hell, it's not a competition," he said publicly, when asked how he felt about being subsumed. But for many years, in the privacy of his own thoughts, he found himself gloating over the Sheriff's failure to find the killer. He was actually ashamed by such pettiness—made worse by what seemed like a passive-aggressive investment in their not finding those who were responsible—but couldn't help himself. It was personal. Those kids were like family. He felt stymied that he couldn't be the one to personally bring the murderer to justice.

The transition period for the deposed chief was rocky but his ambition to achieve something large, something of greatness, remained undimmed. He was a soldier. He went back to school with a fury, acquiring an M.S. in administration from Central Michigan University. Attended the FBI National Academy in Quantico. Graduated from the Macomb County Public Service Institute Center for Police Management and Leadership Studies. Top of his class in the Northwestern University School of Police Staff and Command. Joined the Sheriff's Office. Was quickly promoted to sergeant and assigned to the Detective Bureau. Promoted to lieutenant. Promoted to chief of staff, in charge of jail operations.

He was a natural leader and a people person. He dabbled in local politics, building a loyal fan base. Did lots of speaking at schools, hospitals and charity events. Became a Democrat and ate as many rubber chickens as the fundraisers could throw at him. Buddied up with the lieutenant governor. There was still a lot of goodwill toward the former chief, not just in Macomb but in surrounding counties, even after all those years. Folks never forgot the elegance and compassion he brought to the impossible task of the nightmare in Saggerty Falls. There was a case back in the seventies, the Oakland County Murders. Four schoolkids were abducted and their bodies found posed, in different clothing. To this day it remained unsolved, but those who were old enough to remember wished there'd been a competent, avuncular figurehead like Lieutenant Caplan to soothe the collective nerve. Macomb wasn't nearly as high-end as the westerly Oakland County, yet with his warm and easy blue-collar charm, Owen would have fit the bill. He fit it for Saggerty Falls, best he could—until they took the job away from him three months into the investigation.

Twelve years after the abduction of the Rummer children, Owen Ca-plan was elected Macomb County sheriff; four years later, he was voted in for another term. It wasn't even close.

Now he presides over an undersheriff, four captains, thirteen lieutenants, a handful of corporals and twenty-five sergeants. Some of those he appointed and others floated to the top, or near it, in accordance with the arcane mysteries of civil service. Under him are 225 sworn deputies, with another 250 at the Macomb County Jail in Mount Clemens (thirteen hundred prisoners strong), where Deputies Daniel Doheny and Lydia Molloy began their careers. The sheriff is responsible for maintaining that institution.

He insisted on being directly involved in the hiring of his deputies and had the heart and energy to do that. He felt responsible for their successes and failures, which made him an exemplary sheriff, an exemplary man. Owen trusted his instincts, even when he didn't fully understand where they were heading—such as now, with Daniel and Lydia sitting across from him.

Deputy Doheny wasn't exactly a loose cannon, but certainly had his moments. As a fellow veteran, Owen could see that he was wrapped too tight; the kid went through some bad hoodoo in Afghanistan. And Owen knew all about the major melodrama that occasionally flared between Daniel and his eternally soon-to-be-ex-wife. Still, there was something about him that made the sheriff want to give him a shot.

Lydia was actually a bigger question mark, but Owen absolutely knew she had heart—the Tim Hortons shooting proved it. When a lightbulb went off in his head to throw them together in a squad car at the substation in Saggerty Falls, his gut said, *Hell, absolutely.* Either it'd work or it wouldn't, like anything else in this world. (But it'd sure be fun to watch.) He enjoyed creating micro-labs where his deputies could flourish, learning both from their mistakes and gold-star actions. Instinct told him that Molloy would be a good complement to Doheny, providing the balance that seemed to be MIA in his Special Ops problem child. She was no pushover either. In a way, the sheriff was glad it was Molloy who had pulled the trigger on the nutjob. That it went down like that made it easier for him to enlist them in tandem for his new enterprise.

"I might have a special assignment for you two," he said. The sheriff had summoned them to his office on Elizabeth Road in Mount Clemens. The deputies nervously glanced at each other. They liked and respected their boss but had no idea what he was up to. "How would you feel about that?"

They thought he was being sarcastic and prepped themselves for some kind of demotion.

"If you're going to put me on a desk because of the shooting," said Lydia, "there's no reason to punish Daniel too."

"I'm not putting either one of you on a desk."

"You want us to go to middle schools and talk about gangs and the perils of medical marijuana?" said Daniel, smiling.

"Not even close."

"*I* know!" said Lydia, as if she'd solved a riddle. "You want us to play ourselves in a movie."

Owen grinned and sat back, letting them have their fun.

"The only role I'd consider," said Daniel, "would be the sequel to *Space Jam*. Funniest movie ever!" His laugh was strident and too young. "Michael Jordan and the Looney Tunes characters? Are you kidding me? Fucking best movie ever!"

Lydia looked at him sideways, rolling her eyes and trying to laser-beam the "crazy horseplay" caveat of Rule Number Three into his head. Time to deflect. "What do you have in mind?" she asked.

"I'll let you know. What I guess I want to hear is that you both won't mind a change. And a challenge."

Daniel looked at Lydia and grinned. "You up for a change?"

"Life would be boring without it."

"Good," said Owen. "Okay, we're done."

He wasn't sure why but decided not to go further. But in that moment, he understood the real purpose of seeing them: putting them in a room together so he could read their energy. He smiled to himself because "reading energy" was a strange, tried-and-true technique that he'd put to effective use over the years, having picked it up from his gifted former partner, Willow Wylde.

As they stood to leave, Owen said, "Oh—there's just one more thing." They knew what was coming: the sheriff's signature way of ending all his meetings. "Get the fuck out of my office."

After work that night, they changed into civilian clothes and went to a coffee shop off the beaten path. Whenever they wanted to dish about Annie and the Meeting but were too amped to go home, they enjoyed having dinner at an anonymous, unfamiliar place.

"*Space Jam?*" said Lydia. "*That* was awkward. You are such a spaz."

"You could at least have brought up *Harriet the Spy.*"

"Oh my God," she giggled. "*Harriet the Spy!* We need to rent it, Daniel, like, we need to rent it *tonight.*"

"So what do you think Owen's cooking up?"

"Haven't got a clue."

"Maybe *The First 48*'s gonna do Macomb and he wants us to star. Wouldn't that be cool?"

"We're not homicide detectives, Dumbo. In case you haven't noticed."

"There's lots of those kind of shows that follow regular cops around."

"I don't think Annie would approve." She took a bite out of her tuna melt and got serious. "I saw the shrink today for the last time."

"How'd it go?"

"She was a little . . . concerned. You know—that putting a bullet in Crazypants didn't seem to 'bother' me. She said I had what's called 'flattened affect.' Thinks I'm gonna have PTSD."

"Those people just want return visits. It's all about billable hours."

"She's probably on salary, don't you think? But it was kinda helpful, overall. Kinda sorta. I guess. And I did have this realization . . . that the first thing that went through my head when I shot him—I mean the *very* first thing, Daniel, that went through my head was, *I'm not here for this.* It was like hearing a really loud voice."

"'Not here for this.'"

"You know, like, I know I'm supposed to kill—*someone*—but not *this* turkey. It was just . . . very, very weird. When I was standing over the body looking at him, I had this *other* thought: *I'm done.* 'I'm done.' It was like I'd had some kind of . . . *moment of balance*—and at the same time I was thinking *I'm not here for this* I was also having this feeling that I *had* done what I was here for, accomplished my 'mission,' my whatever—that I'd finished what I was meant to finish. Even though I totally knew I hadn't, that it was a fake *moment of balance*! And that I wasn't finished at all."

"That was my first thought too—when I got stabbed. I mean, a variation of that."

"Are you serious?"

"I was thinking that if I died—if I die, I . . . fail. Not that I would have failed in stopping him or protecting *you*—but I would have failed to have done what I was meant to."

"So weird, right?"

"I'm telling you, we're a fucking Netflix series."

"Maybe. It's either *Black Mirror* or some manga comic—I just don't know which."

They left the restaurant and walked to the car.

The street was dark. As Daniel opened the door of the driver's side, a man with a hairnet over his face leapt out and grabbed Lydia's purse. The strap around her shoulder didn't give and she got thrown to the ground. Daniel ran around the car and pounced on the assailant. Another mugger stepped from the shadows and pointed a gun.

"I'm-a shoot, motherfucker! Give him the fucking purse!"

Daniel lifted the man with the ease of picking up an infant and used him like a shield to storm the man with the gun. In a controlled frenzy, he pounded them both into unconsciousness and would have killed them if Lydia hadn't intervened.

On the drive home, they were quiet until she asked if they should tell Annie what happened.

Daniel said, "Probably," and nothing more.

At home, she rubbed alcohol on his bloody fists. They took bubble baths. As he soaked, she brought him a bowl of popcorn garnished with stalks of black licorice on a tray. After, he wanted to watch *Fear of the Walking Dead* but agreed to rent *Harriet the Spy* instead because she'd been so sweet.

Curled up on the sofa, the siblings fell asleep halfway through.

GOING HOME

I.

Homeroom at Mount Clemens High.

The lame teacher makes a lame joke about Melania Trump.

The lame teacher is still rhapsodizing over *Hamilton*. *Hamilton* is so over!

The lame teacher says the *lamest* shit, like, "I'll take Mary J. Blige over Nicki Minaj every time"—

And she's white!

Honeychile hates her but everyone else loves her.

Whatever . . .

At lunchtime, all Zelda wants to do is keep talking about the crazy asthma attack but Honeychile's so *bored*. Zelda keeps checking in to see if she's okay and Honeychile says, "Why do you keep asking me that? It's annoying!" Her BFF (though not for long if Zelda doesn't *shut the fuck up*) shrugs and says, "Because you're acting weird." "In what way?" demands the scowling Honeychile. "In *that* way," says Zelda. "You're, like, being a total bitch." "I'm being a bitch? I'm the one who almost died, not you!" "I *know*," says Zelda, with a pout. "And I probably saved your life, which is why I can't understand why you're not, like, being more *grateful* and acting like such a total *bitch* to me." "Well," says Honeychile with a crooked, baiting smile. "If you *hate* me so much, why don't you just go away?" "I will! I totally will!"— and Zelda leaves, exhaling the B-word as she huffs off.

Though she probably had a point. Honeychile couldn't quite put her finger on it but she *was* feeling different, if different was even the word. Maybe she hadn't gotten enough sleep. She'd been so unsettled by the asthma attack and what followed that whether she'd slept at all (when they transferred to the den) was a muddle. Her parents didn't want her to come to school, they wanted her to stay at home and rest, but Honey was so insistent—so *bitchy*—that Harold nodded to his wife that going to class might be the best thing. (The nurses there were pretty great and doted over her. Harold would call ahead to give them a heads-up about the night's events.) He grabbed the stethoscope they kept in the first-aid kit and listened to their daughter's chest; no wheezing whatsoever. Under protest, Honeychile demonstrated her lung capacity with a series of long, deep breaths. *See?* she said contentiously. *I'm fine!* Rayanne reluctantly gave in because she didn't want to provoke another respiratory crisis.

She insisted on driving the girls to school, instead of their taking the bus. When she dropped them off, she made Honeychile promise she would go to the nurse's office at the first sign of distress. Honeychile rolled her eyes and said *Whatever* and Rayanne attributed her truculence to the effects of the shot she'd given her, which sometimes happened. Zelda got out last and whispered to Rayanne, "Don't worry, I'll totally watch her." She actually winked at the worried mom.

Alone now, Honeychile tried to break it all down. She felt freakishly disrupted. She wondered if she was about to get her first period (Rayanne hadn't even thought of that). She'd already been twice to the ladies' room to check but there was nothing. What *was* it, then? When she finally realized what had been preoccupying her all morning, her mood grew stranger still.

She'd been thinking of Mrs. Collins from the moment she "awakened," right around the time Rayanne injected her with the EpiPen. Another peculiar realization was that she hadn't given a single thought to Hildy Collins in the years since her adoption—well, *maybe* she had but not much of one. That amazing, beautiful woman! As she ruminated on Hildy, Honeychile felt remorseful for not having bothered to contact the person who'd played the most pivotal role in her young life. She never went to visit; never phoned; never sent a letter of thanks or a *How are you?* text or e-mail. (Did she even have her phone number or e-mail?) She knew that in Hildy's world, the adoptee's cutting of ties would be considered healthy, evidence of a rousing success, but still—the conscience-stricken girl couldn't help but feel that not having reached out was a monstrously indecent thing, an enormous failing as a human being.

Mrs. Collins had been in charge of her case since she was seven years old. She'd stood by Honeychile through it all: the corrupt residential homes, the well-meaning families who shamelessly "returned" her, the lonely hospitalizations and traumatic surgeries. Mrs. Collins was the one who held her hand during those dreadful adoption fair weekends in the parking lot of Macomb Children's Services—prospective parents came to gawk and sample the wares like at some slave auction—because of her strange looks, she was given cloying attention by people who never dreamed of taking her home. When her heart, soul and pride were in tatters, it was Hildy who gathered her up and sewed Honeychile back together again.

Why *was* she thinking of Mrs. Collins, and with the insistence of one possessed? It couldn't be that she wanted to find her birth parents—she never had an interest and still didn't. She was sure of that. Yet even the cliché possibility of a sudden, involuntary curiosity about her origins unsettled and depressed her. She'd read online about happy, well-adjusted adoptees who wake up one day with such an impulse, out of the blue; apparently it was some kind of instinct, like salmon fighting upstream to die in the trailer-trash gravel where they were spawned and abandoned. Honeychile had another seizure of guilt, knowing the anguish it would cause Harold and Rayanne if she announced that finding those pieces of shit was just something she had to do. They'd of course be supportive and understanding but in private would be terribly hurt, even frightened about the results.

The other strange part of her musings about Mrs. Collins was the movie that was playing in her head. She pictured herself making a surprise visit to Hildy's workplace—but arriving by locomotive, of all things. The unlikely express started somewhere in the sky, floating gently down until it stopped right outside the building. In the movie, Honeychile stepped out from a sleeper car, very regal and grand.

She had lots of luggage and a porter helped her down the little set of stairs.

2.

The bus, not a train, took Honeychile to that familiar place. Walking the two blocks to Mrs. Collins's office in downtown Mount Clemens, she began to get excited about seeing her oldest friend in the world.

All this time, the woman who saved her was working just miles away from where Honeychile lived! How is it that they'd never run into each other? (It was better they hadn't, because this way, Honeychile could show her initiative.) Again, she castigated herself for never having had the simple courtesy to acknowledge Mrs. Collins's countless kindnesses—then pushed the thought away so as not to ruin what she hoped would be a lovely reunion. She broke into a smile, imagining Hildy's response to seeing her. Because of her idiosyncratic looks, unlike other children Hildy had placed but hadn't seen in critical years of growth, there'd be no mistaking the spunky, legendary Renée "Honey" Matlock, the unlikely golden child of Macomb Children's Services.

Honeychile recalled the time just after an adoption fair when she told Mrs. Collins about overhearing an earnest husband say to an overexcited wife who was enthralled by the prospect of taking Renée home—"Do you think you're strong enough for the stares and the comments?" "The world can be like that," said Hildy, drawing her close. "The world can be heartless and cruel but not *all* of the world. I want you to hear that, Renée. I really want you to hear and know that." The hug and those words meant every-thing to a throwaway nine-year-old child. When Harold and Rayanne fell in love with her, Mrs. Collins said, "Do you remember what I once told you about how the world can be? How there are bright suns that shine through to light up the darkness? Well, *these* two are bright suns. And they want you. They really, really want you. So now it's up to you, Renée, to be brave. To let yourself feel the warmth of those two loving suns."

Because by then, she had almost given up.

What would have become of her if it weren't for Mrs. Collins? Or Har-old and Rayanne?

She owed all of them so much.

When she saw the building, there was a brief moment of doubt that Hildy had retired or that her office had moved. As she walked in, the light and the look of the place, the whole amazing, complicated feeling of it assailed her again, with its familiar mixed emotions of high and low. There was a metal detector and to her enormous delight, she recognized the guard. Even the name came back to her:

"Lemoyne!"

"Well, well, if it isn't the champion!" (He'd always called her that.) "Now, look at *you*. Look how grown-up you are!"

"I maybe grew an eighth of an inch?" she said drolly.

"Champion, you taller than everybody here. You walk tall!"

"You're the best, Lemoyne."

"Who you here to see?"

"Mrs. Collins . . ."

"Do you have an appointment?" She shook her head. "My champion! Tell you what—I haven't seen her come in yet, but you can tippy-toe back to her office and see if she snuck by. Gonna need to frisk you, though." Thinking he was serious, she lifted her arms. "Ha ha! My *champion*. I'll let you slide, but just for *today*. But I'm gonna get fired if you carrying a pistol."

"Left it at home."

He laughed again, shook his head and said *My champion* as she wandered back.

When she arrived at Mrs. Collins's office, a secretary was on the phone. Honeychile didn't recognize the woman. Secretaries come and go but Hildy Collins stays.

She hung up and said, "Can I help you?"

"I'm Renée—Matlock. 'Honeychile.' Mrs. Collins placed me. Is she here?"

"No, she isn't," she said gruffly.

"Do you know when she'll be back?"

"No, I don't."

There wasn't a trace of friendliness—the lady seemed irritated, even upset—and Honeychile made a mental note to be sure to mention that to Hildy. It simply wouldn't do for a saintly woman like Mrs. Collins to have a mean bitch sitting there, undoing all her great work. "Do you want to leave your number?"

"Is she on vacation?"

"Personal business," she said.

"When you talk to her," said Honeychile, "I'd very much appreciate it if you not tell her I stopped by—I want it to be a surprise. Will you promise not to tell her?"

"I won't tell her," said the woman, with a tortured smile, relieved that the conversation was coming to an end.

After she left, Honeychile thought she might have made a tactical error by asking her not to tell. Being a shitty person and even shittier secretary, now the woman was *certain* to tell Hildy about the drop-in.

She waved goodbye to Lemoyne on her way out, but he was busy watching a mom go through the metal detector. Her toddler watched in fascination and once she cleared the device, the woman swept him up in her arms. Lemoyne patted the boy's head.

"That's a champion you got right there," he said.

3.

On the street, Honeychile made the spontaneous decision to go to Hildy's house. It was about a two-hour walk to Clinton River Drive, over by Shadyside Park.

She'd been to the bungalow-style residence on the leafy street many times before. By the time she got off the bus and rounded the corner for the two-block approach, she was rerunning the tape of her epic betrayal of Hildy Collins and felt miserable all over again. Children's Services employees were discouraged (in some cases prohibited) from inviting children in the system to their homes, for all kinds of reasons—the paramount one being "liability," that heartless institutional chestnut that drained the blood from any human equation. Liability banned teachers from hugging students, and shut down playgrounds because of potential injury on slides and swings. God forbid a woman like Hildy, acting out of *love*, love for her children—lost children, damaged children, broken children—God forbid she invite those innocent, beautiful souls to her home to give them treats (a broken child could choke on a treat and die); God forbid she hold them close (a damaged child might accuse her of unspeakable things); God forbid that her love, a love that healed, restored and renewed, be expressed in the small, essential ways that nourish, allowing saplings to grow into mighty oaks . . . a watering love that provided, sustaining the child until the end of its life. God forbid! Hildy invited Renée into her home and fed her, laughed and cried with her, watched *Tangled* and *The Goonies* and *The Princess Bride* with her, taught her how to bake cookies and put on lipstick, how to look in the mirror at a beautiful girl and not an ogre—*and I repaid her love by ignoring her. Oh! How nasty, how awful! Zelda was right!*

Through her tears, moving toward the house with dread, she said to herself, "I am the biggest bitch in the world! *Soooo* nasty to Mom and Dad last night—just because they were terrified I would die! What the fuck is *wrong* with me?" She shivered with a horrible thought: What if Hildy wouldn't forgive her? Honeychile had told herself she was special (because Mrs. Collins made her feel that way) but had proved by her abominable behavior how very *unspecial* she was. What if Mrs. Collins, in shock and disappointment, realized years ago that Renée was just like all the others, the selfish legions who'd flown the nest never to return, not even for a thank-you or hello. Even worse, what if the squadrons of children Mrs. Collins invited to her house through the years *had* kept in touch, sending birthday cards, get-wells and detailed letters about their wonderful new lives . . . what if they'd even invited Hildy to their homes? And Hildy had come?

What if Honeychile was the single exception?

Oh! Oh! It was just too terrible to think of—

Again, she pushed the black meditation from her head. She wanted only to be joyful, grateful and thankful when she saw her . . . she wanted it not to be about her but about Hildy.

When she saw the sheriff's car in the driveway, Honeychile had a random thought that Mrs. Collins married a policeman, followed by the nervous theory that she'd moved away and a cop was living in her old house.

She rang the doorbell and waited for what seemed an eternity before peeking through the window. She saw Hildy get up from the couch to answer. There were some men with her. One was on a chair, one was standing.

"Renée!" she said, with a startled smile.

"Mrs. Collins!" she exclaimed, hugging the woman close.

"Darling," said Hildy. "Is everything all right?"

She asked with the concern of a mother—of all mothers.

"Yes, yes!" said Honeychile. "I just . . . I was so missing you."

"That's lovely, sweetheart—and I've missed you too. But it's not a good time, Renée. I have some visitors."

Honeychile was finally able to see the woman as she was now, not then. Her face had thickened in the intervening years; it was blank and pasty, half-wet with perspiration and tears. The eyes were hollow and dark, rheumy with worry.

"Is everything okay?" said Honeychile.

Mrs. Collins sighed, exhaling a bitter, fearful breath.

"You see"—she smiled incongruously, in the habit of comforting a child, of soothing others—"well, no. You see, Renée—I can't find my Winston." The girl silently gasped, and again came the smile from the formidable being who'd so tenderly mentored her. "I just—well—you see, we can't find my boy."

OFF THE ORCHARD TRAIL

I.

He wrote the address on the wall of his Port Hope double-wide.

Day by day Willow added doodles and filigrees—with Sharpies at first, then with a set of multicolored markers he picked up in town—to the numbers, street name and zip code of the locale that the handsome woman on the train had given him. The ornamental designs were becoming almost beautiful. Willow never knew he had it in him; *might have to start wearing a beret.* He really did think it was the sort of mural that a woman he was trying to seduce would be impressed by. Trouble was, if he spoke of its true origin, the gal might think he'd gone mad. He was wondering if maybe he had.

He still believed that his drinking was controlled, if *controlled* meant falling short of bingeing. But Dubya was spooked because experience had shown that the illusion of self-will wouldn't last. He had an inkling about what was keeping him at least temporarily from the cliff's edge. He told himself it was because he had a goal—to remember what happened each night in the recurring dream he'd been having since awakening on the train in Pittsburgh. In order to do that, he needed to moderate. Blackouts weren't conducive to memory retention.

The suicidal consequences of relapse had yet to hit him full force; Willow was still in the honeymoon phase of denial. But it sure felt shitty when he telegraphed fake sobriety by getting extra solicitous—almost perky—during phone calls with his daughter. *Ugh.* He didn't want to break Pace's heart for the thousandth time and there was just no upside in being honest with her, other than to expiate his own guilt. (He wasn't even sure if he felt guilty anymore.) The girl had enough on her plate. She and Geoff were setting a date for Larkin's surgery at Children's Hospital in Detroit, and that he could help his grandson swelled Willow's heart. It was a vaccine that did wonders in tamping down his horror of the thing he sensed was lying in wait.

He'd been manically clipping photos of trains from all kinds of magazines, scotch-taping them to the wall on the periphery of The Address, giving the whole of it a blue watercolor wash. He stepped back now to give it a look.

Jesus. This could be in the fucking Whitney.

When the phone rang, he thought it might be Miranda the bodyworker. He was beginning to think the old girl was falling in love with him. Love was a mystery. Sometimes it began with a warm, wet hand towel. Sometimes it ended that way too.

"Dubya?"

"Who's speaking?"

"Your favorite Zen Dyke-ist."

"Renata?" he said, in pleasant surprise.

"Well, shit, Willow. How many other Zen Dyke-ists do you know?"

"You *never* called me Dubya."

"Yeah, well, consider it 'contrary action.' Like the Big Book suggests."

His body both relaxed and stiffened. They'd been through the war together and he wondered if he'd be able to lie. "You in Fort Lauderdale?" he said.

"I am. Home unsweet home."

"God, it's good to hear your voice."

"It's good to hear *yours,* Mayor Wylde. Sunday mornings just aren't the same without your news, sports and weather report. You always put a smile on my face, buckaroo."

"Feels kinda like a dream, right? The Meadows? Like it happened a hun-dred years ago."

"Maybe it did—you know, in our past lives. But I can't decide if it was a dream or a nightmare."

They laughed over that.

"So what are you doing with yourself, kid?" he said.

"Same old same old. Up at three A.M. for meditation. Read the sutras then bike to the zendo by six. Work in the kitchen till eight, then cook some-thing special for the Roshi. Home by four, where I make spiritual use of my valuable downtime shooting up *Sex and the City, Seinfeld,* and the various multiple Bourne identities that are my drugs of choice."

"Nice."

"And you, my friend?"

A grace note of heaviness was in her voice, like she knew.

"Getting used to the world again, I suppose. As pointless as the exercise sometimes feels."

"Still doing the deal?" she asked.

"Well . . ." Renata cut him off with a giggle, having intuited the rest. He was relieved. "Actually, Renny dearest, Dubya ain't doin' the deal so well. Let's just say at the moment that I'm leaning more toward progress than perfection."

"Okay, guy," she said, without judgment. "Wanna share?"

He sighed. "I decided to go to New York to get my old job back. I had some crazy idea they'd be dying to have me. I had no business being there at *all.* And I think . . . Jesus, Renata. I think it must have been one of the most fucked-up trips of my life."

She guffawed. "Been there, done that."

"I won't even get into all the crazy bullshit that went down. I mean, shit you would not *believe.* Long story short: I took the drink. Took the opiates too."

"And how are you doing now?"

"Oh, I guess I'm still into it . . . but not like I was. It's quieted down."

"You know, I had a feeling about you, Willow. And when I kept on having it I thought, 'You know what, Renata? Pick up the goddam phone and call the man.'"

"I'm so glad you did, babe. I really am. You're the first I've told."

"Are you going to meetings?"

"Trying. There aren't too many in Port Hope."

"Well, see if you can find one. They have 'em online too. They're actually supposed to be pretty decent."

"I'll do that," he lied.

"You can probably Skype into one so you can at least see fresh newcomer meat."

"That'll work, so long as they can't see *me*. 'Cause at the moment, I am not a sexy sight to behold."

"Newcomer chicks ain't picky. They're crazier than shit but they ain't picky."

"Yeah."

They hung there awhile just breathing, not talking.

"Just don't die on me, Willow."

"I don't plan to. Not anytime soon."

"You know what they say about a plan."

"I know, 'God laughs.' Guess that's why I'm an atheist—eliminates a major source of sadistic hilarity."

"Hey, you want me to come out?"

The offer surprised and moved him, touching off a reflexive stir in the gonads. She *was* a dyke but he'd known many in his time who experienced the phenomenon of SDC—Sudden Dick Craving. She wasn't Kate Upton, but hell, she could run circles around Miranda the masseuse. In that split second of cold male arithmetic, Willow chastised himself; she was a friend, and a helluva good one. He knew that her intentions were nothing but selfless and altruistic.

"No, I don't think so, Renata. Not at this time. But *thank you*, that means a helluva lot—really. Tell you what, I'll make you a promise. If my shit goes way south, I'll take you up on it."

"If your shit gets wild, Mayor Wylde?"

"If my shit gets wild and purple. And that's a promise."

He was getting ready to wrap it up when the words tumbled from his mouth as if spoken by someone else. "Hey, remember those dreams I was telling you about, the ones I was having before the Meadows?"

"About the train?"

"Yeah."

"I thought they were kind of beautiful."

"Well, I'm having them all the time now."

"Interesting."

"Yeah—they're . . . completely vivid. Hi-def. Like, four-D."

"Sounds more like Higher Power than hi-def to me."

"But instead of just watching the train go by—like from the outside, the way I was doing?—I'm inside now. And there's a woman . . . there's *people*—"

"Maybe it's the Sober Train. It's either that or the DTs."

"I don't know what it is, Renny. But I do kind of look forward to going to sleep. Just to see what's next."

"Well, that's a good thing, Willow. 'What's next' is a beautiful thing. Or can be. We ought to grab on to whatever seems to promise a little bit of serenity. God, I still dread going to sleep. It's so damn hard. But I never was any good at it." She paused. "Ready to make a second promise, Willow?"

"You got it."

"Don't let that peace train derail, okay? You know the Dylan song—blood on the tracks and all that."

"I promise."

"And try to find a meeting. Seriously."

"I will."

"I love you, Dubya."

"Love you too, Miss Contrary Action."

"'May those who find themselves in fearful wildernesses—the children, the aged, the unprotected—be guarded by beneficent celestials, and may they swiftly attain Buddhahood.'"

"Amen to that, kid."

"And in the words of Shakyamuni, 'Keep coming back.'"

2.

A few nights later, at 3:00 A.M., no longer able to dispel the compulsion, Willow drove two hours due south to Armada. He had no say in the matter. He felt like a somnambulist.

He took the M-19, the highway running parallel to his usual route to Pace's home in Marlette, because he got paranoid that his insomniac daughter might glance outside her window to catch his car whisking by.

A ludicrous fantasy but again, he couldn't help himself.

Then all of a sudden, as if teleported in the predawn darkness, he was curbside at the address the woman had given him in the dream: *22147 32 Mile Road.*

He sat stupefied in his ten-year-old Pontiac, listening mindlessly to One Direction, Fifth Harmony, Twenty One Pilots, 99 Souls—all the numerical Top 20 bands of the day.

The windows of the house were dark.

He got that shiver of blueness again and looked out toward the ridge; he couldn't have known that he was only a few miles away from the trail where Lydia Molloy had died and been (provisionally) resurrected. Though he never asked, *What the fuck am I doing here?*, the phantom question's troublesome corollary still loomed—

—*What now?*

He hadn't drank or drugged in forty-eight hours, a goosey sobriety summoned out of respect for what was required of his bizarre, puzzling, fearsome mission. (*Mission* was the precise word that floated to his foggy surface.) Yet amid the chaos of his emotions, he felt deeply connected. It wasn't until somewhere between Marlette and the outskirts of Armada Township that Willow realized he had somehow managed to conjure his childhood self, that preternatural boy who misguidedly thwarted his own eerie gifts for fear of hurting others. As he raced to the terminus on 32 Mile Road, he felt like his mother was riding shotgun and Nana was in the backseat, the aroma of their beings banishing the funk smell of month-old fast-food detritus. The two matriarchs were content. They seemed to approve of the journey their Wylde-child had embarked on . . .

They approved of his mission.

He switched off the radio and listened to choral works on his iPhone playlist. Awash in the sixteenth-century harmonies of Duarte Lobo, he began to weep with the notion that whatever he was doing was either crazy or holy. And for the first time, he understood they were two sides of the same coin.

At seven in the morning, when the first light went on—was it the kitchen?—Willow left his car. He stood on the porch a few minutes, frozen and vacant. He tried to feel his mother and grandmother's presence but could no longer. He looked back at the Pontiac, as if he might see them there, but the vibe was gone.

Should he ring the bell or knock?

He did both.

In a panic, Willow realized he hadn't done an iota of preparation for what was imminent. Suddenly he was ashamed of the arrogance that had propelled him to this freakish endgame—as if not even the simplest plan was needed because it was all just another part of his recurring dream. To save himself and buy time, he thought: *When they answer, I'll just say my name.* But say it to whom? Everything was too real now, grossly undream-like, and he became so shaken by his quixotic act that even his sobriety sobered up. He almost sprinted back to the car, where two options would present themselves: either drive to a bar or drive to a psych ward. Both seemed preferable to the mess he'd gotten himself into.

The porch light went on and the door opened. A man glared at him, his face a grimace of puzzlement.

"Willow?"

The uninvited visitor stared back, his mouth agape. "Owen?"

He almost fainted from the shock.

A woman in a robe appeared behind Owen Caplan, with a look of terror. What was Willow doing here? He looked so strange and awful—it could only mean one thing. "Is it Pace?" she said, heart pounding furiously.

Her carotid looked like it swallowed a tiny frenzied animal. "Willow! *Did something happen to Pace?*"

"No! No, no, no—"

"Is it Larkin? Did something happen to *Larkin* . . ."

The blood had drained from her face.

"No, they're fine," he said definitively. "Everyone's fine."

"Then what is it?" she asked. "What's wrong?"

Husband and wife waited for him to speak. When it became obvious no explanation was forthcoming, Owen took the path of grace and said, "Come in. We just put some coffee on."

AMENDS

I.

They poured him a cup and Adelaide asked if he was hungry. His arrival had been so rash that any pertinent discussion was politely suspended. They'd only moved in a few days ago and the place was a mess, filled with boxes and old and new furniture. She assumed Pace had given him their new address; he must have pried it out of her, because their daughter knew Adelaide didn't want that information "out there" just yet. It wasn't that she had a problem with her ex knowing where they lived. It was more about her growing accustomed to controlling her space, the small and large details of her private life.

She was crawling out of her skin from the effort to keep her mouth shut but followed her husband's gentle lead. She'd leave the interrogation to him. After all, Owen was the professional in the family. Thoughts swirled amid the silences and small talk: *Maybe he's here to get help. Maybe he wants us to check him into rehab. I hope he's not here for money—*

After an awkward twenty minutes, Owen said, "Honey, let me and Willow talk awhile."

The toast popped up and she set it on the table with a rectangle of butter from the fridge. On the way out, she touched Willow's shoulder, and it was a comfort to him.

"Are you in trouble?" said Owen, after she left.

"I—I don't know," said Willow.

He felt better having shakily declared the truth.

"Are you sober?" The guest nodded, eschewing a timeline. "Because you don't *seem* sober. You look hungover."

"I am," he laughed, uncomfortably. "But not from booze."

"Okay," said Owen, staying neutral.

His demeanor reminded Willow of the caring, nonjudgmental counselors at the Meadows.

"Is there something I can do, Dubya—that *we* can do to help?"

Willow hadn't seen the man since the Rummer kids disappeared. (Owen and Adelaide had been hooked up awhile by then.) He'd seen pictures of his old partner on Facebook and whatnot—he wasn't on Facebook himself but had Pace's password—but hadn't gone snooping in a while. And now, sitting in the kitchen like Mr. Vulnerable Hot Mess, with hat, heart and shrinking cock in hand, being stared at like some homeless person trying to wrangle a bed at the Salvation Army (which was pretty much how he felt), Willow held no resentment or animosity. At least he didn't think he did but was too blown out to feel much of anything. Owen Caplan had stolen his wife—well, not really, but that was the spin Willow promoted during the divorce and for years after. He'd managed to make some sort of peace with it.

Twenty-five years or so before, he was an out-of-control Chicago cop who thought the move to Nowhereville would be the solution—what AA calls a "geographic"—so they packed up the debris of their lives and shipped out to Saggerty Falls. Quaint and quiet, the semirural village was free of the corrupting hubbub of the Windy City, and seemed as good a place as any to lose control again. A little more slowly this time, at least. But slow got fast and the Falls became one more place to burn down. As a card-carrying member of the Victims of America Society, he eventually blamed the arson on "the dynamic duo"—his scabrous term of endearment for Adelaide and

Owen. To his reckoning, they were even the cause of his estrangement from Pace, which was only another pile of victim horseshit. It was funny but as the years went by he actually became *grateful* that Adelaide and Owen found each other. Their union saved a lot more grief than everyone had signed up for.

His head began to clear. He knew there was no way he could reveal the weird truth behind his visit. *I've been having a recurring dream that I'm on a train. A lady wrote an address down and told me to memorize it. It turned out to be your house.* Willow thought it outlandish that he'd actually been entertaining such a confessional, right up to the point when Addie left the kitchen.

No, that just wouldn't do . . .

He let his liar's instinct take over instead.

"This isn't easy for me, Owen." He did a little squirming, though most of it wasn't an act. "This is—this is tough. But the reason I came . . . well—I just . . . I really wanted to *thank* you for everything you've done. Not just for Adelaide but for my daughter. For Pace. And . . . even the way you welcomed me into your house this morning—it's just—it was kind. Very, very kind. And I appreciate it. If I was sitting where you were, I don't know if I'd have done the same—probably not! I'da kicked my sorry ass to the curb. So I just wanted . . . I'm here to apologize. To make amends." He emphasized the word, as if putting a tiara on his bogus brainstorm, fully aware that Owen might recognize it as one of the muddy jewels of AA's sunken treasure chest. "I wanted to make amends for all the ways I mistreated you. Both of you. I spent a lot of years getting high. I was a terrible husband, a terrible father and a terrible cop."

"You had your moments. We all do. But I always thought you were a *great* cop. Had the potential, anyway."

"Thank you for that." He closed his eyes in penitence. "What I feel the worst about is giving you a shitty rap because I couldn't admit to myself how badly I'd fucked up. *Repeatedly.* It wasn't you, friend. And it's just . . . it's taken me a long, long time to admit that. Not just to myself, but to someone else."

It was ironic but in all the years in and out of 12-Step, this was Willow's first real amends. What always stopped him was the fear that the targets of his abuse would either laugh in his face or shower him with justifiable invective for his transgressions. But Owen simply listened, respectfully taking it in, his attention seemingly genuine. Willow felt lighter, even dignified, in spite of himself.

"I guess I'm kind of a hardheaded S.O.B."

"You can be," said Owen, not without affection.

"And I know an apology can't make up for all the crap I pulled, not even close. But I'm hoping . . . well, it was just important for me to say it to your face. Having said *that*, I really do want you to know that I came for you and for Adelaide, not for myself. I'm not proud of my behavior but I guess I'm not ashamed anymore, either—at least I don't want to be. I know that might sound like a self-serving contradiction but it's true."

"Dubya, if there's one thing I've learned in getting older it's that it becomes harder to hold on to stuff. It either gets *easier* or it gets harder, and believe me—I'll take the letting go over the holding on, all day long. I once heard someone say, 'Do you want to be right or do you want to be happy?' You know what? I'll take happy. People like to say life's too short and the trouble is by the time we *get* it, we're just about done. I've been on the life's-too-short program awhile now."

"I'm trying to get there," said Willow. "I guess it's like the scene in that movie, 'I'll have what you're having.' I'll have what you're having, Owen—without the orgasm. Oh, what the hell, I'll take the orgasm."

They laughed.

"Well, thank you," said Owen. "For everything you said. I appreciate it. It couldn't have been easy to get that off your chest." Willow made a show of wiping cartoon sweat from his brow. "Helps explain the urgency of your arrival."

"I couldn't hold on to my shit anymore." Willow felt relief all the way around; he was buying his own malarkey. "I kept telling myself I'd give you a call but I woke up in the middle of the night and said, *Nuh uh, a phone call ain't gonna do it. Too easy.*"

"I'm glad. And glad you're sober, Dubya. I guess there's always enough blame to go around. Now I have something I'd like to say, in the spirit of clearing the air. The truth is, Adelaide and I never got together until both of you were one hundred percent certain that things were . . . irreparable."

"I know that. I mean, actually, maybe I didn't! Thanks for telling me— but I'm okay with it now. With all of it. And Jesus, Addie deserved . . . you both deserve having someone in your life."

He meant it. Willow felt great warmth toward his former partner. In the middle of the strange madness of the situation, he was blessed. "Sorry for barging in—I know y'all just moved and all. Guess that was selfish but what else is new. Seems to be my strong suit! I'm trying not to make it all about me, Owen, I swear I am! Guess I can't always pull that off."

"Don't worry about it."

Willow blotted a for-real tear from his eye, half-wondering when he'd be shown the door, having said his peace and all. His host's impulse *was* to move on—but in a most unexpected way.

"Want to know what's weird?" said Owen. "The weird thing is that I was planning to get in touch with you." Willow flinched. "I spoke with Rafael Leguerre, your old boss at NYPD."

"Uh oh."

"He had good things to say about you, friend."

"Oh really?" said Willow, trying not to sound sarcastic.

"Yes, he did. See, our funding just came through and we're about to start a Cold Case Task Force. I've wanted that for a *long* time. A head-hunter brought us a slew of supervisor applicants but one day last week I thought, 'What about ol' Dubya?' Hell, you actually did that for a few years in the big leagues. Macomb ain't Manhattan—we'll be the little Cold Case engine that could—but you'd bring a shitload of valuable experience to the party, Willow. I think it'd fit you like a glove." He chuckled and said, "The glove might have a few holes in it, but hey . . ."

"Wow," said Willow. "Does Adelaide know about this?"

"Just a little."

Which meant it was likely she knew everything. At the minimum, she'd given Owen her seal of approval; if she hadn't been cool with the hire, it never would have been broached.

"Call the job offer an amends of my own," said Owen. "Not just to you, but to a lot of people. We are not saints. The point is that we are willing to grow along spiritual lines."

The last thing he expected was Owen laying quotes on him from the Big Book. "Are you in the Program?"

"I'll have fifteen years in July."

"I don't even know what to say."

"Just say you'll be at the Macomb County Sheriff's Office in Macomb on Friday morning—sober. Because we're going to make you pee in a Dixie cup."

MYSTERY TRAIN

The kerfuffle with the odd-looking girl on the train rattled Annie more than she would have liked. For the first time in years, she went to the special cabinet—a low-lying mahogany piece of chinoiserie that her mentor bestowed her on his passing—and retrieved the diary she kept during her apprenticeship.

His name was Jasper Kendrick Sebastian and he rescued her. The voices she heard as a girl—always those of children—had become a screaming cacophony; to make them stop, she tried more than once to take her own life. By the time she was three years into her stay at Swarthmore Psychiatric Hospital in Ann Arbor, friends and family had abandoned her. Then one day came a visitor, a tall, gaunt man with sunken cheeks and the strangest eyes she'd ever seen. They looked right through her—into her soul, so the cliché went—like sovereign creatures unto themselves. Jasper told her he'd been searching for members of his family and discovered that she was a cousin, a ruse that enabled him to get past the door of that awful, terrible place. He made the trip from Detroit twice on weekdays and on Sunday afternoon. They didn't talk much at first but his presence soothed her, and the awful, terrible staff approvingly took note. The voices in her head diminished. The softening of Annie's unruliness gave her caretakers less work. (She even became polite.) In just eight months, she was transferred into Jasper's care. It seemed like he had done this sort of thing before.

When she walked out the door, he was her legal guardian.

Like Annie, he once was a teacher, a professor of English literature at Bryn Mawr. But while his ward had been scandalously expelled from her profession, Jasper retired "in order to take up my new, unlikely vocation." The halfway house that he founded in the Corktown area of Detroit was presumptively for psychotic women, but Annie learned that too was a ruse. He told her that all the ladies who lived there were "special, just like you."

He called them Porters-in-Training.

One day, when he felt she was ready, he expanded on the topic.

"The world, *as you know*, is a very mysterious place. For example, those people at Swarthmore—not the patients but the staff—well, of course they have their lives: private lives and working lives. There isn't any mystery at all to their working lives; most despise what they do and have come to despise the very people they're meant to help. There's no mystery to their private lives either, for the most part . . . I'm not talking about secrets, Annie, because they have plenty of those! Those kind of secrets aren't mysteries. And what about the patients? You were one, not too long ago. Many are damaged, some more than others. There are those who are there for the short term—a crisis of self-harm, a depression that got out of hand, the dangerous manias of bipolar illness, that sort of thing. 'Malfunctions,' *yes*, and sometimes *interesting* ones—but mysteries? I don't think so, not in the sense I'm discussing. Are you following me, Annie?"

"As best I can."

"Good. Now, in regards to schizophrenia, in which this house purportedly traffics," he sniggered. "Well, there *is* mystery regarding its origins. I don't mean genetics because everything is genetics. What I really mean is . . ." He literally scratched his chin and meditated. "I may have erred in my little premise. What I meant to say is that *all* is mystery, *everything*, even the most commonplace, the most familiar, the most mundane. All is an absolute, inscrutable mystery! Even the working lives of those incompetent people at Swarthmore, even that: a complete and total mystery."

He paused, as if it were an opportune time to reprise the question—*Are you following me, Annie?*—but demurred.

"I'd go as far as to say it's a miracle that any of us are able to function . . .

not bodily functions, which seem to carry on perfectly well with or without our cooperation, but the functioning of our minds. It's a miracle the whole lot of us don't wind up in Swarthmore, completely insane—yet we don't. Another mystery! We do our grocery shopping and laundry, we go to the bank and obey traffic signals. (Some of us!) We fall in love, get married, have children and so forth." He threw her an impish look. "You've been dreaming of a train, haven't you, Annie?"

She thought about it—it wasn't a conscious thing until he asked—and startled herself by saying, "I have."

"Now we have two mysteries! The first is the recurring dream of the train, a mystery wrapped in the mystery of a dream. The second mystery is my knowing it. In your dream, someone—some*thing*—wrestles you into a cabin, no?"

"Yes!"

"And you wait, you wait very patiently, frightened and bewildered, until a man comes in. A tall, gaunt gentleman much like myself, no? He offers you a tray of refreshments. He seems to know what you'd enjoy: ginger cookies and herbal tea. Your favorites, no? You have this dream for weeks until one night the man tells you to look at the other side of the coaster where you set your tea. You turn it over and find an address written there. He asks you to memorize it. That was the very way I came to be Porter," said Jasper. "In the same fashion you've begun *your* journey. Except in my case, I came to Portership much later in life than you—sometimes that happens. It's not ideal but it can't be helped. My tray," he said, with a parenthetical gleam in his eye, "came with my favorites: bar nuts and a Tom Collins! That's how it happened. And it's been happening forever, the baton passed from Porter to Porter. The longer I've been doing this, the more certain I am that what I said earlier is correct: the only thing we can be sure of is that it's all one great mystery—no one knows anything nor ever will. And *that* is the least mysterious thing we shall ever be able to comprehend."

Annie skipped to the pages that she wrote just before he died.

Jasper was in hospice care, ending his days on Earth. He was in an upstairs room of the halfway house, tended by Porters in various stages of tutelage who hadn't yet left for cities unknown. (Among the ladies were a few men, though Jasper said male Porters were far more rare.) He told Annie that a half year before—around the time he scooped her up from Swarthmore— he became aware that he too was departing, "though on a more pedestrian path than our children do after their *moments of balance.* I'll be leaving in a most conventional way, and so be it. There's nothing to be done." He said that she would know when her own time had come—when she was dying—"by signs and wonders. Things will begin to go . . . haywire."

"What do you mean, 'haywire,' sir?"

"When a Porter passes the baton, there's a period of 'haywire.' Inexplicable things will occur—within that which is already inexplicable, of course. Only someone *new* will be able to set things right again. It's always been like that. We don't know why; we don't ask because we know nothing."

She set down the pages and thought of the rambunctious girl—and of Dabba Doo, the gentle, eccentric, barefooted man who wore the same tweed suits favored by her mentor, and had stayed too long. She thought of Maya and Troy, the brother and sister, and how murdered siblings had never arrived in toto before—and the agitated older man whom she'd recently wrestled to his cabin with the help of the shadowy Subalterns. A fully grown man, on the children's train! She unaccountably had brought him a Tom Collins—*Jasper's* drink—but the offering infuriated him and he knocked it off the tray, much like the odd-looking teenage girl had with her lemonade.

He was the only one aboard who wasn't awash in blue . . .

She thought of all those things and knew what she had always known, but long forgotten:

The time that Jasper foretold had begun.

HAYWIRE

I.

When Lydia and Daniel got there, Annie hadn't yet arrived.

The landlords mingled sheepishly, helping themselves to coffee, lemonade and cookies, or just sat in their seats staring straight ahead. The group had never been together without the Porter, who was always there to greet them. Some thought Annie's tardiness had something to do with the Meeting having been changed to midday from its usual evening spot.

Lydia spontaneously approached Dabba Doo.

"How are you?" she said, shy and brave at once.

Interaction among guests was rare and he was pleasantly surprised. His eyes were pale green and she was drawn to them. He looked to be about sixty, the oldest landlord in the room.

"I'm very well, thank you," he said.

"I guess Teach got stuck in traffic, huh?"

"She does take the bus, which makes her subject to the rather dependable delays of the Metro."

"I wonder why she doesn't have a car."

"It would be more convenient, I suppose."

"Where does she live?"

"A closely guarded secret," he said affably. "Perhaps an automobile isn't within her budget—though she never struck me as the driving type."

"Well, I'm glad she takes a bus and not a bicycle."

"Dangerous, those! This mad push for cyclists' rights has certainly emboldened them. They tend to make the mistake of believing they're indestructible. It breeds entitlement."

"Why are you called Dabba Doo?" she asked, emboldened herself. It felt nice to make a new friend.

"I was a fanboy—to put it mildly!—of *The Flintstones.* Loved running around the house all day screaming *Yabba Dabba Doo!* I didn't have all my teeth and 'dabba doo' was all that came out. Everyone thought that incredibly amusing. It stuck."

"How old were you when you were . . ."

Murdered, she meant, without supplying the word.

It felt like a line had been crossed but she couldn't help blurting it out; something about him gave her permission. He seemed so familiar, readymade, so much like family. Maya (she felt less like Lydia just then) felt a closeness toward him that was different from her feelings toward the other fellow travelers, an intimacy almost like the blood-closeness Lydia felt for Daniel. Dabba Doo grew thoughtful and when it looked like he was about to answer, Annie strode in and the Meeting began.

Right away, Lydia noticed something "off"—the Porter looked pale and sweaty, half from hurry, half from something else.

There weren't any new guests (Daniel had been the latest), and Lydia surveyed the faces in the room during Q&A time: Daniel, of course, and Dabba Doo . . . the attractive Nordic-looking woman named Violet who worked in IT . . . José, a jovial, portly fellow who didn't at all look like a "José." (He was some sort of engineer and was fond of wearing heavy Pendleton shirts, even though he had a perspiration problem.) Rounding out the tribe was an African-American yoga teacher in his thirties called, of all things, Rhonda. The absurdity of such a creature having that name made Lydia giggle.

Most of the landlords' shares were concerned with the subtle, occasionally unsubtle "differences" noticed in them by confused friends and family.

Each had been told they were "acting weird," and some had been urged to seek professional help. The accusations usually fell into two camps: the landlords were perceived as being either inappropriately juvenile or clinically depressed. Some at the Meeting spoke of the rage of lovers who either felt they'd been spurned or suspected they were being cheated on.

Violet, who Lydia thought looked like a model, was in the middle of some very sticky business.

"I'm just having . . . a lot of problems!" she exclaimed. Everyone laughed because "a lot of problems" was definitely the theme of the day. "I mean with the men I've been seeing. Or dating. Or having relationships with or *whatever.*" José went "*Ewwwww*" and Rhonda said, "Get over it, girl!," eliciting more laughter. "I know! But the problem is, I'm still having feelings toward them. *Some* of them. *Violet* doesn't . . . but I mean, I'm even still 'doing it' with some of them." The whole room yucked and tittered. "I'm *trying,*" said Violet. "But some of them are just so *insistent.*"

Dabba Doo said, almost folksily, "Well, how many of them *are* there, Violet?"

"Not too many. But one of them's kind of my . . . fiancé."

Hilarity ensued until Annie took control.

"It's a process," said the Porter. "And it can be messy. But the mess *will* go away. Your priorities will assert themselves. People's feelings are going to be hurt, you can't avoid that. But you're not here to soothe hurt feelings, you're here for a purpose. Sometimes you might forget that, but your purpose won't forget *you.* So take the time during the day to read your *Guide*— and be patient."

Rhonda raised his hand and she called on him.

"There's something I'm really struggling with, Annie. I can't quite . . . It's something I'm trying very hard to understand. Not so much to understand, but to—" His voice trailed to a whisper as he looked at his feet. "I'm trying to remember how I was killed."

A few in the group audibly gasped. His frankness jolted but at the same time was cathartic, because many had had the same thought but weren't courageous enough to give it voice.

"Thank you, Rhonda," said Annie. "How long have you been with us, about three months now?" Her delivery was matter-of-fact.

"Ninety-five days," he said.

"Three months is about right for that particular question."

Was the Porter rattled by what Rhonda had asked? It *seemed* like she was but Lydia couldn't be sure. When Annie began a worrisomely pro- longed cough, she brought her a glass of water.

"You may never know," said the Porter, after she'd taken a few gulps and sufficiently recovered. "You may never have the answer, Rhonda, or learn the details of how you died. What I can tell you is that sometimes— quite often, actually—such knowledge comes at the *moment of balance.*"

"That's so unfair!" cried Rhonda, sounding for all the world like a little boy being deprived of a puppy. "It just seems so important!"

"*Seems* so important," said Annie, putting on her wisdom smile. "I sug- gest, Rhonda—I suggest to all of you that you don't waste time and energy trying to remember those terrible details. They'll either come back or they won't, but really have no importance. Why would you *want* to know? I think it's merciful you don't. That's my belief."

"But what happens," said Lydia, the words erupting from her throat, "if we never find the people who did this to us? What happens if there *is* no *moment of balance?*"

Annie wasn't prepared to respond. It was a riddle she made note to mull over later—not the question per se (she had asked her mentor the same thing during her apprenticeship), but that it'd been asked by one of the train chil- dren. It was one more thing the Porter had never encountered and she put it in the "haywire" file.

José piped in.

"You said the *moment of balance* comes in three or four months, but Dabba Doo's been here for *seven.* Is he having trouble? I mean, finding the responsible party?"

The eyes of the room fell upon Dabba Doo, who looked bereft. Maya thought it quite rude of José to have spoken about her new friend in such a way—as if he wasn't there.

"First of all," Annie said sternly, "we do *not* discuss other individuals during the Meeting! That's called 'cross-talk.' We don't stick our noses in business that's not our own. Is that understood?" José shook his head contritely. "The last thing I will say on the topic is that it takes as long as it takes—and that's *everything* you need to know. This isn't a competition! And Maya, in response to your question, all I can say is that I've been doing this a very long time and what you asked about has simply never happened. There is *always* the *moment of balance.*"

Lydia smiled nervously (Maya had receded for the moment), not wishing to get on Annie's bad side. Troy supportively put his hand on his little sister's.

"All right, let's move on. As some of you get closer to fulfilling your purpose, there's much to cover. And we have a birthday today! José's time is done and he'll be leaving us."

The group broke into congratulatory applause, which was more about getting to eat chocolate cake than it was about saying goodbye to one of their own.

2.

The high school was buzzing with the news of Winston Collins, whose disappearance was trending on social media. He was a student at the Mount Clemens Montessori Academy, only a few miles away.

Honeychile said nothing about her connection to Mrs. Collins and her missing son, not even to Zelda. Her anguish was multiplied—not only did she feel an overwhelming sense of guilt for having banished Hildy from her life, but she also vividly remembered meeting Winston on her first visit to the house. She'd been so happy to be invited! It was a privilege not extended to all of Hildy's "children," and she and Winston played well together. Honeychile was seven and he was four. While he tried explaining to her what he'd been building with his Legos, Honeychile's driver, a volunteer from

Children's Services, helped Mrs. Collins prepare an array of treats in the kitchen.

As hard as it was, she decided to smooth things over with her BFF and apologize for being such a bitch. They arranged a sleepover, this time at Zelda's. Honeychile said that she had an "extracurricular activity" in mind during tomorrow's school field trip to the city, a plan that per usual was shrouded in secrecy. The truth was that Honeychile couldn't have told Zelda what she was up to, because the plan was obscure to her as well.

"Tomorrow?" said Zelda.

A busload of freshmen were being taken to the Detroit Institute of Arts.

"Yup. We're gonna go AWOL."

"Oh my God, we *can't*, Honey. They'll *expel* us—"

"No they won't. They won't even know we're gone."

"What are we going to do? Are we going to the movies?"

"Fuck no. Movies are so boring!" said Honeychile.

"Since when do *you* think movies are boring?"

She was right—movies were Honeychile's big love. She could sit in the den for hours on end watching old films on the Turner channel. But since the asthma attack, *Jake and the Never Land Pirates, Dinosaur Train* and *SpongeBob SquarePants* had supplanted the Technicolor TCM classics. Which puzzled Zelda, but her BFF was nothing if not unpredictable.

It was one more thing she loved about her.

Honeychile stood mesmerized in front of a giant painting called *Massacre of the Innocents*, by an artist called Rubens. Infants were being stomped and slaughtered and she wondered why on Earth it was happening and who the hell had let it. She actually became furious. She wanted to enter the roiling, chaotic, color-saturated image and intervene, but felt a persistent tug at her shirt—Zelda was saying it was lunchtime and they had to go, because everyone was making their way toward the cafeteria.

After the teachers' head count, Honeychile seized the moment and told Zelda to follow her to the bathroom—

And suddenly, they were outside in the bright sun.

With the efficiency of a soldier in a military operation, Honeychile hailed a cab, yanking in her startled BFF. She handed the driver a slip of paper. As he punched it into his GPS, Zelda, pale as a ghost, kept saying *Oh my God* under her breath. She was numb, afraid, titillated. They were in the taxi for seven minutes but to Zelda it felt like a century. Honeychile gave the man money and leapt out, not waiting for change. Zelda was paralyzed until her friend shouted, "Come on!"

When she caught up, Honeychile was standing stock-still, staring up at the stone church. She took off again and Zelda followed her through the portico.

"What *is* this?" she said. "Where *are* we?"

Honeychile was oblivious, pausing again at the stone arch of a hallway of rooms before dashing forward again. An odd-looking young man in a loud tie and threadbare, short-sleeved shirt waylaid them as she entered the corridor.

"I'm sorry, but this is a private event."

"This is *not* private!" said Honeychile. "This is a *public space*."

"You can't come in. It's by invitation only."

"And who the fuck are you?" she said, while Zelda nervously hung back.

"I'm Bumble. And I'm the sentry, *for your information*."

"Well, buzz off, Bumble—" She tried moving past him but he blocked her way. "You cannot do that!" said Honeychile, outraged.

"What is going *on*?" whispered Zelda, terrified. "Honeychile, we are *trespassing*. We could get arrested!"

"We are not trespassing! Stop being such a wuss! We have every right to be here and Bumblebee here knows it."

She flung a look of utter contempt at the sentry, who grimaced. There was no way he was going to let this *child* get the better of him. They literally began to scuffle—with a shocked Zelda attempting to wrestle her friend away—when a door to one of the rooms of the corridor opened and a woman appeared.

"It's all right, Bumble," she said coolly to the flustered, resolute young man. "I'll take care of it."

He begged off. When she looked at Honeychile, the Porter's features softened but she couldn't shake a residue of surprise.

"He said I wasn't invited," said the girl. "But *you* said I *was*, in the *dream*. I'm Honeychile Devonshire and I'm invited!"

"Yes, you are. And I'm so glad you found your way."

Zelda muttered, *What the fuck?*—soft enough not to offend.

"The Meeting's nearly over," said Annie. "But you're welcome to join us."

Honeychile triumphantly walked toward the open door before turning to her BFF. "Come *on*." Now it was Annie's turn to block entry. Honeychile instinctively knew the formidable woman wasn't to be trifled with; there would be no tussle, as with the short-sleeved boy.

"What's the matter?" asked Honeychile.

"I'm afraid your friend has to wait here."

"What do you mean? She's with me."

"Bumble was correct in saying that the Meeting is by invitation only. You're invited but your friend is not."

"If *she* can't come, then I *won't*."

"That's up to you."

She continued with her tantrum but Annie was unyielding.

Well, *this* was certainly a new wrinkle. The world was playing by haywire rules now, of which several indicators gave proof. In the Porter's experience, landlords were never younger than, say, twenty (a rarity, at that; the oldest had been seventy-three). But the one who called herself Honeychile couldn't have been more than fourteen. Far more disconcerting was that she was the same ungainly child Annie had been grappling with on the train! The children in the cabins were *always* in the form they'd been in at the time of their death; that one of them would show up in *this* world, in that *same* form, without a landlord's loaned body, was incomprehensible.

The queerest thing of all was that Annie had been expecting her—which was the reason she'd changed the time of the Meeting to lunch hour. She didn't have a real understanding of why, but realized now it was to accommodate the girl's school-day schedule.

The question remained:

Was she a murdered child? Or an adult, recently deceased?

The whole little melodrama was baffling, yet Annie knew from experience there was nothing to do but acquiesce. And better the prideful, stubborn girl huff away than make a further scene. A troublesome thought intruded—that the Meeting and its location were no longer secure.

"Come on, Zelda," snarled Honeychile. "We're going back!"

(And they did, arriving unnoticed just as the students were finishing lunch. The girls had hardly been away thirty minutes.)

While the others at the Meeting had timidly remained in their seats, frightened by the loud voices outside, Maya crept to the doorway to see what was going on. The feisty, peculiar-looking interloper captivated her in the same manner as Dabba Doo. Annie watched the diminutive girl sprint away, tagged after by her bewildered friend. Then, like a mother, the Porter straightened Bumble's tie and thanked him, apologizing for the visitor's rudeness.

"She'll get her manners back in time," she said.

The sentry was already over it, prideful about having faithfully discharged his duties. "She better!" he said, with a snort.

Annie turned to see Maya standing in the door. She smiled and held out an arm, shepherding her in.

As the Meeting resumed, Annie's thoughts played lightly over the eventful hour. It had only been at the last minute, leaving the SRO, that she'd had the impulse to prepare a *Guide* for the "angry girl" from the train. (She had visited her every night in the cabin for a week now, and there was only marginal improvement in her rebellious behavior.) Finally, Annie was forced to shove the coaster with the address of the Divine Child Parish into the pocket of Honeychile's robe. The Porter wouldn't have been surprised if she turned out to be a mirage or an aberration, disappearing one night from the train as mysteriously as she had arrived—so obviously a part of "haywire" and all. She hadn't really expected her to ever make it to the Meeting . . . but if she did, Annie never imagined the girl herself would come, in that body, that *train body*, and not in the form of whatever adult would be hosting her. The children from the other side simply couldn't exist in this world without that protective shell.

If the girl wasn't a child of the train and if she wasn't a landlord— meaning, not dead—how had it been possible for her to board? The Porters were the only living ones allowed. What *was* she, then? With that haunting, recurrent thought, an unexpected voice rose from Annie's depths to thoroughly confuse her:

She's a mutation, neither landlord nor child. Some sort of hybrid—

Just before the Lord's Prayer, she announced to everyone that the location of the Meeting would have to be changed. She said that Bumble would let them know and gave no explanation.

Everyone filed out.

Bumble was stacking his last chair—the only one that remained vacant during the Meeting. He picked up the pamphlet resting there and handed it to his Porter. Annie no longer knew if it was meant for the enigma that called itself Honeychile. She'd written *Winston* on the cover, with a gold star dotting the i. Alongside, she'd whimsically written a word to personalize it (as she had with Lydia's unicorn), though she didn't know what it meant:

Rise

book two

The Spirit Room

———◆———

Rule Number Seven: You will have many
questions, but please do NOT involve THOSE
OUTSIDE THE GROUP in any dialogue about
these very PRIVATE issues. PLEASE WRITE
DOWN ON PAPER any questions you may have
and SAVE THEM FOR THE MEETING. (PS!
When you're feeling overwhelmed, it's always
good to work. Most of you have employment . . .
jobs can be a WONDERFUL distraction!!!)

—from the Guidebook

MOVING DAY

I.

After his heart-to-heart with Owen, he would have preferred going home, but the couple insisted he crash in the guest room. Adelaide said, "It'll give us a reason to unbox one of our magic Internet mattresses—otherwise, it might sit there for months." He was brutally fatigued and it made perfect sense to him to pass out on a Casper because he felt like a baby ghost himself. For the first time in weeks, his sleep was dreamless.

Willow awakened late in the afternoon, mulling over the eerie circumstances that brought him to the house in Armada. He patted himself on the back—if he couldn't, who could?—marveling at the ingenuity of his spontaneous amends. *Got myself out of some serious shit right there.* An unfortunate side effect of his actions was that he was forced to make amends to Adelaide as well.

That was tough but he took one for the team.

He splashed water on his face and thought about taking a shower, but that just didn't feel right. Addie must have heard the flush. She tapped on the door and said, "Soup's on!"

Willow let her serve him. It was the most marvelous thing in the world to feel zero acrimony toward this woman, almost like a complete absence of personal history. It was a turn-on. He may as well have been an exhausted firefighter being served by a MILF whose house he'd helped save.

"Pace knows you're here?"

"Not at all," he said.

"But she gave you our address—which is *fine*, by the way . . ."

"She didn't."

"Okay," said Adelaide skeptically. "Then how—"

"I can find stuff out. I'm a detective, remember?" he said impishly. "Was a detective, anyway. Who's about to be one again. Allegedly."

"Kind of amazing, huh?"

"And hey—thank you, Adelaide."

"For?"

"I'm assuming the whole Cold Case thing wasn't Owen's idea."

"That's one hundred percent not true."

"So you didn't plant a seed that became a mighty oak?"

"I'm all thumbs. And they ain't green, my friend."

"Well, thank you anyway. It's coming at a good time for me, Addie. I mean, a not-so-good time that might have a shot at becoming a good one again."

"I'm so glad about that, Willow. I really am. You know, I always wanted the best for you. Contrary to your beliefs."

"Sorry I was such an asshole, kid."

"Can you stop with the amends already?" After a moment, she said, "But Jesus, you *were*." She laughed, a little too long. The laugh that was once so sexy to him.

Still was . . .

He got shy, clammed up and ate his eggs. She nibbled on some fruit and they sat awhile, enjoying the anomalous company. Willow thought: *This is what it would look like if we were still together. A sleepy kitchen morning.*

"How's work?" he said.

"Great! I kind of run oncology now."

"Pace mentioned that."

"I know more than the doctors," she said pridefully. "At least that's what the *doctors* tell me."

"Got 'em wrapped around your un-green thumb, huh?"

"That's me, Dub. I just stick it out like a hitchhiker and *bam*." She watched him finish his meal, noting a daintiness, which touched her. The moment and certainly all the years had humbled him. "Guess you'll be looking for a place in Macomb?"

"I'll find something online," he said.

"I can help with that if you need me to."

"I think I can manage. I'm the bachelor-apartment king."

"You oughta see if our old place in the Falls is available," she said with a smirk. She'd meant it to be funny but realized it wasn't. "Mount Clemens might make the most sense. That's where your office will be, no?"

"Yeah. We'll see—maybe someplace by the lake. And, Addie . . . I'd prefer you didn't mention any of this to Pace—the job opportunity *or* my little drive-by this morning. Not just yet. Okay?"

"You got it, Dub. Seen our grandchild lately?"

"Just a few weeks ago. He's a kick and a half."

"They haven't been here in a month and I'm jonesing for my Larkin. Might have to bushwhack 'em."

It was clear that Pace hadn't told her about the boy's condition. After all the hospitality and goodwill, Willow had mixed emotions about withholding the news, but in the end convinced himself it wasn't his information to give. It was their daughter's.

He got his things together and she walked him to the car.

"Guess we'll be seeing a lot of each other," he said drolly. "You know—extended family dinners, Sunday brunches. Watching *Game of Thrones* and Super Bowls, that sort of thing."

"For *sure*. Don't forget the extended family vacations! And I'm not a *Thrones* gal, I'm a *Homeland* gal. It makes me so tense I almost throw up."

"You always liked negative excitement."

They hugged, heartfelt. She stopped herself from saying, *All this could have been yours*—another attempt at humor that would have laid an egg. She watched him pull away.

"Hey!" shouted Adelaide, running after him. He stopped and rolled down the window. "I'm going to get you a Casper for your new digs! Easy and great, right? My housewarming gift."

2.

He found a little place for $775 a month on Craigslist, an apartment on Beech Drive in Sterling Heights with a "terrace" off the dining room big enough to wedge yourself in for a smoke. (Though Miranda the bodyworker might have a problem.) It was a twenty-minute drive from Mount Clemens.

The weekend before he moved, Willow organized the Port Hope trailer and scoured it clean. He wasn't ready to sell; there wouldn't be any takers anyway. It wasn't so much a teardown as a blow-away. Down on his knees at 2:00 A.M., the gusts off Lake Huron shimmying the walls, he took a Brillo Pad and scrub-a-dubbed the kitchen floor, cackling to himself that it was just the kind of OCD ritual folks were known to engage in pre-suicide. At least he could laugh. Whistling along with the wind while he worked, he ruminated on his ex . . .

They met in the early eighties when he was a rookie cop in Chicago. Addie was a waitress, with that Jewish/Italian thing that always made him hard. She was funny too—she was *biting*, another thing that got Willow off. He was all about waitresses and changed coffee shops whenever the affairs blew up, which they inevitably did. But it was different with Adelaide. They knew what they had but tried to keep it light. They didn't even move in together until she was pregnant. Didn't get married either, not until a couple of years after Pace was born.

A decade flew by like a dirigible on fire. Ten years of booze and coke, of stealth waitresses and skimming money from small-time drug dealers, of beating the shit out of arrestees during joyrides back to the station—Brave Old Cop World before the nightmare of political correctness and nonstop social media surveillance put a stake through its black heart. His suffering wife began a last-ditch pillow-talk campaign about how much better their lives would be if they got out of Dodge. A homeboy who worked violent crimes in the 4th District (and grew up in Macomb County) told him that the police department in Saggerty Falls, Michigan, was currently recruiting. "Dubya, you just might be overqualified for the job." When it looked like Willow might be fired for his latest tomfoolery, he and the Chicago PD parted ways, with both parties pretending to be amicable.

The village had a goofy Thomas Kinkade flavor, sans water mills and thatched-roof cottages. The houses were all newish, the neighbors awe-some and the schools decent—which meant it took all of fourteen months for Willow to lose his mind. He kept a grip on his insanity by playing musi-cal waitress chairs, but there were only so many coffee shops in the sur-rounding townships. Adelaide knew what was going on. He'd begun to think that she always did, and wasn't sure whether to love or hate her for that.

At least he appreciated the company of the man he shared a squad car with. Owen Caplan enjoyed a drink himself and was simpatico to his part-ner's borderline behaviors. But Owen was destined for greatness—which included Willow's wife. "I guess the best man won" was how the loser chivalrously characterized the soap opera in the years that followed the di-vorce. He got a lot of mileage out of all those three-minute sad-funny shares, honed to perfection in sundry rehabs and midtown Manhattan 12-Step meetings. Women really seemed to go for his sly, self-deprecating line of bullshit.

He moved out of the house in '97. Pace was thirteen, that vulnerable, invulnerable age when a girl hates her mom and needs her daddy. Like every couple who separate, they still held out hope, trying to keep it together for the kid, the pension, the fraud of makeup sex, the whatever. Willow hung around for another year. But there always comes that moment when the stoned, exasperated husband throws something at a wall and it bounces back and glances his wife; or he makes a menacing macho move and she backs away in fear, stumbling, and hurts a wrist while breaking her fall.

Then one of those events—pick one—becomes alt-fact legend, passed on to the neighbors, the coworkers, the children and generations to come.

Your father hit me . . .

Not to say that men don't beat and kill their women. But Willow Millard Wylde wasn't remotely capable of that.

After the split with Addie, he and Owen still rode together but his cohort started getting squirrelly. A little weird, a little distant—like Adelaide!—then one day Owen was pulled from the car and partnered with someone else. Owen evinced mild outrage, acting like he'd been blindsided, but Dubya knew he requested the change. Willow thought it was chickenshit, but it didn't really rock his world. He just kept drinking and whoring his way through his shifts, going through the merry motions, because he knew it was all coming to an end, *some* kind of end. And soon. His daughter hated him because he basically ignored her existence. Everything fell in Adelaide's lap: Pace's abortions (three), Pace slicing up her thighs (an X-Acto), Pace stealing unused drugs from the room of the dying father of a girl she babysat (Dilaudid), Pace's correspondence on the Internet with a fifty-something teacher in Fort Wayne. When Adelaide caught Willow driving her to a ballet lesson drunk, she put the plug in the jug and filed for divorce. In six weeks' time, he said goodbye to all that—the waitresses, the marriage, the whole shitty postcard of a town—and decamped to Manhattan to become prince of the city.

He said goodbye to Pace too and never forgave himself.

The last thing he did before departing Port Hope was to paint over the mural composed of Owen and Adelaide's address that he'd colored the wall with on his return from the disastrous outing to New York. Like some magnificent coral reef, the numbers and letters had grown into explosive, abstract glory. Somehow it wouldn't have been right to leave it behind unattended. But Willow had high hopes for the fresh canvas of the new place in Sterling Heights.

He was already feeling inspired.

3.

A photo montage—

Willow in his Port Hope double-wide, contemplating his navel . . . staring at the ceiling while being serviced by Miranda . . . scrubbing the floor like a man condemned. Willow in Armada, sweaty and disoriented, on a fresh-out-of-the-box Casper, staring at the ceiling of his ex-wife's guest room. Willow in Sterling Heights, staring at the ceiling of an empty utility apartment from a thrift-store futon (the Casper was on its way).

Such was life—a succession of random walls and rooms, of tiny spaces that we convince ourselves provide continuity, secrecy, safety.

He'd met a few neighbors during the move, the most notable being an attractive RN named Dixie Rose Cavanaugh. Even the name got him horny. He hoped she didn't work alongside Adelaide at Macomb General—that would be such a bore. Another was a Viet vet who still managed to climb on his Harley and ride off each day at exactly 11:50 on an excursion to Early World Diner, where all the wounded warriors hung out. A clockwork public lunch dropped them into the babbling brook of humanity and broke the spell of loneliness. It was pretty much the only thing left on their schedules, that and field trips to the VA for whatever was slowly or quickly killing them.

A week ago he showed up at the administrative building of the Macomb County Sheriff's Office and peed in a cup, just like Owen promised. Good ol' Charlie Powell did the test. *How 'bout that?* Took out the dipstick, gave it a glance-over and pronounced, "Dubya, you're clean." Willow had always called him Charles in Charge, from back in the day. When Owen bailed on their partnership, he and Charlie rode together, becoming the Falls' new Starsky and Hutch. Years later, by the time the former Saggerty Falls PD chief snagged the brass sheriff's ring, Charlie'd already had a few heart attacks. Owen pulled him out of his retirement and depression, anointing him as his de facto assistant and all-around man Friday. Charles was back in charge.

Sheriff Caplan was supposed to accompany them on a tour of the building on Gallup Street in Mount Clemens but texted that he couldn't make it.

The Cold Case Task Force took up the first floor and climate-controlled sub-basement of a nondescript edifice housing nondescript departments that performed nondescript county services. He and Charlie strolled through empty rooms—most of the rented furniture was yet to arrive—but there were folding chairs and a beat-up metal desk in the space designated for Willow's office.

At least there was a guard in the lobby. Greeting him on that first day, Willow couldn't help thinking such a fate could have been his. Maybe still would be. Becoming a badge monkey might just be the pot of shit at the end of the rainbow.

"It ain't Trump Tower," said Charlie. "But we'll get the place looking half-decent. Central heating works like a champ. Hang a picture or two, get some carpet. A little paint job."

"It'll do till they realize how important we are."

Charlie smiled warmly and said, "It's real good to see you again, Dubya. Life sure takes some funny turns, huh?"

"Oh, don't you know it. Though I *have* learned that some turns are funnier than others."

"Guess we've both been through the ringer."

"I feel like I'm still *in* the ringer," said Willow with a chuckle.

"I heard that. When the dust settles, let's grab a drink. Not a *drink*," he revised, in a nod to Willow's sobriety. "Dinner. Play some catch-up."

"I'd like that, Charlie. It's been too long. You still enjoying your whiskey?"

"It's wine now. My cardiologist insists," he winked.

"We used to do our shifts half-drunk," said Willow nostalgically.

"Half? I don't think so, Dubya."

"Maybe you're right. It did make the time pass, didn't it."

"Not fast enough," said Charlie. "Kinda sweet to have the dysfunctional Dream Team back, cooking on a burner or two."

"We can thank Papa Caplan for that."

"Oh, I thank the man every single day—say my prayers to him at night too. Owen Caplan saved my life—I'd have been home on the porch, waiting to die. Probably dead already. He's the best man I know."

Willow said that he wanted to take a look at the basement storage on his own, and Charlie gave him the key. "The files were just transferred so it's a bit of a mess down there."

"We'll sort it out," said Willow.

As the old friends parted, they shook hands.

"Charles in Charge," said Willow, in an affectionate adieu.

He began to hear a low chorus the moment he pressed B, and when he stepped from the elevator it was loud as a church choir. The cacophony of blended children's voices was manageable and didn't frighten him, as it had on first exposure to the Spirit Room in Manhattan. There was nothing to prove anymore and nothing to run from; at least that's how it felt in this moment. (He knew all moods and feelings were subject to sudden, radical change.) The sheer *blueness* of the space came back to him, the same mordantly transcendent, otherworldly color and the attendant feelings it evoked, feelings he'd made it his life's work to suppress.

This time, he surrendered.

There were haphazard stacks of cardboard boxes marked by county names, surnames, case numbers. Closing his eyes, the detective (for that's what he was again, officially) stood and swayed, unpacking at last the psychic gifts he had stowed away as a young boy, unspooling them with the steady, battle-scarred hands of a man who'd paid a heavy price for denying them. He didn't bother to look through any of the files. Nor did he desultorily examine the plastic bags harboring swatches of stained fabric, human hairs and crime scene photos—bodies in forests, bodies in automobiles, bodies in open fields—the effluvia of cases so cold and forgotten, they were deader than the victims themselves.

He closed his eyes and stood straight as an anchor's chain, formally assuming the position of choirmaster.

4.

When he got home, Willow went straight to work.

A virgin wall meant only one thing: mural-time!

Some folks took pictures; others threw pottery or played chess online. The more adventurous took tango classes, dancing with like-minded strangers on a Saturday night.

Hell, said Willow. *I'm just gonna paint my walls.*

It was a perfect time to pour himself a drink, but he resisted.

This time, he'd bought oils and watercolors at an art store in Mount Clemens. His apprenticeship with crayons and Sharpies was over.

He was just finding his groove when he got the text from Adelaide: *uhm, still coming, dub?* He'd completely forgotten about the late-afternoon shindig at Macomb County General that she invited him to. He couldn't blow it off—it was important, for lots of reasons, that he attend. He set down his palette, already van Gogh–thick with ocean waves of color, grabbed his coat and dashed.

He knew it was a little paranoid, but on the drive over all he could think of was bumping into the cute little RN neighbor. He pictured Addie introducing them ("Willow, meet Dixie, my bestie!") and then raising an eyebrow when Dixie said, "Oh my God, your ex just moved into my building! Isn't that funny?" He was starting to feel his sap rise for the first time since he left the Meadows and didn't need any complications. Willow had big plans for him and Nursie—shitting where you eat be damned. He made a mental note to ask Dixie what hospital she worked at the next time he ran into her, so he could stop obsessing over the unforeseen.

The lobby swarmed with visitors. Trays of cheap crudités circulated, and cheap wine too. Willow clutched a can of half-cold Diet Coke.

"There you are!" said Adelaide. She was out of her nurse's uniform.

"Hey there, Addie. Don't you look chic. Owen make it?"

"He's around here somewhere."

"What's the occasion again?"

"We're just thanking some folks who do a lot around here for no pay.

Doing amazing shit for love, not money—what a concept, right? Hey, how'd it go today? Wasn't it your first day at school?"

"It went really, really well."

"How's Sterling Heights? Are you settling in?"

"Oh yeah. Just got my Casper. Thank you for that."

"Awesome! Still in the box?"

"It has been freed."

"*Excellent.* And how do you like your digs—I mean, your Cold Case digs."

"The place isn't turnkey but I like my office quite a bit."

"Well, look at you!" she said proudly.

"Charlie Powell showed me around."

"I guess it's old home week."

She saw someone across the room and grabbed Willow by the hand. When they got to the woman, Adelaide said, "Willow Wylde, meet Annie Ballendine—World's Greatest Volunteer."

Annie blushed. "I don't think that's true but you're very sweet, Adelaide."

"It *is* true. But I probably shouldn't say that too loud or the others'll get jealous. Annie . . . *this* is my ex-husband, believe it or not."

"Oh my goodness!" she said. "How nice to meet you."

He smiled and shook the volunteer's hand. She seemed to wince at his touch before flashing a warm smile. Willow swore that she muttered *It's you* under her breath.

CLOSURE

A few hours after José received his birthday cake, he had a massive heart attack and died at home, in the middle of watching *Dancing with the Stars*. Despite their best efforts, paramedics were unable to bring the engineer, known outside Annie's Meetings as Tim Norris, back to the land of the living. It was Tim's habit to unwind in front of the television from 8:00 P.M. to 11:00 while his wife sat beside him, catching up on old *New Yorkers*.

Only after he passed did certain things begin to nag. In the last three months, she noticed a change. Some of it was just silly—like Tim's new-found love of Frosted Flakes in the morning (he was always a no-breakfast guy), an anomaly that she wrote off as a quirk of middle age. And those songs he'd started to sing, in Spanish no less, in a funny, childish voice. He said that a Mexican coworker had been giving him lessons. But some of the changes had a darker feel, like when she called his name and he wouldn't answer and she'd find him sitting in the basement rec room, brooding in the dark. And the "work-related" day trips he'd taken to Lansing, Flint and Battle Creek, in the ten days preceding his death—what was that about? He was employed by the City of Detroit and had told her that his bosses wanted him to do a little "fact finding" to see how other cities and townships conducted their business. *Fair enough*, she thought at the time.

Another strange thing was that Tim somehow got it into his head that he had a drinking problem, which was absolute nonsense. He *never* drank hard liquor and only had a half-glass of wine a few nights a week. But one day (and yes, she thought it was three months ago) he announced that he'd be attending AA meetings two or three times a week, not far from the house. She did her best to interrogate him about that, jokingly asking if he'd been stashing bottles of liquor like Jack Lemmon did in one of their favorite movies. He was closemouthed and adamant about his decision. She never liked interfering in his private life and thoughts—oh, they talked a lot about mutual interests and worries; it wasn't like they hid things from each other—and in the end, she thought, *Who am I to say? If Tim thinks he has a problem and if those meetings make him happy, I'm all for it.* And they *did* make him happy; whenever he returned from AA, his mood seemed buoyant, lighter. She loved having dinner ready for him when he got home, with the kids already in bed. It felt romantic.

It crossed her mind that he was having an affair. They hadn't been physical in months, but that was never high on their to-do list. They were spooners. And besides, her husband was cuddlier than ever. She knew in her heart that unfaithfulness wasn't a possibility.

What she couldn't have known was that Tim had actually died months ago and the reason he made those day trips was to find the person who had murdered the child he'd joined forces with. Battle Creek and Lansing were false starts—in private conversation, Annie assured him that things sometimes took a moment to "geographically come together"—and he finally found his man in Flint. The killer was about thirty-five, on parole for exposing himself to a child. As he strangled him, the boy José receded while the brute strength of Tim Norris, enhanced by what felt like superpowers, took over. (Tim looked into the man's eyes the entire time.) As the life went out of him, José the child could finally remember what had happened.

Ten years ago, in Kissimmee, Florida, a man outside a convenience store waved him over. He was dressed like a policeman, sort of, but his car was a regular one with a dent in the door and duct tape holding a headlight in place. He told José that something happened to his dad and he was there to take him to the police station. He wasn't an aggressive kid and when the man's tone became forceful, José got in. They traveled on dirt roads for an hour before pulling over. The man took him to a barn and said, "We're going to do some things that you're probably not going to enjoy—but that's life. Sometimes you have to do things you don't enjoy." At five in the morning, José died from internal hemorrhaging. He was buried in a swamp.

All of the details flashed before Tim's and José's eyes as they strangled him. Tim saw the faces of two other children the man had killed too—one in Louisiana, one in Kansas—and felt their release, prompting the engineer-landlord, not the child-tenant, to offer a simple prayer: *May you rest in peace.* When he loosened his hold on the murderer, he was flooded with emotions belonging to José; for the first time since melding with Tim Norris, the boy yearned for his Kissimmee home. How he missed his parents! Tim and José cried for the hour it took to get back to Detroit and sang the popular song, José's *papi*'s favorite, that his family used to sing on weekend road trips:

> *Dale a tu cuerpo alegria Macarena*
> *Hey, Macarena!*

Drawing on Tim's more developed sense of regret, José felt a pang of guilt. Why hadn't he bothered to contact his mother and father, his sisters? To see what they looked like now, where they lived, and if they were in good health? It didn't seem "natural," it was so selfish, so *mean*, even though Annie had already addressed the topic. She reminded all of them how the *Guide* informed them that those who returned wouldn't give the parents and siblings they'd left behind much thought, and while that seemed callous, it was "as it should be." Spying on the family one lost would only be a distraction, an encumbrance to effecting the *moment of balance.*

That day, they drove directly to the Meeting from Flint so that José could take his birthday cake. The Porter knew at a glance that José had fulfilled his purpose.

When he saw Annie, he was distraught, blurting out how he wanted to see *mi papi y mi mama* and what should he do? In her experience, the urge to visit family was nothing new—she encountered it in 90 percent of her children after their *moment of balance.* She took his hands in hers, noticing that he'd lost his blueness, which was expected when a mission was complete.

"I'm afraid there isn't time for that, José," she said gently. He bowed his head in sadness. "But your family will always be with you and I think you know that. They're with you now." José nodded and she knew the landlord Tim was helping the child to make sense of her words. "When you take your cake, don't forget to thank Tim. And Tim—when you get home, don't forget to thank José as well! Make sure. Sit in the driveway before you go in and thank him. It's so important to thank those who've helped us in this world. In *any* world."

José grew stronger during the Meeting, no longer preoccupied by the family he had lost. He sat listening to everyone with a smile on his face, and all of them could see that he had been released. When he blew out the can-dles, he thanked the landlord-tenants for their fellowship, and then he thanked Tim, saving Annie for last. He spoke to her in Spanish. The others became emotional, even though they couldn't understand his words.

The Meeting ended with a raucous "Macarena" and the song stuck in their heads for more than a few days.

HEAR ME, WILLOW

I.

Willow went through a thousand head trips about all the ways he was
going to maneuver his neighbor into bed, then *bam*—there they were under
the sheets, moaning and grinding away.

Nurse Dixie outmaneuvered him.

And he felt alive again, *no shit.*

—take *that*, Miranda!

She was almost thirty years younger, and it wasn't just the freshness of
her body that excited him. (Not that it wouldn't have been enough.) No, it
was the pure psychology behind her attraction, or his interpretation of it,
anyway: that she likely had a thing for older men. Something about that
theory was as hot as it was self-serving. And it wasn't just the daddy thing
that turned him on. It was the boldness of a youngster who said *fuck* it, who
grabbed the old bull by the horns and took the perilous leap into AARP
World. She wasn't a knockout, but Jesus—the sly twist of her mouth, more
pronounced than Adelaide's, sent him over the edge.

The staying power of the things he loved in women always amazed
him. The hair on their arms, the way they laughed or got shy when he looked

in their eyes as they fucked, the sounds they made in bed while trans-
ported to another place. Women were a wild and messy feast. He loved the
way they talked, the words they chose, hell, he loved the way they *farted*.
The staying power of lovemaking itself amazed. By all rights, fornication
was a foul, dumbly repetitive, crazy-stupid act, and that it managed to con-
sistently transcend dropped the detective's jaw. The way it could heal, the
joy it brought, the intense spirituality of it—that fleeting fusion with all humanity. Willow got all misty and mystical just thinking about its divine
puzzle.

"So how long you been a cop?"

"Longer than you've been on the planet."

In the short while they'd known each other, they hadn't really spoken all
that much. Getting into bed hadn't required the usual investment of time-
consuming nonsense, which only spiked his crush. And now, just *talking* with
the lady was one more aphrodisiac.

"Are you retired?"

"Not really," he said. "I kind of have a new job"—he said it like that
because he still couldn't believe it—"that's why I'm here in Macomb."

"Aren't you a little old to be playing *Fast and Furious?*" she said, with a
crooked smile.

"Those guys aren't cops. But you tell me," he said, referring to recent
events.

"Well . . . you were pretty furious—and not *too* fast, I'll give you
that."

She winked, cuddling up. They made out a while.

I could fall in love with this woman . . .

He got up to pee and then Dixie did the same as he went to the kitchen
for Diet Dr Peppers. She came into the living room and sprawled on the
couch, fishing a roach from her purse.

"You smoke?"

"Nope."

" 'Cause you're a cop?"

" 'Cause I'm sober."

"That's cool. Mind if I indulge?"

"Actually, if you want to do that, Dixie, I'd appreciate it if you went outside." He was matter-of-fact, not mean.

"No worries."

She put the roach away and lit a cigarette instead.

"Temptation can be . . . tempting," said Willow, trying not to sound defensive. "'The phenomenon of craving' and all that."

"So you're in AA?"

"I try to be."

"I've been to some meetings—mostly Al-Anon. It's *crazy* how many nurses and doctors I know are drug addicts. But I never really drank because it gives me migraines. My dad's an alcoholic, though. And I never liked painkillers because they make it hard to poop. I *do* like weed but I don't get too crazy. I take it mostly for my headaches."

"Are you having one now?"

"Nope! You haven't given me a migraine—yet." She stared at the wall opposite them. "I *love* that you painted on that! I promise I won't tell the landlord or you might have to arrest yourself." She scrutinized the creation. "What is it?"

"What does it look like?" he said. "I mean, to you."

"A fence?" She tilted her head. "Like, a fence lying on its side? It's hard to . . . It's kinda dark in here. But is it—"

"Train tracks."

"Ah! Okay. Yeah, I can see that."

"It's kind of whatever you want it to be."

She smiled and said, "C'mere, Rorschach," then kissed him. Despite his older-man tricks, Dixie had all the power—it wasn't even close. It was ridiculous the amount of power a woman had. "Willow . . . such a sad and beautiful name. 'Dixie'—I mean, what does anyone think of? Dixie cups and rednecks. But *Willow* . . ." She began to softly sing, stroking his neck with her perfect, slender, chewed-up fingers. He'd always liked a nail-biter. "'*Willow, weep for me. Willow, weep for me. Bend your branches green, along the stream that runs to sea . . .*' Mom used to sing us to sleep with that."

"Your voice is really beautiful."

"Ya think? You're lucky I wasn't stoned! My singing tends to be a little more dramatic when I'm high."

"That'd be okay. I like drama."

"Careful what you wish for."

2.

After she left, around 10:00 P.M.—she had to get up at 5:00 for a morning shift—Willow lay on the couch, his mind wandering.

He thought of how good it would have been to smoke that weed. How good the sex would have been . . . not that it could have gotten much better. Replaying choice bits from their rumble in the jungle, he felt himself becoming aroused, like some kind of teenager. *There's hope for you yet, ol' boy.*

He went to the bedroom and tried to sleep. Sniffed the pillow where her head had been. Sniffed the sheets and started playing with himself, but his heart wasn't in it. He was restless.

Hungry.

Without thought, he got up, got dressed and drove straight to the Early World Diner.

It was a quarter full.

Random folks: a solitary older woman, three kids with piercings and spiky hair, an old vet (not his neighbor) out way past his bedtime. Prolly got some bad news from the VA. Willow ordered fried chicken, a lifetime ritual he liked to indulge après sex.

The solitary woman walked toward him. When he glanced up, she smiled.

"Willow?" she said, eyes twinkling.

"Yes?"

"Annie Ballendine, 'World's Greatest Volunteer'—we met the other night at the hospital."

"Oh! Yes—hi," he said, his own smile fading.

She shook his hand and then plunked herself across from him. "You surprised me the other day."

"How so?" said Willow, perplexed.

"I wasn't expecting you so soon. But there you were. I came to you tonight—*here*," she said, laughing, "because I didn't want any *more* surprises!"

She charmed and terrified him all at once. "I don't really know what you're talking about."

He was still trying to be affable. He wouldn't want Adelaide to get a bad report.

"I understand," she said. "I felt the same way when Jasper—Mr. Sebastian—paid me a visit my first time. But I didn't have the luxury of being in a cozy little coffee shop, enjoying a lovely late-night meal. I was 'in hospital,' as they used to say. The nut ward."

"What is it that you want, Annie?" he said, with an edge to his voice.

"What do I want?" She smiled. "Well, what I want is just one thing."

Willow felt himself softly come asunder. He didn't know what was happening (yet absolutely knew). The part that was ignorant dug in and spun its wheels. Would she ask for money? Blackmail him over some old felony? The spinning tires splattered mud in a frenzy, deepening the rut. Was she the mother of some douchebag he put behind bars, here to exact an explosive, fatal revenge?

But the part that *knew* stiffened, and made him wonder if he would be able to survive the ordeal that was coming. What ordeal, though? Instinct only told him so much. He felt like he'd been punched in the gut, waylaid by imperial powers commanding him to drop everything and set off on an expedition to climb Everest, without oxygen.

Their booth contracted, like the cabin of a train.

"Give me one thing, Willow," she said.

"And what's that?" he said numbly.

"Your attention. I want your attention."

REUNIONS

I.

He felt hungover when he got to the office in the morning.

They talked—Annie talked—for more than an hour, while he listened, insensate. Willow figured he'd retained only 10 percent of what she said, if that. He spent the morning cautiously revisiting the few snippets he was able to recall, fearing a more comprehensive effort might somehow prove injurious.

His wheels stopped spinning; they'd fallen off entirely.

What the woman described was nothing short of madness. He had already begun a heroic struggle not to be sucked into the vortex, but to Willow it was insane that he even felt susceptible. He wondered if he'd been poisoned. *She shook my hand before sitting down . . . maybe that's when I absorbed the pyschotropic powder.* As a detective in New York he'd interviewed every crackpot known to man, sometimes climbing deep inside their heads; Annie had climbed into his. He dredged up a phrase from college psych books—*folie à deux*—a term that defined the sharing of a delusion or mental illness by two people. *Maybe this is what that looked like. Or the beginning of it . . .*

At the moment, the only thing that offset the disorienting outlandishness of Ms. Ballendine's bullet points was Dixie. When his thoughts became too crazy, he flashed on their carnal moments and it settled his nerves—the sole shared delusion he was up for.

During Annie's monologue, he wanted to bolt but his feet were encased in cement. He was shocked when she spoke of the train, reminding him that it was the place where they first met. "You had a Tom Collins—remember?—*that* was a new wrinkle." She even referred to his wall paintings, saying that many years ago she'd been compelled to do a mural "in the same theme myself, in the room where I lived during my apprenticeship." She discreetly paused whenever Willow zoned out; though it didn't have much effect, Annie occasionally touched his hand, to comfort. Then she would ask if he had any questions, like a doctor trying to interview a patient who'd just had surgery and was still under the fog of anesthesia.

"You don't have to know the 'whys and wherefores,' because there aren't any, not really. At least none we can understand. But what *is* important to know, as a *father*, is that you're going to be a father *again*. Which is marvelous, isn't it, don't you think? And it's important to know as well that you have arrived—you've disembarked and you're in the station now, whether you know it or not! We don't have a choice about such things. I'm just like you, Willow. I didn't have a choice either. And like you, I'm no one special—but I *can* show you what to do, where to go, how to *be*. That is my privilege and my honor."

She patted his hand and then stood to leave.

"You'll be fine," she said. "You just need a moment to integrate. And thank you for giving me your attention! It's really all that I wanted."

2.

The new recruits were waiting for him like anxious children in detention when Willow walked in.

Jesus. They're just kids.

What was Owen thinking?

"They're greener than green," the sheriff had said. "But I'm telling you,

Dubya, they certainly have the aptitude. Mark my words—in a few months, they'll be known far and wide as the Cold Case Kids." Like an amateur soothsayer, he added, "I have a feeling about those two."

Back when they were partners in Saggerty Falls, Owen had been awed by Willow's reluctant necromancy. "You, my friend, are spooky," he'd say. There was that time his beloved Rover disappeared and Willow said he had a "feeling" about the dog's whereabouts. The next day, he led them through a mile of forest to the animal, accidentally shot dead by a hunter. (Owen futilely tried to get the visiting detective to track the missing Rummer kids the same way.) The sheriff's lame prognostication about the greenhorns becoming Cold Case legends served to put Willow on notice that hey, Owen Caplan could be spooky too—real schoolyard pissing contest shit. In an *oh shit* moment, it occurred to him that Adelaide was the secret sauce behind Owen feeling competitive.

After all, Willow got there first.

"The sheriff said you worked Cold Case in Manhattan," said Lydia, nervously taking the lead.

"That would be correct."

"He mentioned you had 'special talents,'" said Daniel. He'd been staring at Willow from the moment he walked in, as if trying to place him.

"More like special needs."

The three of them laughed and everything got better. Willow realized he was as jittery as they were. It'd been a long time since he had anyone under his wing, and he wasn't sure he was up for it.

"That was actually my nickname in New York. 'Special Needs.' True story." The couple smiled, warming to him. "So, what do you think of your new job description? It's a helluva change from being out in the field. You're definitely not going to have the kind of action you had recently."

"That's probably a good thing," said Daniel.

"Sometimes when you have an encounter like that, you get a little taste and want some more."

"Not me, sir," said Lydia. "That's not my purpose."

He thought the phrasing was odd. "And what do you think that purpose might be, Deputy Molloy?"

As she began to reply, Daniel cut her off. "To bring justice and closure to those who no longer have a voice."

"To *be* their voice," said Lydia, with gusto.

"Well played," said Willow. "It's long hours, with not a lot of satisfaction. Cold Case isn't glamorous. On TV, they solve everything in an hour—and I mean everything. In the real world, you might work on a case for a year and still be trying to tree the wrong bear."

"We have three to five months, six at the outset," said Lydia mechanically.

"How's that?" said Willow.

The deputy awkwardly explained away the remark, as if it were a joke about being gung ho.

Well, she's an odd one.

"Let me tell you something," said Willow. "You crack a case in six months and you'll be up for some kind of medal."

"One thing doesn't make sense to me," said Daniel. "This is kind of a big deal, right? The money comes through for a Cold Case team and the sheriff handpicks *us*? No offense to my partner and me, we're going to do an amazing job, one hundred percent. But why pick us? And not—I don't know—a couple of seasoned detectives?"

"Don't look a gift horse in the mouth," said Lydia, annoyed.

"Sheriff Caplan had a feeling about you. And as for the 'seasoning,' I guess that's where I come in. Don't think too hard about it."

"We're honored," said Lydia. "I know we'll learn a lot from you." She turned to Daniel and said, "Any other brilliant questions?"

"Nope."

"More will be revealed," said Willow.

The Cold Case Kids smiled at each other; indeed it would.

In the Spirit Room, their lighthearted demeanor changed.

Willow noticed the temperature of the space growing colder. The detective started getting "feelings" of his own that he couldn't identify. He had planned to dip the deputies' toes in the water by sifting through the contents of a box or two but hung back and watched.

The familiar blueness of the room that sometimes wafted like smoke appeared for a moment—a long moment—wrapping itself around Lydia and Daniel in an embrace of curiosity before migrating to their heads, where it sparkled in excitation like a swarm of cobalt fireflies.

Willow was entranced.

Deputy Molloy was the proactive one. Deputy Doheny monitored her moves in a way that seemed almost chivalrous. She looked like she'd fallen into a trance. She ran her hand over the topmost boxes of the stacks, putting Willow in mind of a professional medium the department once hired when he worked homicide in New York. There was an elegance and focus to her movements that was almost balletic. The area became an enormous stage; the detective had a sense the orchestra was tuning up.

Daniel joined her as she lingered by the box scrawled RUMMER/JULY 4/'00. She lifted the lid and pulled out a tiny T-shirt found at the scene of the roadside abductions. He took it from her hand and held it to his much larger chest, turning to Willow with a smile to show him what was written there:

BE EXCELLENT TO EACH OTHER

RISE

I.

She noticed a change and it was scary.

For all Honeychile's gregariousness and sporadic outbursts of affection, Zelda, in the role of codependent bestie, was a close observer of her brilliant friend's *other* moods as well. She understood that what the world (or student body) judged to be standoffish, bitchy, embarrassing or sometimes outright ridiculous—her nickname at school was Funnychile, not meant to be endearing—was simply a misunderstanding of Honeychile's deep insecurities. It made Zelda so sad! She wanted to "fix" her friend, but lately their enmeshment wasn't meshing so well. The BFF's usual words of support had no effect.

Zelda spoke to her own mother about it, using her as a sounding board for her latest theory that the change in Honeychile's personality might possibly be related to her cleidocranial dysplasia. She'd done a fair amount of Internet research on the subject, though as yet couldn't confirm or deny. Each time she came across a dreadful user comment on various message boards that invoked horror-film scenarios of what could or probably already *had* happened to the brains of people afflicted with the condition, she comforted herself by watching YouTube interviews with Gaten Matarazzo, the amazing star of *Stranger Things*. He was smart—*more* than smart. He was, like, the smartest kid in the room.

Just like Honeychile.

When her mom offhandedly said, "Maybe she's just manic-depressive like your uncle Walt," Zelda went down that Internet rabbit hole faster than Alice herself.

What was it? What was wrong with her bestie?

The teacher expelled Honeychile from class because not only did she start humming "Rise," but actually started to *sing*. Really belted it out. The kids were shocked at first and then began to laugh, which only seemed to inspire her. WTF? Zelda knew that Honeychile was a total Katy Perry *hater*—she liked Pink and Alessia Cara and Twenty One Pilots (and maybe parts of the Chainsmokers and Sia), but held Katy in outright contempt. She was always schooling Zelda on people she'd never heard of, like Amy Winehouse and Nina Simone and that amazing YouTube video of a bald woman who stared right at you the whole time as she sang this incredible breakup song.

And that crazy place they went that day at the museum! It was fun for a little but then it got seriously fucked-up and weird. In the cab, Honeychile told her that she was "just looking for a friend" and wouldn't answer when Zelda kept asking, "*What* friend?" Finally, Honeychile said, "The friend I'm looking for is dead, okay? And I'm going to fucking hunt down and *kill* the person who did it!" She seemed utterly serious before dissolving into peals of laughter, like the theatrically silly girl Zelda once knew. Then the laughter turned into creepy cackles. "I'm writing a movie about a girl with superpowers who avenges death," she said, her voice all different and really, really young-sounding. Zelda just shook her head and let it go; all she wanted was to have her friend back. She was afraid, not only because she felt like she was losing Honeychile, but because she suddenly realized how much she meant to her.

The morning after the "Rise" incident at school, Zelda sat up in bed as if struck by a thunderbolt. The answer had arrived in the exact same way her teacher said that answers came to famous scientists in their sleep. She googled her brainstormy diagnosis and confirmed her suspicions:

Honeychile had multiple personality disorder!

2.

The texts came one after the other—

YOU SING LIKE KATIE PARY.

YOU LOOK LIKE KATE PARY.

ACCEPT U HAVE NO FUCKING TITS

AND U R SO FUKING UGLEE AND NOT FAMMOUS

+++YR VOICE IS SHIT THEN +++++YOU R A FUCKTARD/DEEFORMD HORE

UGLY BITCHCUNNT

UGLIEST DEEFORMD CUNTBITCH HOREMONNSTER—

—but Honeychile was oddly unaffected. She thought the whole bully thing was tiresome and overplayed. Anyway, she could give as good as she got, laying low her detractors with a laser-beamed Funnychile aperçu. She liked to pretend her words had the same effect as in that awesome episode of *Stranger Things*, when Eleven made the bully pee his pants.

She had a pretty good idea who sent the texts, but at the moment couldn't really be bothered. She had a lot of other things to distract her— like all those new, amorphous feelings and memories that *definitely* weren't hers . . .

In the morning, she awakened from a dream that she was somewhere else—in a bedroom that wasn't hers, surrounded by a menagerie of stuffed animals and a wall of magazine cutout collages of Kendall Jenner and Bella Hadid and . . . *Kaia Gerber*—Kaia Gerber! How did she even know who Kaia Gerber was? That she was Cindy Crawford's daughter! How did she even know who *Cindy Crawford* was? But she did. In the room, there was a mosaic of pictures of Marc Jacobs, all buff and tatted, posing with Neville, a bull terrier in a bow tie. How did she know what Marc Jacobs fucking looked like and that his dog had two hundred thousand followers on Instagram? But she did . . . in the dream, somewhere close by, was a woman with no face, making breakfast—eggs and toast, so real that Honeychile could smell the smells. Who was she? Her biological mother? Maybe that's why she went to visit Mrs. Collins after all, and not because she missed her. To find her real mom . . .

There were darker thoughts too.

But were they thoughts? Or were they feelings—

Weren't the two things the same?

Honeychile hated the corrective dental surgeries she'd undergone, dreaded them, and told her parents that she refused to have more. But now she had the strange sensation that she was having surgery again, somewhere *else* on her body, somewhere down below. Between her legs . . . And that she was being—buried? Buried! She could smell the mud as it burrowed into her nostrils, and tiny seizures of lancing coldness shot through her at the most inopportune times, even when she wasn't dreaming. Like when she was on the toilet or when Rayanne came into the kitchen to try to talk to her about whatever.

And that nasty woman—the one who sicced those freaky creatures after her on the train. *The train!* Night after night she found herself onboard, hurtling through darkness. Sometimes she saw children in the corridors, but they were so much younger . . . She couldn't make heads or tails of it. And that meeting at the church! Why wouldn't the nasty woman let Zelda in? That wasn't very nice. Even more vexing to Honeychile was that she really wanted to join the gathering, was *desperate* to, and as much as she hated that woman, she loved her too . . . It made no sense at all, but Honeychile had the feeling that she belonged there, and ached to meet the people on the other side of the door. Something about it all felt like family . . . so, so crazy! Since that afternoon they went AWOL from the museum, she'd had more dreams of being on the train, but those awful, shadowy creatures no longer wrestled her into the cabin. She'd been behaving herself.

That beast called Annie kept handing her slips of paper but instead of running, Honeychile crossed her arms and rebelliously shook her head, refusing even to look at what was written down.

T his is what she heard when eavesdropping at Harold and Rayanne's bedroom door after they thought she was sleeping:

"I'm so worried about her."

"What now?" said Harold.

(He probably wasn't even looking at his wife—just reading a book and being chill, which was his way.)

"You mean you haven't noticed? Have you seen that weird shiver that she does?"

"Maybe she's getting sick," he said. "Did you take her temperature?"

"She is *not* getting sick, Harold. It's like—like she's . . . somewhere else. Like she's some*one* else."

"Hey, it's called 'fourteen,'" he said. "Fourteen-year-olds *are* someone else—a lot of the time, anyway. Fourteen-year-olds don't know who the hell they are. So they try on different outfits."

"No no *no*. You don't know what I'm saying. Something isn't *right*. My God, have you seen the drawing? In her room?"

"I don't go in her room. Probably not a good idea for you to go in either."

"It's *Katy Perry*, Harold!"

"Who's Katy Perry?"

"Like, her *nemesis*. She drew it right on the wall. It's huge!"

"Fourteen-year-olds are artistic," he said with a shrug.

"Well, I think something is *wrong* and I think she should see someone."

"Maybe she should see Katy Perry."

"It isn't *funny*, Harold. I'm serious."

Maybe I should see someone, thought Honeychile as she crept back to her room.

Yes, I should—I *will*.

Tomorrow!

3.

She sat on the couch with her head against Mrs. Collins's breast, enfolded in the ravaged woman's arms.

Her son was irretrievably gone—Hildy knew it in her heart—but for a series of moments, holding the distraught girl as she sobbed inconsolably, the grieving mother had the strange sensation that it had all been a dream, that Winston was here with her now, with *them*, as she rocked her unexpected houseguest like she used to rock her boy. How strange. She would take her relief wherever and whenever she found it.

It felt good to be a mom again.

When Honeychile asked if she could visit his room—"my room" was how she put it—Hildy said she would get her a blanket and she could nap right there on the couch. But the girl insisted, tenderly pleading, and to Hildy's surprise it felt right.

She looked in on her an hour later.

It would be impossible to describe the emotions that played across Hildy's face when, in dusky darkness, she saw the shape of the girl's small, misshapen body beneath his favorite quilt—bolstered by an army of stuffed animals and watched over by wall-pastings of Kendall, Kaia and Bella torn from the pages of W—dead asleep.

MISSING CHILDREN

I.

As he left Sterling Heights for the Caplan home in Armada, Willow passed a middle school with a PLEASE BRING WINSTON HOME! banner strung across the gymnasium.

Along the way, some of the houses had a smiling picture of the boy on lawn stakes. Over the weekend, hundreds of volunteers went poking around the banks and foliage of the part of Clinton River that wound its way through Mount Clemens. As a cop, Willow knew it was futile and that he was likely dead.

It was way too soon to bring a date to the barbecue.

He wanted to feel the way men do when they walk into a party with a beautiful woman on their arm but didn't think that would fly—especially not with a gal, technically speaking, who Willow hardly knew. He hadn't yet earned that kind of goodwill, and showboating Dixie would just make him look foolish. He didn't want to offend his ex either; young pussy had a way of stirring the pot. At the same time, he kicked himself for not inviting her, because Dixie had the knack of generally chilling him out (more so since the insanity with Annie), a talent that definitely would have come in handy at the backyard hullabaloo. He kicked himself one more time because his concerns about Adelaide felt codependent, flashbacking him to the worst parts of their marriage.

"There he is!" said Owen, standing at the grill in full barbecue regalia. "How do you like your meat?"

"Young," whispered Willow, uncharacteristically macho. His thoughts still lingered on Dixie and he felt a tad unruly.

Owen laughed and licentiously prodded at a sizzling patty. "Speaking of which. Had any lately, Dub?"

"Nope. Been sending everything back to the kitchen."

"Well, at least you put an order in. Trouble with you is you're too picky," said Owen. "You didn't *used* to be that way."

"I didn't used to look this way."

They chortled and then Adelaide waved Willow down. He dutifully went over.

"Well, hey there, Dubya!"

"Hi, Addie."

"You good?"

"I am excellent."

"That's what I like to hear. And thanks for coming to our event the other day. I know you hate that kind of thing."

"No worries. I actually had a nice time." He stared at his shoes a moment, wondering how to approach it. "That lady you introduced me to . . . you know, the volunteer—"

"Annie?" she said brashly. "Little old for you, isn't she?"

"Very funny," said Willow. "I was just curious." He had to circle around to it. "You know—are all those people retired? The volunteers? Or are they independently wealthy?"

"Well, *Annie* isn't. Makes the drive from Detroit twice a week. I think she takes the bus. They're selfless people, most of them. Annie's a saint."

He was stymied over what direction to take next. Just what was it that he wanted to know, what was it he was trying to find out? Willow was at a total loss. At least it felt good talking about the woman—it got her out of his head, made her less of a chimera.

A few couples settled into the picnic tables. Most of the men were cops. Willow and his ex joined them as they fed their faces and shop-talked. The wives were used to it.

"A friend in California told me about a pretty wild case," said one of the men. "All these folks were being murdered in Atlanta. I'm talking straight-out executions. This happened, oh, I think over the course of two or three years. Not thugs or gangbangers or drug addicts—just folks who'd given information on homicide cases. Not CIs. Regular people. Witnesses, what-ever. It wasn't even a Crime Stoppers deal, just members of the community calling in tips from what they heard on the street. *Some* were probably do-ing it for the reward, but most were just trying to make the community safer. Gettin' bad guys off the streets. And none of the murders were con-nected. Zero. No one in homicide could figure it out. For a while, they thought it was a serial deal. Know what they all had in common?"

"What was that?" said Owen.

"Every one of the vics had been interviewed on a reality cop show. There's a hundred of 'em now. During interrogations, when the shows aired, they were heavily blurred out, voices altered, the whole deal. To protect their anonymity. Now *here's* what's amazing. Turns out there's a guy work-ing at the editing facility out in Hollywood—"

"The blur-out guy?" said Willow.

"That's right. There was *one guy* who had that job. The motherfucker was selling pre-censored images to the criminal community."

"Jesus," said Adelaide. "That's like an Agatha Christie. Or whoever's writing that kind of thing now."

Guests came and went, replenishing their paper plates. When the talk fell to Winston Collins, the women didn't want to entertain the hardboiled husbands' certainty, backed up by stats, that the boy was killed within hours of his abduction. To placate the ladies, one of them half-heartedly said, "He'll probably turn up." A wise guy couldn't help adding, "Parts of him, anyway."

A few of the wives asked Owen if his office had any leads, and he shook his head. "Something'll break," he said. "Just a matter of time." Willow was familiar with that kind of optimism, or at least its compulsory public face. One of the men brought up the infamous, unsolved Oakland County murders that took place an hour southwest—four kids between the ages of ten and twelve were killed in a thirteen-month period between 1976 and '77. But the "Oakland County Child Killer" was never found.

"Maybe the guy's still doing his thing," said a wife. "And living in Macomb."

"Possible, but unlikely," said her husband. "He'd probably be in his seventies by now."

"Let's get our cold case expert's opinion," said Owen, turning to Willow.

"Oh, you find serial killers who are 'active seniors.' I'm sure there's a few out there who are wearing Depends. It's atypical but it happens. They don't usually lay low for forty years, then pick up again. But as the man said, anything's possible. It's more likely that he's dead."

"Or she," said Adelaide.

"Or she," echoed Willow. "It certainly wouldn't be without precedent for a woman to be involved. The prime suspect in that Oakland deal shot himself in the head, though, didn't he?"

"That would be Christopher Busch," nodded Owen. "There were a *lot* of 'prime suspects.' And speaking of cold cases, how'd you like my deputies?"

Willow suddenly felt remiss for not having called his boss to compliment him on the recruits. "Good people," he said. "They're green, but sometimes green's a good thing. A *very* good thing. You just may be right. I think there *is* something special about them."

"Willow's heading up our new task force," said Owen to the others, mostly for the benefit of the wives because the men already knew. "He very courteously allowed me to lure him out of retirement. He was the Big Apple's Cold Case king."

"Your wish is my command," said Willow.

"The king and the genie," said the wise guy. "*There's* a pair to draw to."

"I don't mind playing genie," said Owen. "As long as there isn't any rubbing involved."

"I'll try to keep my hands to myself," said Willow. Everyone laughed. "You won't believe who they chose for their first case."

"JonBenét?" said the wise guy.

"Troy and Maya Rummer."

"You are shitting me," said Owen, genuinely surprised.

"Oh my God!" said Adelaide. "Dubya, are you being for real?"

He got a pang, thinking it was probably something he shouldn't have casually announced at a barbecue. But the cat was out of the bag.

"It came down to the Rummers and two other cases, but that's the one they stuck with. Almost insisted on it."

"Funny," said Owen. "Those two were working at the substation in Saggerty Falls when I pulled them for the task force."

"They did have an awareness about the abductions," said Willow. "But I don't think it was something they'd ever given much thought."

"Well," said Owen, almost meditatively. "What are *your* thoughts, Willow? About reopening the case?"

For a moment, he wondered if the sheriff might have a problem with it, though he wasn't sure why. "At first I thought it wasn't a good idea—too personal. To *me*, not them. So I'm going to let 'em run with it."

One of the women theorized that the recruits' selection of the Rummer kids was probably influenced by the disappearance of the Collins boy.

"That may be true," said Willow. "But I've found that in cold cases, there isn't always an obvious correlation or rationale behind the circumstances of *why* we investigate what we investigate. It's not always about going into a file and identifying, say, a glaring error in how an unsolved crime was prosecuted, or following a lead that was never pursued but should have been. It tends to be a little more mysterious than that. Or can be."

"Somebody put this man on the lecture circuit," said Owen, without sarcasm.

"I can't tell you," said Willow, "how many times I've heard a cold case detective say 'I don't know' when some journalist asked what it was that initially caught their interest."

"That was an awful, awful time," Adelaide said solemnly. She turned to Willow. "You heard what happened to Elaine Rummer, didn't you?"

"No," he said.

"She went out of her mind," said Owen.

"Can't blame a mother for that," said Adelaide.

"Shot herself in the face with a rifle—and lived."

"Recoil saved her," said one of the cops. "Happens more often than you'd think."

"What doesn't kill you," said the wise guy, "tends to rearrange your features. They call that the penny-saver's facelift."

"She's had a bunch of surgeries," said Owen. "They did a pretty good job too, from what I hear."

"It's a funny way to take yourself out," said another cop. "Particularly for a woman."

"Are you being sexist?" said one of the wives.

"On the contrary. Women usually aren't that stupid."

"I would have overdosed," said Adelaide. "I'd have taken ten thousand sleeping pills. There is no way I would have been able to bear what she went through. There is just no way."

"ODs aren't foolproof either," said Willow. "Do it wrong and you can end up strapped to a chair in a nursing home."

"Believe me," said Adelaide. "I'd have done it right." She clenched her jaw. "Believe me."

2.

Is there a hell more specific than the chaos following the disappearance of a child?

If *two* children vanish (a brother and sister, ages nine and six) from a cookout on Independence Day, in a pastoral village in the late afternoon—is it possible for hell to double and become worse? If all happy families are alike (families whose children never disappeared), is each unhappy, disappeared-child family unhappy in its own way? Or is there a sameness to their torment?

The question and its queer permutations haunted Willow, not merely because he happened to be in Saggerty Falls when Troy and Maya Rummer went missing. For years prior, like many parents, Willow and Adelaide shuddered over the possibility of their child being snatched by the bogey-man. Pace had just turned sixteen when it finally came true—for the Rum-mers. It was like some nightmarish wish fulfillment of the collective unconscious. He was living in New York, working in the narcotics division, the occasion of his return to the place he once called home being to surprise his estranged daughter on her Sweet Sixteenth.

Elaine and Ronnie Rummer, friends and onetime neighbors, had warmly spearheaded the welcome wagon on the Wyldes' arrival from Chicago in 1993. A few years later, when Troy was almost five and Maya had just turned two, they agreed to let twelve-year-old Pace apprentice in the art of babysitting. The Wylde girl proved such a quick study that she effectively became Troy and Maya's big sis, and a second daughter to the Rummers. When they disappeared, the abyss of evil that opened at Pace's feet was intensely personal; the shock of what happened to her babies brought the hormonal girl's relations with the dark side to a level that was more than flirtatious.

Willow extended his stay for a week after Troy and Maya fell off the face of the Earth. In the first few days, Owen, now Saggerty Falls' chief of police, begged Willow to use his "spooky" ways to help find the children. Dubya tried, but shamefully came up empty; he had suppressed those gifts for too long. At that point, Owen and Adelaide had been "out" for eight months—apparently the two began seeing each other while he and Owen were still partners. In the shock-time of the abductions, Willow stuffed his animosity in view of the greater tragedy and greater good—but mostly be-cause he wanted to be there for Pace, who was suffering. He didn't want to add to the burdens she already shouldered.

Among other off-color hobbies, she'd been secretly (then not so secretly) cutting herself. It started when she was fourteen. Willow and Adelaide kept as close a watch as they could. But he was hundreds of miles away and it was his ex who waited by the phone for the dreaded call from police stations, hospitals and morgues; it was his ex who crept into Pace's room to sigh with relief when she confirmed, after tortured observation, that their daughter was asleep and not dead. When Pace didn't come home for days at a time, it was his ex who visited the police stations, hospitals, morgues . . . and when she could take no more (to his credit, Owen tried his best to be a father figure, but Pace wasn't having it), she called Willow, usually while he was in bed with one of his snitches, whores or whatevers, shouting *You're a piece of shit who does not care about your own daughter!* In his heart, he knew he was a good father, but actions were the only thing that mattered.

The road to Hell was paved with men who knew they were good fathers . . .

When Willow returned to New York immediately after the catastrophe, he started having the dreams—not of Pace being dead, but that she was gone and he would never see her again. Never! The idea was enough to drive a person mad; no wonder Elaine tried to blow her head off. *Not to have a body to bury* . . . though was it better to *have* a body? Were the moms and dads of the Oakland County Child Killer's victims—or the parents of April Millsap, whose body *was* found a few years ago by the tracks of the Macomb Orchard Trail, not far from Owen and Adelaide's home—were they better off? How could one know? To have or not to have a body . . . that was the question. Not having one to bury was a primal terror—that a beloved was out there rotting, their soul anchorless and defamed. Willow recalled a case in Minnesota where a killer led investigators to the remains of a ten-year-old boy he murdered in exchange for not being charged. (He was already in jail for other barbarities and would never get out.) The parents agreed to the deal because having a body meant that much to them. They no longer cared that the record would declare for all eternity that no one— *no one*—was officially accountable for the rape, mutilation and extinction of their shining star.

Willow wondered if he would do the same. Would he plea bargain with God Himself, if it meant bringing the closure that he imagined would be provided by a body? Closure! Symmetry! *Balance* . . . He hadn't seemed to care enough when she was alive; might caring too much when she was dead be the ultimate selfish act? When God fulfilled his request and her body was retrieved, plucked from earth or water or the barrel the killer encased it in, when He laid Pace at his feet, where would that leave Willow? Would he realize what he'd done and put a shotgun to his face? The travesty of demanding back the girl who had hated him in life and now would hate him in death for calling her back as if she were his property, like a teenager grounded for violating curfew, seemed like the worst desecration, unholier than letting her be, letting her go.

He dreamed those dreams of losing her for years, but they stopped right around the time of his first dream about the train.

THE NEW AGE

When would he see Annie again?

The peculiar thing is that he wasn't dwelling on it, any of it, not really. Willow noticed that in himself. He simply knew he would see her soon, whatever *soon* meant. He didn't seem to be obsessing on the outrageous weirdness either, which struck him as more than peculiar, there being more than enough outrage and weird to go around. The only thing that really mattered was that he didn't feel crazy anymore. (There'd been a moment when he thought he was going over the edge.) He couldn't explain why; it wasn't as if the bizarre encounter at the Early World Diner was fading—it wasn't. If anything, Annie and the things she had told him were becoming more real. Taking root. Maybe that's what she meant by her last few words. That he needed time to "integrate."

Maybe that's what was going on: he was *integrating*.

Well, bring it. He had to laugh (intermittently), which he thought was probably a good thing.

Smile while your brain is breaking . . .

He began to diligently work with the Cold Case Kids, schooling them on what Rafael, his old NYPD boss, called the "black art." They'd certainly done their homework. Each day, he grew more persuaded that Owen's instincts were correct—the greenhorns were made for the game. They were surprisingly au courant in the latest advances in forensic science, which were many in the years since Willow had been active. He struggled to keep up. Lydia and Daniel were some kind of prodigies—plus, their generation had an entirely new, comprehensive, unpredictable way of perceiving and interpreting the matrix. Not only was the detective impressed, but he was slowly coming around to *I can learn from them too.*

Did they ever sleep? When he arrived at the office in the morning, the guard often said they'd been there for hours. Evidence and material pertaining to Troy and Maya Rummer's case were meticulously deployed in a conference room, and when Willow came in they usually ignored him, standing hypnotized in front of blurry school photos of the bucktoothed boy and freckly, pigtailed girl. The plastic bag with the BE EXCELLENT TO EACH OTHER T-shirt was pinned to a corkboard, same as the unicorn-themed fifth birthday card Maya had faithfully carried around for a year before she died. (It was found in the basket of her bicycle.) Its horn was made of gold sequins but only a threadbare sprinkle was left. Ninhydrin had been used to reveal a latent palm print, less than two square inches, on its cover. Lydia and Daniel already ran a photograph of the palm through APIS, the Automated Palmprint ID System, a database that hadn't been available until 2005. There wasn't a match.

On the table was a small stuffed unicorn, also found in the basket, removed from its smothering baggie as if by order of the American Society for the Prevention of Cruelty to Mythological Animals.

Maya's bike lay on the floor, replicating its position in the ditch, in crime scene photographs.

Troy's bike was never recovered . . .

The files took up half of the long table. Another section was devoted to Persons of Interest, beginning with Ebenezer the neighbor, whose house the kids were heading to for lighter fluid on that fateful day. There were other POIs, paroled sex offenders living within a fifty-mile radius, though none ever panned out.

Willow thought it compelling, even auspicious, that the newbies chose the Rummer case—yet sometimes it seemed like the case had chosen them. Though it was against his interests, he couldn't help but think of the crime as unsolvable, destined to be no more than an invaluable laboratory of learning—training wheels, so to speak, before they were confident enough to ride full-speed on the twisting roads of Cold Case country. Of course he hoped that he was wrong, because Willow knew that he couldn't afford to have a five-star failure right out of the gate, especially one with so much resonance in the community, so much personal history and emotion. To cover potential losses, he already planned to introduce a few more cases that he'd chosen himself. He would wait awhile; he didn't want to dampen their enthusiasm. Still, the restive freshness and idiosyncratic focus that both deputies brought to their task were encouraging. They showed seriousness and passion in regard to finding the party or parties responsible, and demonstrated a rare, innate understanding of the sacredness of the work. For the work *was* sacred to the detective—which was why his failure in New York had dealt such a terrible blow.

One day, when the kids were on a lunch break, Willow wandered into the war room for what he called a hover. He knew one could get lost in the details and that it was important to get a bird's-eye view. It was corny but he had shown them a video of a seagull treading air, staying still while buffeted by the currents. The detective told them they should do just that—remain still in the windstorm of data, without losing the ability to scan the horizon and take off in whatever direction that was needed.

He let his mind drift, glancing at the corkboard as he played back that afternoon at the Rummers'. Ronnie went to find the kids to borrow lighter fluid from a neighbor. When he came back to the grill, they bullshitted awhile. Stomachs were growling and Ronnie got mad that Troy and Maya were taking so long; Willow could remember his face darkening, as if by a shadow. Ronnie jumped in the Camaro and went looking. Then all hell broke loose. A few days later, they drank some beers in Ronnie's garage, a small reprieve from the hourly onslaught of fresh agonies. That was when he told Willow what was going through his head as he hightailed it down the road to find them—crazed-parent images, like his children being cut down in the middle of a field by a Cessna as it made an emergency landing.

The detective walked to the window. He saw Lydia and Daniel in the pocket park across the street, in deep discussion. He wondered what they were saying. He was growing inordinately fond of the two. Willow had never met anyone like them but didn't even know what that meant. He thought of sucking on a cigarette but reached in his jacket for a Nicorette instead. He'd lost the craving for drink and drugs—maybe all it had taken was the new gig. Someone showing a little faith.

He bent down to gather a balled-up scrap that missed the wastebasket. He unfolded it, for no particular reason—a stick figure drawing of a girl with flaming red hair. Below it, also in a child's scrawl, was *hoo hert me?* For a moment he thought it was evidence, but there was no stamp or penciled case file number. They wouldn't be crumpling up evidence and tossing it anyway. He retrieved more drawings from the basket. One was of a small boy, with a cartoon bubble drawn above his head that read *PAPA!!!!*

As he left the room, Lydia's purse caught his eye. He looked out the window again; the novices were slowly on their way back to the building. He rummaged through the bag, a compulsion he'd had for as long as he could remember. His mother rapped his knuckles when she caught him, but he didn't think that was fair because he never intended to steal. The habit persisted, occasionally getting him in trouble with girlfriends. He justified the quirk as the naturally curious predilection of a born detective.

He pulled a folded paper from the side pocket, focusing on one of the paragraphs:

Rule Number Three: As time goes by, you will find that you are becoming more "yourself." But *remember*—while ADULTS are PLAYFUL, and CHILDLIKE qualities are usually tolerated and enjoyed, do NOT call ATTENTION to yourself with too much CRAZY HORSEPLAY! Listen to your Landlord!!!!

That was unexpected—he didn't peg Lydia as a New Agey "inner child" workshop-type.

(But that part about landlords . . .?)

He stuffed it back when he heard their footsteps in the hall.

RIDERS ON THE STORM

I.

Each day after work, at Lydia's place in Richmond, they threw themselves on the couch and measured their progress. It was Friday, the end of a week that had brought them to their knees.

They were scared.

It wasn't because they didn't yet have the leads they hoped for (it was still so early in the investigation)—no, it was something else, something ominous. They shared a disquieting sense of pending doom, as if any day the rug of the *moment of balance* would be yanked from beneath their feet, banished forever. Inexorably, their initial, almost religious feeling of purpose was being stripped away, replaced by indifference and accidie.

A listlessness, a sickening blankness, crept in like a fog.

"It just doesn't make sense," said Lydia. "I mean, aren't we supposed to know what we're doing by now?"

"Like I'm the expert?" said Daniel.

"Well, aren't we kind of *supposed* to be the 'experts'? And you *know* what I mean, Troy. By now, we're supposed to at least already have some sort of an idea—"

"I know what you mean." He was ruminative but noncommittal. It just wasn't a fun thing to talk about.

A few days ago they began calling each other by their child-tenant names, but only while at home. The Porter told them that would happen—a "cross-over day" when the children became not so much dominant as *present*, and began to assert themselves within the borrowed brains and bodies of their landlords. From then on, adult and child would enhance each other, preparing the way for the *moment of balance*. (In speaking of that process, the landlords often used a word not in the children's vocabulary: "synergy.") By blending beings—Lydia with Maya, Daniel with Troy—the end result would be far greater than its separate parts.

"I still can't shake this feeling," he said.

"What feeling."

"That I've met him before."

"Who."

"Our supervisor—Detective Wylde."

"Well, he's an old friend of the sheriff, isn't he? You've probably seen him around."

"*Maybe*," he said, elongating the word.

"They used to work together in the Falls."

"I know, I know." He paused to organize his thoughts. "I'll tell you something else that's been troubling me," said Daniel. "Don't you think it's weird that we're cops?"

"Weird like how?"

"And not just cops—*cold case* cops."

"What are you trying to say?"

"It's just that . . . everything Annie's told us about the *mystery* of it all, everything we've learned at Meetings—let me ask you this." His smile became ironic. "When the train brings everyone back, does it drop them off to enroll in *detective* school? Are all the other kids, like, secretly going to night classes to learn about investigative techniques? Because that's what we're doing, isn't it? Where's the so-called mystery in *that*?"

"I guess we *are* the only ones. Who are cops, I mean."

"You better believe we are! Fucking 'Macarena' *José* wasn't exactly Sherlock Holmes."

"Please don't use bad words," she said. "But I still don't know what you're trying to say."

"Come on, Maya! Don't you think it's just a little bit strange that out of everyone in the group, we happen to be the ones who are actual cold case cops? We solve old murders for a living!"

Something clicked in her head. "Oh my God," she said, with a shiver. "That is *totally brilliant*. But what does it mean?"

"I'm not the expert, sis."

"We have to talk to Annie—"

"At the next Meeting. We'll talk to her after."

"I don't want to wait—let's find out where she lives!"

"Down, girl. Don't go off the deep end, Freckles."

"It's a little too fucking late for *that*," she exclaimed.

"You swore, you swore, you swore!" he said, in delight.

"*Lydia* swore!"

She blushed, clapping a hand over her mouth in prudish repentance. She started to giggle and Troy did too until both were practically rolling on the floor.

After they composed themselves, he said, "You know, I did kind of talk to Annie about it already."

"What!"

"Just a little . . ."

"When, when, *when*?"

"The last time we saw her."

"Oh my God, what did you say?"

"What I already told you . . . but I hadn't really thought about it as much as I have now. I said, 'Annie, if after we get here we're just supposed to *know*—you said it's this mysterious knowledge that just comes—if *that's* supposed to be what happens, why are my sister and I, like, in *training* to be cold case cops?'"

"And what did *she* say?" said Lydia-Maya, rapt.

"The Porter was, like, *stumped*. And it wasn't some teaching moment either—you know, when she goes all Yoda-'more-shall-be-revealed.' Which was what I was expecting. She *could* have said that being cold case cops was just random—a random thing that didn't *mean* anything. But she didn't. Nope! Wouldn't go there. It was like my question had seriously fucked her up."

He anticipated Maya swatting him for the expletive but she ignored it, staring out the window in the same way she did when her brother used to read to her from a spooky fairy tale book.

That night, Lydia sat bolt upright, startling him.

"Oh my God," she said. Her face was wet with the tears she'd shed while dreaming.

"What's going on?" he said, groggily.

"It's here!" she said, blissed out.

"What?"

"It's here, I *know* it . . . I know now—" She paused and he waited for her to speak. "We need to get up! We need to go . . ."

"Go where?"

"We need to go to the airport."

"O-*kayyyy*," he said. He looked at his phone; it was a little after 4:00 A.M. "So where to? Barcelona? Paris? How about Barbados?"

"St. Cloud."

"St. Cloud, Minnesoda pop?"

"This isn't a joke, Daniel!"

She leapt from bed and stripped off her PJs. The Daniel part liked to see her nude, but the Troy part looked away. He sat up and started to sing. "'Don't know why . . . there's no clouds up in the sky, stormy weather . . .'"

"It's no *sun* up in the sky, not 'clouds,' doodie-breath. And it's going to be cold, so dress accordingly."

"Can I have a little coffee first?"

"At the airport," said Maya.

"Is the airport even open?"

"The airport's always open."

"Why don't I just buy our tickets online?"

"You can buy 'em on the *way*."

"May I be so bold as to ask what's in Minnesoda pop?"

"Rhonda."

"Who?"

"*Rhonda's* in Minnesoda pop." She'd already turned on the shower and was sitting on the toilet to pee. "Rhonda from the *Meeting*," she yelled. "He's there—I *saw* him. Rhonda's in St. Cloud."

2.

There was a 6:10 A.M. flight to Minneapolis–St. Paul; Metro Airport in Detroit was an hour away. The sky had no moon and they felt as if they were plunging through the black tunnel of a dream. It was almost like being on the train again.

"Do you want to tell me exactly what you saw?" said Daniel. "In your vision or your whatever . . ."

"Just him: Rhonda. He was rushing to meet someone in St. Cloud. He was going so fast—"

"Who was he meeting?"

"More shall be revealed," she said, almost gleefully.

"Do you think it's connected? That *he's* connected? To us?"

"He has to be," said Lydia. "It felt . . . too strong."

"Do you know anything about Rhonda? What year she was murdered?"

Lydia knew what everyone else did about their fellow travelers: next to nothing. The Porter stressed that individual history (of landlords and ten-ants) was none of anyone's business and a distraction from the *moment of balance*. What purpose would such knowledge serve, anyway? God—or as Annie called it, the Great Mystery—was definitely *not* in the details.

"I don't know a thing about her," she said. "But *he's* a yoga instructor. I asked him once and that's what he told me. Rhonda's landlord, I mean."

Daniel stared at the road ahead, deep in thought, with that connect-the-dots look. Lydia loved watching his wheels turn.

"Remember at the Meeting," he said, "when Rhonda kept saying she wanted to know how she died?"

"I do," she said pensively.

"I thought that was twisted. I mean, to be so insistent about it." He paused. "I sure the fuck don't want to know how *I* died."

They were in the air about two hours. Lydia raised an eyebrow when Daniel ordered a drink. He got the message and the tiny bottle sat unopened.

The same irrefutable feeling that his sister experienced now saturated him: that Rhonda held the key. But could he trust such a thing? Before this, the nascent "visions" that presented themselves as exciting clues to the identity of their killers were ultimately exposed as no more than phantasms, a distorted series of headlines featuring the memories of the child-tenants Maya and Troy and their landlords, Daniel and Lydia. For example, Troy would find himself standing at a door that he was certain would open into the *moment of balance*, only to realize it led to rooms filled with the dark secrets that his landlord, Daniel, had suppressed: the hauntedness over murdering an innocent child in Afghanistan, the irrational guilt over the crib death of his son, his rage toward his estranged wife, even his shame at being impotent on that night he'd been scheduled to lose his virginity at age fifteen. The same thing happened to Maya, but for her the door was a beautiful wooden gate leading to a profusion of gardens. Each path she took uncovered *Lydia's* secrets—the two abortions, the pain of an extramarital affair she'd had in her early twenties with a woman who was violent and possessive, her guilt over shoplifting at thirteen and lying to the police, knowing that her best friend would be taken to jail because of what she had told them.

They landed in the Twin Cities, rented a car and embarked on the hour-long drive to St. Cloud. It began to storm and they were quiet. Maya was behind the wheel. Daniel found a station that played classical music. They listened to Gregorian chants crackle in and out of reception.

About twenty minutes in, she swerved to an off-ramp.

"Hey now!" he said. "Starship *Enterprise* is off course." He pointed far right. "St. Cloud's *thataway*."

"We're not going to St. Cloud," she said. "We're going to Jacobs Prairie."

3.

After teaching his 6:00 P.M. class at the studio called Lotus in Midtown Detroit, the African-American yoga teacher known at the Meeting as Rhonda—but to his students (and the DMV) as Ganesha Ashanti Sinclair—went to the movies at a local revival house. "Ganesha" was the name bestowed upon him years ago by a guru at an ashram in Bangalore; when he returned from his South Asian sojourn to Detroit, he added "Ashanti" in homage to his Ghanaian ancestors. The appellation suited his sportive, free-spirited nature and made him smile. It seemed to make a lot of people smile.

About an hour into *The Man Who Would Be King* (he'd always been fond of Kipling and loved any adventure story that took place in a faraway land), he left his seat to buy more bonbons. His students still couldn't believe that their Ganesha, who treated his body like a temple, had developed a thing for the frozen chocolate treats that were Rhonda's favorites. In the last four months, they'd noticed a host of new quirks, reflecting a childishness in him that struck some of them as puzzling or even pretentious. Many, though, took the new behaviors as a refreshing indication that their teacher had entered a higher, if playful, spiritual plane. He was on his way back into the theater when he bit down on one of the ice-cold nuggets and simultaneously had a stereoscopic vision of the man who had killed him—killed Rhonda, rather—and where that person could be found.

He immediately left.

He drove toward I-75S on a route that allowed him to skirt the toll roads. Flying under the radar was paramount because Annie cautioned her flock about the importance of not being identified or linked in any way to the homicide called the *moment of balance*. (She aimed this caveat more toward the landlords; their child-tenants would not possess such savvy.) The Porter said there would be terrible consequences if one was caught in the act or traced to the crime itself. Even though the landlords would have expired by then—traditionally, the "second," final death occurred in the hours following the *moment of balance*—such a revelation would cause unnecessary hurt, shock and confusion to their surviving loved ones. Annie referred everyone to the section of the *Guide* that addressed itself to the essentialness of respect shown not just to landlords but to the friends and family of those borrowed bodies as well. The Porter said that "invisibility and discretion" were almost as crucial as the deaths of the child-killers themselves.

Because of the storm, his eleven-hour drive from Detroit took fifteen. It was Ganesha who planned and strategized the trip, the way adults do; Rhonda, child and tenant, provided energy and purpose, the propulsive *vision* informing the whole enterprise. As he navigated the blurry hodgepodge of rain-slicked highway and staccato brake lights, Ganesha meditated on his life. What an amazing journey it had been! His twin brother was in prison, a quarter way into a sixty-year sentence, but the yogi had taken a different path. Ganesha was gay and didn't come out until his early twenties, after traveling to India. He spent three years exploring the continent before being graced to find his guru. Now thirty-one, he taught yoga five days a week and on Saturday nights played jazz piano at Cliff Bell's (when they'd have him). He collected pottery and had even been looking into classes with the view of designing his own when his tenant, Rhonda, arrived.

If one *didn't* embrace the amazing journey of this life, then what was the point? He was sorry he'd be leaving the world so soon yet had no regrets. Now it was the amazing journey of death he would embrace.

Annie said that when the *moment of balance* was nigh, nothing would matter but the task at hand. And it was true: something took over with cyclonic force. In the early days of Rhonda's emergence, Ganesha experienced the same turbulence of doubt, bewilderment and anxiety common to all landlords. In those first Meetings at the Divine Child Parish he was hesitant, ruled by the instinct of self-protection, until it slowly dawned on him that the "self" he'd spent a lifetime maintaining and protecting was disappearing. An illusion . . . In the same way one experiences contentment at the end of a long prayer, Ganesha Ashanti Sinclair became aware that his body was effectively gone and clung to it no more; how arrogant to think it ever had been "his," even after being evicted from it 118 days before! (His guru always told him that we are only "renting" anyway—"Body like hotel," he'd say.) His strange new predicament was no cause for panic, because something truly miraculous had happened and Ganesha knew he was blessed and would soon slip into the masterpiece of the Great Mystery itself. There were so many gifts along the way! He'd learned to love his tenant as well, that tragic little girl, raped and murdered at age eleven. He'd laughed at her sweet, funny ways, marveled at her memories, laughed with her until they were as one. Now, hurtling toward the *moment of balance,* he couldn't find "himself" at all—the very liberation his guru had always spoken of. His only duty now was to serve, to help Rhonda find her way.

To free them both.

The desolate farmhouse was an hour and a half northwest of the Twin Cities, in the unincorporated community of Jacobs Prairie, along Stearns County Road 2 near Cold Spring.

The sixty-eight-year-old man who murdered Rhonda Whittle in 1984 was in the middle of attacking a fourteen-year-old runaway he'd met on the Internet and drugged at a motel when the wiry black yogi, his Ford Escort left a half mile outside the farm's perimeter, began an unstoppable jog toward the house. His locomotion was so powerful that when he crashed through the heavy door, it broke off its hinges. The girl's assailant jumped from the bedroom window and ran to his weathered old Mercedes turbo-diesel. (The cracked pink phone of the abductee still lay in the backseat along with her jeans and underwear.) The old man always left the key in the ignition and a weapon under the floor mat of the passenger seat.

Ganesha sprinted through the house, ignoring the still unconscious runaway, her arms and legs tied to bedposts. Just then, the bathroom door opened. Standing there was a thirty-something woman with the sixty-something death's head of a meth addict. She held out her hands in submission. "He said he wasn't going to hurt her! I didn't know, I didn't know!" She shouted it over and over, as if repetition would inspire belief. Ganesha leapt like a tiger, butting her head until it pulped before jumping out the window himself.

The old man dug beneath the seat for the gun, but it was tucked out of reach.

He looked in the rearview as Ganesha appeared, muttering *Crazyass nigger picked the wrong one to fuck with* as he fired up the Benz and peeled out. He would circle back and run him over. While reveling over his escape and the anticipation of the kill, he was startled by a jolt—his pursuer had impossibly leapt atop the trunk and was holding on to the groove at the base of the rear window. *Piece of shit fuckin' nigger!* The old man fishtailed, but at sixty-eight his reflexes weren't primo and the ground was sludgy from the rain. He lost control and shimmied into a tree. Staggering out, he saw that his stalker had been thrown from the car. He went to open the Benz's back door so that he could get the gun out from under the passenger seat but by the time he did, Rhonda was upon him.

"Ain't keep no money here! Ain't keep no money here!"

Rhonda smiled and the old man had his first real look at the assassin, a skinny, preternaturally calm young black, his scalp slick with blood from the bedroom battering.

"What do you want?" he said, terrified.

His pursuer answered in an eerie, little girl's voice, "Please don't hurt me please, Mister! I just want to go home! I want my Mommy."

The panicked quarry backed away (he was able to because Rhonda allowed him) and then ran—not to the house but toward the road bordering the eighteen-acre property.

Seeing the approaching car, the old man quickened his faltering pace. Someone was either lost or trespassing—no one had visited in years, not by consent or invitation, except once when a cop asked some dumb questions— and for the first time in the decade he'd owned the place, he was glad of it. *More* than glad because he wasn't in the best shape. He was having trouble breathing and his feet were so numb with cold that he was beginning to have trouble standing; the old man knew that if he stopped moving it would be the end. When he saw that two people were in the car, he grew hopeful. He scrambled toward them, yelling *Halp! Halp!*, and took a quick look over his shoulder.

The nigger was gaining but taking his sweet time.

"Halp!" he screamed, as Lydia and Daniel emerged from their car. "He's trying to kill me!"

Rhonda was on him in seconds.

She held him down and whispered in his ear. The old man listened in horror, pivoting his head as best he could to mutely plead to the trespassing couple. They remained at their car, watching. In the anarchy of coming death, he feebly grappled with a question: *Why don't they help? Are they a part of it? They all come to rob and kill me?* He ran out of the time required to solve such a riddle. His attention returned to the still-whispering assailant, blood from his lacerated scalp now dripping into the old man's mouth, covering it in red lipstick like the smear of a mischievous child who'd broken into her mother's makeup kit.

Maya took a small step toward them, but her brother put his hand on her arm, gently holding her back.

It was the old man's turn to whisper, but only Rhonda heard his last words.

4.

Ganesha was listless while Daniel washed him in the tub.

Lydia tended to the runaway, who was still asleep. She was joyous that the girl would live. *She'll never have to go to a Meeting,* she thought. *She'll never be on the train having lemonade.* She loosened the straps that bound her but didn't remove them. Lydia worried that after they left, she might start thrashing and fall from the bed, hurting herself.

Daniel dragged the dead woman to an adjacent room so the girl wouldn't have to see that when she came to. He wore gloves—a chapter in the *Guide* warned about leaving evidence, though being a cop made his precautions automatic. He wasn't sure how careful Rhonda had been but strongly doubted that the yoga instructor was in the fingerprint database of criminal offenders. When they thought he was in good enough shape to drive, they walked Rhonda to his car. Lydia had the temerity to ask him what all the whispering was about. The landlord Ganesha told her that Rhonda wanted to know the details of how she'd been killed. She wanted to know what the old man had done to her. The old man told her that she'd been drugged—apparently his M.O.—which was why Rhonda was so confused about what happened and kept bringing it up at Meetings. From the moment she was abducted to the moment she died, the little girl didn't have a sentient thought.

It never occurred to Ganesha *or* Rhonda to ask Daniel and Lydia what they happened to be doing there; nor did it occur to the siblings to pose the same question themselves. The excitement of the day superseded the meaning behind Maya's mirage of an appointment near St. Cloud that crystallized into the powerful vision of a remote farm in Jacobs Prairie, sixteen miles away. But Daniel sensed that something was troubling her. He had an inkling of what it was but chose to let it go.

At the gate, Lydia told Daniel to hang back because she wanted Rhonda to leave first. Rhonda waved to them as he drove out. On the highway, they stayed as close to him as they could, but when they got past the 94, he was swallowed up by traffic.

"We lost him," she said.

"Don't worry. He'll be fine."

"Are you sure? He was super shaky."

"Well, duh. But that's probably normal."

"What the fuck is *normal*."

"I mean normal for right after a *moment of balance*. We'll see him at the Sunday night Meeting."

"Ya think?"

"No *way* he's going to miss getting a birthday cake."

Twenty minutes outside Minneapolis–St. Paul International, the bossy little sister directed him to veer off the highway. She wanted to stop at Waite Park, "where Lydia's parents are from."

"Not a great idea," he said.

He knew that Lydia hadn't seen them since they came to stay, a few days after she killed the Tom Ford lookalike outside Tim Hortons.

"I didn't say I wanted to *visit*," she said. "I just want to see the house."

"What's on your mind, babe? Is there something about what happened back there that you're having a problem with?"

"A problem?" she said acidly. "Damn *straight* I'm having a problem. I'm having a problem that Rhonda killed someone he wasn't *supposed* to."

"The woman?"

"Yeah, the *woman*."

"I get that. And it's a shame. But shit happens."

"Really? That's just part of the deal? I don't *think* so. Annie never talked about it. Annie never said, 'Oh, by the way, sometimes innocent people die during the *moment of balance*. I'm sorry, Daniel, but it just doesn't feel right.'"

"I hear what you're saying," he said, trying to placate.

"That's *not* what we're here for. We're here to make responsible parties accountable."

"I see your point." He was drawing on a technique that he learned in couples therapy with Rachelle. "But shit, Lydia—you don't know anything about that woman at the farm or the evil shit she was up to."

"And I don't *care*. She could be the biggest scumbag in the world, but she wasn't involved in what happened to Rhonda."

"Maybe she was."

"That's bullshit and you know it. She was not *involved*—which means she didn't deserve to die."

"Blame it on the Great Mystery," he said wryly.

"Fuck off."

"Are you God now, Lydia? Is that what you think? That all of this—whatever it is that's happened to us—makes us God?"

"I don't want to talk about it anymore."

She'd been guiding him through the streets and finally told him to park. Lydia slunk in her seat. It was raining but the storm abated. She stole glances at a redbrick house.

"Stay down," he said.

"Why should I?"

"Oh come on," he chastised. "The day's been complicated enough."

"I'm still Lydia," she sighed. "And I miss my mom and dad. Don't you miss yours, Daniel?"

"They've been dead awhile. Not a lot of love lost."

"Sometimes I miss them *so much* . . . and what about *our* parents? We never even drove by our old house in the Falls. Why *haven't* we, Troy? For fuck's sake, it's five minutes from the substation!"

"You know what the Porter said. It's a distraction to our mission."

"I don't care about our mission!"

"You know you don't mean that, Maya."

"I'm sorry, I'm sorry!" she cried. "But don't you want to see it again, Troy? Don't you want to play there? Don't you want to see your room?" He solemnly touched her hand as she wept. "Don't you want to see them again? Mom and Dad?—"

"Maya—it's time to go. We really need to get home."

"Home!" she said, bitterly. "Wherever that is."

As he pulled away, Lydia gazed longingly back at the house where she'd spent her childhood. "I guess I should be grateful—they had me a lot longer than Maya's parents did . . ." He was about to turn the corner when she shouted, "Wait! Go slow, go slower, Daniel, please? I know that . . . I have a feeling I'm never going to see them again—" The sobbing overtook her and Daniel knew the best thing to do was get out of there. He sped through the intersection as she stared helplessly out the rear window.

It didn't look like anyone was home anyway.

SAVASANA

I.

When they arrived at the Sunday Meeting, Rhonda was sitting in his usual place in the semicircle of chairs. (Daniel winked at Lydia, as if to say "Told you so.") Thus far, José was the only one who had graduated, but his absence made the room feel empty. There hadn't been any newbies in weeks and when Maya asked the Porter about that, she said, "It happens. Actually, when you and Troy got here, we had more customers than usual."

Then, in she walked—tousled, tiny, on edge.

Maya caught a glimpse of her on the afternoon the Meeting had been disrupted; when Annie rushed outside to see about the fuss (and to rescue Bumble), Maya left her seat to watch the little drama from the door. Now the very same girl tiptoed in, looking about as peculiar, morose and defeated as could be. Annie appeared surprised, digging in her purse for the newcomer's hibernating *Guide*, even before she stood to give her a proper greeting.

She was short and malformed. It seemed like she didn't have any shoulders, let alone a collarbone, and was very, very young, at least as far as Meeting standards went. She nodded a painfully shy hello to the group so they'd at least stop staring. Maya was instantly charmed, in spite of herself. When it came "Winston's" turn—the name Annie introduced her by, though Maya heard the girl call herself "Honeychile" on the day she tres-passed with her school friend—she candidly explained what was wrong with her. "I lisp on account of my still having baby teeth." Then she puffed up her chest and proudly announced, "I have the same thing as Dustin, from *Stranger Things*." No one but Violet (who blurted out, "I *love* that show!") seemed to know what she was referring to. Winston-Honeychile went on to share her puzzlement at "whatever the *fudge* happened to me," adding that she thought it was "really scary but kind of cool." Annie told her they'd talk more about it privately when the Meeting ended.

Maya found herself paying extra-close attention to Dabba Doo when it came his time to share.

He wore his customary professorial tweed ensemble—and was shoeless, as usual. It was Maya's opinion that *all* children liked to go barefoot; she idly wondered why Dabba Doo was the only one who had the brilliant idea. (She got the feeling Annie would put a stop to it if any of the others fol-lowed suit.) He told the room that he was becoming depressed—"not really depressed but a little *worried*. Not worried, but . . . *concerned*"—about the fact that he'd been there for so long yet didn't seem to be any closer to "crossing the threshold." He was afraid that he'd reached an impasse. Maya and Troy exchanged glances because Dabba Doo was expressing the same fears they were having themselves. "I can't help but feel," he said, "that the passion I had in the first months about reaching my *moment of balance* is beginning to fade. It pains me even to say it! But I *do* feel caught between worlds, so to speak—I seem to be half who I *used* to be and half Dabba Doo—half landlord, half tenant! I find myself sitting at home waiting for that child to just *take over* and give me marching orders! But he won't, he won't, he won't. The boy just *won't*, and I'm starting to worry he may never . . . oh, I know he's *here*, it's not that he's gone away. I feel his feelings, think his thoughts, I even eat his precious gummy bears—which by the way, I have always loathed! But I only eat the green ones." Everyone laughed. He turned to the Porter and said, "All that opens up a hornet's nest of ques-tions, doesn't it?"

She smiled uncomfortably (so it seemed to Maya) and said, "I think it'd be best if we spoke after the Meeting"—an aside that was on its way to becoming code for the Deep Shit Ahead zone.

"I guess I'm kind of having the opposite problem," said Violet. Annie actually sighed with relief—at last, some good news! As the young woman spoke, Lydia assessed her perfect Scandinavian features with a covetous adult eye; she'd always wanted to have that kind of beauty. "I've been feel-ing so strong and confident . . . what's the word? *Resolute.* I think my *mo-ment of balance* is getting really close. It's just a *feeling* but it's really, really strong . . . All I can say is, you better get my birthday cake ready, Porter! And can it please be angel food?"

Everyone oohed and ahhed, spontaneously volunteering the kind of cakes they wanted for their birthdays. After refreshments ("Winston" sat alone with her untouched lemonade and cookies), they read aloud from the *Guide* for a while. Then it was time for Rhonda's birthday speech.

He wore a skullcap to cover the gashes on his head. So much seemed to have gone wrong of late that Annie could hardly conceal her thrill that a *moment of balance* had been achieved in the midst of "haywire"—that another one of her children had lost their blueness and would soon be reboarding for the final voyage.

"I want to bless everyone in this room," he said, before turning to Win-ston, who stared timidly at the floor. "And I'd like to say a few words of welcome to the newcomer. It *is* scary at first but then gets cool, like you said. It gets *very* cool. So, trust the process. And trust the *Porter.* She'll take care of you. Annie takes care of everyone!"

Maya caught Dabba Doo smiling at her and bashfully smiled back.

"It was wonderful having you here," said Annie. "You were—*are*—a lovely, supportive presence."

"Back at ya," said Rhonda.

"Now, who would the landlord Ganesha wish to thank?" she said.

"Well, I'd like to thank my guru, the man who put me on the path to Kriya Yoga. Annie, I know you've said before that what we do in this room isn't related to the spiritual—not directly—but I can't help believe there's karma here too. There: I said it! Whatcha gonna do, throw me out of the

Meeting?" The room tittered, without exactly knowing why. "Too late for that! I guess I've already thrown *myself* out . . . And of course I want to thank—and say goodbye—to my folks, who gave birth to me. Would never have gotten this opportunity without 'em. And I especially want to thank my twin brother, who's more or less doing life without parole. God bless you, Curtis. May you find peace in the madness of incarceration, and I know that's possible. Because we're all in some kind of prison. Most of the time it's our heads. But even our bodies are prisons . . . So I guess it's time to say goodbye to *this* body. I'm so grateful I had these extra few months to honor it."

Annie smiled at the wisdom of her pupil's words. Still looking into his eyes, she said, "And Rhonda? Your turn. Who would *you* like to thank?"

"First and foremost, Ganesha Ashanti Sinclair—oh my God, you rocked! Though I wish I'd had a landlord who was older . . . That's probably just Ganesha still trying to say, 'Don't take me, girl, I'm too young to be a land-lord, take someone else!' But it's true, Annie, I *do* wish it wasn't Ganesha. He was way too young to have had a stroke. My grandma had one but she was sixty-eight. And she didn't even die!"

Winston sporadically glanced from the floor to the players, uncompre-hending but taking everything in.

"It's time," said Annie. She nodded to Violet (Lydia realized who she reminded her of: a less voluptuous Scarlett Johansson) and the gorgeous techie skipped to the table, eagerly lighting the candles Bumble had already stuck in the banana cream cake. "Tell us what song you'd like—your choice."

He scratched his chin. "Well, it ain't gonna be 'Macarena,' I can tell you that." Everyone but Honeychile laughed at the remark. "Tell you what," said Rhonda. "Let's do something *different*. Since I won't be seeing y'all again."

"Just make sure we know the words," shouted Daniel.

"Oh, I think you might," said Rhonda. "Obscure as they may be." Vio-let sat the cake down in front of him, on the little table the sentry brought over. He closed his eyes and softly began.

"'Happy birthday to me, happy birthday to me'—"

The others joined in, and sang the roof off.

He blew them out to raucous applause and then drew the palms of his hands together in prayer.

"Namaste," he said softly.

2.

After the Meeting, the Porter spoke quietly to Winston while a few others lingered. Maya and Violet girl-talked in a corner and Daniel made cordial conversation with Dabba Doo.

Annie draped a mothering arm around the girl's shoulderless shoulders. The poor thing was shaking. The Porter made the required *more shall be revealed* pitch but felt like the captain of a ship with broken masts. She told Winston how brave she was to have returned and urged her to keep coming back—yet had nothing more in her arsenal. Winston let her cheek be kissed before slinking out the same way she slunk in. Maya smiled pitifully at her as she passed by, a smile that seemed to say, "So sorry about the absolute *clusterfuck* you've found yourself in—that we've *all* found ourselves in!"— but was focused on speaking to Annie. Accosting the Porter, she said, "I have something I need to say."

"Dabba Doo is next, Maya. You'll have to wait your turn." Sometimes she had to talk to them that way. They were children after all and needed to mind their manners.

Maya balled up her fists in a fury and said, "Rhonda did something very, very *bad*."

"Please lower your voice!"

"She killed someone she shouldn't have—"

Annie looked like she'd been stung. "What are you saying?"

"Someone was there—someone else during her *moment of balance*—who had nothing to *do* with Rhonda's murder! And she killed her anyway."

"That just isn't possible," said Annie, in disbelief.

"It *is*, it *happened*. Ask my brother!"

The ship was foundering and the Porter felt herself going overboard. At the moment, further details—like how Maya and Troy had come upon such knowledge—were insignificant.

"It was *wrong*," said Maya. "That's not supposed to happen, Annie—is it?"

"I'm not sure." She was wondering how much of "haywire" to divulge when her mouth broke the impasse. "But all of this may have something to do with my leaving."

"Leaving? For where?"

"I'm—I'm dying, Maya."

"No!" she cried.

"*Please* lower your voice."

From across the room, Daniel and Dabba Doo turned to look before self-consciously resuming their conversation.

"What do you mean, 'dying'?"

"I don't know when, but soon."

"Can't you come back? Like we did?"

"It doesn't work that way."

"Why not?"

"It just doesn't, not for Porters. Anyway, I've been preparing. I've known about it a long, long time."

"But what will happen to *us*?" she implored.

The little-girlness of her entreaty broke Annie's heart.

"You mustn't worry, darling. You'll be well taken care of." Maya was weeping now. "There's already someone coming—do you hear me, sweetheart? Someone's coming to help and soon you will all meet the new Porter . . . and when that happens—when the new Porter's here—everything will be made right again. So please be patient and please don't worry! Be patient and *trust*, can you promise me that? Because you—well, you and your brother don't have much time." She grabbed Maya's wrists. "And if you stop trusting, you won't find the person who did this to you. Do you understand that?" Maya shook her head. "And I'd appreciate you keeping this to yourself. I'll talk about it with everyone at the next Meeting." Maya nodded distractedly. "I don't want the others to know until I know a little more myself. You can tell Daniel—I expect you will—but no one else, because it will only upset them. Do I have your promise? That you'll keep this to yourself until the next Meeting?"

"Yes."

"Thank you."

Maya screwed up her face in sorrow and remorse. "I'm so sorry! I didn't mean it when I asked about what would happen to us! I didn't mean to be so selfish."

"Stop it now," said Annie, hugging her. "I *love* you and everything is going to be fine. See you Tuesday. Now run along."

The Porter nodded to Dabba Doo that she was ready for their conference. As Maya walked to the door, she passed Dabba Doo and her elbow brushed his.

"*We need to talk,*" she whispered.

3.

For the final time, Ganesha Ashanti Sinclair went home to his subdivided loft in Core City, not far from Cliff Bell's, the club where he occasionally played jazz.

After the *moment of balance,* he felt less like Rhonda—though it wouldn't have been accurate to say that he felt more like Ganesha either. All identities, all forms, were receding. Annie once told him, "After the *moment* is done, you will come to know a new kind of serenity." She said the feeling would be unlike any he had experienced "in this life"—and it was true. He tried comparing it to the peace he'd felt at the ashram in Bangalore but this was something else, otherworldly and indifferent. Impersonal . . . Again, his heart and thoughts touched upon his parents, his twin and all the people he had loved. He recalled his enemies too, real and imagined, closing his eyes to watch the magic lantern of characters pass before him—an extravaganza of poignant beings caught in the majestic dance of suffering and bliss, of birth and death, choreographed by the Source. Everyone was alive but everyone was already dead, like the tale Krishna tells Arjuna in the *Bhagavad Gita*. He felt so privileged to have been chosen.

He made a final cup of tea.

He unfurled the yoga mat on the floor of the sparsely furnished living room. Before he lay in savasana, the corpse pose, he examined the grain of the wood floor that he had proudly sanded himself. It contained the universe.

Such was the last wonderment he had on Earth.

TRESPASSERS

I.

In his life, Willow had worn love in all sizes—small, medium and large. A few times, he'd tried to wear all three at once.

But *no* woman had ever been kinder to him than Dixie Rose Cavanaugh. She felt his woundedness and was mindful of his moods, knowing when to go toward him and when to back away. (She hadn't become a nurse for nothing, he thought.) Neither wanted to swamp each other—they were happy to have separate places to retreat to—but both thoroughly enjoyed their overnights a few times a week. That worked out anyway because Dixie's migraines forced her into solitude and darkness, sometimes for days. She was a night owl and liked to read for a few hours before she slept; while she perused her Kindle, she multitasked by petting him with a free hand until he passed out. The first time she did that, after an hour of hypnotic caresses, he guiltily said, "It's okay, babe. You don't have to." Dixie said it calmed her. "I do it to my cat," she said, with a bewitching smile. "It chills us both out." He came to believe that it wasn't a codependent, OCD thing, and only an expression of love. *What a concept*, as Adelaide liked to say. He didn't believe that Dixie loved him and told himself that he didn't really care. But he was starting to get feelings and wasn't sure what to make of that. It seemed too easy, too simple, too perfect.

Maybe that was true love's secret.

Once, in the middle of the night, she did something extraordinary. As he lay back down after having a pee, Dixie's hand reached out from deep sleep to stroke him. How was that even possible? He tried returning the kindness by holding her in his arms when she had "pre-migraine night-mares." She yelped while dreaming, and he would shush her and rock her until her screen went blank. She never remembered the demons that gave chase. Her dark side appealed to Willow and made him want her more.

He thought about Dixie, and all the women in his life, to distract him-self during the half-hour drive to Farmington Hills. He needed to occupy his brain because he was on his way to see the Rummers, an errand that filled him with trepidation. Willow had been astonished when he learned they still lived so close to the ground zero of the Falls; for some reason, he imag-ined they would have moved to the farthest ends of the Earth. Wasn't that what *he* would have done? Maybe not, because the detective knew it was human nature to stay close to the land of the ghosts one still loved. Even the peasants of Chernobyl refused to leave, their desire so strong that the gov-ernment could do nothing to prevent them from staying.

In a different set of circumstances, the Cold Case Kids would have been the ones making the trip to interview them, but it was incumbent on Wil-low to make the pilgrimage. He'd been with them on that hellish day and all through the hellish nights that followed, and owed them that much. The cruel, inescapable truth was that upon the disappearance of their kids, Elaine and Ronnie Rummer became sacrificial goats, spit-roasted and carved by the parents of Saggerty Falls and beyond. For a few weeks, it felt like the entire nation embraced the myth of the burnt offering because one couldn't help having the primitive belief that those children's abduction and likely slaughter were an inoculation, a protective necklace that could be worn to ward off the same fate befalling one's own.

The detective wanted to get the lay of the land as well—to reopen his heart and strange gifts to the tragedy. When he made the call from his office, he wasn't sure how they'd respond. From what he had learned about Elaine at the barbecue, he doubted that she'd be in any kind of shape to meet, and Willow had actually begun to worry that the news of dredging up the case might cause a domino effect ending in her suicide. He was grateful when Ronnie, not Elaine, picked up the phone. They small-talked and Willow tested the waters. He asked about stopping over to say hello.

"Of course, Dubya, come on by! We'd love to see you."

He sounded weirdly insouciant but Willow didn't want to read too much into it.

T he day had turned windy and haunting.
      As he stepped from the car, a premonitory image flooded him (as they often did), but without blue mist, without "the Blue Death." Simply that of Elaine in bed, cocooned in darkness, a bright patch of light at her feet.

Ronnie Rummer opened the door before he could knock.

They hadn't seen each other since the event and the week of its aftermath. In the overeager way of old friends long separated, they took each other's measure, downloading the version they saw before them while tweaking, updating and deleting the one they'd been carrying in their minds' eye. Ronnie had a little more work to do than Willow in that regard, because the detective's rugged travels on Alcohol Road had done some damage to the vehicle. Dubya's awareness of his own haggardness was rekindled in Ronnie's wide-eyed look, even as his gaze softened with warmth and affection.

The man was genuinely glad to see him, almost deliriously so, and it struck Willow that his former neighbor may not have had a visitor in a long, long while. What really took him aback was his host's sheer normalcy, if one could call it that—he was so affable, so upbeat and well-groomed. Willow had imagined stepping into the broken house of a broken man, but realized in an instant how silly that was, and overwrought; the wound never heals yet people find ways to move on. What about Elaine, though? Her "way" must have wreaked all sorts of havoc on the man . . . Still, it *was* a bit

topsy-turvy. If they'd been put together in a lineup it was Willow, not Ronnie, who'd have been fingered as the casualty and lost soul.

They shared a pleasant half hour, with Ronnie doing most of the talking.
He extolled the quiet life in Farmington Hills and waxed proud over the
tool-fitting business that "allows me to spend most of my time at home,
which I've come to view as the best revenge." When he finally asked after
Adelaide, Willow said, "She's great. You know, I actually work for Owen
now"—a segue designed not only to get the old *scandale* of his divorce above-
board and behind them but to serve as entrée to a discussion of the revisiting
of the case. Ronnie didn't bite, which seemed strange. If he already knew
that Willow was heading up the task force—hence the house call—he wasn't
yet ready or willing to go there.

They were getting nearer to the heart of the visit when Ronnie said,
"How's Pace doing?" Willow almost whipped out his phone to show him his
daughter's picture—Larkin's too—but thought better of it. He didn't want
to rub the continuity of life in his face. Ronnie told him that Pace had been
sending birthday and holiday cards for years, something she'd never shared
with Willow. Through it all, the elephant in the room was Elaine's absence.
He would ask about her in a minute; first things first.

"I don't know if you read about it in the paper but the City Council
voted to fund a Cold Case unit. Since I had somewhat of a career doing that
in Manhattan, Owen asked me to come aboard."

"Well, isn't that something?" he said, with that Stepfordy smile. The
detective got the sense he would have reacted the same if he told him he'd
been knighted by the queen.

"And we've decided to reopen the case."

"Uh huh"—again, with a curious, shiny affectlessness.

"It's kind of interesting how all this came about . . ."

His words trailed off because at the moment he was about to explain
how it wasn't his idea at all but that of his recruits, Willow realized the
intense irrelevance of those details.

"Well, we've made our peace with it, Dubya," said Ronnie, this time
wincing a smile. "Elaine and I made our peace, best we could. One thing I

have to say is . . . I just don't think I'd be here—well, I *know* I wouldn't, and I think I can speak for my wife—we would not be here without the Lord Our Savior. He provided comfort in our darkest hours. And boy, we've had a number of them."

"I don't doubt."

"We *still* have those times—but through His mercy, they're fewer and farther between."

"I've been circling 'faith' myself the last few years," said Willow, trying to make a bridge.

"Come to church with us! We have a marvelous pastor."

"I'd like to, Ronnie. I'd like that very much."

"If the Lord has shown me anything, it's that all happens for a reason. I know that's become a cliché but most clichés have tremendous power, have you noticed? We call them clichés because they contain essential truths that sometimes are pretty tough to wrap your head around. The more simple a truth is—well, it's human nature to either ignore it or make it complicated. So we turn these beautiful truths into greeting cards. But our—the children . . ." His voice broke. "There was a reason and it's not for us to know. It's for Him and Him alone. And that's enough for me. It wasn't at first—oh, not for a *long* time. I was too damn arrogant. But it is now. It's enough. How little we know, Willow. How little."

"I don't think we're meant to."

"That's right, sir. Because He's too big and we're too small. More will be revealed—there's another greeting card phrase for you, but it's a good'n. If I wasn't in polite company," he said with a wink and a laugh, "I'd say more will be revealed *on Judgment Day*—but I wouldn't want anyone who was listening to think I'm a kook."

"Nothing kooky about you, my friend. I heard a lot of wisdom there."

Willow felt comfortable enough to dance around some memories of that afternoon. He lightly touched on the Persons of Interest—Ebenezer Jamison and some known felons who lived in the area at the time. He even brought up Grundy, Roy Eakins's challenged son. He had to start somewhere and you never knew the quality of light that would refract through the prism of someone else's memory. The detective was open to both the hard facts *and* what he called the "ineffables." It was part and parcel of the black art.

"Ebenezer was short a few cylinders but didn't have a mean bone in his body," said Ronnie. "I'd have never sent the kids over there if he did. And Grundy? They jumped the shark with that one. When Grundy Eakins got thrown in the mix, that was the day I knew in my heart that we'd never find who took my babies. That big lunk of a damaged boy? And he was *there*, at the barbecue, remember? I told Owen, 'You're grasping at straws, come on, man!' None of those felons and perverts ever came to a hill of beans. The one thing I do know, Willow, is that it was someone outside the community. From the outside—the palm prints proved it! Whoever did it is in jail or running a successful business or dead. Only the Lord our God knows."

Every man in Saggerty Falls had given a palm print to the department for comparison to the one found on Maya's unicorn birthday card. At the time, it struck Willow as an emotional, largely symbolic act of solidarity, though in later years it bothered him that the women of the Falls hadn't been asked to do the same.

Willow started to feel like he was flying a little too close to the flame. He made the decision to come back with Daniel and Lydia in tow, and mentally prepared to take his leave.

That was when Ronnie said, "Would you like to see Elaine?"

"Well, yes!"

"She apologizes for not coming out. I'll walk you back and you can say hello."

2.

Ronnie brought him to the bedroom door and disappeared.

Willow's heart was in his throat. He let his eyes adjust and then saw her lying there, just like the image he'd had before Ronnie greeted him at the door. Was she sleeping?

"Come in, come in!" she said, without moving a muscle. Like a ventrilo-quist's dummy . . .

He walked to the bed.

"Hi, Ellie."

"Well, for goodness sake, Willow, take off your damn shoes! Lordie, do you know what kind of gunk lives on the bottom of our shoes? I read about it online and it's worse than a crocodile's mouth. Worse than a toilet!" she laughed. "That's why I love the Japanese culture. They take their shoes off when they come home, leave 'em right at the door. That's just common sense, don't you think?"

"I do, absolutely," he said with a smile.

Same old feisty Elaine.

(The patch of light at her feet was the little television.)

She turned her head to look at him. "Willow Wylde—my, my, my. How good it is to see you."

"Nice to be seen," he said, falling back on the AA retort.

"And how kind of you to visit! I haven't seen my husband so excited since the gal from Mary Kay tried to sell him—well, it must've been the *whole line*. She was here for three hours. If I didn't know Ronnie better, I'd have thought . . . maybe he was interested."

He chuckled and said, "I made a play for *you* a few times. And I wasn't even working for Mary Kay."

"No, but you were drinking like a fish. You were a *naughty*, naughty boy."

"Still am, I hope."

"That remains to be seen," she said flirtily. "Now, do you remember me trying to hook you up with Penny Lancaster?"

"Oh do I."

She got titillated. "Do you mean to say, naughty man, that something happened between you two without my knowledge?"

"Why don't we put it this way: something happened, but we were so wasted at the time that it may have been without *our* knowledge."

She howled at that. From the side of his eye Willow caught a glimpse of

Ronnie lingering in the hall. It probably did him good to hear his wife laugh with abandon.

They bantered some more and then got quiet while Elaine stared at the TV. One of those girl-chat daytime talk shows was on, with too much innuendo and energy. She paid strict attention, tittering along with the studio audience. It gave Willow a chance to sneak a look at her disfigurement. The nose was mutilated; a scar like a yellow lightning bolt bisected her face. Reading glasses rested atop a head that was bald in patches. (Afterward, when Ronnie walked him to the car, he jokily apologized for "my wife's wacky hairdo.") Elaine later explained that when Troy and Maya were taken from her, she started pulling it out by the handful, and the habit persisted.

When a commercial came on, she lowered the volume and said, "Have you been well?" The question came from the heart.

"Yes—pretty well," said Willow. "I guess you could say I've had my time in the 'dark wood' but I'm beginning to see the light. At least I hope it's the light."

"And not the flames of Hell?" she said with a laugh.

How to speak in front of these people, this woman, of dark woods and light, of renewal? Yet it didn't feel like a faux pas. He could see that Elaine appreciated the intimacy.

"You know," she said. "I have my reasons for wanting to see you—oh, of course I wanted to see you, Willow, I love you—but that's not what I mean." She struggled with her thoughts. "You see, I've been *thinking* of you, I've been wanting to *tell* you something. And when Ronnie said you called and were coming for a visit, I thought, *Well, that's interesting. See how the universe works?* Did my husband give you his spiel about everything happening for a reason?"

"Most definitely."

"It's become the official mantra around this house."

"A pretty good one too."

"When Ronnie said that *Willow Wylde* was coming to call, well, I just *knew*. Because it's been on my mind—I didn't even tell him about it. I've already put my husband through enough." She grew thoughtful. "How I love that man. Ronnie likes to say that God never gives you more than you can handle, but I think our Creator might have said that before He made *me*."

She patted a spot on the bed and told Willow to come sit. When he did, she leaned over and began to whisper, as if aware that her husband might be within earshot.

"What I wanted to say . . . what I've been *feeling*, Willow—and I can't pinpoint when it started—"

She turned to him full-face and he saw her ruined features in the half light. Her skin looked like the polished stones he used to collect as a boy, embedded with ordered, fossilized rows of spindly creatures.

"I *feel* them, Willow! I feel my *children*, I know that they're here! And it's—I know that I sound like a character out of . . . like JoBeth Williams in *Poltergeist*. It's a *wonderful* movie and it *speaks* to me. Lord forgive me, but *Poltergeist* speaks to Elaine Rummer! When that gust of wind blows through JoBeth and she says that she *felt* her baby—she could *smell* her—that her baby's smell was all over her . . . well, it's the same, Willow, it's the very same with me!" Tears filled her eyes. "Look at me, Willow! *Look at me.*" She took his hands in hers. "Who could live after that? Who could do what I've done to myself and live—what I did to myself and to *Ronnie*? Well, I can tell you, for the first time since it happened . . . I can tell you for the *first time*, Willow, *now*, that I want to *live*. Does that make any sense? Do you believe me, *can* you believe me? You see, JoBeth saw her baby again and I know I won't see mine. This I know. But I *feel* them. And I want to *live* so that I can *keep* feeling them. I can smell them, Willow, I can smell my babies!" She laughed with joy as she wept. "Because they are *here*. I don't know how and I don't *care* to know but they are *here*. And that's what I wanted to tell you, that's what I *needed* to tell you. I had to tell *someone* and the Lord chose *you*." She turned away and laid her head on the pillow. "I am not a madwoman."

"I don't think that, Elaine. Not for one second."

"Then God bless. God bless you and yours."

Ronnie quietly appeared. Willow presumed he'd been eavesdropping and prudently decided it was time for his wife to rest. Elaine saw him and smiled. She'd exhausted herself.

"Troy wanted to be a policeman, didn't he, Ronnie—did you know that, Willow? Oh, he'd have made a fine one. He was always protecting his sister. One day he cut a little sheriff's badge out of tinfoil and followed Maya everywhere she went, shooting all the imaginary bad guys! Isn't that the sweetest thing? And did I ever tell you about the time I came home and Maya was in the garden looking terribly sad? You remember, don't you, Ronnie. I went over and said, 'What's the matter, darling?' and she led me to a spiderweb. Lordie, she was so unhappy! It wasn't really a web anymore—looking at it, you could hardly see what it once was. Maya was crying her little eyes out. She said that she touched it with her fingers but was too rough and it broke. That's what she told me, 'I broke it.' Then she said the dearest thing: 'Do you think the spider will mind?' I said, ''Course not! He'll make another one.' And Maya just looked at the web and looked at me and said, 'Well—I guess it's better than coming home to nothing.'"

She laughed and Willow shivered with emotion.

"Sweetheart," said Ronnie, "how about a nap? I'll cook a little something for dinner. If we're so honored, maybe Dubya will join us."

"Oh, please do!" said Elaine, turning to their guest.

"That's awfully kind but I think I'll have to take a rain check. I really should be getting back."

Elaine reached out and touched his hand again. "Thank you for coming. And thank you for listening to the ramblings of an old broad."

"It was so good to see you both," said the detective.

"G'bye, Willow Wylde. I'd let you kiss my good side," she said impishly. "If I had one. But as I say to Ronnie, hey, it's better than coming home to nothing. Though maybe it isn't."

He stopped at Early World to mull over the impressions of the afternoon—to integrate—and happened to sit in the same booth he shared with Annie, World's Greatest Volunteer.

Was he was on his way to becoming that too?

The Underworld's Greatest Volunteer . . .

He sensed the presence of Nana—sometimes beside him, sometimes sitting straight across, like Annie had—and it felt as if she were trying to say something to soothe him and somehow persuade, like she used to when she snuck into his room after the *ague*. But he couldn't make sense of her words.

It was nighttime when he got home.

He parked the car and sat listening to Mahler awhile, lingering on the image of the bedridden Elaine—the tragedy and, yes, the power and delirious beauty of that orphaned woman's confessions.

Grundy Eakins was rattling around in his head.

As he walked to his apartment, he detoured to Dixie's. He was about to knock, then thought, *I should probably take a shower and make myself pretty.* That's what Dixie was always saying, "Gimme a minute so I can make myself pretty." When he turned to leave, she ran out.

"Hi, babe!"

"Hello there, Darlin' Dixie."

"Sorry I didn't come over after work . . ."

"No worries."

"I could see you through the drapes but you were on the couch, all lost in detective-like thought. I didn't want to disturb."

"Saw me when?"

"An hour ago?"

"Go back in the house," he said, drawing his gun.

She did as she was told.

As he got closer, he saw that his front door was ajar.

He slowly pushed it open.

From the sofa, wrapped in darkness much like Elaine was, Annie said, "I'm running out of time—we both are. Soon all will be lost."

SINGLE ROOM OCCUPANCY

Annie invited him to her Skid Row SRO. He didn't want to go; he didn't want any part of this phantom that had invaded his untidily tidy life. She looked ill and her frailty laid siege to Willow's defenses—but that wasn't what compelled him to obey. As they drove in silence, he remembered something from an AA meeting at a church in downtown Wickenburg, during his stay at the Meadows. A woman shared that a normie asked her why she drank. She surprised herself by answering, "Because I have to."

Willow accepted the invitation because he had to.

Since their "official" meet-and-greet at Early World he'd done a lot of integrating, like it or not. During his workday, the conversation at the diner (hers, anyway, because she'd done all the talking) played nonstop in his head like esoteric Muzak; by night, it became a babble that disrupted his dreams. She'd had the audacity to announce to him his destiny—that he was to become midwife to wayward souls who returned, like so many pint-sized samurai, to dole out bloody, high-toned "moments of balance"! Apart from the complete, unfettered lunacy of it, the scenario sounded like nothing more than straight-up old-school revenge. He resisted succumbing to her bizarro entreaties and explanations, not wanting to sign up for her or anyone's folie à deux.

Yet as days went by the mysterious world she spoke of became less farfetched and the messenger took on indisputable gravitas. It wasn't only that she spoke of the train he rode in his dreams night after night (he could actually remember her bringing snacks and Tom Collinses to his cabin); no, it went deeper. Annie told him secret things no one else in the world could have known. She knew everything about his experience as a boy at the time of his grandmother's passing. All his life Willow had been hearing voices and communing with the dead. She told him that he possessed "powerful gifts," and he couldn't help getting puffed up when she said he'd been chosen to enlist in a strange mythology, one that would force him to swap the role of cowardly spectator for some kind of Joseph Campbell–sized uber-hero.

As batshit as it sounded, he couldn't deny his excitation.

I invited you to my home because that's what *my* mentor did. His name was Jasper—Jasper Kendrick Sebastian—and he ran a kind of boarding-house for people like me. Like us. A place where Porters trained under one roof. I'm not sure such a thing exists anymore; that was a different time. But it's always a different time, isn't it? One day Jasper took me to his room. I thought he was up to something nefarious! See, I was still having all sorts of doubts, just like you. But when I sat at the edge of his bed—the place where he slept and dreamed—all those doubts left me, just drifted away. I finally stopped fighting, stopped trying to understand. We say 'more shall be re-vealed,' not 'more shall be understood,' no? We're funny creatures. We buy a ticket on the train but don't think to ask where the paper for the ticket came from. We don't ask who set the price or how the engine operates or if the conductor will come to work. We never ask 'Why?'—we don't even want to know how it is that we awakened on *that* particular day and de-cided to take the train and not the bus—though we usually took the bus . . . all the dumb little things we never ask that come together to form 'consen-sus reality.' But aren't there a multitude of *other* realities? Ones we never notice? Doesn't that stand to reason? You see, we come to accept the world we live in, *this* world, and all of its phantasmagoric mysteries . . . but when presented with a new world, suddenly we're afraid. And we foolishly go about trying to 'understand' it, to make *sense* of it. That's how we adapt. When Jasper opened that new world to me, the world of the children, I became obsessed with *understanding* what it was all about. Which didn't work out so well! So finally, in spite of myself, I surrendered. I stopped trying to 'understand'—stopped wondering about my place in it. I stopped asking why the train existed and where it came from. How it 'worked,' why I'd been chosen . . .

"Those questions will fall away, Willow, I promise. You'll come to see there *are* no answers, not to why the dance began or when it will end or who made the steps. You'll stop asking why you have a certain partner—and when another dancer cuts in you won't protest. You'll just dance."

He felt a preternatural sense of calm as she spoke and for a moment contrasted the stillness of the room with the sounds of the street, with the known world's busy, beguiling banality.

"I didn't have your strength, Willow. I didn't have your special gifts. I certainly didn't have your life experience! You were able to push away the voices you heard by sheer will—I know the booze and drugs helped—but I couldn't, and the voices led me to Swarthmore, where I thank God Jasper found me. Once he took me in, I flourished. And there I was, released and rescued—saved!—but *still* I kept wondering, 'What exactly is this strange man asking of me?' Mind you, he'd been clear about the nature of my duties from the beginning: to orient and stabilize the children, to prepare them for their *moment of balance*. Nothing more, nothing less. But that wasn't good enough! We *are* funny creatures, Willow. Mad, arrogant creatures. Even from my dingy, forgotten room at the hospital, I was arrogant.

"The day he invited me to his room, I surrendered. The most poignant thing"—she dabbed the wetness in her eyes—"the most poignant thing was that in an instant I became a mother. I couldn't have children in *this* world but I became a fertile queen in *that* one, a mother to the lost boys and girls. And my heart rejoiced."

Without warning, her demeanor became grave and her expression hardened. While she was speaking, Annie managed to summon a girlish youthfulness; now she looked sickly again, deathly so. Her features grew taut, the face floating before him like a memento mori. Her jaw began to clench and tic.

"But something has gone terribly wrong . . . Jasper warned it would happen when my Portership was ending. He said that was a dangerous time—when things would go 'haywire.' He was reluctant to say more but I saw in his face that he'd been through such a time himself. It was the only thing he *couldn't* teach me and now I see why: it's up to the Porter to set things right. The battle is his or hers alone and no one else can fight it."

She leaned in close. He smelled her warm breath, fragrant with the spice of desperation.

"We need to move quickly! The train is about to derail—I worry that it already has. Only you can help the children already here. And the ones who are coming."

"But *what* has gone terribly wrong?" said Willow, in alarm.

All of his doubts had dissolved and he was fully inside Annie's dream.

"A brother and sister returned *together*, which has never happened . . . and one of my boys, Dabba Doo, has been here far too long—three times longer than he should, and that too has never occurred." Willow flickered in and out. One moment he was all in; the next, he saw her as if through the wrong end of a telescope. "And *worst* of all," she said, "I've begun asking myself those same useless questions again, the ones I had early in my apprenticeship. I know it's the fault of 'haywire' but knowing doesn't seem to make a whit of difference . . . I fear that I'm losing my faith, and I cannot afford for that to happen! I will *not* betray my mentor in such a way, nor will I betray *you* or the children under my care." She took a deep breath that he imagined being her last. "You see, Willow, I'm not well—the truth is, I'm dying. That's why you've come to me, to us. That's why you're here—"

"I'm so sorry," he said.

He felt a measure of shame, because the panic of abandonment that seized him at the prospect of her leaving him had temporarily eclipsed any feelings of empathy about her condition.

"You said you were asking yourself questions, Annie . . . what sort of questions?"

"I probably shouldn't say—you're too new, and it isn't right to burden you . . ." Her need to confide overruled the hesitation. "My children have never failed to achieve the *moment of balance*—but lately I've caught myself wondering, 'What happens if they don't?' What if they fail in their task of finding the ones who killed them? And what if the landlords—the bodies they've borrowed—are destroyed before they're able to assist them? If they're struck by an automobile or somehow disabled—which has never happened and in itself is unthinkable! It's a loss of faith I tell you . . . a Pandora's box of *What ifs* has blown open and hard as I try I cannot slam it shut . . . What if those who return confront their murderers, but the *moment of balance* somehow gets botched—and they're murdered *again* by the very one who once destroyed them? Is or isn't that a possibility, Willow?" She literally shook in distress and he couldn't discern if she expected him to answer. "And *larger* questions come, that aren't even germane. For example, are children the only ones who seek *moments of balance*? Why wouldn't everyone who'd ever been murdered do the same? And if that were true, it would stand to reason that Meetings are being held throughout the world"—she was hysterical now—"thousands and thousands and thousands of them! When I asked my mentor, he said that may well be true but that it wasn't my concern . . . which it isn't! Because we're meant to deal only with that which is in front of us, Willow; to ask for more is egotism, arrogance, faithlessness. But I *have* begun to reconsider all these things, I can't help myself!—can't sleep at night—worlds of Meetings I can never attend or know of, as if any of it makes a difference! These questions, these doubts are merely a symptom of 'haywire,' can you see? My mind is cluttered and disordered . . . Just this morning I was wondering: If my children don't complete their tasks, *then* what happens? Do those responsible for their deaths get away scot-free? That would be so unfair! Yet the very idea of 'fairness' is a notion of *our* world, not theirs, not the world of mystery—or is it? Can you see the quandary? I've even begun to question the *moment of balance* itself . . . because in the end, isn't the whole notion of 'getting away with' or 'not getting away with' murder a meaningless thing? Mystery cannot be fair, Willow, mystery just *is*. Mystery isn't meant for such a crude concept as fairness . . . and yet—*what will happen to the children*? What will happen to them if they don't succeed? Will they be in limbo? Or is 'limbo' just another crude and meaningless concept, a concept of *this* world . . . I tell you, it haunts me! I am haunted just like the mothers who lost their murdered babies . . ."

Annie went on to say that if she failed at her duties, she'd be killing her wards as surely as those who had slayed them. Then she calmed herself, apologizing for the outburst.

"Not a wonderful way to pass the torch to a new Porter," she said. She poured her tea with an unsteady hand, took a deep breath and smiled. Worry returned, furrowing her brow. This time it was as if she were think-ing out loud. "And there's a girl who's far too young. Adolescents are *never* landlords, they're too unstable to effect the *moment of balance*—too many hormones. And this one's unstable by nature . . ."

"Okay," nodded Willow, numb and overwhelmed. It was another way of saying *that's enough now.*

"There's only one thing I seem to know—just one thing."

"What's that, Annie?"

"It's time that you be properly introduced."

She closed her eyes and a charming little smile played across her face.

"It's time for you to meet the children."

DYSPHORIA

I.

Dr. Jacqueline Robart's supervisor told her about the girl. Jacquie was his go-to when it came to troubled teens.

Because of a genetic condition (and resultant physical deformities), Renée "Honeychile" Devonshire had played adoption roulette longer than most. Three years ago, Hildy Collins finally found her a home. Jacquie had profound respect for the woman whom professionals in the field called "the adoption whisperer." She was a legend, routinely placing kids thought to be hopeless, violent or mentally ill in environments where they blossomed. Renée, a member of "Hildy's Girl Squad," had apparently done very well—until now.

Jacquie met with her parents while the client waited in the anteroom. From what the shrink could see, Harold and Rayanne were a warm, loving, somewhat overprotective couple who'd become concerned with their daughter's erratic behavior. They spent the first five minutes kvelling over how smart and funny Renée was and how well she'd done in school, considering her special challenges. Her lisp, short stature and overall appearance made her an easy target. "But lately," said Rayanne, "everything has changed."

She was often reported as truant and sometimes didn't come home for supper. She'd been a straight-A student, but three of her teachers told the Devonshires they might have to fail her. Rayanne said she had a heart-to-heart with Zelda, one of Renée's closest friends, who confided that she too was "worried sick." The therapist was glad to hear Renée still *had* a friend, which bode well in its small way. By the time kids wound up in her office, they'd often left friends far behind or acquired new ones of the dangerous kind. The Devonshires insisted that drugs or boyfriends weren't an issue, but Jacquie didn't give their remarks much weight because it was common for parents to deny or downplay the experimental, sometimes criminal behavior of their kids. Children who'd been in the system as long as Renée were pretty genius when it came to concealing their inner and outer lives.

At the end of the interview, Jacquie walked them out. She smiled at Renée and shook her hand, inviting her in.

The office was friendly and inviting, announcing its "safe place" status by a few stage-managed accoutrements—a print of a Basquiat graffiti painting, a framed photo of Eminem (the therapist hadn't found the time to replace him with a more up-to-date avatar), and a drawing of Jeffrey Tambor's character from *Transparent*.

Renée was sullen and fidgety, like all the kids who came through the door.

"I'm Jacqueline. My friends call me Jacquie and you can too, if you like."

"Okay."

"I like either one. Your mom said everyone calls you Honeychile. I love that! Very Southern. Have you spent any time in the South?"

"No."

"It's pretty amazing. Especially New Orleans—for Mardi Gras. I think you'd love it. Is it all right to call you Honeychile? Or would you prefer Renée?"

"Whatever."

"Then Honeychile it is," she said with a smile. "How are you feeling?"

"About?"

Jacquie saw straight off that the girl was smart. Her native intelligence shone through. "About being here. Probably not the most fun thing you're going to do all week. It can be kind of a drag at first."

"At first? They said I only had to come once."

"Fair enough. Then let's make the most of our visit. Do you know why your mom and dad wanted you to come see me?"

"Not really."

"Okay. That's fair enough too."

"I know what you can call me!" she said, in a playful burst of enthusiasm.

The therapist welcomed the girl's change in mood. The first half hour was always the toughest. It usually took at least three sessions for defenses to begin to drop.

"You can call me *Winston*."

"Winston?" said Jacquie. "Okay! And who's Winston?"

"Winston is who I *am*."

"So you're a boy."

"Well, a *girl* wouldn't be called Winston. Maybe a cigarette, but not a girl."

Honeychile giggled and Jacquie noticed that her voice had changed. It was thinner, reedier, childlike.

"And how long have you felt like a boy and not a girl?" She grew silent and the therapist gave her a nudge. "Sometimes little girls feel like they're in the wrong bodies. Sometimes little boys feel that way too. Is that what you're trying to tell me, Winston?"

"*Yes*."

"Good—and that's *okay*. I'm so glad you're sharing this with me. Have you shared it with anyone else?"

"Nope. I was gonna share it with *Hildy* but I didn't."

"I love Hildy. Are you still in touch?"

"*Yes*. But I was scared to tell her I was Winston."

"Why were you scared? That's something Hildy would understand. And support. Why were you scared to tell Hildy?"

"Because I'm her *son*. They hurt my mouth and pee-pee with a sword, then put me in the ground."

Jacquie's heart quickened. In a few stroboscopic seconds, the stunned woman put it together: "Winston" was the name of Hildy Collins's missing child. Her diagnosis caromed from gender dysphoria to psychosis.

"You're Hildy's son?" she said, almost stammering.

"*Yes*. But I can't find who kilt me."

Her voice and her language were regressing further.

"You can't find them?" said Jacquie. All she could do was fall back on her training, to echo and mirror.

"That's why I didn't tell *Hildy*."

"That's why you didn't tell Hildy."

"Because I can't *find* them. I'm s'posed to find the bad people but I *can't*. And I'm scared to tell *Annie* 'cause she'll be so mad."

Annie? Was she dealing with a multiple?

"And who is Annie?"

"From the choo-choo. She brought lemonade and cookies. She *sent* me."

"Annie sent you?"

"To hurt the people who kilt me. But I can't *find* them. I know I'm in the *marsh*-muds but not who kilt and burying me."

The girl grew quiet and so did the shrink.

Jacquie took some long, slow breaths, trying to decide, in a rare in-over-her-head moment, just where to go next. Before the session ended, she needed to bring her client back from whatever world she had gone to. She needed to get proactive and take control.

"Winston . . . can I talk to Honeychile? I'd really like to have a few words with Honeychile. Do you think I can do that?"

"Honeychile is *dead*."

"She's dead?"

"She die of a *asthma*. That's when Winston the tenant come."

"Winston came . . ."

"When Honeychile die in a asthma attack!"

"When Honeychile died from asthma—?"

The girl nodded, disembodied, like a bobblehead soothsayer.

"But I see you," said the therapist. "I see Winston *and* Honeychile—won't you let me talk to Honeychile again?"

"You can talk to her *dead body*. Only her dead body is here. But if I find the people who kilt me, you won't see her dead body *no more*. She'll be *completely dead* and go away forever!" Honeychile's glee turned to despair and she began to hyperventilate. "But I can't *find* them! I can't find the people who kilt me—and Annie is going to be *very, very* mad!"

2.

They tailed Dabba Doo from the Meeting and sat in the car in front of his modest New Baltimore home. Lydia wasn't really sure what they were doing there—it'd been her idea to come—but Daniel trusted her instincts, even though they'd gone somewhat askew when it came to Rhonda and the incident at Jacobs Prairie.

"I've been thinking," he said, "did you really want to go see the old house in the Falls?"

"*May*-be," she said, without taking her eyes off the house.

"You're the one who brought it up."

"I know, but it's . . . weird. Sometimes it's the *only* thing I think about—and sometimes it's the furthest thing from my head. Like, *zero* interest."

"Do Mom and Dad still live there?" he asked, sounding very young.

"*No*," she answered, almost contemptuously. "But right now can we please just focus on what we're doing?"

"What *are* we doing? Why are we here?"

"I don't know . . . it's just a *feeling* that maybe there's some way Dabba Doo can help. Anyway, it can't get worse than it already is."

When they knocked, he threw open the door with a frisky smile, as if he'd been waiting for them. Lydia noticed how everyone at the Meeting tended to be like that—friendly and funny in an open, sweetly eager way, not only because they were scared and drew strength from the fellowship, but because all of them were longing for playmates.

"Hope you're not starving," said Dabba Doo as he walked them to the living room. "Afraid I don't have much to offer in the culinary department. I do have gummy bears. You may have all the reds and the yellows you like, but *lay off the greens.*"

"I'm a red gummy man myself," said Troy.

"Then there shall be no controversy. Take a load off, kiddos!" He planted himself on a beanbag chair in front of the TV and his visitors sat cross-legged on the floor.

The local news got everyone's attention. A man and woman had been murdered at a farmhouse in Minnesota. They were holding a fourteen-year-old runaway captive; the police floated a theory that the couple may have been killed by "one of their own," a third accomplice to the kidnapping. They were digging up the property because the girl said that her assailant had threatened to bury her where the pigs slopped. "You'll meet a lot of new little friends there," he told her. They showed the sty being disinterred by backhoes—sets of human remains had already been uncovered. Local politicians expressed outrage when the dead man was revealed to be a Person of Interest in the disappearance of a young girl in Soddy-Daisy, Tennessee, eight years back.

Her name was Rhonda Whittle.

"Yabba Dabba Doo!" squawked their host when he heard the reporter say Rhonda's name. "Now we know what the yogameister did to earn that birthday cake. Well, good on him—I mean her!"

Maya shot a glance at Troy, telegraphing that she was about to get real.

"We were there," she said. "At the farm, when it happened."

"You were *not*," said Dabba Doo, excited as could be.

"Saw the whole deal go down," said Troy. "Rhonda's *moment of balance.*"

Dabba Doo was beside himself with merriment. "Well how in the world did *that* happen?" A lightbulb went off. "Ha! *I* know—you were after him too! That busy sonofabitch killed you and Maya!"

"He didn't," said Maya, shaking her head.

"He *didn't?*" said Dabba Doo, half-confused, half-disappointed.

"No—I just had this *feeling* we should go there. This *vision* came to me out of nowhere that Rhonda was on his way to a farm in Minnesota. So I went with it."

"Well look at you, Young Miss Marple!" said Dabba Doo, duly impressed. "Now, isn't that something!"

"We couldn't just sit home anymore," said Maya.

"I heard *that,*" said the host, suddenly vexed.

"I guess," said Troy, "we've sort of been having the same kind of trouble that you were talking about at the Meeting. It's like the radio signal used to be clear but now everything's gone static."

"Can't find the frequency, huh?" mused Dabba Doo. "A bit worrisome, isn't it?"

"And about what you said earlier," said Maya. "We really *were* hoping that whoever Rhonda was going to see *was* the same one who—"

"The same one who killed us," said Troy.

"You're sure that he wasn't?" said Dabba Doo.

"We're sure," she said.

"How do you know?"

"Because when it happened"—she turned to her brother for ratification—"when Rhonda had her *moment of balance,* we didn't feel anything."

"It wasn't like we even wanted to join in," said Troy. "There's just no way it could have been him."

"Well, well, well," said Dabba Doo. "Things are definitely getting curiouser and curiouser . . ."

"Besides," said Maya. "The Porter said it never happens that way. You know, whole *hordes* of us hunting down the same one."

"Like *The Walking Dead!*" said Dabba Doo. He gobbled a fistful of green gummies and reflected awhile. "I'll tell you what it sounds like to me— sounds like a few wires got crossed."

"That's exactly what I was thinking!" said Maya.

She *knew* Dabba Doo would help make sense of it all; that's why she'd been drawn to visit.

"And I hate to say it," frowned their host. "I mean no disrespect—but I'm beginning to lose faith in the Gospel According to Annie. Something's off. Have you seen her lately? She looks like hell."

"She's just a little run-down," said Lydia, biting her tongue so as not to spill the Porter's secret.

"More shall be revealed!" said Dabba Doo. "As our friend Mrs. *Porter* house likes to say. Though maybe more won't!" He laughed again, acciden- tally spitting a gummy onto the carpet. He grabbed it and plunked it back in his mouth. "What concerns *me* is that I don't know how much lon- ger I can keep the balls in the air. Hell, I don't even think of the *moment of balance* anymore—I'm just worried about the old ticker." He tapped his chest. "I can feel it winding down. I've tried asking Annie about it. 'How long can these fucked-up dead bodies keep going?' 'Course I didn't put it quite that way but it's a damn good question, huh? And boy, does she not want to go there! Tell you something else: I'm starting to feel more like my old landlord self, and that's *very* confusing. Isn't it supposed to be the reverse? It's like my tenant—Dabba Doo—he's still in there somewhere but the kid's gone *real quiet.* Giving me the silent treatment. Sometimes I feel like I swallowed him," he said. "Aren't I supposed to feel like he swal- lowed *me?*"

Maya started to go quiet too; Lydia was ready to go home. What he said about swallowing his tenant had frightened her. She felt guilty as well for having gone around Annie—she hated being disloyal and knew the Porter wouldn't approve of their mutinous outing. She was still glad they came. It *was* good to have a playdate, especially with someone who shared the same purgatory.

For his part, Daniel tried his best to hide the brutal funk that had descended during their visit. He couldn't put his finger on it. It seemed to be a mixture of rage and abject fear, an indecipherable storm of emotions and physical reflexes incongruously reminding him of two things: Daniel's inadvertent slaughter of the boy in Afghanistan—and Troy's strange feeling of déjà vu that time they first met Willow Wylde in his office.

As they left, Dabba Doo said, "Let's hope it's just a glitch in the system and everything turns out fine. We'll all have our *moment of balance* and ride El choo-choo into the sunset together."

"I hope you're right," said Lydia.

"All roads lead to Rome," he said. "History doesn't repeat itself but it often rhymes. That's Mark Twain but I take credit for it all the time."

3.

After her session, Honeychile again waited in the anteroom while the therapist told Harold and Rayanne in no uncertain terms that their daughter was having a psychotic break and urgently needed to be hospitalized. They listened in shock and disbelief. Mindful of client confidentiality, Jacquie omitted much, though what they were hearing was more than enough to leave them terrified.

When the couple stepped outside the office to speak with their daughter in private, Honeychile vehemently denied the account of what transpired. "I think she's *loaded*," she snarled. "The *shrink's* the one who needs a shrink!" Indeed, to the untrained ear, Dr. Robart's redacted version sounded like the ravings of someone who was high or unbalanced, especially so because the irascible client offered no evidence that would support such theories.

The family left, angry and unresolved, without a goodbye.

Jacquie immediately called her supervisor for counsel; she was flummoxed enough to begin to doubt her own perceptions. Had the girl been putting her on? Her colleague remained annoyingly noncommittal, "not having been in the room." Jacquie defensively dug in: while it *was* possible she had been "played," she insisted that the girl's pathology was too real, too complete, too *something*. Still, she was embarrassed at being so dramatic. Either she'd been hoodwinked by a brilliant sociopath—or met an authentic "multiple" head-on, the likes of which come along once in a career, if that.

When they hung up, she gathered her thoughts. She anxiously drummed her fingers on the desk, replaying gory highlights of the session. In her agitation, Jacquie had forgotten to run something else past her boss. She was about to ring him back when she stubbornly thought: *I'll figure this out myself.*

She wavered a moment before deciding to err on the side of professional prudence, not legal obligation.

She called the police.

O wen and Dubya were having their twice-a-week shoot-the-shit lunch, not at Early World, which Willow would have preferred, but at Owen's favorite, KFC. The sheriff admitted to having a full-blown addiction to the $5 Fill Up, faithfully ordered with two hundred grams of coleslaw. KFC coleslaw got him crazy. The whole beggar's banquet, washed down with a mix of lemonade and iced tea, really made the man happy.

They usually touched on personal things before getting into cop talk. This time it was their prostates. Owen confided that his PSA "went rogue" and he needed further tests. He hadn't mentioned it to Adelaide yet. (The woman loomed large for these two men.) When Owen asked about Willow's romantic life—he seemed to have an abiding, vicarious interest—the detective said it was "great," without mentioning Dixie. But it was interesting to him that he *did* have the urge to talk about her; he'd been feeling a tug of a desire to promote his girlfriend to someone, anyone. He felt that pride of alliance and burgeoning love that compels one to share. He just wasn't comfortable yet with Owen putting his shit on the street and gossiping about it to Adelaide.

When it came time to cut up Cold Case business, the sheriff made his usual rape kit backlog pitch. "It'd do wonders for the department if we nailed a few of those, Dubya. My educated guess is, we'd see a serious bump in funding. We need the rah-rah goodwill *and* the political muscle that would provide. I don't want 'em to shut us down in nine months. Hit a few home runs with those kits and it'll go a helluva long way. Don't get me wrong—*anything* cold we can put to bed is going to be a big win."

"Understood."

"Solve a few and we can add some new hires."

"Well, that'd be nice. I actually have my eye on three more cases but I'm still training the newbies. We're stretched a little thin."

"I know—but good."

"I went and saw Elaine and Ronnie Rummer."

"Is that right?" said Owen, his interest piqued.

"I thought they needed to know we've reopened the case."

"And how'd that go?"

"Ronnie's found religion."

"Did you see Elaine?"

"Yeah."

"How was she?"

"Okay—I guess. I mean, it was interesting. Not what I expected."

"What about her face? What'd it look like?"

"Not like it used to, that's for sure. But it's not some Phantom of the Opera deal."

"And was she rational?"

"Very much so. But I may have caught her on a good day. I was kind of surprised she wanted to see me. When I talked to Ronnie on the phone before I went over, he didn't mention her at all. Not a word."

"The man has hoed a tough road."

"Tough isn't the word."

"There's probably some serious caregiver burnout in there on top of everything else."

Willow shifted gears. "How's the Collins boy investigation going? Any breaks?"

"Don't ask. We get a hundred tips a day—'sightings.' You know the drill. He's in Chicago. *Nope*, someone's one hundred percent certain they just saw him in Seattle. *Nope*, he's with some vagrant in Florida living under a freeway. And the vagrant looks suspiciously like Jimmy Buffet. *Nope*, he's tied to a leash like a monkey, to a busker in Times Square . . . Wait! He's frolicking in the surf with some shady family in Cuernavaca."

"There's no surf in Cuernavaca, Owen."

"Not according to our tipster. Hell, we got a call from a psychic in *Moscow*."

"At least it wasn't a Russian hacker."

"I might have more luck with one of those. But you will not *believe* the latest. Yesterday, a therapist calls. Says she had a session with an unstable girl who claims to know where Winston Collins is buried."

"What kind of therapist?"

"A shrink—totally legit. I checked her out."

"*Dios mío.*"

"It gets better. The girl tells the shrink that she's some sort of zombie— you know, 'Hey, Doc, I'm actually dead but I know where the kid's buried because I'm *channeling* him.'"

"Makes sense to me," Willow said drolly. "And what do you plan to do with this valuable information, Sheriff?"

"What do you think I'm going to do?"

"'Press delete'?"

"Hell no. My men are out there digging as we speak."

Willow couldn't help but laugh and Owen broke into a smile himself. "It's called desperation, Dubya. Desperation with a healthy scoop of public outrage and political pressure." His phone rang and the sheriff knitted his brow as he listened. "On my way," he said, then hung up. "Let's go."

"What's up?" said Willow.

"A kid just got stabbed to death at Mount Clemens High."

4.

The ambulance sirened away as Owen and his cohort roared in. The area around the crime scene had been cleared. A few crying students loitered behind the yellow tape, hugging one another.

A skittish flock poured from the main building, shepherded by teachers. The little (some not so little) lambs blinked in confusion as they emerged to survey the scene. Some pointed to the slick of bright red blood smearing the pavement at the foot of the steps.

Hysterical parents, alerted by calls and texts while the school was locked down, arrived in panicky droves. The police wouldn't let them park. A few jumped from their cars, demanding to know if their kids were all right.

Willow couldn't blame them.

Owen was briefed by one of his deputies. The victim was a football player. A student had been arrested. The deputy pointed to a witness, a distraught student named Zelda.

Willow and the sheriff walked to the squad car where the suspect sat cuffed in the caged backseat. They peered in. Her eyes were closed. A funny-looking thing—tiny too. How the hell did she nearly cut off the head of a muscle-bound gridiron king? Owen tapped the trunk, signaling the driver to take her away. The sooner she was gone, the faster calm would prevail.

"Jail or hospital?" said Willow, knowing the answer.

"County General. I have been duly informed that the perp discussed the possibility of self-harm."

"She did appear to be an unhappy camper," said Willow.

"Being a leprechaun amidst jolly green giants'll do that to you. Makes you want to slash some throats. You know what's funny, Dub? Back in the day, this would've been some kind of world news. Now? It's just a blip on the Internet—or whatever they call blips on the Internet. Something to tweet about. When it comes to schools, people only really pay attention when you've got a ten-plus kill count. Or they're little bitty kiddies."

"Different times for sure."

"To put it mildly," said Owen derisively. "It's like that line in *No Country for Old Men*. 'It's the tide, the dismal tide . . .' "

" 'It's not the one thing.' "

"God, I love that movie."

Another deputy urgently interrupted.

"Sheriff? They found Winston Collins."

"You are shitting me."

"They just dug him up."

CROSS WIRES

I.

They went straight to the marsh from the school—it was turning into that kind of day.

The body had been found in New Baltimore, about twelve miles north-east of the high school, in a boggy area of Anchor Bay not far from Walter and Mary Burke Park, where Owen watched fireworks as a boy. The area was public enough (downtown shopping and popular beaches were close by) that both men wondered if the killer was trying to make a statement.

It took a moment for the startling connection to be made: the girl who provided the information that led to the discovery of Winston Collins's body was the very same who stabbed the star athlete to death. In the sheriff's mind, Renée "Honeychile" Devonshire was quite possibly a double-murderer.

Owen phoned Dr. Robart from the exhumation site. When she asked him certain details about what they had found, it was compelling enough that the sheriff broke confidentiality. He told her that toilet paper had been stuffed down the boy's throat and all of his teeth removed. When he shared about the penis being severed, the therapist said that Renée, "speaking as Winston," had told her the killer "hurt my mouth and pee-pee with a sword."

He needed to speak with the parents right away—but most of all, he needed to interview "Honeychile." Unfortunately, that would have to wait. When he called the hospital, they said she'd become violent and was hallucinating. The doctors were bombing her with antipsychotics.

Standing on the sidelines of the dig, Willow's thoughts drifted to the bedroom of Elaine Rummer—then back to the Cold Case conference room with its files and baggies, its corkboard and spilled evidentiary detritus. He floated there awhile before dipping his toe in the stream of subconscious memory, whose waters lapped up on the old Rummer place—

July 4, 2000.

Their photos weren't on the corkboard, but he could already see them there, pinned in his mind's eye:

Roy Eakins and his ungainly son, Grundy.

2.

Harold and Rayanne camped out in the family waiting room of Macomb County General's psych wing.

They wouldn't let them see their daughter and Rayanne was right behind Honeychile in losing her mind.

She blamed herself for not having listened to the therapist. Harold reminded her that he hadn't believed the woman either—how could anyone have? Rayanne attacked it from all angles. One minute she was attributing the surreal, horrendous events to some undiscovered neurological quirk of cleidocranial dysplasia; the next, indicting Honeychile's birth parents for being a "minefield of shitty genes," something she'd always believed but never dared declare out loud. She even went after the bully football player, impugning him for sending those cruel, disgusting texts to their daughter. (They'd looked at her phone before handing it over to the police.) When Harold gave her a look that she'd gone too far and was being unchristian, she grew quiet and relented, though without becoming contrite.

Rayanne said *We need an attorney* and Harold said *We'll talk about it later.* Rayanne wondered if they should reach out to the parents of the dead boy and Harold said *Too soon, talk about it later.* She broke down and said *Oh, Harold! What if they put her in jail and throw away the key?* and Harold said *They're not going to do that, Rayanne.* She wrung her hands and said *They never allow an insanity defense, never!* and Harold said *Maybe not on TV but they do in real life, they do it all the time.* He said it like a seasoned criminal lawyer.

Zelda came by with her parents and sat with the Devonshires awhile. Zelda's mom and dad were kind, but standoffish. Later Rayanne told Harold it was "obvious" Zelda's folks never liked their Honeychile, never liked the way she looked or acted, never liked her "bad influence." *Did you see how far away they sat? Like we had shit on our shoes.* Harold said she was being too sensitive and that Zelda's parents behaved just fine.

Two cops came into the waiting room after Zelda left. When they said they were here to see their daughter and just wanted to say a quick hello, Rayanne's eyes sparkled for the first time since the world turned on end.

"Please," said Rayanne, in the quietest, sanest way she could muster. "Please tell them it's all right for us to see our baby. She's probably so scared! And please come back! Come back and tell us how she's doing?"

Lydia promised she would.

They wore their old deputy uniforms, a strategy both cagey and naive, thinking they could bluster their way into visiting the girl under cover of "official business."

Why had they come in the first place?

This time it was on Daniel's instigation.

A few days before the high school killing, he awakened from a deep sleep with an overwhelming *feeling* (like the one Lydia had about Rhonda) that "Winston," the new girl from the Meeting, was in some kind of danger. When they learned Honeychile had been arrested for murder, the vision was validated. The two of them rehashed Dabba Doo's theory that wires had been crossed and decided more *would* be revealed—once they got into a room with her.

But the head nurse wouldn't allow it.

The frustrated deputies returned to the waiting room. When they told her, Rayanne was stoic. She knew what she was about to say was futile but couldn't help herself.

"Did she ask for us? Did they say that she asked for us?"

"We didn't talk all that long," said Lydia. "The nurse kind of had her hands full."

The deputy wisely kept to herself the only intel they were able to gather: that Honeychile *had* been screaming for her mother—whom she alternately referred to as "Hildy-Bear," "Mommy Bear" and "Mrs. Collins."

The next morning at the office, Willow laid into them.

"What the *fuck* was that little stunt about?" Lydia and Daniel stared at the floor and took it in the neck; there was nothing else to do. "Do you know the *shit* I got from the sheriff about you going to see that girl? What did you think you were doing?" They remained silent. "Open your mouths and give me some fucking *answers*. Now!"

"She's—a family friend," said Lydia, without looking up.

"A family *friend*?" said Willow, his rage building. "Really?"

Daniel improvised. "We know her folks, that's all. It was . . . an emotional decision and we were wrong."

"It was *dumb*," said Lydia. "Totally inappropriate and we're sorry."

"How do you know the family?"

Daniel made an executive decision that the only way out of the shit was to go deeper in. "I know the dad from a veterans' group. I work with a PTSD group."

"Harold and Rayanne called us from the hospital," said Lydia. "They sounded so frightened. My heart went out."

Willow was still red hot. "What in hell did you think you could accomplish by seeing that girl?"

"It was stupid," said Lydia. "They wouldn't let her see her parents and then we thought that if we could get in to see Honeychile for a few minutes, we might be able to calm the girl down."

"Calm her down," said Willow, stunned by their idiocy.

"Maybe make it easier for Owen and his people to interview her," said Daniel, in futile damage control.

Willow looked like he was going to have an embolism.

"They wouldn't let the *parents* see her—they won't let the fucking *sheriff* see her—but somehow *you* two, the casual acquaintances and *bleeding hearts*—somehow you thought, *We'll ride in like the cavalry and save the day for the department!* That it'd be just a *wonderful* idea to drop in on the prime suspect of an ongoing homicide investigation and potentially *contaminate* said investigation. Is that what you're telling me?"

"I know, I know," said Lydia, in star-spangled *my bad* mode. "It's totally crazy and effed-up, and, sir, we completely apologize."

"A terrible judgment call," added Daniel.

Willow shook his head in disgust and resignation.

"I'll *tell* you who you're going to have to make those apologies to: Sheriff Owen Caplan. You better hope and pray he's not going to hang your asses out to dry. And not just from this *unit*—you better hope he doesn't ask you to turn in your guns and badges, *period*. That man went out on the line to put you here and you go and do something so *stupid*, like a couple of *kids*—"

"We're sorry, sir," said Daniel.

"It won't happen again," said Lydia.

"Damn straight it won't. I'll fire you myself."

3.

The sheriff spoke to Zelda at the Mount Clemens office of the Detective Bureau, with her parents present. He would have liked to have done the interview at her home but needed everything on video. Honeychile's best friend was completely unglued, crying nonstop. He was joined by the detective lieutenant heading the case, but Owen was taking charge for now.

About fifteen minutes in, he asked Mom and Dad if they would mind waiting outside. They didn't, of course, because he'd already had a private conversation about it with them. He said there were things a teenager tended not to talk about if their parents were in the room. They understood.

"Zelda," he said, softly sympathetic. "I know this has been very, very hard on you. It's a terrible shock and I know that you're worried about your friend. But I want to assure you that right now she's in the absolute best place she could be, getting the best of care."

"K," said Zelda, sniffling and avoiding his eyes.

The detective lieutenant sat back, doing his best to become part of the wallpaper so as not to antagonize the girl.

"Can you tell me a little bit about Renée?"

"We call her Honeychile."

"Right—Honeychile. From everything I've heard, she sounds like a very good person. A sweet, decent girl."

"She *is*," said the loyal friend. "Oh my God, she's the *best*."

"That's why what happened is so hard to understand. Because I've talked to a *lot* of people about her. And they say she's a wonderful, funny girl. A joy to be with. That's not up for argument—that's a fact."

Zelda nodded. She was getting calmer, which was good. It was all about building trust.

"What really *bothers* me," she said emotionally, "is that people are saying—*some* people—that she was on *drugs*. She is so *not* on drugs, she *hates* drugs. She never even tried marijuana!"

He pushed a box of Kleenex her way.

"Okay. Okay. And I believe that. I really do believe that, Zelda. And I understand how hurtful it is to hear people make false accusations about a friend."

"They are *so* false!" she said, blowing her nose.

"What I need to know—what I'd *like* to know, if you'll help me—is if there was anything you noticed that was different about her, different about your friend. In the past few days or weeks. If she was hanging out with any kids or even *grown-ups* that you didn't know. At school or *outside* of school—"

"Not really," she said, nonplussed.

"I need you to think about it. Really think. Because it's important—if you want to help your friend. If you want to help Honeychile."

"All I want to *do* is help her!"

"I know. I know that. And you're helping her *right now*, Zelda, just by meeting with me and talking with me in exactly the way that you're doing. I just need you to think about what I asked. And it doesn't matter if it's a big thing or a small thing, Zelda, you can let me decide. All I want you to do is go back in your mind and *think*—we can meet again too—go back and search your thoughts about Honeychile's activities and behavior over the last few weeks."

"Well . . . she did start acting kind of different—"

"Okay. Good. Tell me about it."

"After the asthma attack."

"She had an asthma attack."

"A really *bad* one."

"When was that?"

"Maybe a week ago? Oh my God, we thought she was going to *die*. Maybe she got scared that it would happen again. Maybe she started acting different because she thought it was going to happen again and that she would die. It was really, really *bad*."

"Can you tell me *how* she was acting 'different'?"

She shook her head and he didn't want to press.

"Did Honeychile ever mention Mrs. Collins?"

"The woman who placed her?" said Zelda.

"That's right. Did she ever talk about her?"

"Not really—but I know she really loved her."

"Did Honeychile ever talk about Mrs. Collins's little boy? She had a son named Winston. You probably heard what happened to him." Zelda nodded. "Did she ever talk about Winston?"

"I don't *think* so—"

"Did she ever tell you about going to visit Mrs. Collins?"

"No . . ."

"Are you sure? That would have been sometime recently. Are you sure she never mentioned going to see Mrs. Collins?"

"She didn't!"

Owen believed she was telling the truth. Still, he followed the theme. "Did Honeychile ever say anything to you about Winston, before or after he disappeared? Anything at all? It's important, Zelda."

"No."

"She never said she was upset about what happened? That she was upset for Mrs. Collins and wished she could find the people who were responsible for what happened to her little boy?" Zelda kept shaking her head. "Did the two of you ever go to the beach together?"

"Not really."

"'Not really'—does that mean 'maybe'? Try to remember. Did you ever go to New Baltimore? The beach over there? I used to go when I was a kid. There's a pier there and a park. Did Honeychile ever take you there?"

She shook her head once more, then said, "There *was* something—it sounds really dumb . . ."

"If it's 'dumb,'" he said, smiling, "which I promise it *won't* be, then we'll laugh about it together."

"Honeychile asked if she could sleep over. After she had the asthma attack. We'd been fighting so much I thought it would be really nice. The next day, we went to the museum in Detroit. Five classes went. And we . . ."

"Go ahead, Zelda."

"Am I going to get in trouble for this?"

"You're not going to get in any trouble, I promise."

"Well—Honeychile said there was someplace she needed to go, so we left. I don't want to get thrown out of school for this!"

"You're fine. No one has to know but you and me."

"We left—I mean, while everyone else was still there. But only during lunch hour! We were totally back in time and no one even found out."

"Where'd you go?"

"To this church—we took a cab."

"You went to a church . . ."

"I don't think she ever went there before, but it was like she knew *exactly* where she was going. But they wouldn't let us in."

"Who wouldn't let you in?"

"These *people*. It was weird, I can't explain! This woman . . . actually, they wouldn't let me in, they were going to let *her* in but the woman said I couldn't come. Honeychile told the woman *no way*—that *she* wasn't going to go if *I* couldn't go."

"You said that she told a woman. What woman?"

"She was older and wore a long dress. And jewelry—like turquoise jewelry? She said I couldn't come with. She wasn't, like, *mean* about it, she was really *nice*. She said I could sit outside and they'd bring me cookies and lemonade. But only Honeychile was allowed to go in."

"Then what happened?"

"We left."

"Did Honeychile tell you who the woman was?"

"I don't think she even *knew*," said Zelda. "It wasn't like they were friends."

"Did Honeychile tell you what was going on? After you left?"

"She *wouldn't*. I kept asking but I finally gave up." Zelda's face contorted in a mask of misery. "It wasn't her *fault*, what she did! Everyone hated him! He was a bully and everyone hated him!" Her entire body seized. "I'm *sorry*, I'm *sorry*! I *know* he shouldn't have died, no one deserves to die, but he was so *horrible*, he texted such horrible *things* to her! People don't have a right to do that either, do they? And I know she probably didn't *mean* to hurt him like that—she probably didn't even know what she was doing! Because she's a really, really good person! And I just want to *see* her! I just really need to see her! Can't I see her? Why can't I see her! Why can't I see her?"

He knew the interview was over.

RESURRECTION

I.

The entity known as Dabba Doo sat in front of the television at the end of a long day, as was his habit. All of his days were long now—almost beyond belief.

He was not a child; nor was he a man.

Neither a landlord nor a tenant be . . .

He was a diver who'd spent too much time in the lower depths, with no decompression chamber waiting.

His memories were a miasma, a stew dissolving into broth. His physical body, such as it was, flicker-faded. Intermittently, his breath became labored and he could feel his very blood coursing its last lap. When he asked himself (with growing infrequency) what it was that had happened to him, he was baffled, and dropped the thread. What he lived for, if *living* is the word, was the Meetings—communion with those who were like family now. For the first time in his life, he loved and felt loved in return.

But even that was beginning to flicker-fade—

His son and daughter-in-law saw the change in him and searched for evidence of a stroke. They wanted him to get a check-up but he refused. He never left the house anymore, except for the hour-and-a-half round-trip to the Meetings in Detroit.

Then—one morning after a morose and hectic sleep—something happened that seemed like a miracle. He began to remember everything about his old life, a life that'd been slipping away since the murdered boy Dabba Doo settled in with his childish ways, his childish memories.

He remembered he once was a hunter. He was a schoolteacher too, but he had always been a hunter, and childhood memories—not Dabba Doo's—returned to cosset him. When he was small, he hunted insects, chickens, snakes and mice, before graduating to cats and dogs, household and stray. At twelve, he stole onto a neighbor's property at midnight and killed a young horse. Thinking about the foal's dissection gave him a hard-on. That hadn't happened in a long while, not since his child-tenant took up residence.

He tried to conjure the hunting life after his teenage years but had trouble. But the miracle had arrived, the miracle of becoming himself again, and those memories, *his* memories, would soon come as well. He knew there must be a purpose to everything he'd undergone in these strange, epic months, that all had been orchestrated by a force greater than him—some fierce, wild-hearted god.

Roy Eakins died and was reborn as Dabba Doo, but now the child-tenant was collapsing and something new was taking its place, staking its claim. Dabba Doo slept most of the time now, in a little royal bedroom deep inside the castle of what Roy Eakins was becoming.

He felt as if he were in the midst of being granted a third life. He was convinced he was changing into something extraordinary and that it would be a mistake to wait passively for his destiny to unfold. He came to believe that had been the whole problem, the reason he'd been there the longest: because he hadn't seized his destiny. He just sat in Meetings like an addled coward, waiting for it to seize *him*.

Now he knew what he must do to be whole—to retrieve the memories of the hunt.

V iolet answered the door in her business suit. She smiled in friendly puzzlement—she'd never seen a landlord outside of the Meeting before. It was a fun thing but flustered her.

"I was in the neighborhood," he said. "Thought I'd stop and say hello."

"Yes, hi, of course! Come in!"

She was winding down after her workday and he smelled wine on her breath. The insurance company paid her well; the condo was beautifully done. She made a joke about being sorry she didn't have any gummy bears, "not even green ones!"

He laughed and said, "But I'll bet you have angel food cake."

"My favorite," she said. "And I do!"

"I'm Roy, by the way. Roy Eakins. That's my 'street name'—my landlord name."

"I'm Sarabeth Ahlström," said the one he knew as Violet.

"Lovely apartment. My lord."

"Thank you."

"I guess I had to come to Dearborn Heights to see how the other half lives."

"Ha! Well, do you approve?"

"I more than approve. I envy."

"Can I get you a drink, Roy? It might dull the pain."

"I'd like that. Whatever you're having will be fine."

She went to the fridge to get ice.

"Hey, is this kosher?" she called out.

"The wine? Well, if it ain't Manischewitz—"

"You're silly! I mean, are we landlords supposed to fraternize?"

"Rules were made to be broken. The Porter's sure got a lot of them."

"Yes she *does*," said Sarabeth.

"Let's break 'em one by one."

"I won't tell if you don't."

"Mum's the word. I don't think we can get in *too* much trouble—what's Annie gonna do, put us in detention? It's kind of tough to punish a dead person."

Sarabeth laughed out loud. "You're a wicked man!"

As attractive and even flirtatious as she was, it was clear that sex wasn't going to be part of the program. From what she'd shared in Meetings about her tangle of spurned lovers, Sarabeth had been a very busy girl before she died. But she'd been around too long now; her child-tenant, Violet, was dominant, killing off the landlord's body's memory of desire.

"Here you go, Dabba Doo," she said, handing him his drink. "A little dab'll do ya."

He laughed and said, "You better call me Roy—Dabba Doo's underage and providing a minor with alcohol *will* get you in trouble."

"You're right! I stand corrected. Or sit corrected."

She was a little drunk.

"You know, you're awfully young," he said. "Do you happen to know how you died? That always intrigues me. Some of the landlords seem to know, others haven't a clue."

"Well, I have a suspicion," said Sarabeth. "I was in the air, flying back from Europe, when it happened—when I felt Violet come. Maybe a blood clot? I googled it. Deep vein thrombosis. I thought maybe that was—"

With a surge of energy, Roy sprang up and broke her jaw, knocking her off the designer loveseat. He crouched over her as she lay stunned on the vintage flat-weave carpet.

"So many things are becoming clear," he said, in a pensive, almost decorous tone. "Have you had any of the same feelings?" He spoke with the openness and vulnerability of an old friend seeking to ratify common experience. He thought she said *Why* through the bubble and gristle. "Why? Because I can!" he laughed. "Sorry—*hate* people who say 'Because I can.' Just hate it." He rabbit-punched her stomach until she vomited blood. "Haven't done *this* in a while," he mused, climbing off her. "Can't even remember the last time I hunted a full-grown. The little ones were always my thing. Which is perhaps ironic."

Sarabeth clung to consciousness with just enough awareness to feel Violet trying to escape. The child-tenant cried as she ran through dark corridors, searching for her cabin on the train.

"And just so's ya know, I had nothing to do *whatsoever* with the fool who murdered your precious tenant. What's sad, though, is that Violet's killer is about to get full amnesty—gonna go free as a bird. Right? 'Cause let's face it, if a kiddie blows his *moment of balance*, he's seriously fucked in the revenge department. No tickee, no momentito de balancia. Pardon my French."

He pulled her pants down. The underwear was soaked in bright blood and Roy peeled it off with the sunny industry of a nurse redressing a wound.

"You said you thought you were getting close to your *moment* . . . sorry to rob you of that. Wonder who the bugger was. Oh well. Hey, you know what Violet is? Violet's a rude little *cunt*. There you are, flying around in planes, business class no doubt, occasional upgrade to first, enjoying your life, drinking fine kosher wine, making a shitload of money—doin' *all* kinds of quality fucking (you *know* you're the hands-down hottie of the Meeting, right? Though Maya's a close second)—there you are at the top of your game and *wham!*—a-hole Violet moves in so she can play her dumb shitty game of afterlife retribution. Tsk, tsk. That's an interesting theory about the thrombosis, and you might just be right. I think I had a heart attack, which is more age-appropriate for a fogey like me. I remember driving along, don't recall where to, and I suddenly had these *killer* chest pains, the whole radiating, achy-arm, elephant-on-your-chest classic. Probably the Big One—what the cardiologists call 'the Widowmaker.' I did a little googling myself. I pull over and pass out and the next thing I know I'm awake and just fine—relatively speaking! Off I go, putt-puttin' down the road. And right *then*, I started to feel him: the incredible shrinking loser and party-crasher, Mister Dabba Doo. What a pain in the ass he is. No wonder some pedophile whacked him! Dabba Doo: now *there's* a bigger cunt than Violet. And *wham!* A week or so later, my butt's sitting in a Meeting. Wham, bam, thank you, Annie!"

He took off his clothes. Roy wanted to hear music but her audio setup was too hard to figure out.

"Hey, but Annie's a helluva gal, don't you think? She hasn't looked too spiffy in the last few weeks, have you noticed? Maybe she's got a thrombosis goin' on herself."

He stayed with Sarabeth and Violet until past midnight, long after both departed.

book three

Local and Express

————— ⦿ —————

For the *children*, when your time is done, it is VERY important to THANK YOUR LAND-LORD—they've been such CARING roommates!!! Remember, without THEM, you would never have been able to have your *moment of balance*. For the *landlords*, when YOUR time is done, THANK your BODY!!! (For the wonderful times it pro-vided.) NEVER FORGET that it gave you so much more time than your child-tenants had! And THANK the FRIENDS and FAMILY that you LOVED . . . and thank this beautiful BLUE EARTH.

—*from "The End" (the Guidebook)*

VISITATIONS

Once upon a hill, we sat beneath a willow tree
Counting all the stars, and waiting for the dawn . . .

—Charles Strouse and Lee Adams

I.

Willow's day (and night) was full.

He planned to leave work after lunch and drop in on Adelaide before driving down to New Baltimore to keep his appointment with Roy Eakins. Then, in the evening, he would pick up Annie and attend his first Meeting, at the Cross of Glory Lutheran Church in Detroit. (After Honeychile had trespassed, the circumspect Annie moved it from the Divine Child Parish.) Willow had mixed emotions about that.

But mostly, he was scared shitless.

A nagging sense of folie à deux made him shudder—that he was entering into an irreversible pact with a deranged woman. He pictured himself back in AA (he hadn't been to a meeting since moving to Macomb) and imagined his share before the packed room: "I started drinking again because I got stressed over a new job. I couldn't handle being the scout leader of a troop of dead kids whose mission was to hunt down and kill their own murderers."

The macabre fantasy made him laugh, and he was glad he still could. He sensed that his laughing days were coming to an end.

He knew that Owen wouldn't be home when he stopped over, which was best. He wanted to talk to Adelaide before his appointment with Roy, though the detective wasn't even sure what it was that he wanted from her. He was flying by the seat of his pants—or maybe Roy Eakins's pants—and none of it seemed particularly promising. What else was an over-the-hill, in-over-his-head cold case fuck-up to do? At least Roy was affable when they talked on the phone. It sounded counterintuitive but if the man had been closemouthed or even nasty, Willow may not have had the energy to further pursue. But Roy had always been affable. Like Ronnie Rummer, he actually sounded excited that Willow had called.

From Adelaide's, he would pick Annie up at the SRO in Detroit. She was getting weaker and the bus ride to the Meeting had become too challenging. She told him to come at 7:00 P.M. He got nauseous just thinking about it.

Since he'd ripped them new assholes, the Cold Case Kids had gotten down to brass tacks. Lydia even approached him with a few rape kits, breaking her monomaniacal focus on the Rummers. When the detective told them about his visit with Elaine and Ronnie Rummer, they listened attentively, not in that weird way they tended to whenever Willow began talking about Troy and Maya's parents. In general, they played their emotions close to the vest. Only once did Lydia betray an inner turmoil—when he shared that Elaine tried to kill herself on multiple occasions, the last effort ending in a disfiguring shotgun wound to the face. Willow thought that might have triggered something about Lydia's own mother, but didn't want to pry.

Before he left to see Adelaide, they met in the conference room so he could hear a plan of action. He could see they needed a kick in the pants. (The detective was starting to worry that he hadn't properly been doing his job.) It haunted him that he had always failed as a mentor, from his daughter on down—which begged the surreal yet pressing question: *How the fuck am I going to be of any use to Annie?*

He scrutinized the corkboard as the rookies spoke of the leads they had chased, admitting with some chagrin that there wasn't anything that looked intuitively promising.

"Then stop looking for intuitive," Willow said sagely. "Intuitive can be overrated. Look for the *real*—connections that are real. Let 'intuitive' take care of itself."

They nodded gravely, like freshmen in Wizard School.

"Here's something obvious," said Willow. "Maybe *too* obvious but I'd have been on it six ways from Sunday." He touched the fingertips of both hands, as if encircling a crystal ball. "The serial killer in Jacobs Prairie . . . that's not too far from here, right? Are there any dots to connect?"

Lydia brightened—finally, they could please their teacher.

"We looked into it," said Daniel drily.

"And?" said Willow.

"Timeline doesn't work."

"He was in jail that summer," said Lydia. "Failure to pay child support."

"You could have told me about that."

"Sorry, sir," said Lydia.

"Cold case folks from all around the country have gotten their knickers wet over that little shootout," added Willow.

He stared at the pinned bag with the birthday card inside. Adorned with a sequined unicorn, it had been found in Maya's bicycle basket, the one Elaine helped decorate with red plastic roses. The police surmised it had been picked up from the ground where it fell, then fastidiously replaced. It bore two prints: a tire track from the bike itself, and that of a human hand. In a show of solidarity and love, the community offered up their palms—hundreds of them. Willow had already returned to New York when he heard about the voluntary effort, and while it touched him (a three-page feature, "Palm Sunday," ran in *People*), the cynical cop knew better. He thought it was a colossal waste of money and manpower. He tended to agree with Ronnie Rummer. Whoever grabbed those kids was likely transient, and long gone by the time Saggerty Falls staged its compassionate act of theater.

"I keep seeing that card. What's it still doing here?" he said gruffly. The deputies were perplexed. "Send it to the lab. See if they can get some DNA off the print."

It had never been swabbed. In 2000, DNA was only something in the air.

"Yes, sir," said Lydia.

"Seems unlikely, though, doesn't it, sir?" said Daniel.

"I'd like a dollar for every time 'unlikely' turned out to be a grand slam."

"Yes, sir."

Since having their backsides spanked, they'd been *sir*-ing him to death like child actors out of *Oliver!* It amused more than it annoyed. He returned his gaze to the Ouija board of clues.

"Have either of you come across the name Roy Eakins? Or Grundy Eakins?"

"The teacher and his son?" said Lydia. "Sure. I read his interview—the father's."

"The boy was developmentally disabled," said Daniel.

"That's right," said Willow.

"He was ruled out," said Lydia. "He was at the barbecue all day."

"They both were—they never left. Why do you ask, sir?"

"I'm interviewing Roy this afternoon."

"Really," said Daniel.

"Like us to come along?" said Lydia.

"No, I think you can sit this one out. I'm not even sure why I'm going. Definitely no need to show up with the whole cavalry."

"He was cleared," said Daniel. "He submitted a palm print. They both did—to my knowledge."

"What do you hope to learn?" said Lydia.

"I don't know," he shrugged. "It's just one of those intuitive things."

"'Intuitive' can be overrated," she said impishly.

Though he had no reason to, Willow parked around the corner from the Caplans' driveway, so his car wouldn't be visible—old stalk-and-skulk habits die hard.

But there was something else to his skullduggery; when it came to Adelaide, being surreptitious gave him an erotic charge. He'd been fantasizing about her again. He couldn't have been happier about his sex life with Dixie Rose, but the idea of seducing his ex-wife (with the twofer of cuckolding Owen) set his heart aflutter. Some of it was sore loser's payback—it would cut the sheriff to the quick—but mostly, it was the pure, verboten kick, the Blueberry Thrill of it all. Addie was great in bed, one of the few women he'd met who could come on a dime. So many of his lovers after the marriage (and during) seemed to have trouble in that department. It was practically an epidemic. After a while, a man couldn't help thinking he was the problem.

As he walked the half block to Adelaide's, his cell phone rang. It was Owen. *Jesus, the man's telepathic.* He informed Willow that he was having his first interview with Honeychile in the morning. Then he dropped something that righteously pissed Willow off. The sheriff said he'd learned that Lydia and Daniel were in uniform when they stopped by lockdown "to have tea and crackers with my suspect. Do you make them wear deputy uniforms to work, Dubya?" Of course he didn't and Owen knew it. Willow could tell that his boss was more irritated than anything else—there were too many things on his plate just now—but the Cold Case rookies' costume party had been enough to warrant a mention. "You might look into that," he reprimanded. "You bet I will," said Willow.

He hung there on the sidewalk a moment, wrestling with the impulse to call the Devonshires, which probably wasn't a good idea. Then he said fuck it and dialed them anyway.

Harold picked up.

Willow hadn't thought it through—not his specialty—and had to do some tap dancing. He introduced himself as a detective, omitting that he worked Cold Case. He apologized for interrupting Harold's day.

"What can I do for you?"

"I'm sorry we couldn't get you folks in to see your daughter that afternoon."

"Well, someone finally made that happen," said Harold. "But I appreciate it."

"We had a couple of deputies who were upset that the hospital was being—well, going a little too 'by the book.' You may even have run into them while you were there."

"Oh yes. They came to see us while we were waiting. They were very kind."

"Do you work with veterans, Mr. Devonshire?"

"Excuse me?"

"Have you ever done any work with PTSD veteran groups?"

"No, I haven't."

"Sorry for asking," said Willow, milking his acting chops. "One of the deputies is a vet and he said that you reminded him of a fellow in his group."

"Why were you calling again?"

The query sounded borderline tetchy; the last thing Willow needed was for Mr. Devonshire to call in some kind of complaint, as far-fetched as that might seem.

"I really just wanted to see how y'all were doing and wish you my best. Have a good evening and sorry to have bothered."

"No bother at all."

H ey there, mystery man," said Adelaide, inviting him in.
God, she was gorgeous. For the first time, he noticed a melancholy to the observation, though not over what he'd lost. No, the sadness came because Dixie had stealthily put a yurt up on the precious, long-barren land where he and his ex once lived. Willow hadn't built on the property for years and Addie had the feeling he never would. She took comfort as well in knowing he'd converted the acreage into a memorial park—and Willow drew comfort in knowing that she knew.

It was complicated.

"Wassup, Dubya?"

"Not a helluva lot. Just doing the Cold Case deal."

"Owen said that you went to see the Rummers."

"Yup. That'll put a dent in your mood."

"Poor things," she said. "God."

"Speak of the devil—I think Ronnie found Christ."

"Well, I guess if you can't find your kids, you have to find somebody." She winced. "Forgive me, that was awful."

"You're dark, Addie. It's what I miss about you."

"You don't miss me, Dub. You might think you do but you don't. Which is probably a good thing."

"Why do you say that?"

"You might miss the 'me' you had before things went south . . . but things went south a long-ass time before we busted up." She grew thought-ful. "I'm sorry for all the hurt, Willow. I'm sorry for my share."

"We're still standing."

"That's right. We didn't take each other down—not that we didn't try." *Oh! That gorgeous, crooked mouth when it smiled!* "And we have a beautiful daughter to show for our troubles."

"Yes we do. And a beautiful grandson."

"I'll drink to that," she said. "Note I said I'll drink, not you."

It was so easy with her, but he needed to focus.

"I've really been traveling down memory lane with this Rummer case. Hey, remember Roy Eakins?"

"Roy? 'Course I do."

"Whatever happened to him?" he said.

"No idea," she said. "He moved away—not for a while, though. It must have been about a year after the kids disappeared. I heard he was teaching at some fancy school somewhere . . ."

"They were at the barbecue, weren't they? I mean, Roy and his kid."

"Well, I came late, remember? I declined the invitation—I wasn't too thrilled when I learned you were riding back into town from New York on that surprise birthday puppy. Turned out to be a pretty good gift though, huh. Anyway, I only went over when I heard the kids were missing. When Pace and I got there, it was already after dark."

Of *course* Adelaide hadn't come till later; he'd blocked that out completely. He thought he was being so crafty with his little fishing expedition, but suddenly he felt old, senile, inept.

"It's funny, though," she said. "On the way to the Rummers', we passed them on the road—Roy and Grundy. I'm just now remembering . . . You know that dirt road, how slow you had to go? There were cop cars coming and going, just—craziness. Folks with flashlights running in the fields . . . Do you remember the chaos, Dubya? Truly, truly horrible. And a car came toward us with two people *fighting* inside, like literally punching each other in the front seat! And I kind of pulled over—I'm just remembering this now—I thought it might be a couple of drunk kids but it was Roy. He slowed down—I think he probably must have seen it was me and felt he needed to explain. Gave us that big smile of his, which was weird considering the circumstances. Said something about Grundy having a nosebleed and how he had to get him home. You remember that boy. He was way *off.* Roy should have put him in one of those places they seem to have everywhere now, but I guess back then the choices were limited. I mean, he either had to keep him at the house or throw him in some county snake pit— *anyway*, he was trying to be a good dad, which I think he was. Grundy was always acting out, hittin' his head against walls, remember? He was a 'helmet' kid. And I think that's probably why—well, I *know* that's why it didn't work out in the romance department. It was too much work. Not so sexy when it came to the dating game. Poor, poor Roy. He had to concoct a whole system just to deal with that kid, it was seriously a full-time job. Quiet time for bad behavior, rewards for good . . . Grundy just sat in the car staring out the windshield with his bloody nose. It was a good thing he got him out of there, because his behavior was unpredictable. I don't think he was ever embarrassed—that's what I loved about Roy—but he knew that Elaine and Ronnie had enough to handle. *That's* the understatement of the century."

It was getting late and Willow needed to leave if he wanted to get to Roy's on time.

"Is that why you came to see me, Willow? To noodle around about Roy?"

"Maybe a little bit. Maybe I got a little nostalgic, in general."

"I guess we're a cold case that can never be solved."

"It's always tougher when there isn't a body."

She laughed out loud at the innuendo. Willow flashed on shoving her against the living room wall and sticking his tongue down her throat. He wondered if she'd submit. How long would it take for her to push him away? Would it be a push? Or a kick in the balls? Maybe she'd do that thing ex-wives in the movies do and go limp in his arms while breathlessly muttering, *We can't—we can't—it's not fair—to Owen—please stop—don't stop!* . . .

"Like I said, Dubya: you don't miss me. You miss the *idea* of me, the idea of *us*. Now go home, take a cold shower, and call your daughter. I'm sure she'd love to hear from you."

He smiled, kissed her cheek and left.

T he drive to New Baltimore took half an hour. He could have taken Armada Ridge to County Line Road but chose the southernmost route instead—29 Mile Road, then left on Avenue of the Waters—so he could pass directly through Saggerty Falls. (Visiting Adelaide had awakened something.) Since his return to Macomb he hadn't made an expedition to the place where he and Addie once lived—let alone to the Rummers, a fact Willow found both understandable and strange, in light of the fateful decision on the part of his deputies to reopen the case. In New York, it was always his habit and instinct to visit the scene of a cold case crime, under the aegis of a ritualized mystical reconnoitering that for him was mandatory. But he'd stayed away from Ronnie and Elaine's (even the path where Maya's bicycle was found), a fact that suddenly seemed worse than disrespectful. It felt like some sort of sacrilege, some sort of travesty.

Willow shivered as he crossed the border of the village. He made the five-minute detour to Creekview Street, where the Rummers had that barbecue on the day the Earth stood still. He put on Elgar's Cello Concerto in E Minor for dramatic effect and it worked: as he entered the cul-de-sac, the large, Windsor-style home, painted in brighter hues than he remembered, hove outlandishly into view like the star of a movie doomed never to be released. The neighborhood hadn't changed all that much. It looked like people were making more money now, which didn't really make sense—making it how?—shiny new muscle cars and ATVs grandstanded in the driveways, and even the decorative accoutrements on the faces of the houses looked added on, as if for a promotional brochure.

A redheaded little girl in pigtails stopped to take in the stranger, straddling her bike as she eyed him. For a moment, he wondered if she were a hallucination but rejected the thought because he saw no blue mist, no Blue Death. He wondered who lived in the Rummers' house now. He turned his car around in the bulb of the dead end and got back on Avenue of the Waters for the short ride to Roy's.

He watched the girl in his rearview. She stared after him like an admonishment, and the old shame returned, the shame of leaving Pace behind.

Roy came to the door in a three-piece tweed suit and bare feet.

He gave Willow a bear hug and then, with comic swagger, ostentatiously waved an arm toward the dining table, where humble sandwiches and chips had been laid.

"You've won everything behind Door Number Three! And *those*, m'lord"—he showcased a bowl of gummy bears—"are for dessert: my favorites, may I add, the *green* ones, in honor of your visit. Took me an hour to do the sorting."

He'd actually lit one of those fat fragrant candles, and that cracked Willow up.

It's like a date!

Maybe Roy turned fag.

The detective acknowledged the brief bluish steam that rose from Roy's chest before dismissing it as an aberration. Hadn't the same kind of misperception occurred when he first took Lydia and Daniel to the Spirit Room?

It'd been eighteen years since they'd last seen each other, and nearly that long since Willow had even thought of him. Eakins looked remarkably young and vital—far healthier, thought Willow, than himself. (And Roy was much older.) Roy farcically snatched away the beer he'd set down when Willow informed that he was sober, replacing it with a Dr. Brown's Diet Cream. His eccentric, guileless amiability was endearing; there was something so childlike about him that Willow felt like he'd stepped into Pee-wee's Playhouse. He had always liked the man but the reality was they'd never had much contact, apart from the few open houses he attended at his daughter's school.

"Man, I was jazzed to hear from you!" said Roy.

His ardent demeanor recalled Ronnie Rummer's, and made Willow think loneliness must be going around. "It's good to see you, Roy. And thanks for the awesome spread."

"I had a marching band but I think they must've got stuck in traffic," said Roy with an exaggerated frown.

"I'll bet you did. It's very welcoming and I appreciate it."

They chitchatted awhile—it was a little tricky because Willow didn't want to show his cards. (Not yet and maybe never.) Roy asked if Willow was still living in New York and he said no, he'd "moved back to the area," to be closer to Pace. "I've already missed too much time with her." He shifted things over to his host. "And what have you been up to all these years, my friend?"

"No good, I'm afraid," said Roy, before growing serious. "After what happened with those kids—the bottom kind of fell out. You know what I mean. The Falls lost its charm. The media practically moved in! Too much attention, and all of it negative. I knew I didn't want to be there anymore. I wasn't sure if I even wanted to teach. Not there, anyway. Not in the Falls. Bloom was off the rose. The rose was *dead*, quite literally, I'm afraid. Oh, I didn't want to be the party pooper—that wouldn't have been fair to the parents *or* my students—so I hung in for about a year. That year was a *bummer*. But it wasn't about me. I had an obligation. As a *quasi-educator*, I had a duty, a responsibility to the community. I really felt that and still do. Did a lot of hand-holding, something that comes naturally to teachers, if they're worth their salt. And then I moved on. Took me awhile to find my footing. I taught for a few years in public schools, in Flint, then Grosse

Pointe—did a little private tutoring on the Gold Coast. Hedge-fund guys who took a shine to Amercan history! You know, rich captains of industry who wanted to add a little scholarly sex appeal to their fund-raiser dinner conversations. They paid *very well*, by the way. Oh, I was the go-to guy for a while! Socked away a lot of money. I'm still living off those savings."

Roy was curious about Adelaide and, without being mean-spirited, made a passing reference to the cause célèbre of her remarriage. He asked after Pace as well, recalling what a wonderful student she was. "The best and the brightest," he said.

"How'd you wind up here?" said Willow, friendly and open-faced. "In New Baltimore?"

"Sweet little community," said Roy. "I like being close to the lake." Willow was about to bring up the matter of the Collins boy being found in the local marsh when Roy beat him to it. "And now that poor kid gets dredged up off Anchor Bay. It just never stops, does it, Willow?"

"Doesn't seem to."

"The madness of the human species . . . makes you want to burn your membership card, doesn't it? But I don't feel like moving, not this time. It was different with Troy and Maya. I guess that's because they were my students. My kids. It was personal."

Suddenly Roy's face grew rigid and cold, like an effigy of stone. Willow thought he must have been experiencing a wave of unanticipated grief, but it was something else that would remain unknown to the detective: for the first time, saying their names aloud, Roy Eakins realized with a shock that the Rummer children had *returned*, embodied in the eponymous landlords from the Meeting—and they had visited his very home! How was it possible he hadn't realized who they were from the moment they appeared, by *name*, at the Meeting? But there were so many elisions . . . so many things he was only just beginning to remember. He was becoming *awake*, ever since he managed to become dominant over Dabba Doo.

A conundrum asserted itself, and he wondered: Do they know who I am?

"Hey," said Willow, breaking into his reverie. "How's your boy? How's Grundy?"

"Doing remarkably well—the kid up and got married."

"Is that right?" said Willow with genuine surprise and a measure of relief on Roy's behalf.

"Oh yes he did, to an *angel*. And there's wonderful news from the heavenly quarters."

"Oh?"

"Mrs. Angel is gravid with young. She's expecting."

"Isn't that something!" said Willow, masking dismay with delight. "Just fantastic. Congratulations." He couldn't process Grundy as a functioning human being, let alone a dad, but supposed the two weren't mutually exclusive. "You know, I recently became a grandfather myself."

"Did you now?" said Roy, beaming.

"He'll be five in a few months. That's another reason I wanted to move back."

"It's funny," said Roy. "We worry and worry, and in the end they seem to turn out all right."

He knocked on the wood table and then got up and did a slapstick jig, knocking any wood he could find.

"Does Grundy live nearby? Here in New Baltimore?"

"He lives up in Wolcott Mills—used some of that hedge-fund tutor money to buy him and Mrs. Angel a foreclosed farm. Now, *Grundy*, you'll recall, had his share of problems. Did he ever! Thought I was going to lose him. For many, many years I thought that. Then he straightened up and flew right. Oh, he still crashes into windows now and then but he never broke his wings, and that took courage. I respect that. The kid hung in and came out the other side. We both did."

"Here's to coming out the other side," said Willow, raising his Dr. Brown's. "Well, I'd love to see him. And meet the wife and mom-to-be. I'm in Sterling Heights—that's twenty minutes from Wolcott Mills."

"Would that be an official visit?" said Roy hostilely. "Police business, Sergeant Friday?"

Willow's gut flipped and his mouth went slack.

Roy clocked the reaction and burst out laughing. "What I'm *saying* is that there may still be a few open warrants on the boy from the bad old days—desecration of public property, public masturbation and the like. Oh, he was a handful!" Willow smiled in relief. "I'm afraid before I could make that visit happen, I might need a promise of full immunity."

"Request granted."

"Now, mind you, these were youthful crimes."

"I'm sure the statute of limitations has run out."

"Then a visit shall be duly granted, m'lord!"

When Roy asked if he'd retired, it appeared that he wasn't aware of the recent task force hire. At the same time, he thought the query was likely a ploy, because the creation of the Cold Case unit had been all over the local news. Still, he couldn't be sure. He decided it was best to play a game of his own, even though it could backfire.

"Almost there," said Willow. "I'm counting the days."

"Well, come over and count 'em with *me*. Anytime."

"I just might do that."

"Tell you one thing I was counting—the number of green gummy bears you ingested, which was nil. Which means there's more for me. Which makes you my new best friend."

He wrote down Grundy's cell phone and handed it to Willow, nodding at the empty can of Dr. Brown's. "One for the road?"

"I'm good. I *would* like to take a whiz before getting into traffic."

"Always a good idea to drain the snake. Down the hall and hang a left."

As Willow walked away, Roy took a step forward and yelled, "Hey!" He drew the detective's attention to his bare foot and, like a magician doing a trick, slowly moved it aside to reveal the scrap of paper with his son's number that Willow had somehow already managed to lose. Roy picked it up and put it in his hand.

"I don't have athlete's foot. I promise."

Willow was about to enter the toilet when Roy sprinted forward, vigorously blocking his way. "Oops, forgot! Powder room's out of commission—been waitin' on a plumber for three days. Use the one by the washer."

Sarabeth's bloody panties were in the sink, which wouldn't necessarily have been a good thing for Roy.

Or Willow either.

2.

Annie had bad dreams.

To ban the nightmarish images, she dried her face and said the new mantra while looking in the mirror—the slogan that had involuntarily supplanted "More shall be revealed." It reminded her of something in a Victorian children's book:

"All will be most very well."

And all *would* be most very well—for she had found her man, her Porter, and the children would be protected now, which was all that mattered. The tradition would be unbroken. More turbulence was expected, of course, more thunderclaps, marvels and wrinkles, but even with "haywire" factored in Annie knew in her depths that the Great Mystery compassed them and held them close. Considering the current messy state of affairs, such knowledge was grandly counterintuitive, but she'd long since learned to trust the unchallengeable feeling of serenity that thankfully had returned to engulf her. It was an *old* feeling and she was glad it'd come back again; she'd been without it for months now.

Her own apprenticeship had taken over a year, and was devoted to learning Jasper's methods of preparing her for the profoundly disorienting things that Annie would encounter—now she had only weeks, if that, to tutor Willow Millard Wylde. At first, she feared he would never agree to come to the Meeting. Part of him was so distant and unbelieving, and there was an angry part too, that seemed, unthinkably, to be courting his own death. They were so different that way! There was much about him Annie didn't understand nor felt it her business to. So when he accepted her invitation, she said to herself, *We're halfway there. We're more than halfway . . .*

She primped and got ready for her visitor.

Again, Annie looked in the mirror (the one beside the Murphy bed was full-length) at the doomed, blessed woman who stared back: hard-set, timelessly feminine features, bluish porcelain skin, delicate chain of the necklace that her mentor gave her subtly rising and falling to the artery's faint pulse—then a rap on the door startled her.

She looked at her watch: only 6:30 P.M. . . . *He's half an hour early!* Poor thing's probably shaking in his boots. *Lord, how terrified I was when Jasper brought me to my first Meeting.* She remembered actually soiling her underwear when a landlord requested a hug, knowing it was a dead thing—and a dead child!—who'd been asking. It was funny now but it wasn't then. She opened the door and her face froze.

It was Owen Caplan.

"Hello, Annie" was all he said.

She smiled back with warmth and confusion. They'd met a number of times because he was Nurse Adelaide's husband but she didn't really know him. He was the county sheriff, she knew that much.

"Owen, hello! What—what brings—?"

"Sorry to bust in on you like this but I couldn't find a phone number."

"Well, that might be because I haven't a phone!" she said jovially. With flustered concern she asked, "Is something wrong? Is Adelaide all right?"

"She's fine," he said. "And forgive me again, but it's a little urgent and I wasn't sure when I'd see you."

She was mindful that Willow was on his way but it was still early enough. "Come in!"

The SRO building was ramshackle but he noted the elegance she'd brought to the tiny, immaculate room. A lovely kilim carpet spanned most of the floor. Atop a low table was a dark stone vase of white roses.

"I don't have a sitting room," she said humbly. "Though I should say all I *have* is a sitting room—as you can see."

"The reason I'm here is to ask about Renée Devonshire."

Annie looked at him quizzically. "Who is that?"

"A student at Mount Clemens High. She killed a boy there on Thursday. You may have heard what happened."

"Oh Lord. I didn't—I haven't. I'm afraid I'm not much of a newshound. But how awful, how terribly awful."

"I came because we learned that Renée dropped in on some sort of meeting, in Detroit. At the Divine Child Parish on Lafayette Circle. Do you know it?"

"Yes, of course."

"Your name is listed as the person who rents that space for an AA meeting at the hour Renée visited."

"I did rent that space, but had to give it up."

Annie already knew what she'd tell him. She had rehearsed the probability of such an encounter in her head for years. "It's not AA, Owen. That must be some sort of clerical error. It's where I teach—or taught—my class."

"What sort of class, Annie? Do you mind me asking?"

"Not at all! You see—I've never even told Adelaide this—I teach creative writing. It's a bit embarrassing," she said, charmingly contrite. "But, well, I always wanted to write. And I *did* write—tried to, anyway. I think it's safe to say that, over time, I became painfully aware that the public, not to mention the publishers, weren't beating a pathway to my door. In fact, they were beating a pathway away from it! If it said 'by Annie Ballendine,' well, people just seemed to become . . . allergic. And I couldn't blame them. I didn't have the talent. But I found that I might have the talent to teach."

"I'm sure you're a wonderful teacher."

"I'm not licensed, Owen. I don't even have a degree, so I hope you're not here to arrest me."

He knew she was kidding but still wanted to allay any concern. "Of course not. What kind of writing is it, Annie?" he asked, more curious now than interrogatory.

"Oh, all sorts. Mostly poems and short stories but my kids have been doing a lot of memoir work, which is still very much in vogue. It's actually a wonderful tool for self-discovery. But I encourage my students in whatever they feel drawn toward. They *do* write a disproportionate amount of stuff about childhood . . . People don't seem to want to grow up!"

"Sounds pretty great. And as far as I know, you can hang up a shingle without legal repercussions." He winked. "Oh: the girl Renée was also known as Honeychile. Does that ring a bell?"

"'Honeychile,' yes!" She made a split-second decision to be candid, or as candid as she could, because she didn't want to get tripped up if Owen had something else up his sleeve. "I *do* remember, it was such a cute and unusual name. She came—when was it, a few weeks ago?—and I'm afraid it didn't turn out very well." Her nose wrinkled when she said the last, as if hinting at bad behavior. "She's quite young, no?"

"Fourteen."

"Well, I have no *idea* how she found my little workshop. I'm prone to bursts of enthusiasm—I go around town putting up flyers and they wind up being read by all sorts of people . . ."

"Do you remember if she came alone?"

"I don't believe she did," said Annie, cocking her head in recollection. "I'm pretty sure she came with a friend."

"And what happened?"

"May I be frank?"

"Please."

"I thought she was . . . *unstable.* You know, I'm a pretty good, quick read on folks, especially children—though I never had any of my own. And this girl wanted to just *barge in.* Since the class was already in session—well, I thought it would be disruptive, and unfair to the others. And . . . she didn't have the tuition." An anxious look mottled her features. "I only charge ten dollars, Owen, I hope that's all right?"

"That's fine," he said, smiling.

"It's really just to cover rent at the church and pay for cookies and lemonade. And coffee!" she amended, to make things sound more adult.

"You should raise your prices! The sheriff gives you full authority."

"I hate turning away *anyone* who wants to write." She literally wrung her hands. "I felt sorry for that child . . . but from what you told me, I'm rather glad I didn't let her in. God knows what might have happened."

"Well, thank you, Annie. And sorry again to bust in on you."

"Don't be silly. And please give my love to your better half."

"One more thing," he said, fishing something from his pocket. "We found this in Renée's room. Have you seen it before?"

She took it from his hands and blanched. It was the *Guide*.

"She doodled on it—your name's right there, see? 'Annie Ballendine.' And another name—there. It says 'Dabba Doo.' Maybe she's a Flintstones fan."

"Might it be her diary?" she said, playing the naïf.

"I don't think so. As you can see, it's printed out. Which would be un-usual for a diary."

"Well, it *is* a puzzle, isn't it . . . Maybe it's some writing that she was planning to share at my class? A fantasy story or something? Oh dear. Now I feel worse for not letting her in."

"What's strange is that she wrote 'Winston' on the cover. Though it seems to be in a different handwriting . . ."

"Winston?"

"The name of a boy who was murdered a few weeks ago." There was, of course, no reason for him to discuss Honeychile's connection to the discov-ery of Winston's body.

"Another murder? Lord, Owen! What's happening to the world? You're not saying *she* had anything to do with—"

"I'm not saying that at all. But she did kill a boy at school. There's no question about that."

She looked at the *Guide* and read "Winston" out loud. "It *is* odd. It is *very*, very odd."

"Thank you for your time, Annie. And good luck with your students."

Zelda, not Honeychile, was mostly responsible for Annie's decision to change venues—it never bode well for an outsider to know the location of a Meeting. And in the end, she'd been correct; it was Zelda who made it possible for the sheriff to connect the dots that led him to the Porter. If he had actually shown up while a Meeting was in session, the consequences could have been catastrophic.

Ten minutes after Owen departed, at seven on the dot, Willow Wylde knocked on the door. Because he was in law enforcement, she assumed that he knew the sheriff, but had no idea of their long history and close ties. She was going to tell him about the unexpected visit, then thought better of it when she saw his face.

She'd been telling him that the Meeting would be a "great adventure"—but he looked scared to death.

RELAPSE

I.

Three new landlords sat on folding chairs, primly waiting, when the Porter walked in with Willow in tow.

All had been on the train, of course, but Annie never got the chance to visit their cabins—another detail belonging to the "haywire" file, for in the past such a transgression would have been inconceivable. It grieved her because she so prized those precious first encounters with the frightened, fidgety children, when she dispensed treats and soothed them as best she could. It was the time she felt most like a mother. And how dreadful that they would leave empty-handed tonight, without her having had the chance to prepare their *Guides*! It was simply unheard of. She always knew who was on the way, taking great pleasure and care to inscribe their names on the pamphlets' covers. The Subalterns were forced to step in for her, personally delivering the address of the Cross of Glory Lutheran Church to each. And there was another strange thing: once the children left the train, it usually took anywhere from a few days to a full week for their landlords to appear at the Meeting—but these three arrived on the very same day they had become tenants.

When it came to characterizing the shock and gravity of recent events, the word *haywire* fell woefully short.

Annie shook it off and struggled to focus on the task at hand. She was passing the baton to a new Porter, just as her mentor had done with her, and was determined not to let the children *or* Willow down. No, that simply wasn't an option. But there was something Annie couldn't shake, evoking what her head called "the black panic"—with a vertiginous shudder, she realized that Dabba Doo and Violet weren't in the room. (Troy and Maya were merely late, which had happened twice before and raised no red flags.) As she linked their absence to the information the sheriff had provided about "Winston," it was suddenly all of a theme and her worst fears were confirmed.

Last night, during feverish sleep, she caught a glimpse of tiny Violet on the train—running *from* her, not toward her. But how? It wasn't possible! The children weren't allowed to board again until they'd had their *moment of balance*. Violet shared at the Meeting that she felt her *moment* was nearing ("You better get my birthday cake ready, Porter!"), but it hadn't yet happened . . . though *could* it have? Could it be that "haywire" made the Porter miss it? As the passenger compartments rounded a bend, she saw the pajama'd little girl wrench herself from the Subalterns' restraining arms and then leap into an abyss with a bone-rattling yowl. Her dark braids, weirdly lit by moonlight, gave only the briefest hint of how far she was falling. Like a somnambulist—or the heroine of a horror film—Annie perilously began to make her way toward the window that Violet had jumped from. As her pace quickened, the Porter dashed past the cabins of the frightened children who so desperately waited for her to come to them—the very ones in this room tonight—but there wasn't time . . . And why were all of the windows of the corridor wide-open? They gaped like the throats of dead birds. The Subalterns were gone now and the light in the corridor sickeningly flickered. As she ran, Annie stepped on a trail of sticky things, a bumpy carpet leading all the way to where Violet had vanished.

When she took off her shoes, she saw them in the cold, stroboscopic light, stuck like cleats to her soles—crushed green gummy bears.

. . .

Annie's presence was of course an enormous comfort, anchoring Willow as he floated in the half dream, half nightmare of the Meeting. (He was startled to see *everyone* wrapped in a blue haze.) She introduced him as a "special friend." He didn't catch anyone's name; he could hardly remember his own. She knew he was in distress and occasionally reached over to pat his knee, as if to say, *You're doing just fine.* She apologized to the newbies for not having brought their *Guides* (a "snafu," she said) and promised to hand them out at the next Meeting. The room was dark, save the glimmering candles that Annie asked Bumble to light, in her wish to soothe the *Guide*less freshmen.

After ten minutes passed, Lydia and Daniel slipped in, nodding cursory apologies to the Porter for their tardiness. They took their seats and scanned the candlelit room, registering surprise at so many new bodies (including the one sitting next to Annie). The half-light blurred the faces, but they were still able to make note of the absence of old colleagues:

Violet, Dabba Doo and Winston.

As the Meeting came to a close, Lydia wondered if Annie had done as promised, before they'd arrived—if she had told the group she was dying. She decided that the Porter probably hadn't; there were too many new ones and it would have frightened them. All stood and held hands, while the first-timers nervously took their cues from Annie, Lydia and Daniel. As he joined in the recitation, Willow noted with irony that it was the first time the Lord's Prayer had given him succor. When it was done, Annie smiled and said, "More shall be revealed," before adding, "And all will be most very well!"

When the sentry turned the lights on, Willow, Daniel and Lydia locked eyes. Lydia gasped, "No!" and fainted; Daniel propped her up so she wouldn't fall. Willow, dumbfounded, muttered, "How? How?" Annie watched it unfold and then shooed the others from the room.

"You can't be!" said Lydia, as she roused, clambering from dream to dream. She turned to Annie, pleading, "He *can't* be dead!"

Daniel, still possessing the cool nerves of a combat veteran, shook Willow's trembling hand. "Welcome! What's your name?"

"Willow Wylde," he said by rote, in a complete state of shock.

"Not your landlord name," said Daniel. "Your *child* name."

"He doesn't have one," said Annie, in slow realization that the three somehow knew one another outside the Meeting.

"I don't understand," said Daniel, confounded.

"He's going to be your new teacher."

"But what do you *mean*?" said Lydia.

"Willow is the new Porter. He'll be taking my place."

Daniel screwed his eyes at the detective for a good, long look. "*Now* I know who you are," he stuttered. "Now I remember . . . I *knew* that I knew you!" He took a deep breath and declared, "You were a friend of our father's." He turned to Lydia and said, "He's Pace Wylde's dad."

"Pace?" said Lydia. She looked like she might faint again.

"Pace! Our *babysitter* . . ."

Willow could hear Daniel's words but nothing made sense; like a corrupted hard drive, his brain had frozen. Lydia dropped to her knees, sobbing uncontrollably as she clung to his legs. Willow turned to Annie, in helpless supplication. "I don't understand! Please! Help me—"

"Well," she said calmly. "They seem to know *your* name—but you don't know theirs." She helped Lydia to her feet. "It is my honor to introduce you," said the Porter, not fully cognizant of the havoc that her words were about to cause, "to Troy and Maya Rummer."

It was Willow's turn to collapse.

The siblings came together, helping him to a chair. Daniel brought a cup of lemonade while Lydia knelt beside him. As his consciousness flagged and rallied, he weakly smiled.

Then Daniel knelt too, and brother and sister each took one of his hands in a crowded pietà.

2.

Willow told them to meet him at the Early World Diner.

They got there first. After half an hour, Daniel began to think their boss might not show—that the shock of the revelation was likely too much and he had probably jumped ship. He understatedly added that if the detective *didn't* come on board, "it's going to open a fairly serious can of worms."

Then Willow walked in, shifty-eyed and ashen. He sat down almost reluctantly; for a few minutes no one spoke.

"First of all, I am *never* going to call you by those names," he said at last. "*Maya* and *Troy*—that's the last time you'll hear me say them."

"Fair enough," said Lydia, in sympathy.

"We get it," said Daniel.

Compared with Willow, they were old hands at the game, and they knew he had some serious catching up to do. They were actually surprised that he was doing so well—um, considering.

"Secondly, I have some questions. Forget the *big* questions—I can't even go there. I'll lose my fucking mind."

"We hear you," said Daniel.

"Don't *humor* me," said Willow brusquely. He composed himself and was about to speak when the waitress approached. They ordered coffees. When she left, he said, "What part of you is Lydia and Daniel—and what part is . . . those *kids*?" The absurdity of the question made him bridle halfway through the asking; he was grinning like a dyspeptic clown.

"Well, sometimes it's hard to say," said Lydia.

"Try me!" he said cynically.

"And by the way," she said. "The Porter—Annie calls us 'landlords.' Lydia and Daniel are the *landlords* of Maya and Troy."

"That's the lingo," said Daniel.

"And Maya and Troy are the 'tenants,' " she added.

"*Whatever*," said Willow.

"As to your question," said Daniel. "Sometimes it's more one than the other. Landlords and tenants switch off. But at a certain point the tenants take over. At least they're supposed to."

"Sometimes I feel more like Maya—is it okay to say the name?"

"Say it all you want! *I'm* just not going to say it."

"Fair enough," said Daniel.

"And stop saying 'fair enough'!" he barked. "I hate that."

"Sorry, sir."

"Sometimes I feel more like 'Maya' than 'Lydia.' What my brother— what Daniel was saying is that we *do* feel all those little-kid kind of feelings, but we're still the main—we're still the adults. *Daniel and Lydia* are the adults in the car, and *Troy and Maya* are the ones along for the ride." She turned to Daniel and said, "Does that make sense?"

"Absolutely. It wasn't like that at first, though," he said, continuing the analogy. "It was like the kids were in the trunk! *Very* confusing. Then one day they sort of popped up in the backseat. Now sometimes they're in front, giving directions!"

"Or trying to," said Lydia, in a nod to their recent crossed-wires trouble.

The veins in Willow's head looked like a blue candelabra. "But I *knew* you," he nearly shouted. "I knew *both* of you—I knew your *parents*. How could you not have recognized me?"

"Troy did!" she said gleefully, as Daniel smugly looked on. "He *totally* did. He was always telling me that he thought he remembered you from somewhere . . ."

"Yup—just couldn't put it all together. Plus, you don't exactly look like you used to. You got fat and your face changed."

Lydia tittered at the indiscretion.

"That's right," Willow snorted. "I'm a fat, ugly slob."

"Sorry about that, sir. You actually don't look too bad."

"I think you're handsome," said Lydia.

"And as far as not recognizing you," said Daniel, "Maya wouldn't have because she was too young. When exactly did you move away, sir? Didn't you move to New York?"

"In '97," said Willow.

"Well, there you go—she was only three . . . and we only really saw you *occasionally*, when you dropped by to see our folks. But I was six then and old enough to remember. And the Fourth of July, the day we 'went away,' was the first time we'd seen you in a long time."

"Oh my God, *Pace!*" exclaimed Lydia. "We loved Pace! She was the bestest babysitter!"

It seemed to Willow that Maya was talking now, not Lydia, and he felt on the verge of cracking up.

"How is she?" said Lydia.

"Fine," he said tersely. "She's good, she's well."

Wonderful. I'm giving updates on my daughter to the dead.

"Why'd you leave her? Why'd you go away?"

The general question cut to the quick and he chose to ignore it. "But what about Lydia and Daniel—the 'landlords' or whatever? If they had to die in order for Maya and Troy to—what *happened* to them? Do you know how they—how *you*—" The pronoun-jumping was exasperating. "Do you know how they, you, whoever, died?"

Lydia went first. "I think when I was hiking, on the Orchard Trail. I fell and hit a rock with my head. A totally freak, stupid thing. That's when I first felt her—felt Maya come."

"What about you?" he asked Daniel.

"Heart attack—one night at my wife Rachelle's. The thing nobody knows is that I had a heart attack a year and a half before, right when I was about to apply to the Academy. A pretty bad one. But I wanted to be a cop and there was no way I was going to let that stop me. A doctor friend of mine lied and gave me a clean bill of health. Actually, he was someone Rachelle fucked"—Lydia didn't like the language and looked at him askance—"and I blackmailed him into doing it." He tilted his head, ruminating. "I guess it's okay to tell you that now. I guess there can't really be any official repercussions. I mean, now that you know I'm dead."

The detective let the attempt at wit slide. "And what about your parents?" he asked.

"What about them?" said Daniel.

"Don't you have the desire to see them?"

"But see who?" said Lydia. "I mean, *which* parents?"

"Whomever!" said Willow, exasperated.

"Well, if you're talking about Daniel," he said, "we weren't all that close. I barely saw my folks *before* I died,"

"And if you're talking about *Lydia*, I still talk to Mom a couple times a week."

"And Elaine and Ronnie?" To make himself clear he needed to break his own rule, but at that point didn't really give a shit. "What about *Troy and Maya's* parents. Didn't you both want—don't you want to see them?"

"Not really," said Daniel, shrugging.

"We've *talked* about going by the old house," said Lydia, answering for Maya. "In Saggerty Falls. But it feels somehow we'd be more like tourists or lookie-loos . . . I know it doesn't sound logical but I guess we just haven't had the urge. Annie said we probably wouldn't, at least not until our *moment of balance*. She said that's the way it works. The trouble is, once you've had your *moment*, there usually isn't any time left. You know, for a visit."

"And what about—didn't Lydia and Daniel have boyfriends, girlfriends? Lovers?"

Lydia blushed. "Well, I don't know how the others handled it—the landlords at the Meeting—but we lucked out. The word kind of spread that we were an item, so people left us alone."

"That is *so creepy*," said Daniel, in his high voice.

"And how do you feel?" said Willow, trying to get a grip—and failing. "I mean, *physically*."

"I guess sex is no longer a priority," said Daniel.

"Gross!" said Lydia.

"But the Porter told us that's kind of par for the course."

"No, I meant physically, in *general*," said Willow. "I mean, your bodies . . . how do they maintain—"

"I see what you mean," said Daniel. "You'd think it would be the opposite but we're actually *stronger*. In some ways. Right, Lydia?"

"Yeah, it's weird. I stopped getting my periods—"

"Yuck," said Daniel.

"—and Maya didn't even know what that *was*. I only had it once, then it stopped. Thank God."

Daniel sat up straight. "Annie said that the closer you get to the *moment of balance*, the tougher your body becomes. She said she didn't know why."

"That's just the way it works," said Lydia.

"Like you get . . . *fierce*," he said. "Like Rhonda did, right?"

"Yeah, whoa!" said Lydia. "That was *crazy*. Rhonda was totally like the Terminator."

"Who's Rhonda?"

"Just a guy who used to come to the Meeting," she said.

They told him about the events at Jacobs Prairie and for the thousandth time that night he was pole-axed. The detective in him (or was it the Porter?) wanted to know if they'd left any prints or evidence behind. They said they'd been careful about that because the *Guide* stressed the importance of not leaving clues at the scene of a *moment of balance*.

He excused himself to the men's room.

Willow splashed water on his face and stared at the haggard, blown-out man in the mirror. He went into the stall, sat on the toilet and phoned Dixie. She was expecting him but there was no way he was in any shape to go home. He told her that he was "into it" at work and that she shouldn't wait up. Dixie said okay but that she probably wasn't going to sleep until whenever, and if he saw her light on he should just come over.

When he returned, they were tucking into cheeseburgers and milkshakes— like hungry kids, he thought.

"I think I'm gonna take off," said Willow.

"Okay," said Daniel. "And thank you."

"Thank me for what?"

"For helping us," said Lydia. "Annie said that you're really, really special. We need help, sir! We've been having a lot of—problems."

"Give the man a moment," said Daniel to his partner. "Let him integrate."

"See you at work tomorrow," said Willow, standing to leave. The hum-drum remark was meant to mimic normalcy. "Oh: I *did* want to ask you about Honeychile. What was that all about? Why did you try to go see her?"

They suddenly realized he had no idea that Honeychile was a landlord, just like them. The only person who could have provided him with that information was Annie—and apparently, she hadn't. Lydia and Daniel were seized by the same troublesome thought: What if Annie didn't know that Honeychile had stopped coming to the Meeting because she'd been arrested for murder? Could it even be possible that Annie wouldn't know? Because didn't she know everything? Another thought followed: Why hadn't they shared with her what they knew about the crime? (Both of them were aware something had gone wrong—that the death of the football player had nothing to do with "Winston's" *moment of balance.*) It was a strange and unaccountable oversight on their part, indeed, and each felt a shiver of guilt at the omission—made somehow worse by their clandestine visit to Dabba Doo's.

Lydia decided to blurt the whole thing out. But as she began, Daniel gave her an elbow, forcing her to amend. "Uhm, I don't know—it was just a *feeling* I had," she said, improvising a dumbed-down version. "Like when we flew to St. Cloud to look for Rhonda."

"Right—just a feeling," said Daniel. "We got it into our heads that Hon-eychile might know something about how Troy and Maya died."

Only a short while ago they were crying in Willow's arms, so it felt odd to still be lying to him about certain things. The detective was too beat-up to explore any further.

"I understand you wore your old uniforms when you stopped by at the hospital."

"Sorry about the boner," said Daniel, snickering at the word in spite of himself.

Willow's irritation at their antics gave him a second wind. "Well, *do* you think she knows something? About who killed you—I mean, your *tenants?*"

The one who was asking was half detective, half Porter, and Willow was startled by his commitment to the new reality that lay behind his words.

"*Mayyy-beee*," said Lydia. "I think maybe she does."

"*Oh* yeah," said Daniel. "There's something there, mos' def. We can *feel* it."

"The sheriff's interviewing the girl tomorrow," said Willow.

He had nothing more to add. Shattered by the night's events, he was only able to spit out a bullet point.

"It'd be *really good* if we could talk to her. I mean if that's at all possible." Lydia said it offhandedly, not wanting to press her luck. "Because we've kind of been chasing our tails. But Annie said that was going to change, now that you're here."

"You said you had a 'feeling,'" said Willow. "Did you even *know* that girl? I checked with the family and that story of yours about the veterans' group was complete bullshit."

Their hand had been forced. So be it—they would have told him tomorrow anyway. Probably.

"I guess Annie isn't all that well," said Daniel, speaking more to Lydia than to Willow. "She's been really sick. Maybe that's why she didn't know about Honeychile's arrest. Because it's definitely something the Porter should have already known about—she'd have *felt* it."

"What are you talking about?" said the detective.

"What I mean is that it would have been up to her to tell you, not to us."

"We were just being respectful," said Lydia. "By not telling you. Respectful to Annie."

"Tell me *what*?" It was maddening.

"Honeychile is a landlord," said Daniel. "She used to come to our Meeting."

"Only for a few times," said Lydia. "That's how we know her."

"Do you mean," said Willow, "that killing the boy at school was part of her *moment of balance?*"

"Nope," said Daniel. "And that's the problem."

"We think she killed the wrong one," said Lydia.

"Yup. I kinda think that when she took out Mr. Letter Jacket Asshole, she made a total raging boner."

He started giggling again.

"But we didn't call her Honeychile," said Lydia. "I knew that was her name from when she tried to break into the Meeting that time—but it's not what we called her. You *never* use landlord names in a Meeting."

"That's a total no-no," said Daniel.

"Everyone called her Winston."

3.

Eleven P.M. now.

He was drinking.

The bar on North Avenue had an unfortunate name:

Dickweeds.

It was empty—just him, the barkeep and some other drunk in a booth. He was on his fourth Tom Collins but didn't feel it. There was a phrase in Alcoholics Anonymous that applied to the experience of someone who tried boozing again after being exposed to 12-Step work: "AA ruined my drinking."

Willow thought that's what had happened to him, but with a caveat: *Dead children ruined my drinking.*

The bombshell that Renée "Honeychile" Devonshire was a player in Annie's permanent floating ghost dance was disturbing but presented itself (to the part of him that was a detective) as a puzzle—perhaps *the* puzzle that needed to be solved. The old, familiar feeling of being "in the zone," that smell of cracking a stubborn case, had returned with a delicious vengeance. Under the radical new circumstances, Willow wasn't really sure what that feeling meant, he didn't know what *anything* meant, yet the rookies' revelation reflexively stirred the thing that had always protected and served him: the sleeping giant called Hope.

The story they recounted about Rhonda and the murders at Jacobs

Prairie aroused an entirely different emotion. Willow had a toe in both worlds, but the toe in *Annie's* world was badly stubbed. The panic that caused him to hoist a drink at Dickweeds wasn't merely rooted in the abrupt and phantasmagoric upheaval of his life—it was more prosaic. Simply put, if he didn't tell Owen what he was now privy to, he would technically become a coconspirator, an obstructer of justice at the very least. Because not only did Willow know the identity of the killer (the name of "Rhonda's" landlord could be uncovered easily enough), but he knew the witnesses as well—Cold Case deputies who worked directly under him! By not intervening in a murder they could easily have prevented, they were as guilty as the perpetrator himself.

Yet Willow the inchoate Porter understood everything, or at least was beginning to. While the *Porter* had no allegiance to the traditional, so-called truth and its attendant morals and jurisprudence, the *detective*—the veteran cop and professional, the provider for hearth and home (Pace, Larkin)—bridled at the potential consequences of criminal malfeasance that went along with a course of nonaction, nudging him toward accountability and the fantasy of telling his superior all. But what would he confess? That he'd become a sorcerer's apprentice? That he was communing with the dead? It was a conundrum that he knew had no resolution.

And what about Grundy Eakins? Willow hadn't even been able to summon the energy to drive out to Wolcott Mills, which (as a detective) was unforgivable . . .

There were so many things to drink about that selecting merely one seemed the greatest of luxuries.

Deep in his cups now, he meditated on karma. He used to talk about the concept with Renata, the opinionated Buddhist; they spent many an hour in the smoke pit at the Meadows, inhaling nicotine and confabbing in the 110-degree heat. She believed karma didn't exist, "because there is no 'you' and there is no 'me.' How can there be retribution when there's no 'doer' of the deed or crime? What they call *karma* is just more sisboombah Catholic bullshit." For him, the dialectic was a little rarefied. He was old-school and believed there was balance and symmetry to the universe, call it what you will. She scoffed and said that was just a pretty way of saying "eye for an eye." Maybe she was right.

He was about to order another drink when the man in the booth got up. Instead of passing Willow, he stopped right beside him—it was Charles in Charge. The detective felt a shudder of shame and paranoia. Charlie of course knew that he was sober. After an awkward hello, Willow decided the best defense was a strong offense. He pointed to his glass and said, by way of explanation, "I just got a piece of very bad news."

"Awfully sorry, Dubya." He put a hand on his old friend's shoulder and warmly said, "Take good care now."

It was just like Charlie not to pry. He was about to leave when Willow gripped his arm.

"Charlie, I'd appreciate it if you didn't mention this to the sheriff."

"No worries." The man's word was gold. "Hope it's nothing with Adelaide or the family."

"No," said Willow. He at least had to disabuse him of that. "Nothing like that. A friend of mine passed away."

"I'm sorry to hear."

"It's all good," said Willow, world-weary.

Charlie patted the detective's shoulder again. "You good to drive?"

"Yeah, I'm good," he said, then touched his arm and smiled. "I love you, buddy." And he really did. As Charlie left, Willow said, "Charles in Charge," like he always had when they parted, as if in benediction.

T he detective did what he told himself he wouldn't.

He knocked on Dixie's door.

And her light wasn't even on.

She was pleasantly surprised and literally pulled him over the threshold by his lapels. She smelled the liquor and said "Oh" but kissed him anyway. She didn't have it in her to be judgey, even if she knew how serious the situation might be. All she said was "You okay?" as she helped strip off his clothes. His

pants got caught around his legs and he stumbled like a cartoon drunk, bracing his fall against the couch. Dixie laughed, saying, "Whoa there!" and he
blurted out, *I love you.* "That's what they all say after last call," she said.

He came on like a lion in bed but that didn't last. Inside five minutes he
was cradled in her arms, his body convulsing in tears. She let him do that
while she stroked and shushed.

"Talk to me, baby. What's going on?"

"It's—*those kids*. The Rummer kids, Maya and Troy."

Saying their names out loud, saying anything about them, ambushed
him. He had mentioned the case to her weeks ago in the most impersonal
way, without naming names, and now he felt immense shame at pimping
the innocents as an excuse for his relapse, much like he'd summoned the
"death of a friend" with Charles in Charge. The horror and sadness of it
tore through Willow's very soul.

"How they must have suffered—" he said, in agony.

"I know, I know . . ."

"I *knew* them, Dixie! I never told you that, but I knew those kids, I
knew their *folks*—who are destroyed, by the way. I went to see them and
they are completely destroyed. My daughter *babysat* those children!" He
closed his eyes. "When I think of what happened to them—that it could
have happened to Pace . . ."

"But it *didn't*, sweetheart. It didn't. And I'm *glad* you're letting this shit
out. It's okay to cry, babe, you have to, you *need* to. We need to cry! And I
know how you hold that in, I know it's part of your job not to show how
much you hurt. You've been holding so much in for so long—your whole *life*.
So let it out, babe, just let it out. I'm here. I'm here. I'm here . . ."

As he nodded out on the bed, he prayed he wouldn't dream of the train.
Leave me in peace, he thought. When Dixie solicitously asked if he wanted
to sleep alone, Willow realized he'd said those words out loud, and it stabbed
at him that he might have wounded her. "I didn't mean that for you, babe . . .
No, I want you here. I need you here." She smiled, quizzically, as if she
didn't quite believe him. "Okay," she said.

"I'm a hot mess, huh," he said.

"Yeah, but you're my hot mess. At least tonight you are."

He kissed her cheek. "Thank you, Dixie."

"We aim to please."

"Watch your aim, babe. Wouldn't want any more casualties."

"Too late for that," she said.

DECOMPENSATION

I.

While a small part of him yearned to go back to the Meeting, Roy Eakins knew that he was done—with the Porter and the landlords and the whole deal. It was the "residual" of his child-tenant that tugged at him to return, because he missed his playmates.

But Dabba Doo was gone forever.

It would be challenging now to make the journey to the Cross of Glory Lutheran Church even if he wanted to. The drive would be too rough. He wasn't physically well and his weakness surprised him, because of late he'd experienced a cascade of strength and well-being that he attributed to the killing of Violet and her landlord, Sarabeth. He still had power surges—moments when he felt almost superhuman—but the "hangovers" that followed were getting worse. He wet his bed every night and lately the sheets were stained by his stool. When Roy used the machine at CVS, he thought it was broken; he had no blood pressure at all. His urine was black and he had episodes of blindness in alternating eyes; except for the beloved, dreaded gummy bears (he was even losing his taste for those), he could hold down only broth. His skin was splotched by purple starbursts. He thought of seeing a doctor and then laughed when he imagined the fellow entering the examination room to tell him the test results came back, revealing that he was dead. Like one of those good news–bad news jokes.

With careful thought and determination, he'd traced back the moment when Dabba Doo moved in, nearly ten months ago to the day, after a lethal heart attack. How and why his ruined body continued to function was a thing that he ceded to Annie and her Mystery talk: there are more things in heaven and Earth, and all that. But now he felt as if he were dying *again*. That excited him because he couldn't help believing that if he could fool death once, he might do it twice. Perhaps he was meant for bigger things.

Perhaps he was meant to become Death itself.

His attention drifted to the photos pinned on the wall:

A blurry image of Sarabeth Ahlström (he'd written *Miss Shrinking VIOLET* above it) from her LinkedIn profile, poorly printed on his antiquey HP . . . Deputies Lydia Molloy and Daniel Doheny (*TROY and MAYA-oh-my-a!!!*), scissored from an article in the *Macomb Gazette* covering the inauguration of the new Cold Case unit . . . and a yearbook photo of Renée Devonshire (*win-win WINSTON!!*) that he'd found online. The playmates from the Meeting who once elicited such affection were poison to him now. But he needed them—so went the incomprehensible logic of an incomprehensible being—if he was to live.

To live!

For he had come to believe their deaths would act like toxins, in the manner that pathogens of certain snakes, fish and plants can be titrated and absorbed by human beings, allowing them to survive a condition that would be fatal without such intervention.

2.

Renée was still druggy when the sheriff arrived. ("Medicated, but to the minimum," as the doctor put it.) The suspect had "decompensated"—

completely broken with reality. Owen thought that an interview would be futile but he had to try. He brought along Ruthie Levin, an investigator whose specialty was the forensic interview. She was skilled in speaking to juveniles.

She'd been temporarily moved from a padded safety cell to a thick-glassed, sunny room with carpet and sofa. Instead of a hospital gown, she wore the pajamas her parents dropped off. Owen was startled by her appearance. She looked nothing like the girl he'd glimpsed in the back of the squad car that day at Mount Clemens High. She had purplish blotches on the skin above her breasts that one of the RNs said were most likely caused by a reaction to antipsychotics. Still, they reminded him of the skin eruptions of dying children he'd met at Adelaide's hospital.

She smelled like something that was dying.

"Good morning, Honeychile." He thought it was best to use her nickname. "I'm Detective Caplan—and this is Ruthie Levin. We're here to talk with you for just a little. Is that okay?"

When she didn't respond, he nodded to the investigator.

"Hi! And thank you for seeing us today," said Ruthie. "I know it's not easy being here. And the first thing that's so important to say is that no one's upset or angry with you, okay? We just want to get your side of the story. You know, I've been doing this a long time and if there's anything I've learned it's that there's always two sides of a story. And we'd very much like to hear yours."

"That's right," said Owen. "We're not here to judge."

"We just want to know your side. And we're *very* happy to have a chance to sit with you today and just listen."

They waited awhile but she was silent. Just when Owen was about to try a different approach, Honeychile whispered, "Winston was kilt." She stared at the floor, making it easier for the colleagues to communicate by a semaphore of glances, urging or cueing each other to push forward or hang back.

"Who killed him, Honeychile?" said Owen. He didn't think he had anything to lose by cutting to the chase. "Do you know who killed Winston?"

Ruthie discreetly raised her hand, telegraphing him to move slower.

"We're trying to find out who hurt Winston," she said. "And we think you can help. How did you know where we would find him, Honeychile? Where we could find Winston? Because thanks to everything you told us, we *did* find him—and that meant so very, very much to his mom. We really want to thank you for showing us where he was."

"They put Winston in the water," said Honeychile.

"Can you tell us—do you think you can tell us how you knew that?" she said. "That he was in the water? Can you tell us how you knew that, Honeychile? Did someone tell you? Or did you see it? Did someone tell you that Winston was in the water?"

After a moment, Owen said, "Were you there when they put Winston in the water?"

If his eyes weren't playing tricks, he could swear that more splotches were appearing on her calves and forearms, like flowers opening in slow motion.

"Honeychile kilt wrong one! Honeychile the *biggest loser*," she said, and began to cry.

"It's okay, it's okay," said Ruthie, daring to put a hand on the girl's shoulder. Honeychile was oblivious to the gesture.

"He was a mean, nasty boy but did *not* kilt Winston."

"Who was a mean, nasty boy?" said Ruth.

"Boy at skwool. Boy she kilt."

"Why did you kill the boy at school?" said Owen.

"*Honeychile* kilt him, not me!"

"Okay," said Ruthie. "And who are you? Can you tell us who you are?"

"Winston."

"Do you know why she killed him, Winston?"

"'Cause she think he kilt *Winston*," she said angrily. "But it was the bad man who kilt him."

"*Who* was the 'bad man'?" said Owen, powering through despite Ruth's caution. He sensed they'd come as far as they would today—or possibly ever. "Can you tell us about the bad man? Was he alone?"

"I saw woman," she said.

"Was Honeychile with the man?"

"Honeychile *not* with him," she scowled.

"Did you know her? Did you know the woman that you saw?" said Ruthie.

"Woman had wings!" said Honeychile.

"Wings?" said Owen, looking impatiently toward Ruthie.

"Like *angel*," said the girl, her breath becoming labored. "But Honeychile she *fail!* I going to be punished on *train! Porter* going *punish* me! Me and Winston s'posed to *kilt* him—but Honeychile kilt wrong one . . ."

She sobbed, then screamed.

As the sheriff and his colleague stood, two males nurses rushed in to subdue her.

3.

The Task Force gathered in the conference room for a midmorning coffee.

Sitting there with his "kids"—he'd called them that from day one and now laughed at the irony—the detective experienced a cognitive dissonance. From all appearances, things looked, felt and *seemed* normal, though nothing could have been further from the truth. Instead of dissipating, the dream Willow was trapped in grew more real by the hour. He thought of the end of *The Shining*, when Jack Nicholson vanishes into a group photo taken on Independence Day, fifty or sixty years before ("You have always been the caretaker," says the spooky bartender), and fantasized himself entering the mural that he painted on his apartment wall. Dixie would wonder where he'd gone and, when she came to look for him, wouldn't even notice his haunted face staring out at her from one of the windows of the train.

You have always been the Porter . . .

"Daniel," he said. "Let's go over what you remember from that day." It was really Troy whom he was asking, but Willow still couldn't bring himself to use the name. "Start from when your father told you to borrow the lighter fluid."

The deputy shrugged and went blank-faced. "Daddy asked us to go to Ebenezer's. I just remember being on our bikes."

"Do we know what Ebenezer's been up to? Does he still live in the area?"

"He's in a lovely community outside Harrison Township," said Lydia, with a slight smile.

"Go and talk to him," said Willow.

"He makes his home in a quiet little village called Erin Grove," said Daniel.

"It's a cemetery," said Lydia. "Tractor accident, ten years ago."

"A very grave situation," said Daniel.

"You're both fuckin' hilarious," said Willow, unamused.

Suddenly, he thought: What was the point of all this? Of chasing actual clues and Persons of Interest, of sifting through evidence . . . What was the point of a traditional "investigation"? Wasn't the arrival of Troy and Maya supposed to make Lydia and Daniel—wasn't it supposed to confer upon the whole freak foursome some kind of omniscience? For chrissake! These were dead children who'd dropped down from God knows where, like the supernatural hammer of Thor! Weren't they supposed to simply *know* the identity of their killers? And if they *were* supposed to know, why hadn't the deputies made any headway? Willow wondered if it was something he was doing—or not doing—that was creating obstacles, impeding their flow. He felt like an inept counselor lost in the woods with two frightened scouts.

He decided it was all of a theme, in this world and any other: he was failing again. He had *always* failed and now he was failing in the sacred task entrusted to him. And, as in times of challenges past, he wanted out.

"Can either of you expand upon the process or method of how exactly the tenants—how the *children* reach their *moment of balance?*" He still chafed against the essential phrase, enunciating it with a measure of sarcasm. "Do you think you can help me with that?"

"It just comes," said Lydia. "Annie said it's more of a feeling than any-thing else. She said that one day, you just know."

"But what if you don't?" said Daniel, rhetorically. "What if that 'feeling' never comes? Personally, I think something's gone wrong. Because by now we should have known who killed us."

Bingo, thought Willow.

"I'm not sure that's true," said Lydia meekly.

"And what about Dabba Doo?" asked Daniel, continuing to build some sort of ominous case. "In a few months—if he ever comes back—that means he'll have been coming to the Meeting for a year! And from what the Porter said—the *Guide* said it too!—that isn't possible."

Willow wandered over to the corkboard. Staring at the hit parade of evidentiary pinups, he had deep thoughts—though not about the Rummer case. Instead, he asked himself if he felt like a drink. He didn't, not really . . . though maybe it was time to *surrender*, surrender to alcoholism and concede it was booze that provided Willow Wylde his very own *moment of balance*— a custom blend of revenge, symmetry and justice that would never let him down, *one day at a time*, until his trudging-buddy pallbearers (all those he'd abysmally failed) trudged him to the grave.

They joined their boss at the board.

"What are those?" said Lydia, in confusion.

The detective had come in early and thumbtacked two images. One was a photo taken from a 1998 school yearbook of a staffer in a loud bow tie, smiling broadly. The caption read "Roy Eakins, American History. *History doesn't repeat itself but it often rhymes.*—Mark Twain." The other was a re-cent picture of "R. J. Eakins" that Willow clipped from an article in the *Anchor Bay Bugle* about locals who were protesting the installation of park-ing meters with computer chips.

"That's Dabba Doo," said Daniel, wide-eyed.

"Dabba Doo?"

"From the Meeting," said Lydia.

"He stopped coming, which is weird. Because he hasn't taken his birth-day cake," said Daniel.

"Jesus," said Willow, under his breath.

In the detective's view, Roy had never been a viable contender in the leading role of the Rummer murders anyway. And yet, after the uneventful visit to the tidy home in New Baltimore, Willow had been surprised when his gut stubbornly refused to acquit the schoolteacher of the crimes. Now, though, learning that Eakins was de facto *dead* seemed absolute proof of his innocence. Willow couldn't believe he was capable of such berserk logic: as far as he knew, the children of the train only sought revenge on the living. If Roy *had* killed Troy and Maya, how could they balance the scales if he was already dead? He would definitely need to have a talk with Annie about that, if only for curiosity's sake . . .

Now that he knew Roy was a landlord, he felt hoodwinked. It gave him the willies just thinking about being "entertained" by a charming cadaver on a pleasant afternoon. The damn thing even made him a sandwich. It made him feel unclean.

"Do you really mean to say," said Lydia, "that *Roy Eakins* . . . is Dabba Doo?" She sounded both like a child whose father had just told her Santa Claus wasn't real, and like an adult who'd been told that he *was*.

"Apparently," mused Willow. "And I wonder why he stopped attending the Meeting."

His detective mind leapt forward. Where there's cremation smoke, there's fire—he had better get on that interview with Grundy tout de suite.

"Hear me out, sir," said Daniel, who hadn't been paying much attention to the exchange. "It's imperative that we speak to Honeychile." It was less a suggestion than it was a pronouncement. "If at all possible."

"I agree, sir. Daniel has a really strong *feeling* about it," said Lydia.

"The sheriff was supposed to interview her this morning," said Willow. "I'll ask how it went—she may not be in shape for that. But if we *do* see her, I'm going to have to tell Owen about it beforehand. I don't want a repeat of that fiasco."

Happy with the new plan, Lydia and Daniel made a shiny little show of getting back to work. Willow blinked at the stuffed unicorn that hung in its

Ziploc just above the photos of Roy. It whispered but he could not yet hear what it was telling him.

4.

After the visit from Owen and his investigator, the patient's transforma-tion was radical and unexpected. She became calm and lucid, nearly present-ing as "normal." She promised to behave and begged to be transferred from protective isolation. Because of the murder charge, they wouldn't allow her to mingle with other patients, but the doctors agreed she could change to a more "mood-elevating" room. Even her skin blotches seemed to fade.

Honeychile said that she wanted to draw, which her therapists encour-aged. Crayons and paper were approved. Through the locked door and wired glass portal, the staff could hear her sing while she sketched. The nurses couldn't believe she had killed a six-foot-tall football player—so tiny, so demure! They smiled as they listened, busying themselves in the change-over to swing shift.

"Girl's got a voice. She should go on tour," said an RN.

"Give Katy Perry a run for her money," said another.

"That's going to have to be some serious running, cause Katy got a *lot* of money!"

As Honeychile put the finishing touches on her butterfly-winged angel, she luxuriated in the melody:

When, when the fire's at my feet again
And the vultures all start circling
They're whispering, you're out of time,
But still I rise

This is no mistake, no accident
When you think the final nail is in

Think again, don't be surprised
I will still rise

The nurses didn't notice when the singing stopped.

W illow told the sheriff that his unit's preliminary investigation indi-
cated that Renée "Honeychile" Devonshire might possibly be in
possession of information of value to the Rummer case. He was prepared to
be vague and lay it off on something "the kids" were chasing down, but
Owen reacted with indifference.

"Have at it, Dubya. She's in the Twilight Zone."

Truer words were never spoken, thought Willow. *You don't know the*
half of it.

W hen Willow and his apprentices arrived for their visit, she'd only
been dead a few minutes.

In the wake of the chaos, the police hadn't yet been called; the staff was
somewhat startled to see that detectives were already on the scene. (Willow
immediately phoned Owen to apprise him.) The nurses looked grim, steeling
themselves for the hassles, controversy and general shitstorm that came with
a suicide on the ward. Hangings were the hardest to defend, almost always
blamed on a lapse in vigilance and protocol. At least the girl's method was
unusual; it would have been difficult to foresee or prevent. She had stuffed
the sheets of an entire roll of toilet paper down her throat and suffocated.

The three of them went for a look.

The room bore the lonely messiness of panicky, failed medical intervention. Daniel ignored the body on the bed, focusing on the drawings that
Honeychile had been working on.

Lydia went straight to the girl. She tenderly touched Honeychile's forehead. "I guess this is what I'll look like," she said, as if talking only to herself. "After the *moment of balance.*"

The poignant moment reminded Willow of one of those high-end sci-fi flicks where androids have existential crises.

"No you won't," said Daniel. "Because she didn't *have a moment of balance.* I don't know *what* she had."

He held up one of her sketches, a finely detailed drawing of a naked angel with huge wings colored like a Monarch butterfly. Above the angel's head, Honeychile had written *RON*.

Willow and Lydia came closer.

"Ron," said Lydia. "Do you think that's the killer?"

Daniel shook his head and said, "I recognize this."

"From where?" asked Willow.

"An album. I'm a metalhead and know whence I speak." He tore a blank page from the back of Honeychile's notebook and then took a crayon and wrote *RON*.

He filled in the blanks, before and after the name:

I R O N B U T T E R F L Y

"See?" he said. "It's from the cover of *Scorching Beauty.* A totally underrated record, by the way."

5.

He told Lydia that he needed a few things from his old place in Smiths Creek, which he actually did, mostly a leather jacket that he missed. But Daniel hadn't been there in weeks and really just wanted to be alone with himself—alone, one might say, with whatever agglomeration he'd become. He was tired of his child-tenant's intrusions and was compelled to reflect on who he once was. He even longed to see Rachelle.

On the way, he stopped at a bar in Richmond for a drink.

Through the weeks, Lydia saw that he was becoming depressed. She was too, and understood why, but handled it differently. "Don't go there," she warned, referring to the dangerous ennui that had overtaken them only weeks before. Both knew that Annie's "haywire" virus was in play, and indeed the stakes seemed higher now; with Honeychile's chilling example, the option of suicide as a response to the anguish of stalemated landlord-tenant relations was in play as well. She gave him little pep talks. She knew the *Daniel* side of him was violently impulsive and urged him to remain cautious—she worried that he'd go off on someone, like that time he beat the shit out of the men who mugged her. "I need you," she pleaded. "We need you. We can't afford your suddenly winding up in jail or worse." Plus, Lydia feared that an innocent person could die, like what happened to that dreadful woman in Jacobs Prairie. "That is not our purpose. So *please* be careful, Daniel. And you have to *share* about the way you're feeling. You need to share about it at Meetings! It's *important.*"

Everything tingled now—he knew that their *moment of balance* was nigh. A vision had come to him that it was Roy Eakins who had killed them yet how could that be? How could they have come so far on the train, only to murder a man who was already dead? Daniel was energized, but depressed; everything seemed possible and impossible all at once. He wanted to talk to Annie but in his opinion, she had grown too weak. He *did* think of speaking to Willow about his overall dilemma but decided the man just wasn't ready. The Porter uniform didn't fit him yet.

He finished his beer and left for Smiths Creek.

He fumbled for the right key (he hadn't been there in a while), and when he came in, the sizzle of a Taser brought him to his knees.

He was shocked a few more times—for fun because he offered no resistance—and as he lay gasping, a rag was shoved in his mouth and sealed in with duct tape. He was lifted up, as if by a crowd of men, and propped against the sofa. The light switched on.

"Hello there, Christian soldier!"

Everything flooded back. That was exactly what his abductor had said on July 4, 2000, after pulling Troy off his bicycle. Then he threw him in the trunk where Maya and her bike already lay. The last thing Troy ever heard was "Gotta run—your dad's making me a badass burger. Catch you and dream girl later!"

"Hey!" said Roy, sidling up to the couch. "I see you're having some trouble with that gag so I'm going to take it out. 'Cause that's the thoughtful kinda guy I am. But when I do, say *one word*, little man, and I will shit down your throat. Promise you'll zip it?" Daniel nodded and Roy removed the rag. "Got a little surprise for ya. Not the surprise I had way back when—not *yet*, anyway." He shoved a handful of gummy bears in Daniel's mouth. "Chew! Come on, ol' buddy! That's right . . . chew, chew, chew, Chewbacca, like the Christian soldier from space that you were meant to be. So sorry they ain't green—I was starting to run out and couldn't spare any. Nobody ever called me the hostess with the mostest. I really should make a candy-store run . . . but no worries, there's *orange* ones and *red*—chew! chew! chew!—those are actually my second and third choices, when I'm in a pinch . . .

"But that's not the surprise I was talking about, no, no, *no*. See, there's a shiny automobile waiting out front. And sitting in the front seat of that automobile is—guess who? Can you guess?" The prisoner shook his head. "*Maya!* Maya is sitting *right there* in the front seat of that shiny car! Hahahaha!" Daniel closed his eyes in anguish. "That's right—Maya the pigtailed Christian soldieress! I *should* say 'Maya-Lydia,' queen of the cold case coppers! The original Dead End Kids hottie! Boy oh boy does little sissy in *all* her incarnations make me come! And here's what's gonna happen next: you will accompany me to said shiny vehicle. Didn't think we were going to stay here all night, did you, shit punk? And listen up, Troy—or *Daniel* or Dudley *Do-Right* or *whatever* you're supposed to be—listen up and listen *good*. If you try to fuck with me during our lovely little stroll to the car, if you try to *run* or *fuck* me in any *way*, my associate has been instructed to lop your Romper Room sister's head off. *And you will watch it happen.*"

Daniel's eyes were fully open now.

"Do you know who that 'associate' might be? Because that's another surprise—can you guess the identity of my partner in crime? Oh come on, at least try. I'll give you a hint: she's old and she's dying and her personal hygiene leaves much to be desired . . . oh, and she serves treats on a train. Or *used* to. That's right, it's the Porter! Little Orphan Annie! She's betrayed you! She betrayed us all!" He laughed like a hyena and then grew contrite. "Just kidding. Not that it wouldn't have been a genius idea, but . . . I didn't have time to pull it off."

He had trouble negotiating the stony path leading to the street but Roy stayed close, holding him up as if helping a friend who had too much to drink.

"And for the record," he said as they walked, "I fucking hate gummy bears. Even green ones, *especially* green ones. And when I say 'I,' I mean *me*, Roy, Roy *Eakins* hates 'em, 'cause I'm the only one left. That's right! I'm afraid my tenant's sailed off into the wild blue yonder—*Dabba Doo has left the building.* Which is why it's a puzzle to me that I *still* crave that sticky shit. Never touched the stuff until that dodo Dabba Doo came along."

H e saw two shadows in the front seat.

As they got closer, Daniel assumed the woman on the passenger side was Lydia and hoped she hadn't been hurt. He couldn't bear to see Maya *or* Lydia suffer—

But it wasn't her.

The windows were open and a man with a deranged smile sat behind the wheel. Roy said, "Christian soldier? I am pleased to introduce Solomon *Grundy* and his knocked-up angel, my daughter-in-law, Laverne."

He opened the back door and pushed Daniel in while his son turned in his seat, tasing the deputy into unconsciousness.

YOU ONLY DIE TWICE

I.

The image of the landlord filled the television screen. The Porter knew her as Violet but the man on the news called her something else: Sarabeth Ahlström. The thirty-five-year-old IT worker at a large insurance firm lived alone and had been raped and murdered in her town house in Dearborn Heights. Police were reaching out to the public for help.

At least it explained Annie's distressing, premonitory dream of some days ago, when Violet jumped from the train into the void. In her experience, the "death" of a landlord before its child-tenant could achieve his or her *moment of balance* had never occurred. (The concept of a "second," simultaneous death of a landlord and its child-tenant seemed the ultimate conundrum.) If one were to apply logic, which of course would be absurd, not only did the reanimation of the dead make no sense, but the presumption that landlords could remain "intact" long enough to serve their vengeful purpose made none either. It stood to reason—and statistics—that a small percentage would be destroyed by fire or accident, even homicide, thus subverting the *moment of balance*. But it was madness to apply rules of probability to the paranormal . . . Annie had always held her mentor's mantra close: that nothing made sense, in this world or the next, nor ever could. That her kids would succeed was inviolable and axiomatic, a part of the Great Mystery she happily took for granted. Perhaps, she thought, this horrific departure from all that she knew was part of the mystery as well.

It had to be . . .

The mess leading up to that *other* unheard-of event—the suicide of the landlord Honeychile—brought what the Porter euphemistically called "a new wrinkle" to the heretofore tidy, time-honored equation: the children of the train now seemed capable of botching their *moment*, not only by killing the wrong party but by killing *themselves*. But the death of Sarabeth Ahlström was even more disturbing—it felt dark and malignant, somehow proactive. She wondered exactly who was to blame for such an aberrant thing, if anyone at all: tenant or landlord? The children, of course, were the original victims . . . yet might their landlords be inclined to "call" victimhood as well? Could it be that in such cases of complete system failure that the fault lay in the emotional makeup of the landlord, in the genetics and neuroses of the organism itself? Annie had grown used to thinking of those bodies as tools and vessels, a means to an end, but what if they were capable of postmortem volition, a kind of kamikaze free will that led to their own deaths or the deaths of others?

What if landlords could be corrupted by the arrival of their tenants or were *already* corrupt at the moment a child entered them—

More "wrinkles" came, furrowing space-time and Annie's brow. There was the matter of Willow having known Maya and Troy before they were murdered—and the additional twist of both children's landlords working for the new Porter in their day jobs! She supposed it to be plausible, statistically speaking, but it was bewildering nonetheless.

Her thoughts returned to landlords; the nature of those beings who had died, only to become the reinvigorated weapons of their tenants. Was it possible for hosts and parasites to become mutual contaminants? You'd have to be a scientist to answer that one . . . perhaps *combatants*, not contaminants, was the better word. Could one act like a cancer upon the other? And if so, was this a symptom of "haywire"? Or had it always been that way, and she'd simply been lucky enough not to have encountered such scenarios? Was there now a cancer in *that* world, like the cancer killing Annie in this one?

It chilled her to the bone.

She turned off the TV. She closed her eyes and in moments was on the train again. Far away, in the middle of the car, a small boy nervously stood at the same window Violet had leapt from. Annie sprinted toward him, at times slicing straight through fog-clumps of loitering Subalterns. As in a classic nightmare, each time she got close, the corridor elongated and she was forced to start over, impossibly redoubling her efforts.

She drew near enough to see that it was Troy.

2.

Willow lay in bed, staring out at a piece of the living room wall. Dixie was asleep beside him. He left the blinds open because he liked the way the moonlight shone on the mural, making the train iridescent.

He finally understood why people turned to painting late in life. Willow used to scoff at that, especially when he read about old movie stars becoming born-again *artistes*. Now it made perfect sense. Call it a hobby, call it a whatever, but he believed he had real talent. Though maybe everyone who took up the brush long after their shelf life expired felt the same. Maybe you kind of had to.

He looked over—Dixie was gone from the world. It was uncanny but amid the chaos and insanity of his predicament, Willow could still see a future with this woman. A selfish worry came with that thought: he wondered just how much time he had left. Being a painter was a voluntary pastime; being a Porter wasn't. The fifty-seven-year-old out-of-shape detective was convinced he'd have a much better shot at living to a ripe old age if he and Annie Ballendine had never met. She'd taken him by force and now he was saturated in unspeakable secrets and death, far more than his natural abilities had ever shown him, steeped in the morbidity and despair of tiny souls in transit. He was certain he would be injured by that world, regard-less of the Porter having extolled the so-called power of his gifts (easy for her to say, and ironic too, because she was dying). And *why* was she dying? Who was to say the cancer taking her out wasn't a direct result of all those years she'd midwifed the dead, giving shelter to the slaughtered innocents whose lives had been pornographically cut short?

Though maybe he'd been wrong to believe that Portership was mandatory—Annie never said those who were "chosen" couldn't simply refuse. What a concept! Suddenly, the idea that Willow could bail was a great comfort. He whispered *I didn't sign up for this* into the ether and felt instant relief.

He shut his eyes, letting the riddle of Roy Eakins wash over him. When the kids told him that Roy used to come to the Meeting, he was flummoxed. It short-circuited his instincts to further pursue the man as a suspect. But now, thoughts came pell-mell, like the turning of a kaleidoscope, and he felt Annie's presence as if she were inside his head. What if a landlord happened to be a child-killer in the life before he was conscripted into Annie's world? What if the very being who was animated by one of the children of the train in order to enact the *moment of balance* turned out to be malevolent, in-fected, impure? And so? So what if they were? Would that necessarily pre-clude a successful result, an effective *moment of balance?* Wouldn't the process itself—the arrival of the dead child-tenant—serve to distill or re-move such impurities? In AA, they say, "Principles before personalities" . . . in the quest for the *moment of balance*, wasn't it "Principles before personal-ity *disorders*"? Yet what if "haywire" meant that things had gone so askew that the unknowable force responsible for selecting those landlord-vessels had become damaged and willfully perverse in *itself*, and was running amok? You'd have to be some kind of psychedelic scientist to answer that one . . . an astonishing corollary followed: Was it possible for a returning child to in-habit the same body of the person it had actually been murdered by? If Roy Eakins *had* killed Maya and Troy, then who was "Dabba Doo," the child who became his tenant? Another of Eakins's kills? Or had Dabba Doo been murdered by someone *else*—and his tenancy in the body of Roy, a child-killer other than the one he sought, was random, coincidental? To complete the brainteaser, if Dabba Doo *was* killed by Roy, then the hapless phantom's *moment of balance* seemed surely, almost poetically doomed: a captive of his predator yet again, he would have no way of killing him because the man was already dead.

Willow called it "haywire squared"—

Dixie cried out in nightmare, startling him from his feverish cogitations. That was when Willow realized he was in the living room, standing before the mural like a sleepwalker. He rushed to the bedroom and held her until the terrors passed. (She never fully awakened.) He gently kissed her head. He felt a stir and thought of making love but was prudishly mindful that she'd set her alarm for an early-morning shift.

As he tucked her foot beneath the sheet, a shock went through him.

"It isn't a palm print," he said aloud. "It's a footprint," he whispered. "A fucking *footprint.*"

He grabbed his wallet from the end table. Folded inside was the phone number that Roy had written down and then stepped on.

I don't have athlete's foot, he'd said.

We'll see about that, thought Willow.

3.

"We're going to go a lot slower than the last time," said Roy. "Tell you one thing: if someone would have told me I'd have the chance to do you *again*, I'd have said they were crazy to their face. But here we are! Will wonders never cease? Your little sister actually went faster than you did— which kind of surprised me, 'cause the Lolitas usually hang in. The lollipops are tougher than they look. Anyhoo, I blame myself for that. Wasn't like it was my first rodeo. Mea culpa. When it's your culpa, you gotta say mea."

Roy never shut up. It took nearly an hour to drive from Smiths Creek to the farm in Wolcott Mills. Grundy and his wife half-carried Daniel into the house. He was barely conscious but could hear and smell a river. When he came to, he was nude, spread-eagled on a bed. They didn't gag him and he immediately understood why. They were far enough away from the world that his screams would never be heard.

The Porter said that in "endgame time," the children of the train summoned superhuman force to confront those who had harmed them. In confused recognition of the *moment of balance* that would soon become a miscarriage, Daniel's tenant thrashed within like a punch-drunk heavyweight. Wishing to protect him from their common enemy, the landlord instinctively shooed Troy away, though with little success.

"I'm rusty so please forgive—haven't done this in a while! Violet doesn't count, not really, but boy oh boy that gal sure gave me the taste again. She's what they used to call a 'ten.' Real marriage material. But you know grownups were never my thang. To each his own." He pursed his lips and grew quiet. "I'm going to make a confession, man-child, and I hope you're flattered. I never told anyone this before—not that there was anyone to tell. Never even told Grundy. Some things just aren't appropriate for fathers to share with their sons. But I'm going to tell *you*. What I want you to know is that out of the baker's dozen—give or take a few cupcakes—you and your sister were my pièce de résistance. Pardon my French toast. And mind you, don't get me wrong, *all* my kids were wonderful; like Mr. Twain was fond of saying, they didn't repeat themselves but they often rhymed. But the Rum-Rum-Rummers stayed *with* me all these years, providing much constipation during sleepless nights. I meant consolation. Pardon my Portuguese."

Grundy laughed (his wife had been banished to the living room) and his father said, "Shut the fuck up."

"You know," said Roy, "this whole landlord-tenant thing has been utterly fascinating—I'm sure I don't have to tell you that—but really, don't you think? I mean, who could have imagined? It's inconceivable. I mean, my dead jaw just drops. Still does. *Definitely* given me food for thought. I was a teacher, as you know, so I'm given to analysis and reflection—unlike my dull-witted son, whom I've sometimes been ashamed to call my own. Oh, he has other 'abilities,' but not in the lucubration department. Put a major crimp in my style for *years*. But I took care of him when the world wanted to flush him. Didn't I, Grundy? Didn't I take care of you?"

"You did, Dad. You took care of me."

"His mom didn't want him. Uh-uh, no way. I got rid of *that* particular problem a few years after he was born. What kind of mother rejects her own son? Yeah, yeah, I had to break his nose a few times—a jaw, a rib—but hey, what's a father for?" He laughed and Grundy did too. "Gave him a hel-luva beating that day you and Maya were in the trunk. See, I was present and accounted for when your daddy sent you for that accursed lighter fluid. I say 'daddy' but what I really mean is executioner, 'cause that's what he was—the man sent you straight to your deaths, but hey, what are fathers for?" He winked. "I briefly recused myself from the happy festivities. Whis-pered to Father of the Year that my boy needed to take his meds and have a little quiet-time siesta, which everyone was used to because wherever Roy Eakins appeared, his gruesome spawn was soon to follow. A package deal, that's all. We got snubbed all over the place but Ronnie and Elaine still in-vited us over, which was very kind. Good people, Ronnie and Elaine. So I took Grundy into the house, threw him in the guest room and told him to keep his mouth shut and stay put. He knew the drill. He was already pretty well-trained 'cause that's exactly what I would do with him at home when I was up to sundry *off-color* shenanigans with my Huckleberrys and Lolitas—once I got Dumbshit into the guest room, oh, it was *on*. When he got older, I'd let him watch, but that's a bedtime story for another day. Not that you'll live to see one. Anyhoo. I knew the shortcut you'd be taking with your bike, so off I went—probably a bonehead move on my part if you think about it, 'cause you never can tell who's watching. But that was before every random asshole was whipping out his phone to piss on the notion of *some* kind of public privacy; a kinder, gentler time. *And* I was younger then—young and in love! Impetuous, that's the word. Have to say I was always lucky that way: lucky in finding my kids and lucky in not getting caught. Lucky in love. But I digress. When I got back, Ronnie was still prattling about some foot-ball game whilst putting the final touches on another round of muy perfecto Rummerburgers—the man had skills! And there you were just fifty yards away in the trunk, having sweet and sour dreams, quiet as two bugs in a rug. You weren't conscious, so that couldn't have been too tough. I couldn't believe how beautifully I pulled that off. *But . . .* I was getting cocky. Careless. That's the cliché, isn't it? Started to scare myself. I didn't want to be one of those dumdums the profilers always say are dying to get caught. I *hate* when they say that because it's *bullshit*. The only people dying to get caught—the only ones dying 'cause I caught 'em—were kids like you! Anyhoo, I thought it best to lay low after our steamy little ménage à trois. Pardon my Middle English. I was like a crocodile: I drowned 'em, grabbed 'em by my tail and sank down deep, deep to the bottom of the river. Could stay at the bottom for years. I seem to be a bit of a departure in that regard. The experts at Quantico don't know quite what to do with a gent like myself. I'm the anomaly, the square peg . . . the square peg who sticks himself in tiny round holes! Hahaha! In rare form today, aren't I, Grundy?"

"You are, Dad."

Laverne appeared, carrying a plated sandwich on a tray, which she offered to Roy. He lifted the top piece of bread. "Too much mayo."

"I'm sorry, Father."

"Don't say you're sorry," he said amiably. "Just scoop some of that shit off. Unless the genius wants it." He nodded to his son.

"I'll take it," said Grundy.

"Waste not, want not. Just make me another, Angel."

"Yes, Father."

She took the plate over to her husband, curtsied and left.

Out of nowhere Roy took a hammer to Daniel's kneecaps. He patiently waited for the screams to subside, like someone waiting for the sirens of fire trucks to subside before resuming quiet conversation. Then, his eyes lit up.

"Holy *shit*, I just thought of something! Grundy doesn't know I'm dead! Whoops! Forgot to tell him! Hey, Grundy! Your old man's been dead for ten months!"

Grundy smiled in confusion. He thought that his father was making another joke, albeit one he couldn't comprehend. Roy had the brief impulse to lay it all out—the story of his death and transfiguration—but didn't have the energy, even though the prospect amused. It would have been pointless.

"I guess that falls under the category of things that aren't appropriate for a parent to share with their chillun . . . Want to know another interesting thing? When you and your sis showed up at the Meeting that first time, I didn't put it together! The Porter introduced you as Troy and Maya, but I drew a total blank—couldn't make the connection. How 'bout that? I finally figured out that Dabba Doo was making me senile! Señor Gummy Bear was gumming up the works . . . That piece of shit . . . but when 'Winston' showed up, now *that* got my attention. See, I'd been out of the game— hiding at the bottom of the river—but that didn't mean that Grundy wasn't keeping me abreast of his repulsive nocturnal activities. The turn of the screw was the day Ugly Girl showed up and the Porter introduced her as *Winston.* Because I was aware of a child who went by that very name who'd been 'involved' in some of Grundy's recent hijinks. He and Mrs. Angel snatched him at the Cherry Street Mall. Grundy told me so during one of his late-night telephonic confessions . . . A puzzle remains: How is it that *you* didn't recognize *me?* I'm much obliged, because it might have made things unnecessarily complicated if you had. Still, I wonder—what gummed up *your* works?

"A most intriguing scenario lies before us, amigo. I'm dead; you're dead. Is that not so? Therein the stage is set for that Holy Grail, that elusive the-orem which heretofore was thought to be unsolvable. Gödel would turn over in his grave. And I sincerely believe . . ." He paused to arduously sup-press a deep cough. "I sincerely believe that we shall soon be assured a place in the annals of history. You see, what we have here is bigger than the inven-tion of the iPhone, bigger than the Internet—bigger than the discovery of fire!" Roy had a sort of seizure and then blew out a dark scab of blood. It took a few minutes for him to recover. "Tonight, my friend, we are pioneers. *Because,* by reason of our both being dead, your murder will have *no killer or victim.*" He broke into a jack-o'-lantern grin. "Isn't that beautiful? The world at last will be provided with the equation it has yearned after for centuries.

"We'll be living *and* dying proof that there *is* such a thing as the perfect crime."

He doubled over, unable to catch his breath. Grundy went to his aid but Roy peevishly waved him off. Different-colored ejecta from his lungs spattered the captive's chest.

"We were in unknown territory *before*, no *shit*, but now are we ever . . . We might even become immortal! I might anyway. Sorry about that"—his soliloquy was interrupted by a death rattle of congestion; it jolted Grundy, who was amazed that his father was able to continue—"God truly *does* reward the worst of the worst. Talk about anomalous serial killers—Our Father Who Art in Heaven is the ultimate. The ultimate outlier! What would Quantico make of *Him*? And the Man Upstairs *knows* I have nothing against you! I didn't have anything against you when you were *nine years old* and I've got nothing against you *now*. It's just how He made me . . . made me a survivor too—I mean, *look* at me. What is there to *gain* from what I'm about to do? What is there to gain from killing you? You're already dead! You and your bratty little soul mate, that whiny scumbag Troy . . . but here's the rub. I can't get this cockeyed idea out of my head that *killing you again* will help me live. Or some alchemical variation thereof. *God* must have put that thought there, no? Even though I'm starting to think it's so much bull because in case you haven't noticed, I ain't feelin' so well. I am *not* the picture of health. But what I was saying . . . is that God ordained that you should die *twice*. Daniel and Troy die twice! Isn't that terribly mean of Him? And I thought *I* was diabolical! What do you think will happen after I kill you for the second time? I'm talking to Troy now, because, well, I don't see a real future for him, unless there's a Hell. Which I guess there is because you're in it now, huh, Daniel . . . So this is for *Troy*: What do you think'll happen after 'sloppy seconds'? Maybe you'll just wake up on the train and the whole cycle will begin again. You know, you'll be sipping your lemonade and then those pesky Subalterns will debark you to your new life . . . where you're reborn in a dog's body! *A dog landlord!* A dog who just had the shit kicked out of him and died in the snow—or maybe you'll wake up inside some stinky homeless woman with pussy cancer. Wouldn't that be fun? No, wait—I know. Wouldn't it just be *insane* if your mommy died—if Elaine finally managed to take herself out—and you came back as *her*? If Mommy were your new landlord? Wow!" Roy mulled over his fantasy. "That's some dark, twisted shit right there."

A noise came from the living room and he disdainfully turned toward his son. "She's vacuuming," explained Grundy.

"Tell that fat, crazy bitch to knock it off or I'll vacuum that kid out of her!"

"Laverne! Turn off the vacuum!"

"I'm too old for this," said Roy introspectively. "Too old and too dead. I think I'm gonna book it, *compadre*. And let my boy take over." He nodded to Grundy, who approached. "Tell Laverne to take me home—I'll sit this one out, much as I hate to. Always best to go out on top. Didn't Seinfeld say that? They offered him crazy-money to do another season but he'd have none of it. Gotta respect him for that."

He left the room without ceremony and Grundy hovered over their quarry.

"I would like to see my . . ." strained Daniel, with great, dignified labor before Troy interrupted—

"I want my mommy!"

The last thing the landlord and his tenant saw was the butterfly-winged angel on Grundy's vintage rock tee.

He hadn't washed it yet; nor did he plan to for the next few weeks.

4.

The suicide of Honeychile unraveled her.

She allowed herself the heretical thought that the wayward girl had shown a courage that was completely justified, a courage Lydia herself might not be capable of. She knew that Daniel was in similar despair—she could *feel* him—and when he told her that he needed to retrieve something from the house in Smiths Creek, she began to worry. After all, he was the one who had the idea to go and see Honeychile. He and the girl seemed *connected* and she wondered how deep that connection went.

Lydia had given up her lightweight opiate habit months ago; she stopped taking painkillers a week after dying on the Orchard Trail. But tonight, she washed down four Oxycontin and three Xanax with white wine. She sat on the couch in the dark and waited for that lush, familiar sense of well-being to come but fell asleep too soon to savor it.

At 11:20 P.M., she awakened bolt upright and thought:

He's leaving me now—

—finally, she knew!

And though her knowledge was flawed, she acted.

S he arrived at the New Baltimore residence of Roy Eakins at 11:47 P.M. The house was dark.

She lifted one of the windows and went in.

She walked to the bedroom.

She heard the sound of lungs in distress (more the sound of gears being stripped) and turned on the light.

He was in bed, propped with pillows so he could breathe.

Was that what he's doing? Because it didn't sound like breathing.

He blinked and smiled. "Hello there, Christian—"

The borrowed life was already leaving his body.

"Where is Troy!" she said, crouching over him like a jackal.

"Well," whispered Roy, with ragged intimacy. "I could tell you he's dead but that would be redundant."

"He *isn't!*" she said corrosively. "I still *feel* him. *Where is he?*"

"You really don't know, do you?" he said woozily, like a wizard toad to a babe lost in the woods. "I guess that's a prime example of what Annie called 'haywire': you managed to get *here*, to *me*, but you still can't get *there*, to *him*. You're botching it just like Winston did—"

She bent back his fingers, breaking them. He yelped but still managed to be jovial.

"It's all about vengeance, isn't it, Maya? I guess I was a little more *pure.* Less . . . *judgmental* than you kids. I didn't have your righteous arrogance. Because I never sought vengeance—what I did, I did for pleasure."

"Tell me where my brother is!" she commanded, stone-faced. She looked ancient and timeless all at once. "Or I'll do *exactly* to you what you did to me."

"I've been thinking. Maybe when I die—*again*—when you 'kill' me— maybe right then, *another* tenant will come along. And a few weeks from now, voilà: I'll be back at a Meeting, with Annie and the gang. Wouldn't that be special?"

"I swear I'll take my time sending you from this world—"

"Do you have any idea how crazy you sound? Send me from what world? I'm not *here*, Chiquita, I'm already gone . . . and you know it. I left ten months ago . . . neither one of us is here! Not *Lydia*, not *Maya*, not *Roy*, not *Dabba Doo*—we're ghosts! The *moment of balance* only works if the one you come back to kill is alive. How you gonna kill a ghost? You dumb *bitch*."

With his last breath he said, "You are so fucked."

She knew that Roy Eakins was right.

BALANCING ACTS

I.

Willow arrived at the Cold Case office early, with a mission.

They hadn't yet sent Maya's birthday card for DNA testing. Willow contacted an eager beaver buddy of his at the forensic science lab—a finger-print expert. The detective was certain that if his friend were able to get a footprint off the scrap of paper that Roy had stepped on (with his son's phone number) it would match the one on Maya's card.

After the messenger came and picked it up, he made himself a cup of coffee, lit a cigarette and opened the computer. A few days ago, he'd requested photos of the crime scene at Mount Clemens High, and he was stunned at the image now on his screen: the football player was wearing an Iron Butterfly T-shirt when Honeychile stabbed him. There it was again, just as it had looked in her sketch at the hospital—the chrome angel, its naked torso sprouting brilliantly colored wings. Willow's wheels started turning. Was the person who killed Winston wearing a shirt with the same design when the boy was abducted and slain? Since Honeychile was Winston's landlord, might seeing the image of the angel have triggered her attack on the student? According to the sheriff, the distraught girl kept saying she had "killed the wrong one" . . . is *that* what Honeychile meant? That she'd lashed out in a case of mistaken identity?

Lydia and Daniel were late. (Meaning, they weren't early.) He'd give 'em that; yesterday was one hell of a day. The death of Renée "Honeychile" Devonshire had been a serious blow, and not just to the investigation. That a landlord had offed herself was a little too close for comfort. Willow closed his eyes. The detective slipped away and the Porter he was becoming took its place. He sunk deep, trying to *feel* his recruits. Daniel was nowhere to be found . . . but he felt Lydia. And with that feeling came a surge of crackling energy—a vision.

He jumped from his chair and literally ran from the building.

He gunned it to the orderly neighborhood in New Baltimore where Roy Eakins lived. Lydia's Kia was parked haphazardly in the drive, block-ing Roy's vehicle. Shit—

Too late!

He drew his gun.

Avoiding the front porch, he skulked around the side of the house, cling-ing to the wall. There'd been a respite from the storm but the sky was dark-ening again. A neighbor in the yard next door just finished taking her clothes off the line; she took her basket and went in without seeing him.

He tried the back door—locked.

He saw an open window and wondered if Roy had escaped.

He climbed in . . .

The house was quiet, like a void where sounds couldn't live. The table where they had eaten their sandwiches was still set. The plates hadn't been cleared.

Gummy bears littered the carpet.

He did some quick cop moves, gun raised while ducking into empty rooms—the sink of the front bathroom was stained with what looked like dried blood—before moving slowly down the long hall . . .

There was a body on the bed. Was it Lydia's?

Motherfuck—

He moved closer . . . It was a man.

It was Roy—

Willow reflexively wheeled around, pointing his revolver at an immo-bile figure in the chair.

"Jesus Christ, I almost shot you!" he said.

She didn't move, didn't blink, didn't say a word.

Was she injured? Was she dead—

He stepped toward her and saw that she was all right, whatever *all right* meant . . .

She was alive.

He swiveled again, drawing his gun on Roy. He moved toward the bed, keeping the weapon trained on the body. The man looked like hell. The smell overtook him now, stronger than any he'd ever experienced—industrial-strength death. He fought the urge to vomit. He turned back to attend to Lydia.

She was still doing her Lincoln Memorial thing: rigid in the chair as she stared into space. Sphinxlike, regal . . . maybe that's what all the chil-dren of the train look like, après *moment of balance.*

"Lydia, are you okay?"

"I failed," she said softly.

"What happened?"

"Eakins was right."

"About what? What do you mean? Talk to me, Lydia."

"I didn't kill him—he died on his own. I just stood there and watched. And he knew that would be the worst thing. He *knew* . . ." She smiled like a martyr on a stake about to be set on fire. "He won. Roy Eakins won."

A thousand things went through his head, half the concerns of a Porter, half those of a professional sworn to uphold the law. *What the fuck am I supposed to do with this? There's a body—need to file a report. I'll say we were following up on a lead—that the print on the birthday card was a footprint, not a palm print—but Owen's going to ask what we were doing here, why we*

came to his house before getting the results—and why didn't I call for backup?
Fuck fuck fuck—and Lydia—what if she dies? Right there in the chair? Be-
cause isn't that more or less the fuck what happens after moments of balance?
Don't they drop dead after the ones who murdered them are gone?

He wanted to call Annie but Annie didn't have a phone. Anyway, she
was dying too . . . everyone was dying. Everyone was dying and coming
back, to die all over again. He wished he had a *Guide*, like the children did,
to tell him what to do. A *Guide* that could dig him out of the deep shit he
was in.

"He wouldn't tell me where Troy was." Her façade collapsed and tears
sprang to her eyes. "I begged him! '*You can't do this to him again!*'—"

Willow shuddered, not from her words but in reaction to the aria that
erupted in the air around him. A castrato's soprano, ecstatic and apocalyptic, pierced the void and a wild, refulgent cerulean blue filled the room.

"I still *feel* him, Willow!" said Lydia helplessly. "He's here, he's here—
he's somewhere here but I can't *find* him, I can't find him! I failed, failed,
failed, I failed like Honeychile!" The look she gave Willow seared his heart.
"What if he's out there *buried* somewhere? Buried but still alive—?"

"I know where he is," said Willow.

He was no longer Willow; Lydia knew what he'd become.

"Porter, tell me! Please, Porter, *please*," she cried plaintively.

Her lower lip trembled as she made her entreaty, like the bravest child
stalwartly holding its ground.

"Please, Mister Porter, please sir, take me to my brother."

2.

A downpour began as they barreled toward Wolcott Mills.

Midmorning now, but dark enough to be dusk.

Willow got that full-circle feeling as they hot-rodded through the middle
of Saggerty Falls, where so many things had begun and ended . . . Maya
looked straight ahead, saying nothing as he drove. He stole glances and was

alarmed by what he saw, or thought he saw: a mountain lion sitting in the passenger seat.

"*This* way," she said, when they got to 29 Mile Road. "Turn *here*"—on Indian Trail—"go *there*"—past the old dam and old mills of the Metropark, bisected by the Clinton River. In ten minutes they were on the muddy road leading to Grundy Eakins's home.

Water pelted the windshield faster than the wipers could handle. He saw a house in the distance, but Maya ordered him to pull over. *Get out,* she said; he hesitated and then obeyed. She slid into the driver's seat and said, *Get in.* He walked around and opened the door. The seat was burning hot, wet with something.

"Grundy Eakins killed Winston Collins," she said, like an oracle. "I'm going to have a *moment of balance*—but not my own. It won't be mine and Troy's, it'll be *Winston's.* And my brother will have it with me, if there's still time. Please put on your seat belt."

She floored it for the quarter mile or so left. When they arrived, the car sailed like a projectile through the fence, crashing into the front porch. The impact was so forceful that even though the airbags deployed, Willow managed to bang his head against the windshield. By the time he gathered his wits, Maya's body was smashing her way through the front door.

The detective's adrenaline overruled his concussion. He lurched from the car and drew his weapon as he cautiously entered. He could hear the begging screams of a woman shouting that she was pregnant. Maya shouted back, "I'm not interested in you *or* your fucking baby! Move! Move! Move!"

Their voices were coming from the second floor.

At the top of the stairs, tools were scattered beside a framed poster of the band Motörhead that was propped against the wall, waiting to be hung. Willow ducked into a dark room and then got down on his hands and knees so that he could peer into the hallway without being seen.

Halfway down, Grundy Eakins pointed a rifle at Maya. She was calm but so was Grundy.

"*Bring me to him,*" she said. "Bring me to him *now* and I'll let you live."

Willow knew she was buying time. She'd been taken by surprise, something he hadn't thought possible—but surmised that shit happens, even during the *moment of balance.*

"Dad didn't teach me to run," said Grundy.

"I know what he taught you," she said acidly. "Listen to me: take me to my brother and I'll let you get away."

"That crying little bitch in the bedroom is your *bro?* Sweet! I'm gonna let you suck me, like he did, though I doubt you'll do any better. Boy's a natural. Sorry—just can't let you go in there. Which, if you really want to know, is actually a great kindness I'm extending. Hell yeah. Because the man's a sight for sore eyes."

"You piece of shit."

"The *real* reason you can't see him . . . is because you're about to be dead."

Willow entered the hall and the pregnant woman tackled him as he fired, ruining the shot. They tussled and then tumbled down the stairs. The commotion was enough to distract Grundy, and Maya leapt, seized the rifle and scuttled it down the hall. The detective lay at the bottom of the stairs—the pregnant woman got knocked out—struggling to remain conscious. He heard an otherworldly scream: Lydia's. It was loud and prolonged enough that he covered his ears in pain. (The pregnant woman did not stir.) He heard hammering and now it was Grundy who was screaming, but this time the screams were identifiably human. When he managed to climb back to the second floor, he saw him in the hallway just outside the bedroom.

Willow walked toward him, gun drawn. Grundy's hands and feet were nailed to the wood floor and his cheek and part of the nose had been bitten off. But he was alive. He went to the bedroom and stood at the door looking in. It seemed like the detective had spent a lifetime following this creature into a thousand rooms, like the eternal sidekick of some horror-film queen. She crouched over Troy, who lay motionless on a stripped mattress stained with blood and everything else.

Willow took a few steps forward.

She was cradling her brother in her arms. "It's Maya! I'm here, sweetheart—your little sissy's here . . ." Both Daniel and Troy were dead.

She shook her head in bottomless sorrow as her eyes played over the body. "What did they do to you! Look what they did . . ." She turned to Willow and with the gentlest countenance said, "He's back on the train." Her smile was beatific. "Troy's waiting for me on the train . . ." She touched her brother's forehead, rearranging the locks of hair, then wiped the blood from his brow. It reminded Willow of the end of a play he saw when he was very young—Shakespeare?—as a boy, he didn't understand what was happening but now he could, and had to look away. Maya stood, passing him in the doorway as she walked from the room.

He watched her go to Grundy.

She took out a pocketknife. "Your father used this," she said. "On my brother and me. I found it in the drawer next to his bed."

"Don't," he wet-whispered, through ragged breath.

"I wonder who else he used it on . . . down through the years. Did your father take it off some Boy Scout he killed? Did you ever get a chance to use it, Grundy? Ever get a chance to use this cute little pocketknife?" He vigorously—as vigorously as he could—shook his head. The exposed rows of teeth on the right side of his face made him into a grinning anatomical model. "Are you sure? Are you sure you didn't use it on Winston?" When he shook his head, she said, "Well, I guess you're telling the truth. Maybe it was a family heirloom Dad was waiting to pass on. Your father's dead now—so you can have it."

Grundy was saying something but Willow couldn't hear it.

"He carved and carved us with that Red Cross knife," said Maya. Grundy's chest began to heave. "Would you like to hear what he did with that pocketknife? I think you would—that'd be like some kind of bedtime story for you, wouldn't it? Well, some other time. I'm going to tell you a better one to help you sleep."

She put the blade into one eye and then the other and Grundy Eakins screamed, not a scream like Maya-Lydia's but not a human one either. Then she looked up toward Willow and the room where her brother lay. "Finish him, Troy!" she shouted, awash in ecstastic, unfathomable horror and resolution. Willow had the sense she was in some sort of fugue state, because even in the magical world whence she came (and would soon return to), he doubted that Troy's or Daniel's participation was an option. Both landlord and tenant had been released—he *felt* it in his Porter's bones.

She went back to work with the "heirloom."

Less than a minute had passed when Grundy's protests ended and the *moment of balance* came, albeit secondhand.

3.

Seven sheriff's cars and three ambulances converged.

It wasn't yet noon; the storm made everything into a dark slurry, a Turner seascape.

Willow sat in the white-trash solarium, shrouded in a scratchy blanket provided by paramedics. His bumpy, bloody head was swabbed and bandaged. Beside him was Lydia in her own blanket, though looking more serene—almost religious. Her face was ethereally calm, like the emblem of a dreamer. The bodies hadn't yet been loaded into the coroner's van and the forensic team was busy measuring, taking pictures and bagging evidence. Laverne Eakins insisted on walking to the ambulance unaided but the request was denied. They cuffed her to the gurney.

After his walk-through of the crime scene, Sheriff Caplan went to the sunroom and stood there, composing himself. His autocratic gaze shifted between them—the disheveled, slightly sheepish cold case detective and the spaced-out rookie. The blood of Lydia's partner had been wiped (mostly) from her face and hair but was still painted on her clothes.

"Can you tell me," he said, "what the fuck went on here?"

Willow sighed before pronouncing the words he'd been rehearsing in his head: "Grundy Eakins killed Winston Collins."

Owen was startled but merely bit down on his lower lip, mindful of a set of circumstances whose gravity could not be overstated—one of their own had been tortured to death. He tabled Willow's news flash. "What happened to Doheny?"

"He got here before we did," said Willow, not that it explained any-thing. He just hadn't had time to formulate a feasible narrative. For now, the best strategy was to state the obvious. "A few weeks ago he told me that he felt Grundy Eakins was a strong suspect. Lydia and I were look-ing at . . . various others. I told Daniel not to pursue until we had a consensus."

"He came here without informing you?"

"That's right. I think the death of the Collins boy hit him hard, harder than he let on. It became personal. I warned him about not getting involved that way. It happens."

Lydia spoke up, to Willow's surprise. "It was PTSD—a PTSD thing. A boy died when he was in Afghanistan and he felt responsible. I don't think that's something you ever get over. I know Daniel didn't."

"Are you telling me," said Owen, "that he came here as some kind of vigilante?"

"He wanted to be a hero," she said, putting a compassionate spin on what in some quarters is called an epic goatfuck.

"I don't know if he was planning to arrest him or kill him," said Willow. "And that's the God's honest truth."

"Jesus," said Owen, shaking his head. "The suspect was *crucified*. And his eyes! His fucking *face*—" He looked at Lydia's bloody hands and said, "Did *you* do that?"

"His father did that," she said. "Roy Eakins did that to him."

"What?" said Owen.

"That's right," said Willow, thinking it best to go with the flow. Buy now, pay later. "His father killed him."

"And how did *you* two get here?"

"I had a *feeling* he might be here," she said. "So I told the Porter and we—"

"Who the fuck is 'the Porter'?"

"I meant my supervisor—"

"We came over together," said Willow. He shot her a glance that said: put a sock in it.

It was difficult for the sheriff to keep a lid on the stew of anger, grief and bedevilment he was floating in. "You had a *feeling* so you just *raced over* to an alleged serial killer's *compound* without calling it in. Jesus, Willow!"

"It happened so fast," said the beleaguered detective. He had always detested that catchall phrase but at the moment was grateful to put it to use. "I'm sorry. You're right, of course you're right. I should have called it in."

"You're sorry." Owen took a deep breath. "Is there a connection to the girl in all of this? Renée Devonshire?"

"Honeychile?" said Willow, with a familiarity that struck the sheriff as odd. "None whatsoever."

"You're saying she didn't know this asshole? That *Honeychile* had zero contact with the Eakinses . . ."

"Zero," said Willow. To sound a little less sure of himself (about everything), he added, "That we know of."

"Let me ask you something else, since you seem to be all-seeing and all-knowing. There was a time we were looking at Grundy as a suspect in the Rummer case—*if* you'll recall." Everything he said had a terminal tinge of mockery. "Has it occurred to you and *Deputy Molloy* that those suspicions were correct?"

Willow touched his bandage and winced, as if to signal that he preferred that the interrogation be postponed. "I don't think so. I don't think he— Grundy—participated." Then it came out. "It was Roy who killed those children."

"Roy?" said Owen, trying to get a footing.

"That's right," nodded Willow. "Roy Eakins killed Troy and Maya Rummer."

"Jesus Christ!"

"I have proof."

"And when were you going to tell me about this? Or do I work for you now?"

"I wasn't sure until last night, Owen."

Willow prayed that the prints he'd sent to the lab would match—if they didn't, he'd be skipping town. Maui was looking pretty good right now. Maybe Woody Harrelson would hire him as a gofer.

"Where *is* Roy Eakins."

"At his house in New Baltimore."

"We need to go pick that man up!" said Owen, waving one of his men over.

"There's no hurry," said Willow. "Roy's dead."

Owen became irate. "You better not be telling me that Daniel Doheny already took care of that!"

"No," said Lydia, calmly. "He died of natural causes."

The sheriff threw up his hands. The confetti of information needed to be properly sorted outside the war zone. "I want you both to clean up and be at my office *within the hour.* You're going to start from the beginning and walk me through to now. Is that clear?"

"Of course," said Willow. "And thank you, sir. I think we both need a moment." He turned to Lydia. "I'll take you home."

"One of my men will take you."

"I'm okay. I'm fine to drive."

"Like hell you are. Leave your car. We'll take care of it."

The detective got paranoid, wondering if Owen was going to turn the automobile over to forensics. He panicked, wondering if he'd left some of the *Guides* Annie had given him in the trunk.

"Take your showers," said Owen. "I'll see you *on the hour.*"

As they walked to the waiting sedan, the sheriff caught up to Lydia. He gently touched her arm, the human part of the baffling equation suddenly making itself known. He knew the deputies were in a relationship.

"I'm sorry about your loss, Deputy Molloy."

"Thank you," she said, warmly. "I'm sorry for you too. It's a big loss for everyone." Her tears had dried up.

They looked up at the police chopper circling above. A media helicopter was keeping a respectable distance.

"Well," said Owen. "The circus has come to town. And you won't believe the elephant shit we're going to be shoveling."

"We're not the heroes," said Lydia, as if she hadn't heard him. "Daniel was."

Somewhat cynically, Owen said, "More will be revealed."

DEBRIEFING

I.

Lydia and Willow lived in opposite directions from Wolcott Mills. The detective told the deputy who was driving to drop him at home in Sterling Heights first, then take Deputy Molloy to her place in Richmond.

As they pulled away, the first thing he did was phone Dixie. He wanted to reach her before she heard about the whole shit show from a coworker who saw it on the news. She asked if he was okay. When he said he was fine but "got a little scrape on my noggin," Dixie told him that she was leaving work and would meet him at the house. He said that wasn't necessary but she wasn't having it. He ignored the repeated calls from Adelaide because he didn't have it in him for a conversation right now. Besides, he knew that her husband would tell her that he was okay, if he hadn't already. Ditto for Pace—Mom would do the same. Willow smiled when he realized he'd been putting Dixie first. That felt good. It felt right.

There were other, more urgent matters. Lydia of course would have no worries—for imminently departing child-tenants, the aftermath of *moments of balance* excluded real-world consequences—but that didn't hold true for Willow. When her body died, which would probably be soon, he'd be left holding a very large bag of brown matter.

They sat in back of the unmarked sedan as if Ubering home, though to him it felt more like they were prisoners. A movie cliché came to mind: they needed to get their stories straight before talking to the sheriff. As they got closer to his house he whispered to Lydia, "I want you to come in with me. Tell him that you don't want to go home—that you don't want to be alone."

With a measure of gloom, he ruminated on Lydia's half-life after the *moment of balance*. Just how long could he expect her to remain in this world? He was new to Portership and so many things were occurring to him, moment to moment, that he hadn't even had the time to write them down, let alone share them with Annie. One of the mysteries among mysteries was the length of time a landlord remained "functional" after their target was eliminated. The case in point seemed knottier than the norm because Roy Eakins, Maya's killer, escaped such a fate—not merely because he expired without her (or Troy's) help but because he was *already dead*. Things were further complicated by the fact that Grundy died by *Maya's* hand and not Winston's, who by all rules of the *Guide* was the only one who had the right to such retribution. Would such "complications" cause Lydia to linger among the living a bit longer than the usual?

The self-serving nature of the speculation coupled with the sheer impossibility of receiving an answer struck him as obscene. On the practical side, he doubted whether the deputy's looming disappearance would dampen the sheriff's ardor about getting to the bottom of things; in fact, it was likely to do the opposite. Apart from the complex feelings Willow had toward Lydia, there was an element of calculation to the question. Part of what he was asking, really, was how long did he have to clean things up before Lydia was gone? All manner of unpleasant scenarios dangled before him. What if Lydia died in his apartment, right in the middle of "getting their stories straight"? He even began to wonder about autopsy results: What might a pathologist reveal about the vagaries of the reanimated dead? That he hadn't raised that particular topic to the Porter suddenly seemed like a glaring omission. It was one more question mark on his long mental list of Things to Ask Annie.

The driver waited outside. He would take them directly to the Sheriff's Office in Mount Clemens as soon as they were ready.

As Lydia stripped off her clothes, Willow couldn't help but say, "Jesus, did you have to *crucify* him? What was that about?"

"It's what he did to me."

"And the whole eye for an eye thing—"

"It's what Roy did to *me*," she said high-mindedly.

"Okay, okay. It just . . . doesn't make things any *easier*."

He brewed some coffee while she showered. Dixie arrived not long after. She hugged him and said, "Poor baby!" then touched the skin around his bandage—a little bit of blood was seeping through. Hearing the shower water turn off, she looked quizzically in its direction.

"That's Lydia—she lost her partner today. Her boyfriend."

"Oh my God. Is she okay?"

"As okay as she can be."

Lydia appeared in the hall, stark naked and still wet.

"Should I just use your towel?" she asked.

"Um, yeah!" said Willow, abashed. He shooed her back to the bathroom. "Go for it! I left a shirt out for you on the bed."

"Thanks!" She smiled at Dixie and then retreated.

Dixie twisted her mouth in a *What the fuck?*

"She's in a little bit of shock," said Willow. "Which I guess is kind of understandable."

It was flattering, even under the surreal circumstances, to watch his girlfriend get jealous.

Dixie shook her head and said, "*Whatever.*" Then, still ruffled: "'I left a shirt out for you on the bed'?"

"Hers had blood all over it."

"Oh shit." It brought Dixie back to the gruesome reality of what went down. "Are you guys hungry?"

"I don't feel like I am. But food's probably a good idea."

"I'll go fix something." She kissed him again and held him tight. "Try and keep your clothes on, Casanova."

After she left, Lydia came and sat on the couch.

"That was Dixie—a neighbor. She's bringing us some sandwiches."

"Are you an item?"

"Sometimes," he said. They were quiet for a while. "So . . . how do you feel?" In spite of himself, Willow wanted to sponge up as much as he could. "What does it feel like? After the *moment of balance?*"

"It feels . . . strange. I feel—strange."

"You mean, like you might be . . . leaving?"

He thought that any moment she might keel over.

"No, not that—though, that too . . . I *will* be leaving, but not just yet. It's hard to explain. It's like I'm not Lydia anymore but I'm not Maya either. It's like I'm no one—I'm no one and everyone. Maybe that's what 'moment of balance' really means. That the balance isn't *revenge*, but the moment you become . . . no one and everyone."

There was much he wanted to ask but they needed to triage, as Dixie would say. There wasn't much time.

"We need to talk about what we're going to say," said the detective. "How we're going to explain to Owen what happened today."

2.

Dixie changed his dressing. The bandage was small and clean and he looked presentable. He even put on a suit. But the deputy was a different story—seeing her through the eyes of the very serious group who was gathered in the conference room, Willow admonished himself for being remiss. She wore a pair of Dixie's borrowed jeans and an oversized T-shirt that Pace had mailed him during his stay at the Meadows. It said CHICK MAGNET and bore an illustration of a cartoon magnet with baby chicks stuck to its end.

They went through the niceties, with pro forma consolations expressed to Lydia for her loss, before getting down to business. (On the way over, Willow reminded Lydia to let him take the lead and to say as little as possible when questioned directly.) The sheriff reiterated they were here to create a painstaking, linear reconstruction of events, "from top to bottom."

"We're waiting for the autopsy report on Roy Eakins," said Owen. "A window to the house was jimmied open." Willow knew he'd be coming around to the question of how they had already known Roy Eakins was dead—but hearing the business about the window, the detective scrambled to make an adjustment to the scattershot narrative he'd been constructing. In a blatant oversight, he'd neglected to realize both his and Lydia's prints would be found on the sill. "But there wasn't any evidence of a struggle," Owen continued. "The body was found in bed, like he died in his sleep." Then he turned to Lydia. "When I asked if Deputy Doheny had anything to do with Roy Eakins's death, you said that he died of natural causes—you said it *right away*. How did you know that, Deputy Molloy?"

Ugh. The question came sooner than Willow expected.

"Because I was there," she said coolly. "We both were."

Willow's gut flipped. *So much for getting our stories straight . . .*

"You were there, with Eakins?" said the sheriff, incredulous. "In his *home?*"

Willow hastily staged an intervention.

"Yes, we were and I'll explain why. I'd only just learned about the footprint—we had a piece of evidence with a print. The birthday card belonging to Maya Rummer." His words came quickly, as if the torrent might somehow stop Owen from taking a swing at him. "The print on the card was always identified as a palm print. But I started to think, what if it isn't? What if one of the experts made a mistake, and a misidentified 'palm print' became gospel—what if it was actually a footprint? So I sent a print of Eakins's foot to the lab."

"And how," said Owen, "did you obtain a *footprint* belonging to Roy Eakins?"

The sheriff hated playing catch-up with his subordinate's breaking news alerts—it embarrassed him as much as it made him suspicious. But

suspicious of what? He was pissed off enough that he was becoming determined to hang Willow Wylde's ass out to dry.

"I went to interview Roy last week at his house. He stepped on a piece
of paper and I confiscated it without him knowing."

"He stepped on a piece of paper!" said Owen, laughing out loud. It jarred
the room because it was more of a seal's bark.

"He liked going barefoot," said Lydia, trying to be helpful.

"How would *you* know what he liked?" said Owen, ready to take a
swing at her as well.

"I mean, apparently," she said, off a glance from Willow. "A lot of people
take their shoes off when they're at home. I do."

"Well, I don't," said the sheriff, turning to Willow. "So you're saying
the prints were a match? That Roy Eakins's footprint was on the birthday card?"

Willow had sweated through his shirt. "That is what I believe the results will show."

"I see," said Owen, grinning like an executioner. "That is what you believe the results will show."

"One thousand percent. That's why Lydia and I went over to see him."

"*Before* you had proof. Makes perfect sense to me! You were going to
arrest him, before you had *proof*—and without backup."

"I admit that may have been a mistake, Owen."

"That's big of you."

"We made—*I* made a *lot* of mistakes. But in my assessment, the man was
only violent toward children. He was absolutely intimidated by adults. I felt
there wasn't any way the situation would have gotten out of hand."

"You didn't think it'd get out of hand because the man was only violent
toward children! With the *exception* of his fully grown son—you know, the
one whose eyes he gouged out. The one he allegedly crucified—"

"I was wrong."

"Jesus fucking Christ, Willow!" A few of the hangmen in the room
nodded their heads in disgust. "And why *would* he kill his own son?"

"I have a few theories about that," said Willow.

"Can't wait to hear them," said Owen. "This is like one of those Jerry Springer shows."

"Maybe Roy had some regrets toward the end—over what his son had become. What he'd made him into."

"Isn't that touching! Willow, you just brought fucking tears to my eyes. Let me ask you something else. How would an old, decrepit guy like Roy Eakins be able to inflict such damage? That killing was ferocious. We'll see what Grundy's *wife* has to say about it," he said ominously. "Right now, she's being a little recalcitrant."

Willow had neglected to consider the surviving witness, and the sheriff's comments put a dent in his mood. "I actually thought that by paying him a visit, we'd have a strong chance of a confession."

"A serial killer's private home is always the best place for that kind of interview," said Owen sarcastically.

"I had a relationship with the man. I'd spent a pleasant afternoon with him a week or so back."

"My friend, you are out of your fucking skull."

"Whereas if we showed up with the cavalry, that wouldn't have been possible. Less likely, anyway."

"So we climbed in through the window," said Lydia.

Here we go, thought Willow, closing his eyes and wishing he were somewhere else.

"You broke into a suspect's house without a warrant!"

"We had probable cause," said Willow.

"We saw him through the window," said Lydia. "He looked like he may have been having some sort of medical emergency."

"What kind of medical emergency?" asked one of the others.

"He was having, uh, tremendous difficulty breathing," said Willow. "We could see that before we went in."

The question of why they never called an ambulance hung in the air (in the blizzard of bullshit), but Owen let it go for now. "And just how is it," he said, "that you ended up at the farmhouse in Wolcott Mills?"

"As I said, Grundy Eakins was a suspect—*Deputy Doheny* thought he was a suspect, and was actively pursuing that lead. Without our knowledge."

"A suspect in the Winston Collins murder."

"That's right."

"All right. I see. Everything's getting very clear. It hasn't been *easy*, but you're starting to make sense. Let me summarize: Daniel Doheny, your *rookie*, decided he just didn't want to work Cold Case anymore—he wanted to crack open a recent homicide. So he left the Rummer murders to you and his girlfriend while he went rogue. Is that what you're telling me?"

"No. The Rummer kids and Winston Collins are connected."

"Ah! So now you're saying Grundy Eakins *did* have something to do with killing Troy and Maya . . ."

"Not directly," said Willow. "Look, Owen, it's possible he may have known about it—about what his father did—he may even have participated in some of Roy's later crimes. But it's still my feeling that Grundy wasn't involved in their deaths."

"Your *feeling*. Well, here's a dumb question, Dubya. I mean, maybe not dumb for you, because you're special. You're like a special genius who does whatever the hell he wants to do and withholds it all day long from the man he's supposed to be reporting to."

"You know that's not true—"

"Can you tell me what it was that made Deputy Doheny think that Grundy Eakins had something to do with the murder of the Collins boy?" He crossed his arms like Mr. Clean, prepared to hear a whopper.

"I can," said Willow. "I can tell you exactly how he knew. It was seren-dipity, but it was brilliant."

"We're listening."

"In cold case work it's important to follow your nose. Sometimes there's no logic or sense to whatever lead you're—"

"Save it for the memoirs, Willow. Or the TED talk."

"Lydia and Daniel kept having a hunch that Honeychile was somehow connected to our case. The Rummer case. And it turned out that she was—through *Winston*, not Troy and Maya. The morning after you interviewed her, we went to the hospital to talk to her. I called to tell you we were going, remember? We got there right after she killed herself. We went into her room and saw drawings—sketches she'd been working on. And Deputy Doheny recognized one of the designs, an angel with butterfly wings. He said it was specific to Iron Butterfly, the old rock band."

"How does that connect her to Winston?"

"Honeychile had some sort of *psychic knowledge* about what happened to Winston Collins. We can't dispute that because she led us to the body. I've seen stranger things . . ."

"Get to the point, Willow."

"The design of the angel she drew in the hospital was the same one that was on the T-shirt of the boy she killed at school."

"And Daniel told me," said Lydia, "that he found pictures on Facebook of Grundy wearing the Iron Butterfly T-shirt. The woman Honeychile drew, with the butterfly wings."

Willow thought they were finding their groove; at least Owen was starting to be reflective instead of derisive. "Deputy Doheny had a theory that Honeychile was fixated on the design because it was on the T-shirt that Winston's killer was wearing when he killed the boy. Dr. Robart said the girl was claiming to *be* Winston—so Daniel thought she had lashed out at the football player because she was triggered by the design. It was *Grundy* who she wanted to kill . . ."

The disgruntled sheriff was peeved that he'd shared the details of the Collins case with his old colleague.

"When the Porter—I mean, Willow—when our *supervisor* realized it was a footprint on the card," said Lydia, "everything fell into place. We knew we had a pair of father-son serial killers on our hands."

"It's rare but not unprecedented," said Willow. "Daniel's idea about the T-shirts started to make sense."

"But how did you end up at the farmhouse?" said Owen insistently.

"The night before, Daniel never came home," said Lydia. "He still kept his apartment in Smiths Creek but always stayed with me. He'd go there to sleep when he was stressed out or needed to be alone—usually during the day. I got worried when I didn't hear from him, so I went over. He wasn't home but his car was there, parked on the street. Which was weird. I didn't know what to do. I went to work in the morning and told Willow about it."

"I probably should have been more concerned," said the detective. "I thought maybe he'd spent the night with his ex, but I wasn't going to suggest that to Lydia. We started talking about the Rummers and I told her the idea I had about the footprint . . . and we went over to see Roy. That's when we found the body."

"And *right then*," said Lydia, hamming it up—not just for Owen's sake, but for Willow's—"I had the feeling Daniel *snapped*. That he might have done something not so smart. That maybe he went to pay a visit to Grundy Eakins."

"How would he have gotten to Wolcott Mills? If his car was still in Smiths Creek?"

"Maybe it wouldn't start?" said Lydia lamely.

Another flaw in the narrative, thought Willow. *But all said, we're doing pretty well.* "We'll have to check cab and Uber records," he offered. There were so many holes in their story that he was counting on the fact that both cases had been solved to ultimately save the day.

Owen called for a break. For the first time, Willow breathed. They'd taken some punches but if they stayed on the ropes the next eight rounds, it would be all right, even if they took a bloody beating. Willow thought anything short of a knockout was acceptable.

Everyone left the room but Lydia, who sat staring at the wall with an ethereal smile. Willow and the sheriff stood outside the door talking in low tones.

"Oh and by the way," said Owen. "Your little theory about Roy Eakins traveling exclusively in children's circles is absolute horseshit. We found a purse in his closet with ID belonging to Sarabeth Ahlström. She was murdered in her condo a few weeks ago in Dearborn Heights. At the time of his death, Roy was wearing a pair of bloody panties and the lab's running tests to see if they belonged to Sarabeth—or someone else."

"Frankly, I'm surprised. Killing adults doesn't fit his profile."

"You're surprised? Fuck *me*, Dubya, I've been nothing *but* surprised for the last few hours."

"Can we not lose sight of the fact that three murders have been solved? Of *kids*? And that two of those went unsolved for almost twenty years?"

"I haven't lost sight of that, Willow," he said, softening. "I haven't lost sight of it at all. And I know they didn't get solved by themselves. I know that and I appreciate that."

"It sure didn't sound like that in the conference room. But thank you."

"I just need to wrap a red bow around it—hell, I'll settle for *twine*—but right now you're asking me to put a ribbon on a pile of horse manure. And it *needs* to get wrapped, Willow, you know it does, you know that's how the game is played. It's all woo-woo dream-catcher at the moment. You've got Iron Butterfly *T-shirts* and *hunches* . . . everyone's having spooky little *feelings*. I run the Macomb County Sheriff's Office, not a psychic fair. And I'm fully aware that cold cases are sometimes solved in methods that are slightly unorthodox. The public *likes* that. But the powers that be are more fond of old-fashioned leg- and lab work."

"We have both, Owen."

"You better pray it's a footprint on that card. And then you need to pray it matches Roy Eakins's—"

"It will."

"—and that Grundy's wife corroborates your story."

"She's a nutjob, Owen."

"Yeah, well. They're everywhere, it seems."

"And do *me* a favor, Owen."

"What's that?"

"Can you leave Daniel a hero? I'm asking you not to go down this 'rogue cop' road. Daniel Doheny was a natural. A brilliant, intuitive investigator.

So leave him a hero—which he was. For real. It won't do his family any good to paint him black *or* gray. It won't do the department any good either. Make him a hero, Owen, and we'll all be heroes."

3.

Not long after they resumed, Owen decided that Willow and Lydia were running on empty. The interview was adjourned so everyone could recharge and begin fresh in the morning.

She probably won't be here tomorrow, thought Willow. *She'll probably be back on the train . . .*

He hoped that wasn't true, hoped it was another lie (he'd told so many today), because of the large place she now held in his heart. He wanted her to live forever. It was selfish but he couldn't help himself. He felt for Maya-Lydia, or whatever she had become, the same protective, unconditional love that he had for Pace. He wondered too: Is it *my* love, *Willow's* love? Or is it the love of a Porter . . .

He realized it didn't matter. Whatever it was contained all love's grisly glory—love's one-and-onlyness.

In the late afternoon, the sheriff called.

Every cell in Willow's body clenched and split apart. Every fear rose up—that he was being arrested for obstructing justice, even for murder and conspiracy; that he would shame his daughter, wounding her so deeply that she'd go back to taking drugs. Maybe Annie had already been detained and started naming names . . . He imagined being locked up on a 5150 for belonging to a cult with psychotic delusions of supervising dead children who inhabited dead bodies . . .

"Laverne Eakins went into labor in jail. It was obstructed—the kid couldn't come out. The doctor said it ruptured her uterus and she bled out."

"Jesus."

"I guess it was a demon seed she had in there after all."

I n the early evening, he picked up Lydia and they drove to the Meeting in
Detroit.

Again, Willow wanted to know how she was doing—but this time with
less subtext about when she might be leaving for parts unknown. Instead, it
had the flavor of what he'd asked a thousand times of Pace, in both troubled
and untroubled times.

When he told her about the death of Grundy's wife, all she said was,
"That's sad."

"There's something I've been thinking about," said Lydia, her brow
pinching up. "I was hoping you might have an answer. I'm not sure Annie
would know, but it came to me that I should ask the new Porter."

"Try me," he said.

"I've been wondering what happened . . . to Winston and Dabba Doo. I
know they were inside their landlords—Honeychile and Roy—but what
happened to them when Honeychile and Roy died? I mean, *finally* died . . .
What happens when your landlords die before you have your *moment of
balance*? Or when someone else has it for you? I mean, I killed Grundy, but
would that be enough? Would that be enough to give Winston his *moment
of balance*? Can you do it like that, by proxy? The *Guide* doesn't talk about
it and Annie never said anything either. And poor Dabba Doo, he never
even found the person who murdered him . . . So where do you think they
went? I know things got 'haywire'—Annie said it got that way on account
of the fact she was dying and you were coming . . . I didn't mean that to
sound like it's your fault! But what happened to Winston and Dabba Doo?
Where did they go? Do you know, Porter? Do you know what happened to
them? Porter, tell me if you do."

He thought it was of note that she evaded the real question: Where did
Troy go? And what would happen to Maya? Because neither one of them
had a proper *moment of balance*, not really. Neither one of them killed
the man who had murdered them. Though maybe bloodline was what

mattered and Grundy could stand in for his father, "by proxy." Maybe the killing of Grundy, though a simulacrum, would be enough to set sister and brother free.

The words poured from Willow without thought.

"Annie talks about the Great Mystery . . . and the mysteries wrapped in mysteries. The mystery of the children who return—and the mystery of evil. I think that whatever Roy Eakins had inside him was so strong that it . . . swallowed Dabba Doo up. I don't know that for sure but I *feel* it."

"But where do you think he is?" she said, with a redundant, childlike sincerity that broke his heart.

"I don't know."

"I know that he's not where Troy is—because I can still *feel* Troy. I know I'll be with him soon! But I can't feel *Winston*. I used to be able to feel the others, at the Meetings. But I can't feel Winston or Dabba Doo."

After a brief moment, the worry inexplicably vanished from her face, erased by that smile she had when already somewhere else, far away from such concerns.

I t touched him that when she sat down next to her brother's empty seat, Maya's serene disposition didn't alter from that moment in the car when all disquiet disappeared. She knew she would soon be departing for the land of the trains; Willow saw the dazzling blueness that surrounded her begin to pulse like a cosmic jellyfish, calling her back, singing to her, loving her. He was certain she could feel its embrace.

He knew Annie saw it too.

A great sorrow, kingly and ennobled, overtook the detective, a palatial melancholy whose bare rooms were filled with the light of grace. Sitting beside Annie, he turned to meet the Porter's gaze. Willow knew that she understood, having witnessed so many children leave this world for the last time after their *moment of balance*. Yet alongside such emotions, something terrifying took hold, more fearful than the panic of his first few Meetings.

It was the sense he was too far in now, that the point of no return was approaching—or had already been passed. *Why am I still fighting this?* Maybe his recalcitrance had to do with Annie having told him that Porter-ship was his destiny. Because whether she was right or wrong, Willow Millard Wylde didn't like anyone telling him *anything* about his own life.

Half a dozen people sat with *Guides* in their laps and Willow was puz-zled that he was able to give each his undivided attention while his head was completely elsewhere. They had so many questions! When Annie gave him the nod to take over, he provided answers, provisional as they were. She smiled approvingly as he spoke, with maternal looks of "job well done."

Maya took her cake and the newcomers were thrilled. (Children being always enlivened by a birthday.) It made no difference that they couldn't comprehend what the celebration was about, though Annie had prefaced it with a short talk about something called the *moment of balance.*

After the Meeting, Annie asked Willow to stay behind. The sentry came in with a scruffy backpack and set it down in front of him. "Thank you, Bumble," said Annie. He doffed his cap and left. Alone now with the new Porter, she pointed to the backpack.

"That's for you to take home. And if I don't see you again, I wanted to thank you. I'm so glad that it's you who's taking my place. I'm not as strong as you are, I was never as strong, and the children deserve that! Did you no-tice something different about this group? There was something so grounded about them, so purposeful. There isn't that sense of *aberration* I've felt for so many months. Nothing 'haywire' about 'em! A healing has already taken place—a balance—and it's because of you. And don't get a swelled head about it either! It has nothing to do with you, not really. Not a thing to do with any person or thing—only to do with balance. Balance and love. Love *makes* balance, you see? Yes, that's what I've learned. And if that's all I've learned, it's enough."

He knew she would die soon and it frightened him. In that way he had become a child like the others.

"I don't know what to say," said Willow.

"You'll have plenty to say and plenty of time to say it in, so don't worry. Oh! There's just one more thing—I seem to always be telling you there's one more thing, don't I? You've been in AA so I'll put it in those terms. You told me once that you never really took the First Step—'We admitted we were powerless over alcohol and that our lives had become unmanageable.' The *surrender* of the First Step is what allows you to begin your sober journey. I know you haven't done that yet, not in this room. You haven't surrendered— I know it! But you're going to need to, Willow, if you want to help these children. You're going to need to finally do a First Step."

"I'm trying, Annie."

"There's a word they use in AA—'Eskimo.' Do you know what it means? To have an 'Eskimo'?"

"It's the person who brings you to your first Meeting."

"Yes! And do you know who your Eskimo is? In *these* meetings?"

"It's you."

"No," she said gravely. "It isn't me. You've still to meet your Eskimo— the one who will allow you to truly surrender." She closed her eyes, as if weathering a storm. Softly, she said, "I pray that it won't be a child." He heard the words but could make no sense of them. Then she opened her eyes and smiled. "God bless you and keep you, Willow Millard Wylde."

The sentry appeared again and took her arm.

Willow watched them go out.

4.

When he dropped Lydia off, he asked if she would be all right staying by herself. She said she would and kissed his cheek. He thought it best to just come out with it, considering the elegiac mood Annie had set, and all that he knew. "Lydia, I have the feeling"—he didn't, really, but wasn't sure how to start—"this is the last time I'll see you."

"That isn't true," she said. "If I'd had a 'perfect' *moment of balance*, you'd probably be right. But things got messed up. I happen to know *exactly* when I'm leaving and it isn't tonight. I'll stay long enough to go to Daniel's funeral; I really did come to love him in the same way Maya loves Troy. Besides, Troy will be there too—hints of him. Because he and Daniel spent so much important time together. So I'll see you Sunday, 'kay?"

"Okay," he said somberly.

She kissed his cheek again.

"Try not to be so blue," she said.

He made love to Dixie that night, saturated in love and death, good and evil, balance and anarchy. She cried when she came, the first time that happened. She was never more beautiful.

They lay in bed and smoked.

"How's Lydia doing?" she asked.

"Seems to be doing okay. Had a bit of a rough day."

"I think you *all* did. I'm surprised you went to your AA meeting."

"It was either that or drink."

"Willow . . . I know she was traumatized—but what was *up* with that little strip show she did?"

"I don't know," he said with a shrug and a smile.

"I mean, did you guys have some kind of deal going on?"

He laughed. "Why do you even say that?"

"I don't know. She just looked so . . . comfortable. Like it was something she'd done before."

"She's just a little Aspergers-y. Kind of a strange affect. If you didn't notice."

"Yeah," said Dixie. "I kinda saw that."

"Cold case cops are weird, what can I say?"

It was her turn to laugh. "*Be* weird—but not *too* weird. 'Cause if some other chick comes out of the shower in her birthday suit, you'll see how weird *I* can be."

An hour later, they were asleep in each other's arms.

· · ·

H e awoke gasping for air and looked at the clock: 1:20 A.M.
He was parched. He went to the fridge and slugged down half
a gallon of orange juice. He wandered to the living room and saw the backpack by the door. Inside was a package wrapped in brown paper and a card
with his name that said "Keep Coming Back!" (It was signed "Annie," the
i dotted with a heart.) He opened the stack of *Guides*. None had the names
of children written on them; if all went well, he would soon meet their
owners on the train.

He stared at the mural and was seized by a dizzying panic. He ran to the
bedroom for his phone. He realized he had left it in his coat and ran back to
the living room. It was slung across a chair and he fished it from the pocket.
He dialed Pace, praying she'd pick up—

—certain that his grandson was dead.

O God, God, God. Larkin is my Eskimo . . .

He kept getting sent to voice mail and resolved to jump in the car and
drive straight to Marlette if she didn't answer in the next sixty seconds. At
this hour, he could make it in forty-five minutes. He was already gathering
his things, thinking about what he would say in the note he'd leave for
Dixie—he didn't want to put her through yet another crisis—when Pace
called back. She'd been drifting off to sleep, her iPhone on mute, when the
light of the incoming call awakened her.

He blurted out, "*Is everything okay?*" She was confused and then frightened by her father's tone. She stiffened and sat up, jarring Geoff to wakefulness. "Is Larkin okay?"

"He's fine, Daddy, we're fine . . . everyone's *fine*. What's going on?"

"*Go check on Larkin.*"

"Hold on."

She sprinted to her son's room with an urgency informed by her father's
history. She still remembered his night terrors when she was a little girl, and
the legendary story of his premonition of her great-grandmother's death had

long been enshrined in Wylde family lore. She touched the sleeping boy's cheek and watched his tiny chest heave with life. Pace tucked the blanket around him and kissed the crown of his head.

"He's totally fine. He's right here, sleeping."

"*Great.* That's great."

"Daddy, what's going on?"

"I'm sorry, babe," he said. "I had a nightmare. Sorry, honey—I'm sorry I woke the house. I didn't mean to scare you." He told her that the bad dream was one of general family safety, deciding it would be cruel to make Larkin the focus. It might put thoughts in her head. "I guess today's events had something to do with it. Guess I blew a fuse."

"I *heard*," she said as she sat at the dining room table. Geoff wandered in and sat too. "You've been all over the news! I've been trying to reach you! I talked to Mom and she said you were okay, but why don't you pick up when I call?"

"It's just been so crazy—and I knew you and Adelaide would talk. I had to turn my friggin' phone off. I was getting calls from the media nonstop. Guess my cell phone number got WikiLeaked."

"But you're okay? Mom said you got hurt."

"Just a scratch. I'm totally fine."

"Daddy, are you *sure*?"

"Absolutely. I'll tell you all about it when I see you. Sorry again to have woke everybody up. My apologies to Geoff."

"Daddy, it's *okay*, I'm *glad* you called. And *always* call, if you have a 'feeling'—or even if you don't."

"Haven't had one of those in a while."

"Well, don't *worry*. Everyone's fine."

"Thank you, sweetheart. Say hi to Geoff and let's plan something soon. And give Larkin a kiss."

"I will. I love you."

"I love you too. Now y'all go back to sleep."

MEMORIAL DAY

I.

It was a week of funerals, wakes and remembrance.

Annie gave Willow's name to the funeral home as next of kin. He was startled when the mortuary called. There was something bracing about the non-etherealness of it, grounding him amid the general "woo-woo," as Owen liked to say. At the same time, he became uneasy, the finality of her death nagging him to reconsider the events of the last few months. Had it all been a dream? The Porter was right: he still hadn't taken a First Step, in this world or the next. And he had his resentments—why did Annie say what she did about praying his Eskimo wouldn't be a child? The remark seemed almost sadistic. He could see himself making late-night phone calls to Pace until his dying day.

When he came to the viewing room, the sentry was standing over the coffin. Willow lingered respectfully in the doorway and was about to step away when Bumble walked over. They shook hands. He said he'd cleaned out Annie's room at the SRO and donated her things to the downtown Mission, as she had asked.

Bumble handed him an envelope.

"Will I be your sentry, sir? Annie said that I probably would but it'd be impolite not to ask."

He was taken aback. "I'm—I'm just not sure yet if I'll be returning."

"She said you might say that too!" he said convivially.

He retreated to the door and stood dutifully on watch.

Willow went to the casket. She was beautiful—smiling that Mona Lisa smile that was so her. She wore the same stunning greenish-blue jewelry and brocaded dress he saw her in when they had their first encounter on the train. It wasn't until later that he realized how much she looked like his grandmother. The errant thought came that Nana had been a Porter. But if that were true, Annie would have known. She probably would have mentioned it.

The public memorial for Winston Collins was a few weeks away, too long for Lydia to wait. (Maya's and Troy's bodies, entombed in the foundation of Roy Eakins's old house in Saggerty Falls, wouldn't be found for three weeks.) As it happened, though, on this day—today—there fell separate services for Renée "Honeychile" Devonshire and Deputy Daniel R. Doheny. Willow hadn't planned on going to Honeychile's memorial until Lydia said that she absolutely wanted to be there. When he mentioned that to Owen, the sheriff was glad. He said he would have liked to go himself but would be attending church services at St. Joan of Arc in Saint Clair Shores for his fallen deputy. Willow told him they'd join up with everyone at the Doheny funeral, after Mass.

He was waiting at the curb to take her to the Devonshires' when Lydia walked out in her deputy's uniform. At first he was uncertain, thinking it a bit heavy-handed for what he understood to be a more casual, kid-heavy, festive gathering at the girl's home. (The parents were calling it a "celebration," that bugbear of a word when it came to heartbreaking occasions.) But then he thought, no—it was a respectful, powerful, purposeful choice. He laughed to himself that even an entity, a moribund vessel inhabited by the spirit of a dead child, had known the right thing to do. The uniform represented those who protect and serve, who sought justice and the restoration of balance. By honoring Honeychile thusly, she was honoring as well the girl who had mysteriously allowed them to recover Winston's body, to help solve his crime. It was the one positive thing that came out of her death.

When they arrived, the house was filled with Honeychile's schoolmates (mostly girls) and their parents. It felt like a party, which was just what Harold and Rayanne wanted. Willow found himself scanning the rooms for Honeychile, which seemed normal, the lines between both worlds having so recently been blurred. The lights dimmed as the movie put together by her best friend, Zelda, began. The montage of Instagram photos and videos of Honeychile being, well, *Honeychile* were greeted by hoots, laughter, applause and tears. At the end came the tour de force: a tribute from none other than Gaten Matarazzo, the young actor from *Stranger Things* who was afflicted with the cleidocranial dysplasia that she shared. The young celebrity had read a story about Honeychile online and after her suicide got in touch with the Devonshires, asking if there was any way he could help. They invited him to the party but he was unable to come, sending a funny, moving tribute instead. "Oh my God," Honeychile's friends kept saying. "She would so die!" The tribute closed with a last group of photos of the absent hostess, accompanied by an eerily beautiful rendition of "Life on Mars?" sung by Honeychile herself, surreptitiously recorded on Zelda's iPhone. There wasn't a dry eye in the house.

They finally found their way to Mom and Dad, who remembered Lydia from the hospital waiting room—the Sheriff's Office uniform helped—and were so touched that she'd come to pay her respects.

"Is your friend here?" asked Rayanne. Lydia looked at her blankly. "The young man who was with you when we met?"

Daniel's death had been big news and while it was likely they knew of it from the paper or television—they'd probably seen his photo—they obviously hadn't made the connection.

"He was unable," said Lydia, not wishing to inform.

"Well, please say hello and tell him he was missed," said Rayanne. Just as they were about to leave, she took Lydia's arm and said, "Can I show you something?"

She walked them to the den—"Honey's favorite place"—and Harold plucked something off a shelf, gently putting it in Lydia's hands. It was a snow globe. On closer inspection, she and the detective saw three figures hugging. Their faces, meticulously traced from photographs, were clearly recognizable: Harold, Rayanne and Honeychile.

"She made this for you?" said Lydia.

"Yes," said the mother, choking up.

Harold stepped in. "That was Honeychile—artistic and loving and so, so smart. That was our Honey."

"Was and still is," said Lydia.

Rayanne seemed to particularly appreciate the remark.

Outside, they passed a woman on the walkway. She stumbled a bit on the steps and the two rushed to support her. She looked at Lydia's uniform and smiled. "Who says the police are never there when you need them?" She thanked them and said, "I'm going to need a walker soon but don't tell anyone." She was only half-joking; she wasn't that old but had the gait of someone who'd prematurely aged. "It's not already over, is it?"

"Not at all," said Willow. "It's in full swing."

"Were you one of Honeychile's teachers?" said Lydia.

"Not by definition," she smiled. "I kind of think she might have been one of mine." She thrust a hand out and said, "I'm Hildy, an old family friend. Hildy Collins—Winston's mom."

"Pleasure to meet you," said Willow.

"And thank you," she said, addressing the one in uniform. "Thank you for finding the man who did that to my son." Her eyes watered over as her voice became resolute. "Thank you for *all* that you do."

2.

Owen went in the direction Willow suggested. Not that he had a real choice; it was either go with the flow or *not* go with the flow, with the latter engendering months of controversy, ill will and bad press.

It was now a matter of permanent record: Deputy Daniel R. Doheny was a hero cop.

The sheriff had his red bow and ribbon—for the public anyway, and the department as well—if not exactly for himself. By stepping outside his Cold Case lane to assist a current homicide investigation, not only did Deputy Doheny find the killer of Winston Collins, but also helped unravel the mystery of the nearly two-decades-old disappearance of Troy and Maya Rummer. Willow's instincts had been spot-on; it was a footprint on the birthday card, not a palm. And it belonged to Roy Eakins. That sort of thing has been known to happen because the ridges of the arch of the foot toward the heel are similar to those on the "knife edge" of the palm. Apparently the technician who did the assessment in July 2000 got it wrong and no one double-checked the results. Dubya really pulled that one out of the hat. He had to hand it to his spooky old buddy for cracking the code.

The bottom line was that the deaths of the Rummer kids, Winston Collins and Sarabeth Ahlström were stamped SOLVED—with five more children's bodies in the process of being exhumed from that hell farm in Wolcott Mills. (Three had already been identified.) As far as Owen was concerned, Roy Eakins did *not* commit the grisly crucifixion murder of his own son, but Laverne Eakins wasn't around to tell any tales. He had a few sleepless nights over that one, because if it wasn't Roy who nailed Grundy to the floorboards, it could only have been Lydia or Willow, and he simply refused to go there. He locked up those suspicions and buried them in a hole deeper than any of those kids had been buried in. For political and personal reasons, the latter of which he was unable to explain, the punctilious sheriff did what he never had in his long, decorated career: he let it slide, even if there was no evidence it was true. Not a drop of his son's blood was found on Roy's hands or clothing as he lay dead in bed at his home in New Baltimore, the place Willow speculated he had gone right *after* killing Grundy. Yet the coroner ruled that Roy had died the night before, with Grundy's death occurring the next morning, around the time of the sheriff's arrival at the farm. But if he wanted that bow and ribbon, Owen had to name Grundy's killer, and name him he did. Neither the public nor the politicians gave a shit about an iffy timeline, because two monsters had been wiped off the face of the Earth. So he hung it on the child-killer dad and felt no remorse. In his heart, he knew that Deputy Lydia Molloy killed Grundy in a rage over the torture of her lover. Owen had even spoken to her about it personally, with compassion, doing everything he could to get a confession, but she stuck to her story. There just wasn't any payoff in making Lydia or the community suffer any further. Owen also knew that Willow was grateful to him for that, and grateful too that the sheriff elected not to further pursue the line of argument in private conversation.

They got to church in time to follow the hearse for the twenty-minute drive to Clinton Township, where Deputy Doheny would be laid to rest at Resurrection Cemetery. (Willow thought it couldn't have been more appropriately named.) The turnout was stately and the pageantry magnificent. Hundreds of officers from Metro Detroit and practically every county in the state comprised the motorcade with its flashing blue and red lights. Lieutenant Governor Calley and other politicians attended as well. Officers came from across the country to honor him. Among the sea of onlookers quietly lining the sidewalks as the vehicles passed—the throngs were there to honor the deputy and the children, all children who'd been harmed, thrown away and forgotten—were wounded vets of many wars. Stories had been written in national magazines about the hero's remorse over the accidental killing of a boy during the time he served in Afghanistan. The articles shared the theme of PTSD and were for the most part sensitively written, each stressing the poetic justice of Daniel bringing a child-murderer to justice.

As they stood at the graveside, Willow grew agitated. He kept stealing glances at Lydia. She'd promised him she would stay—"I'll stay long enough to go to Daniel's funeral"—but what did that actually mean? Would she collapse beside him the moment they lowered the casket? Or would her passing be more in keeping with the drama and elegance of the Great Mystery . . . would he become lost in thought (as he was this very moment) and then turn to find her gone?

To calm himself, he conjured Dixie. Her voice, her sounds, her smells . . . *Should prolly just marry the girl.* A few nights ago, to get him out of his head, she dragged his two left feet to Oilcan Harry's for line dancing. He had more fun than he'd ever had when he was high. Watching Dixie in her boots and cowgirl hat as she ran through the coordinated routine was sexy as fuck. He felt bad for not inviting her to Daniel's funeral but just couldn't see how that would work. It might well be his last moments with Lydia and their experience had been too private, too mystical, too insular to tolerate the presence of a lover. (Besides, the nature of his attentions toward the deputy might easily be misinterpreted.) When he gave Dixie a half-ass plausible explanation for the snub, she backed right off, pretending that she understood. But he knew she was hurt. He would need to make it up to her.

Maybe put a ring on it . . .

They stood with Owen and Adelaide as the box ratcheted into the ground. Willow tried to suppress the ludicrous optics of Lydia expiring and tumbling into the grave.

When it was done, the group walked to their cars. Adelaide took notice of her ex's firm grip on Lydia's arm. Her first reflex was jealousy (which surprised her), but then she chastised herself and actually thought it courtly, if a touch chauvinistic. Of course the real reason behind Willow's ministrations was his terror that Lydia was about to vanish into thin air. As they moved along with the dispersing crowd, they small-talked, mostly about their daughter and grandson. Adelaide said they were having a barbecue next week and told him to mark his calendar. Pace had promised to bring the family down from Marlette. They hugged goodbye and went their separate ways.

About a hundred yards off, Willow saw a couple standing near his car. They were arguing—the woman was, anyway—and the man tried to restrain her. Suddenly, she looked toward the detective and pointed, wild-eyed. She lurched toward them, the man straggling after.

It was Elaine and Ronnie Rummer.

Willow hadn't spoken to them since their children's murders were solved.

He'd meant to and didn't know why he kept putting that off. It was a horrible thing to do—not to make that personal connection—a callous and egregious gaffe, especially after how gracious they'd been during his visit. He flinched, girding himself for impending violence. Maybe Elaine snapped again and was coming after him to repay the insult . . .

Only when the Rummers were upon them did the question arise: How would Maya react to seeing her parents? Or would she have any reaction at all? Perhaps "Maya" and "Lydia" were already gone . . . Again, he was plagued with the image of Lydia conveniently dropping dead on the spot. But Elaine bypassed him entirely and went straight to the deputy, tenderly taking her hands in hers. A shiver went through the woman and she closed her eyes, as in prayer. When she opened them, she said, "It's you."

Ronnie and Willow hung back.

"Mama," whispered Maya, her emotions in check.

What presented itself to Elaine Rummer was a hybrid of her baby girl and a mature young woman—what Maya would have become. "I *felt* you . . . I told Dubya!—I told him that for a few months, I've wanted to *live*. And now I know why! The Lord showed me why . . . I don't know *how* I knew you were here and didn't know how I would find you—*today* . . . Ronnie thought I was crazy for wanting to come! I didn't tell him why I wanted to"—she laughed through her tears—"because then he would have had me locked up again! But I'm not crazy, am I? It *is* you . . . I'm not crazy, am I, Maya?"

"No," she said, smiling. "You're not. And I'm so sorry, Mama, for everything that happened—for how you suffered. That you did to yourself what you did."

"And he—your brother was here too?"

"Yes. He was here today."

"I knew it! I *felt* it. And he's gone now?"

"Yes." Maya looked shyly toward the ground. "We weren't supposed to see you," she said. "There usually isn't time. I wanted—I planned to come visit, even after Troy left. But this morning I knew I wouldn't have to. Because I knew I'd see you here."

Elaine turned to Willow. "Did you know? That they'd come back? Did you know they were here?" The detective somberly nodded and she turned to her husband, ecstatic. "He *knew*. Our old friend Willow knew . . . he knows!"

"I have to leave now," said Maya. She embraced her father to stop him from quaking. "Take care of her, Poppy—and take care of *yourself.* I want you to be happy. Troy and I want both of you to be happy." She hugged Elaine again and told her she loved her.

"Baby, please!" said Elaine. "Can't you stay?"

"I can't, Mama, but I'm here *now*. Remember what I said that time about the spiderweb?"

"That it's better than coming home to nothing," said Elaine, and they both laughed. The woman's ruined face looked beatific.

"Know that I'll never leave you," Maya said.

They left the cemetery and drove toward Lydia's home. When they got to the junction, she told him to take North Avenue instead of the M-19, which would have been a straight shot to Richmond. He did as he was told.

"Do you know what's strange?" she said. "In the last few days, I've started wondering about the terrible things we did—Daniel and Lydia, and Maya and Troy . . . and the terrible things that Rhonda and José and the *others* did too. I mean, wondering about the purpose of it. It's not like I have guilt—not exactly—or even that I've anguished over it . . . it's more of a— meditation. That's the word Lydia would use! A meditation on the purpose of it all. Does that make any sense?"

"Yes." He had a queasy sense of where she was going.

"It's made me question—it got me thinking about the quality of mercy. If the children who came back can be forgiven for the things they did to the people who hurt them . . . well, it made me wonder about Roy Eakins and his son. Isn't it possible they'll be forgiven too? At first I thought that was such a miserable idea, a useless and *evil* idea—to show them that sort of compassion. But is it? How can it be? Maybe it's a *beautiful* idea, because . . . can't monsters be forgiven? How can someone, some *actor* in the Great Mystery, not be forgiven? Is it so wrong, Willow, to be wondering that? And I wondered if I was the first—of those who came back, of the children of the train—if I was the first to have those kinds of thoughts. Though maybe it's just a 'haywire' thought! I guess I'm secretly hoping it is . . . because if you begin to question the purpose behind the *moment of balance*, then who are you, *what* are you? What have you become? Do you think it's an evil thing, Willow, to desire a *moment of balance*? Or worse: Do you think it's evil that such a thing, a *vengeful* thing, even exists? I'm so glad I'm leaving because I really don't want to follow that through to its logical end! What if it *is* a terrible thing, a wrong thing—and what if when your *moment of balance* comes, you choose to refuse it? What if that's actually something within the power of those who return? To say 'no' . . . do you think that's possible, Willow? What if saying no is the next step, part of the evolution of the Great Mystery? What if the Great Mystery has been waiting *centuries* for the children of the train to demonstrate that quality of mercy? I've been thinking about all these things . . ."

Willow had been too but remained quiet. He was about to turn on 32 Mile Road but Lydia told him to stay on North Avenue.

"Where are we going?"

"It's not too far now," she said.

Soon they were passing the canopies of tall trees that stood like stoic guards along the ingress of an ancient castle. The leaves had already begun to change. Banks of wildflowers beckoned from a thousand entrances to the forest. "There," she said, pointing to a dirt road. "Slow down or you're going to miss it!"

He did, and had to back up. They drove awhile before she told him to stop. "This is it. We'll need to walk from here." She climbed into the backseat and stripped off her uniform, changing into the hiking clothes that she'd packed in her duffel. She left the car, jogged in place and then started up the trail. He was still sitting at the wheel, lost, when she called to him. "We can say goodbye here, or you can follow me."

He got out and set after her. It was a rail trail and he felt that was apt. The defunct tracks of a ghostly train came in and out of view, covered over by dirt and clumps of hop clover and spectral Indian pipe. Willow grew winded and a few times she waited for him to catch up. He idly wondered if he would be able to find his way out. He had a fleeting thought that it might be better if he didn't.

She stopped on a high ridge, staring out at the pastureland below and the world at large. Willow knew she was doing as the *Guide's* epilogue suggested—thanking "that big, beautiful Blue Earth, the Mother Earth who nurtured you and those you loved, and to whom you returned for your *moment of balance*. You must thank Her before you take your final leave." When he reached her, he bent over to catch his breath. She let him, before asking if he'd say the Lord's Prayer with her, like at the end of their Meetings.

After *Amen*, she made her final remarks.

"I want to thank Maya and Troy. What beautiful little beings they were—so loved, by so many!—I wish them well on their journey. And how can I thank Lydia Molloy? Such a good woman, such a strong and smart woman. The world will miss her . . . and Daniel the Lionhearted! Deputy Daniel Doheny, I thank you on my brother Troy's behalf. Daniel had such anguish in his life but now he's free. My brother thanks Lydia too! We were both so honored." Willow saw tears in her eyes and had the somewhat clinical thought, *How is it that the dead can cry?* She turned to him and took his hands. "And I want to thank *you*, Willow Wylde, for supporting us, and walking us through every step of the way. My Porter! How lucky we were, and how lucky are the children who are coming! Father! Father! Goodbye—"

And just like that she ran up the hill to seek the gully where months ago she had lain.

3.

He wanted to make love but Dixie wasn't having it.

Her excuse was a horrible migraine that started in the morning. She *looked* like she had a bad headache—he didn't think it was connected to not having invited her to Daniel's memorial, but who knew. When he asked if she wanted to sleep alone, she said no, she wanted company. At least that was a good thing. He got a cold rag and draped it across her eyes, then drew a hot tub for himself.

He was confident in his decision to resign from the Cold Case Task Force. He would tell Owen tomorrow, in person. That was something he wasn't looking forward to, but he knew the sheriff would understand. He hoped the meteoric success of his brief tenure would assuage any disappoint-ment. Willow thought about what he was going to say—he'd thank him profusely for having given him the opportunity and then haul out the "I'm too old for this" trope. He was prepared for the sheriff to try to dissuade him by countering with a bonus or steep raise; in light of recent events, the county's vote for an infusion of funding to the unit was a fait accompli. He would promise to stay on and train a replacement.

As for his duties as Porter, he was done with those too.

His decision was partly triggered by Lydia's crisis of faith. On that last journey together, she had voiced her doubts about the essential validity of the *moment of balance*. Willow had been having those same heretical thoughts himself. Listening to her, he was reminded of something that Re-nata, his Buddhist friend, once told him about the Wheel of the Dharma. The idea was to be free of the Wheel—not to take on another body or some other incarnation, but to reach a state of no-yearning and no-craving, to escape the dogma of justice and retribution, to go beyond hatred, even beyond love. Would the Eakinses be forgiven? *Could* they be? He didn't know the answer but sensed it was irrelevant: there could be no freedom until there were no longer any questions. The truth is that he didn't want to exchange one task force for another, which is what Annie's program seemed to be: just another job with standards, protocols and endgames—

Spec Ops from the Unknown. He remembered that time at Penn Station when he asked about becoming a porter. The man corrected him by saying they called them service attendants now. The little scene wasn't too far off the mark, because that's just what Willow felt like—a drunk with delusions of supernatural grandeur, applying for a gig whose name he couldn't get right.

As he soaked, he reread the note from Annie that the sentry gave him at the funeral home. She included a Wordsworth poem (he'd googled it earlier) about a man who encounters a strange little cottage girl. When he asks if she has brothers and sisters, she declares, "We are seven," even though two are dead—"two of us in the churchyard lie." When the man says that if two siblings have departed, then she only has four, the girl insists he's wrong.

> The first that died was sister Jane;
> In bed she moaning lay,
> Till God released her of her pain;
> And then she went away.
>
> So in the church-yard she was laid;
> And, when the grass was dry,
> Together round her grave we played,
> My brother John and I.
>
> And when the ground was white with snow,
> And I could run and slide,
> My brother John was forced to go,
> And he lies by her side.
>
> "How many are you, then," said I,
> "If they two are in heaven?"
> Quick was the little Maid's reply,
> "O Master! we are seven."

"But they are dead; those two are dead!
Their spirits are in heaven!"
'Twas throwing words away; for still
The little Maid would have her will,
And said, "Nay, we are seven!"

He sunk the note in the bathwater, watching the ink run together.

STATION TO STATION

I.

It went better than he thought.

Then why did he feel worse when it was done?

He wondered if bailing from the task force was a blunder. Yet each time he had such doubts, the detective realized it was a symptom of his general confusion—a mélange of money worries combined with a shudder of fore-boding. The awkward part came at the end, when Owen gave him the Look—the one Willow knew he'd be getting from friends and family over the next few weeks and months, even years—the one that said, *Hope you stay sober!* The Look had nuances akin to regional accents. In the sheriff's, he heard this one: *Bet you've already started—you probably never stopped. Prolly faked your piss test too.*

He painted over the mural of the train with primer, praying the blank space might lend itself to a new chapter. But resigning from Cold Case was one thing; resigning from Annie's Meetings was something else. When he first joined AA, hadn't his sponsor suggested not making any big moves for at least a year? *Don't try to quit smoking. Don't get married. Don't quit your day job.* Drama and instability always got you drunk.

Suddenly, he became wary. What if walking out on his Portership du-ties delivered the coup de grâce?

The same group was there, the ones he had met at his inaugural Meet-ing. There were no new landlords and he was certain that was a direct result of his no longer dreaming about the train. Willow was still the Porter, nominally anyway, and came to understand that he was the portal as well—without his soothing of the fresh arrivals in their cabins, without his in-structions to carefully memorize the Meeting's locale, it was impossible for the children to cross over.

Everyone seemed to be doing just fine. No one really needed the proactive hand-holding that Troy and Maya had required. "Grounded and purposeful" was how Annie had described the fresh batch of immigrants, attributing their simple, clear-eyed confidence to Willow's "healing" pres-ence. He maintained decorum, answering their questions and orienting them, with the help of the *Guide*, in how they should behave in the world. (It felt like he was teaching basic English to foreign exchange students.) Oc-casionally, when they grew agitated, he soothed them as a father would. Without much help, it looked as if one of them, a delivery driver for Ama-zon, was already getting close to her *moment of balance*. Willow was grati-fied and thought maybe that was all that was required of him—to sit there with his healing presence like a factotum, a figurehead, a straw boss. At the end of each Meeting, Bumble the sentry said, "Damn good, Porter. Damn good job."

But what did *he* know?

I'll ride it out till they're done . . . one by one they'll have their moments of balance—*and when I'm the last man standing, I'll burn the* Guides *and close up shop.* "End of an era," he said aloud. Annie's words about the Eskimo still haunted and burned—"I pray that it won't be a child"—but now he had an ace in the hole. The detective was in the process of extricating himself from her world, and when he finally did, her cryptic rules and morbid prognosti-cations would no longer apply.

Dixie had been distancing herself and that troubled him, especially since he couldn't be certain that his impressions reflected reality. Willow theorized it was entirely possible that everything he was going through, everything he'd *been* through, had grossly distorted the way he perceived the world. But he needed to stay cool. He didn't want to crowd her; it was too soon to have a "conversation." Though maybe not having a conversation was distancing her further.

In his struggle to identify the source of her detachment, he kept circling back to Daniel's funeral. He'd been through it a hundred times. It would have been impossible to ask her to accompany him—it was *Lydia's* day, a day of goodbyes—yet more and more the rebuff presented itself as the fatal blow. Women were a riddle that could never be solved by the brick and mortar reasoning of men. In an instant, the consequences of large or trivial actions wrought by male rationale could handcuff love and prefigure its death. In its natural fealty to forgiveness and renewal, the beaten heart of a woman often resuscitated with more devotion than ever. But there came a time—an unpredictable time, cunning, baffling and powerful!—when the heart would not return. The worst thing about love dying in a woman was her ability to stay. It had happened to Willow once before; the woman stayed and it was like living with a ghost. She still smiled, still cooked, still managed to be "fun." He played along, in childish hopes that her mood would pass, because the truth hurt too much. He couldn't admit to himself that it was over until one afternoon he heard her crying behind the bathroom door.

He refused to let that happen with Dixie.

The perfect panacea was the Sunday barbecue at Owen and Adelaide's. He was deliberately casual about the invite, hoping she would appreciate what a big deal it was that he'd asked. He told her that his daughter and grandson were coming, the implication being that the party wouldn't just be their coming-out, but Dixie's unapologetic introduction to his world—his warts and errors, loyalties and elisions. It was only after she said that she'd love to go that he realized what a number it would have done on him if she had declined.

He *would* buy her that ring—today. Desperate times required desperate measures. He wanted to marry this girl. He didn't know how Dixie would feel about that but it was worth the risk. Maybe she'd come back to him from wherever it was she had gone.

He would ask her to be his wife and it would be the proposal of a good man, a vulnerable man, a battered and loving man who wanted her above all else.

2.

It was a spectacular day. The windswept sky ruffled the meadow that abutted the yard, its cool breezes and sporadic gusts cueing the grasses and leaves to shimmer in applause of the sun. The Caplans' home in Armada was close enough to where Lydia had left the world that Willow felt her presence with an adhesion of sadness and sacred delight.

Willow had prepped the crew that he was bringing "a gal I've been seeing," and to his relief, Dixie was treated with great warmth. She rallied, reveling in the mixed company. Maybe some old-fashioned socializing was all that was needed—*that's* right. We never go anywhere, see anyone . . . get too insular and the soil starts to dry up. Add a little sun, water and burgers and we're good to go. As she spoke to various members of the tribe, Dixie made sure to find his eye, smiling that sly, coyote smile. It was the best medicine for both of them.

He was thrilled to see Larkin. His grandson had already had his first surgery (wielding an aluminum tripod cane with a superhero's panache), with another scheduled not too far off. Their daughter ran the whole saga down to Addie a few days before coming to the barbecue, and Mom was chill when Pace informed that Dad was helping on the financial side. Adelaide even took Willow aside at the party and thanked him for making that happen. "I'm glad she has a father she can turn to." Her flattery was of course accompanied by the Look, appreciably more withering than Owen's: *You better not start drinking, because your daughter really needs you now. Don't you dare leave her again!* Addie's Look had layers to it and a measure of *oomph*, due to a bonus subtext of betrayal—when she learned he was quitting Cold Case, she was sorely pissed. Adelaide took it personally, finally admitting what Willow already knew: it was she who had promoted him to her husband for the job in the first place.

Pace cornered him at the edge of the yard.

"We haven't talked about Troy and Maya."

He nodded and said, "It was heavy."

"I can't even imagine. It's so weird that *you* were the one who found their killer."

"Well it wasn't just me, babe. I had a lot of help."

"Dad, you don't need to be so humble."

"It's true. We had some amazing people working on that."

"The one who died . . ."

"Daniel. Yeah. Daniel Doheny. Brilliant."

"It's so *awful* how he died. Those motherfucking Eakinses! I still can't even believe it."

"Oh, believe it. Believe it."

"I loved those kids so much."

"And they loved you. They told me they did."

"What do you mean?"

"Not *told* me," he amended, with a throat-clear. "I mean, it was obvious. Are you going to go to the memorial?"

"When is it?"

"I want to say the twenty-eighth?"

"We'll see," she said ambivalently. "I'd love to but Larkin may have a doctor thingie that day."

"I know Ronnie and Elaine would love to see you."

He could tell she wasn't up for it, and respected that.

"I should call them," she said, chastising herself. "Poor Elaine! Mom said that you went to see them?"

"I did."

"How are they? I mean, now. How are they doing?"

"Better. I think they're better."

"When they disappeared . . . I never really talked to you about it. It was like—like nothing made sense anymore. That's when I got into drugs, I mean heavily. I couldn't handle it."

"I'm sorry I wasn't there for you."

"There wasn't anything you could have done, Dad. I was totally shut off. And it's *okay*. Sometimes shit just gets fixed by itself—or not. I had to go through what I had to go through."

"Glad you made it out the other side, kid," he said, aware that he was echoing Roy Eakins's words to him about Grundy. They hugged. When she responded with "I'm glad we all did," he thought he detected the Look: *I still need you so don't go and do something stupid now that you don't have a fucking job.* Maybe he was just reading into it.

"The one who died—" she said again.

"Deputy Doheny."

"Owen said that his *girlfriend* disappeared? The other cop?"

"She did. Lydia Molloy."

"What *happened*?"

"We still don't know. She's AWOL. The media doesn't know that yet, by the way."

"What do *you* think happened?"

"Personally? I think she was so busted up about Danny that she may have . . . gone off somewhere to self-harm."

"Oh my God. It's like some horrible Greek *tragedy*, right? Someone needs to make a movie about it."

"Too soon," he said, with a smile.

"Who do you think should play you?"

"Well, I love Tommy Lee Jones."

"Tommy Lee Jones is like a hundred years old."

"Bradley Cooper? It's been said there's a very close resemblance."

That made her laugh and she hugged him again—the best medicine.

They sat around the picnic table and dug into their lunches. His ex put his girlfriend right beside her and Willow appreciated the gesture. Dixie talked to all comers, sharing funny RN anecdotes. (Addie had a few of her own.) She was good at listening too.

"I wish we could delete the last few weeks," sighed Adelaide during a lull. "We just lost someone dear to us at the hospital—a volunteer. As if the month hadn't been shitty enough."

"Oh?" said Willow.

"Annie Ballendine. I introduced you at the fund-raiser."

"Was she the one," said Willow, playing dumb, "you called the World's Greatest Volunteer?"

"That's right. And she *was*."

"Helluva lady," said Owen. It occurred to him to share the moment he had with Ms. Ballendine at the SRO—and the odd coincidence of her intersection with Honeychile—but thought it best not to revisit. "Annie the Unforgettable. A kind and selfless woman."

"Oh, but I didn't tell you!" said Adelaide, in a burst of enthusiasm. "I think we actually may have a *challenger*."

"To the World's Greatest?" said Willow.

"Uh *huh*," she said, smiling cryptically.

"I strongly doubt that," said Owen. "Unless ol' Dubya's planning to join up. Now that he's got some time on his hands."

"Very funny," said Willow.

"Don't go all sensitive, Dub," winked the sheriff.

"You will not believe who I'm talking about," said Adelaide.

"A celebrity?" said Pace. "They're always volunteering at hospitals, right? For, like, ten seconds?"

"Nope—not a celeb. Though actually *kind* of, I take that back!" She paused for dramatic flair. "Elaine Rummer."

"No!" said Pace.

"Elaine?" said Willow.

"That's right. She came to see me and it was a complete surprise. Said she didn't want to stay at home anymore stewing in her juices. Said she wanted to work with troubled teens in lockdown—kids who had tried to kill themselves. 'As you may know, that's my specialty.' That's word for word what she said. I forgot how sweet and *funny* Elaine is. And it was so touching because she said that her biggest concern was how she looked—the scars on her face. Which really aren't so bad. I mean, they're not *great* but it's not as bad as they were in my head. She said she'd understand if I had to turn her down because she didn't want to frighten the kids. I signed her up on the spot."

"Wow. Wow. That's great, Addie," said Willow.

"Mom, that is *so amazing*," said Pace.

"That certainly is an interesting turn of events," said Owen.

"You know," said Adelaide. "They always talk about closure, how there never can be 'closure'—*you* guys always talk about it. You're always saying you don't believe in it, that closure doesn't exist. And maybe it doesn't . . . But I want to tell you, there was something about Elaine that I still can't put my finger on."

"I heard they got religion," said Owen.

"It's more than that. You've seen her, Willow. Do you know what I'm saying? Did you notice anything different?"

"Not really."

"It was like she was glowing, from the *inside*. That make any sense? Oh, I know she's had her 'problems,' her mental issues—who wouldn't have. But this wasn't *that*, you know, it wasn't mania, or whatever. It was something else. I felt different just being in her presence. Maybe finally finding out what happened to her kids gave her that. Maybe closure is real."

When they were leaving, Adelaide held him back while Dixie said her goodbyes. She squeezed his arm.

"I absolutely didn't think I'd be saying this," she said, "but your girlfriend's kinda awesome."

"Glad you approve," he said.

"Try not to fuck it up, Dubya. That one's a keeper."

3.

It was dusk when they got back. Dixie briefly came over, then wanted to go home and change. She left her purse.

He couldn't describe the unwelcome shift in her mood but felt the darkness descend in more ways than one. He remembered having the same feeling at the end of certain love affairs, when both parties had the terrible realization that they only came alive for show, around other people. It spooked him, but he powered through—too late to change course.

When she returned, he sat her down on the sofa and told her he had something important to say. Instead of waiting for him to speak, she looked at the wall and said, "You painted it over . . . how come?"

He shrugged and said, "Guess it's time for something new."

"But I *liked* it," she said petulantly.

"You might like what's coming better."

The innuendo didn't register. "I really had *fun* today. Your wife and daughter are so smart! And so *gorgeous*—they don't look anything like you," she said drolly.

"She's not my wife, Dix."

"Oops! I guess what I meant was, once you have a kid together you're kind of in it for life."

"Dixie—" He knew it was going to come out a mess but none of that mattered. "Look, what I want to say—what I wanted to tell you is that I love you and care about you—"

"I know that. Love you too, Willow."

"—and I know I'm an old guy, but what I wanted to say is . . . that I want to be with you until the lights go out."

"The lights?"

"For the rest of my life."

"'Until the lights go out'!" she said exuberantly. "That is *so corny*."

He knew she wasn't being mean, and soldiered on.

"I want to marry you. Will you be my wife?"

He handed her the little box. She opened it and went wild, squealing and shouting, "It sparkles, it sparkles! It's so *beautiful*." He was delighted with her response but she wouldn't take it out. When he told her to try on the ring, she kept saying, "Put it on? Put it on?"—as if it were the silliest, craziest idea in the world.

"I can't put that *on!*"

His heart sunk. "Why not?"

She burst into tears.

"Baby, Dixie, what's wrong? What is it?"

He prayed it was nothing more than an endearing hysteria—her engines flooded by the prospect of being Mrs. Dixie Rose Wylde.

"I have to go *home* now. I have a *headache*."

She kissed him on the cheek and was gone.

He sat there with the ring staring at him from the coffee table like a Jack-in-the-box, trying not to feel like a fool. He quickly did the ameliorative math: *She didn't actually say no, she just said she couldn't put the ring on. (It'll be a funny story we tell our kids.) And: If she does say no, that's fine—she'll probably say yes later. And: If she says no and it never ever happens, that'll be fine too. Plenty of fish in the sea. And: It just wasn't meant to be. And: Maybe she's seeing someone else. Maybe she even has a husband. Maybe she has two husbands. And: I'll move away. Go wherever. Fly out to Hollywood and get a glamour job consulting on CSI. Fuck a few starlets. Hell, fuck Amy Adams, Jessica Chastain and Angelina, now that she's available. And: Get a place somewhere in Holland or Panama City or Bali or friggin' New Zealand where I can live on the cheap. Some place with six-dollar massages. Someplace whores and hash are legal.*

His eyes landed on her purse and the old habit seized him. He picked it up and set it on his knees. No reason to be furtive anymore—not when your bride runs from the altar.

That's when he saw the *Guide* and blacked out.

Lacey Beth was written on its cover.

GHOST TRAIN

I.

He left her alone that night.

Thankfully, she didn't call.

It explained everything: her childlike reaction upon seeing the engage-ment ring—her recent childishness, in general—and the abrupt, adult-informed distress that forced her to flee. Dixie's identity was in the state of panicked free fall commonplace to all landlords. He'd witnessed it firsthand at the Meeting. And of course something else had become clear:

Dixie Rose Cavanaugh was his Eskimo.

Lacey Beth . . .

He pushed the savage, irrational thought from his head that being a Porter had somehow paved the way for the fate that had befallen her; that Willow's role was to blame for "calling" her death. As he went to sleep he willed the train to come, praying he might find answers there. It had been awhile since he'd summoned it and he wasn't sure it would appear. Yet in what seemed like a blink, the Subalterns, resplendent and monkish in their foggy cloaks, were helping him board.

The locomotive departed . . .

It was cold on the train, a cold he'd never before apprehended. As if in ordination, a creature made of shadows placed a beautiful brocaded cape upon his shoulders. Annie told him that one day, "if you are very, very lucky," he would feel its heavy weight. But the detective didn't feel very lucky; no, he didn't feel lucky at all. He felt as bereft and lost as the blue children who sought his feeble ministry.

He made his way down the corridor as the Subalterns lit candles in the sconces mounted on dark wood. He could see them through the glass as he passed—so many children were waiting in their cabins! He wondered if it was a backlog from the weeks he had made himself unavailable.

He went into five of the candle-flickered rooms, one after the other. Each child nervously called out his or her name: "I'm Scooby"—"I'm Abigail"—"I'm Marie-Claude"—"I'm Jimbo"—"I'm Britney"—but there was no Lacey Beth. And what difference would it have made if Willow had found her? What was he thinking? That he could convince the little girl not to become Dixie's tenant? And where would that leave the woman he had hoped to marry? Because he knew too well what the qualifications of a landlord were: they must be dead. Without a tenant to prolong her stay, Dixie would be forever lost to him . . . In a nearly hallucinatory desperation, he thought he might find her, *see* her there, not Lacey Beth but *Dixie* the *woman—his* woman—but he knew that was impossible—and knew as well that "Lacey Beth" would not be present because the children on the train, *this* train, were only meant for him. He was their Porter . . . Still, he kept up his senseless search, yearning to connect with the chimera whom the Great Mystery had assigned to inhabit his fiancée—the child that like a carnivorous flower would slowly then quickly enfold and devour the love of his life, the lady who he now believed loved him back in equal measure. Knowing it was impossible, because Lacey Beth had already disembarked and was living inside his love! He searched and searched, down the hallways and into the cabins that were empty, madly driven to stare into the well of the nascent child-tenant's eyes—the eyes that already shared sight with his bride-to-be!—even with the knowledge that she would inexorably co-opt

Dixie Rose into a seizure of divine violence—Lacey Beth's *moment of balance*—the harbinger of his beloved's permanent leave-taking.

He personally handed the address of the Cross of Glory Lutheran Church to all those he comforted but ordered the Subalterns to deliver their drinks and treats instead.

On awakening, he gathered his paintbrushes and began a new mural.

When she came for her purse in the morning, Dixie apologized for having run away. She started to explain herself and he saw that she was struggling—with so many things.

"I know what happened to you, Dixie."

"You do?" she said.

It was obvious she hadn't a clue what he was talking about.

"Have you been to a Meeting yet?" he said gently. He spoke to her as he would a child. "A very *special* Meeting, where there are others just like you?" She stiffened and grew circumspect. "It's okay—it's okay, Lacey Beth." Her eyes widened at the name. "I know you've been told not to tell anyone about the Meetings, not anyone 'outside.' But it's all right to tell *me*, I promise. Because I know. I know all about it and I'm not from the outside. Have you been to a Meeting? Have you, Dixie?"

She looked at the floor as if caught being naughty.

"Yes."

"Can you tell me how many times?" he said, trying to gauge how far along she was.

"Just once."

"Once. That's good." She's not that far along then.

"Willow . . . what's happening?" Her mood shifted and he was glad that she was confiding. "What happened to me?"

"Something you had nothing to do with."

"I can feel myself . . . but I can feel *her* too—Lacey Beth. She's only eight years old. Someone did something so terrible to her, Willow, it's so terrible what they did! This world is so awful . . ."

"It can be," he said.

"The thing that happened to me . . . to *Dixie*—did it happen to you too?"

"No. Other things happened to me but not the same. Not the same as you, Dixie."

"Can we still get married?" she asked timidly.

"I don't think so. I don't think that we can."

She began to cry. "But I really want to! I wanted to! I was so happy when you asked—I just wasn't expecting it . . . but then *part* of me said, 'That wouldn't be *fair*, that just wouldn't be fair to Willow.' Because I have a *feeling*," she said, trembling. "That I'm not going to be here very long. I have a feeling that maybe I'm not even here *now*—"

She wept and he held her. He didn't know whom he was holding but it didn't matter. In a sense, he was holding himself.

Her tears stopped as if on cue, and she said, "Can we still fuck?"

He gasped at the insanity of the place they had found themselves trapped. "I think it's better we don't, Dixie—in a week or so you won't want to. Trust me. You just won't want to anymore."

"Why do you say that?"

"Because I've met a lot of you—"

"A lot of me?" she said, sounding hurt, and very, very young.

"Children from the train. Someone met you on a train, didn't they?" She nodded. He smiled at her like a father now. "Did they give you lemonade and cookies?"

"She gave me milk and chocolate cake."

"What was her name?"

"Lisbeth. She's from England. She has an accent."

"Did she tell you what her job was?"

"That she's the Porter."

"Well, that's what I am too."

"You?" she said with happy, twinkling eyes—as if he'd proclaimed himself to be the Bunny Rabbit King. "You're a *Porter*?"

"That's right."

"That is *so cool*."

"But there's something important that I wanted to tell you . . ."

"Are you gonna ask me to marry you again?" she said impishly. "'Cause you better watch out, this time I'll say yes!"

"No," he said, smiling. "I just wanted to say what a wonderful time I had with you, Dixie."

"Are you crying?"

"Just a little."

"Why are you crying?"

"I don't know. It happens sometimes."

"I loved you," she said, but this time she spoke like a woman. "And you *were* the one, Weeping Willow—don't you *ever* think otherwise. You were the only one."

Suddenly the commingling of Dixie and Lacey Beth shone brilliant and blue, lighting up the darkness of the curtained room. It was definitive: his home, like Annie's, was now an SRO—Single Room Occupancy—but his heart had expanded, becoming the most magnificent of palaces.

2.

He drove her to the Episcopal Church in Royal Oak, about twenty minutes from where they lived and a half hour from where he led his own Meeting. They walked upstairs. In the hallway at the door, a young woman with glasses put up her hand and shouted, "Halt!" Dixie said it was all right, that her escort was a friend who had given her a ride to the Meeting. "He cannot come!" barked the sentry. Willow thought she may have been autistic; she certainly didn't have Bumble's finesse.

"Trudy, my friend is a Porter!"

"I don't *care*," she snapped.

Dixie turned to Willow and giggled. He smiled and said, "That's fine. I'll wait for you in the car." They embraced. When he was halfway down the stairs, Dixie excitedly called after.

"There's going to be a birthday tonight!"

. . .

He sat in the park next to the church, on a bench beneath the trees. After he told Dixie that he was a Porter, she had all sorts of questions. He held back, thinking it wasn't his place to provide answers. He wasn't *her* Porter, after all. But she was curious about her own death—the death of Dixie Rose Cavanaugh—and he let her explore that. She told him that a few weeks ago she'd had the worst migraine of her life. The part of her that was an RN speculated that her demise might have been due to an embolism, a brain bleed that allowed Lacey Beth to come.

In the car on the way to her Meeting, she said, "If we can't *fuck*, Dubya, can't we at least sleep together? For comfort? *Please?* Can't we at least have sleepovers until the *moment of balance,* when I go away?"

"I don't know."

"We won't do anything bad. But it would be *so nice* to cuddle! I'd like that, Weeping Willow. And you'd like it too."

"We'll see."

Why not? He'd lost his physical attraction toward her, or thought he had. Probably it wasn't a great idea.

He wondered how much time they had. She said he was the "only one"—she was the only one for him too—but he'd already lost her. He knew it was dumb, but he hoped Lacey Beth would take her sweet time finding the one who had murdered her. As a Porter, he realized the selfishness of such a desire. But still . . .

Wouldn't that be grand?

He looked to the second floor. He could see the tops of the heads of the landlords who sat in the Meeting. Then Dixie appeared at the window, searching for him below. When she found him, she waved excitedly, then vanished a moment before returning with an older woman. Lacey Beth pointed Willow out to her and waved frenetically. Willow waved back.

The woman didn't wave but she smiled and nodded.

That must be Lisbeth.

3.

The room was full.

On top of the old group, there were ten new guests.

Ten!

All sat petrified on folding chairs with their *Guides*.

He remembered asking Annie about what struck him as the improbable numbers—how could it be that so many child-killers lived in this general area? She told him "the 'area' can be *rather* large," giving the example of Rhonda, who'd traveled all the way to Minnesota for her *moment*. "That was unusual, but not unheard of—one goes where one needs to go. One of my kids wound up in Vancouver! All in all, though, the system seems engineered for geographical convenience." She also reminded him that homicides spanned decades ("one of the train children hadn't been back for sixty years") and that in most cases, the young ones' lives came to a close "far, far away from our little Meeting in Detroit. So when you say 'general area,' you see, it's a bit more complicated." The spectral dragnet was drawn over a diaspora of perpetrators from the scenes of their crimes, some who fled to escape arrest, others because it was simply their nature to be itinerant. "Of course, Troy and Maya were an exception to that rule. They really *pinpointed it*. Because it's rare that a landlord happens to be employed in the very community where his tenants were killed."

For the benefit of the newcomers, Willow paraphrased from the *Guide*, putting it in his own words.

"A few of you are veterans—but most are here tonight for the very first time. Welcome and well done! You found us and that's the hardest part. It's my privilege to help in any way I can while you're here. You'll have *lots* of questions and I'll do my best to answer them. And I won't have answers for everything . . . but what's most important—and probably the toughest—is that you need to *trust*. There's another word for that: surrender. Now, *surrender* doesn't mean what it does in a war, when an army 'surrenders' and gives up. No. Surrender *here* means that you trust and let go. You surrender to the idea that all of you are here for a purpose. If you can do that, then you won't be afraid. There's a phrase we like to use in this room: 'More shall be revealed.' And it's true. If you don't understand something *today*, it's quite likely you'll understand it *tomorrow*. Just don't try and make sense of it all. If you trust, you'll be way ahead of the game. You'll be halfway home."

An Asian woman in her forties raised her hand.

"Yes, Scooby?" said Willow.

"Will there be refreshments? Like we had on the train? Will there be cookies?"

Everyone tittered and Willow shouted toward the door in mock anger. "Bumble? Bumble!" The faithful sentry sheepishly appeared from the hall. "What on Earth happened to the refreshments?" Willow posed the question in a dreadful English accent, like a demented aristocrat in mid-tantrum.

"I was running late, sir—they're in my car. I was just going to get them."

"Chop chop!" said the Porter, clapping his hands. All of them laughed again. "Now," he said to the group, "open your *Guides* and we'll begin. For those already familiar with the material, it's good to listen. Because in the *Guide*, you'll find everything you need to help you achieve your *moment of balance*."

One of the newbies, a twenty-something with a weight lifter's body, raised his hand.

"Sir? May I ask a question, sir?"

"Go ahead, Marie-Claude," said Willow.

"What is a 'moment of balance'?"

"A-ha," said Willow. "The question of the hour. Don't worry, we'll get to it. But first, let's read from the *Guide*. Would someone like to start? Who'd like to read?"

Britney diffidently raised her hand. She was about thirty, with green hair and a pierced nose. She worked for a CPA. "'Rule Number One,'" she said, holding the *Guide* in her quivering hand. "'Be good to your new body. Treat it with respect and it will return the favor.'"

"We'll have lots to talk about when it comes to your bodies," said Willow. "Because they'll behave in ways that you never had a chance to experience. You'll get some help with that—in Meetings we sometimes say, 'Leave your landlords at the door,' but once you leave this room, it's important to listen to them. They had their bodies a long, long time and can show you everything you need to know." He nodded to a sweaty, overweight woman. "Abigail? Why don't you read next?"

They went on like that and the mood grew less heavy, the child-tenants less frightened. When he saw that too many legs were tapping and glances were being stolen toward the table where Bumble was busy arranging things, he decided that a break would do them good. He rubbed his hands together and said, "Refreshment time!" They mad-dashed for the table and there was much hilarity as they jockeyed for sweets.

Clutching glazed donuts in both hands, Abigail got the courage to approach him.

"What's your name?" she shyly asked.

"My name?" he said blankly, as if he'd forgotten it. "Good Lord, my name . . ."

He clapped his hands again, startling them. Everyone turned and froze.

"Ladies and gentlemen, your attention please! I have been very *rude* and I beg your forgiveness." The awful accent was back with a vengeance. "This audacious young lady"—Abigail smiled bashfully—"just asked me the *most* extraordinary question. She asked me my name! Abigail, I cannot thank you enough . . . And I hang my head in shame before you all. I'm appalled that I didn't properly introduce myself at the beginning of our Meeting." They stared at him in awed anticipation. "My *name* is Willow Millard Wylde." The empty expressions of the more fragile newcomers persuaded him to add, "And I am the Porter."

After a moment of utter silence, Abigail repeated, in a gently mocking baritone (with an accent equally bad, if not worse), "And I am the Porter!" Another said it—then another—then another—as if giddily passing a hot potato. When Marie-Claude burst out with "*My name is Willow Millard Wylde*," the other men frenziedly joined the catharsis in a mass breakout of silliness. Willow let the rambunctious chorus go on for a minute, knowing the value of burning off nervous energy. With a little encouragement, they eventually stopped the horseplay and took their seats. Suddenly they looked wary, as if they'd be punished.

But Willow only smiled, resuming the lesson in his normal voice.

About the Author

Sarah Sparrow lives in Los Angeles.